Masquerade

A Logan Scott Novel

Bryan Alexander

NEWMAN SPRINGS PUBLISHING
320 Broad Street
Red Bank, NJ 07701

First originally published by Newman Springs Publishing 2021

ISBN 978-1-63692-729-9 (Paperback)
ISBN 978-1-63692-730-5 (Digital)

Printed in the United States of America

To my best friend and soul mate

What counts is not necessarily the size of the dog in the fight—it's the size of the fight in the dog.

—Dwight D. Eisenhower,
Thirty-Fourth US President

CHAPTER 1

Looking back, I should've embraced the ancient proverb "Give no quarter, spare no mercy" while I watched the vile and corrupt writhe in pain and castrate the less innocent! All of us were capable of bloodshed. It simply depended on what psychological stimuli triggered that violent act—anger, fear, love, or hate. Most notably, the avarice of villainous thieves topped my list.

What aberrant thoughts I was feeling as I embarked on what should have been another splendid day. My life had twisted into downright shambles just as I was advancing as a noteworthy entrepreneur, working our ideological system, courageous enough to take risks that with hard work were presumed to yield maximum rewards to earn my stake in the American dream. Like most of us, I believed in our government, the courts, the system, and even friends, only to find that most of them craved more, one bleeding in a one-sided relationship, to take but never give.

Unbeknownst to me, the misery I had yet to experience would be set in motion this very normal business day. I was in my clean room lab, testing a new quad-core processor I developed using a newly discovered substance, graphene, as a conformal substrate. Unlike standard coatings used on microchips and electronic components, graphene had yet to reach its omnipotent limit. Simply put, if I were to build the Starship Enterprise today, graphene would be it. It was the strongest material discovered to date. This sp2 hybridized carbon exponentially outperformed structural steel in tensile strength, like, ten to one yet was significantly lighter than paper. It was intrinsically safe, electrically superconductive, and thwarted heat buildup with ease.

So last summer, when Special Operations Command (SOCOM) challenged me to eliminate the performance problems their troops were experiencing in their mobile command centers in the big sandbox, I accepted the project. Electronics and desert heat were like oil and water—they didn't mix. Troops downrange were experiencing overwhelming heat degradation, which resulted in poor performance of their communications servers. Under contract by the army's Communications-Electronics Research, Development, and Engineering Center (CERDEC), my prototype processor was testing off the charts for processing speed, extending operational talk time, and making full use of their communications gear (comm gear).

Last fall, at the Pentagon, the two-star army general in charge of this program stated, "Today's soldier must have a technological advantage. We win wars by outsmarting and outmaneuvering our adversaries, and we need the most advanced technology on the planet to do so."

Startled by the knock on the window of the locked clean room door, I turned to see my admin assistant motioning that I had a telephone call. Normally, she would not bother me and just take a message, but she appeared frazzled. I walked over to the door and pressed the intercom. "What's up, Helen?"

"There's this financial guy on the phone. He insists on talking to you now. He won't take no for an answer."

"Where's he from?"

"He's from Venice Capital out of San Francisco. His name is Nick Audrey. He's on line two."

"All right. Tell him I'll be with him in a few minutes."

"Okay," Helen said as she walked away.

Systematically, I shut down the test, logged out of my software program, locked the prototype in the safe, hung up my clean room jacket, and headed to my office. On the walk to my office, I was thinking, *Why now is some financial guy calling?* I sat down and answered the call.

"Mr. Scott, Nick Audrey from Venice Capital. I just read another article about your latest achievement in perfecting a proprietary architectural securities platform that you've developed to streamline international commerce. I must say, I'm extremely impressed."

"Thank you."

"Seems global commerce just can't grow fast enough. Both *Forbes* and the *Wall Street Journal* say you're delivering tomorrow's technology today and businesses will benefit globally."

"So what can I do for you?" I asked.

"Well, it's more like what we can do for you," he earnestly answered.

"I'm listening."

"Let me be frank. We learned of your need to expand your business through the Economic Development Council (EDC) in San Jose. We're a private equity firm that specializes in young, undervalued companies. We leverage our financial resources and our operational expertise in small companies that have significant potential for global growth. We take an active role in strategy planning to take your company public in twelve to fifteen months. We evaluate offers from several investment banks, hire the right investment bank, structure the deal, and cover the initial public offering (IPO) costs. We inject a substantial amount of operational cash for expansion and growth but only take a minority position. We have a portfolio of companies presently on NASDAQ and the London Stock Exchange. You could be the next Fortune 500 CEO."

"It's been some time since I met with the council, so whom did you hear this from?"

"Oh, you know, word finally gets around in the financial community. Ah, probably at one of the monthly meetings. You know. These committees pass along good opportunities, and since San Jose is part of the Silicon Valley Organization (SVO), your business profile is a perfect fit. One of our backers specializes in telecommunications companies. I'd like to introduce you to him."

"You have my attention," I replied.

"I'd like to visit your facility this Thursday to begin phase one, due diligence. Say, nine thirty to eleven thirty?" asked Nick.

"I will set aside the time. I'd like more information on your company. Please send me your company's portfolio in an e-mail along with your contact information. I'll see you Thursday," I said, ending the call. I buzzed Helen's intercom. "Thursday, this Nick Audrey guy will be here at nine thirty." As Helen made note of the expected visitor, I walked down the hall, stopping at my partner's office. Leaning against the opening, I said, "Just received an out-of-the-blue call from Venice Capital from San Fran. They received info on our expansion needs through the EDC here in San Jose, and they believe we're a perfect fit for going public. One of their staff is coming by Thursday morning. Will you be here?" I asked.

"Ah, yes, I'll be here," replied Rae. "Gee, it's been five months since we submitted our application. I guess someone finally did their job," she mocked.

CHAPTER 2

Raelyn MacAllister, named after her grandfather Lyndal Raymond MacAllister, was a vivacious petite blond whom I had feelings for ever since she joined my company, but love and business rarely mixed, so I settled for being the consummate business partner. I met Rae two years ago at a Chamber of Commerce small business networking event. She had just moved back to San Jose to head the Economic Development Council and was eager to learn about my business.

Rae followed in her grandfather's footsteps in getting a master's degree in business with a bachelor of science in civil engineering. Born in Bellingham, Washington, Rae, an only child, was orphaned at three, losing both of her parents in a head-on automobile collision one rainy winter night. Rae was raised by her loving grandparents Anna and Raymond McAllister thereon on a small ranch on the outskirts of San Jose, California.

As a youngster, Rae was homeschooled until attending Holy Trinity where she excelled in math and spoke Spanish fluently, which she learned from her grandmother. Every summer from age ten on, Rae accompanied her grandfather to his construction sites, working onsite with him all throughout high school and college. Her understanding of engineering principles was better than most. It was just one of her characteristics I found fascinating. I guess all those years of following Granddad around paid off. Her common sense assessments and business acumen continued to amaze me.

All through high school, Rae competed regionally in equestrian show jumping with her Hanoverian horse, Bella. Bella was Rae's twelfth birthday present. Rae's grandparents chose a Hanoverian as they were considered the best breed for show jumping and wanted to give Rae something she dearly loved. She and Bella competed each year, winning three times in her teens. Rae's love for animals and the outdoors was quite obvious when you met her for the first time. She had that healthy glow with the grace and athleticism one attained by exercising outdoors.

After the passing of Rae's grandfather, her last living relative, Rae received a small inheritance. A mutual banking connection convinced Rae to consider becoming an entrepreneur. She had the spirit and wasn't afraid of hard work. This banker friend convinced her to talk to me, and shortly thereafter, she invested five hundred thousand dollars in my company. It wasn't long after her investment that she left her Council job. As she put it, very few people actually enjoyed working. She did and brought her work ethic into my company and had been an asset ever since.

CHAPTER 3

T hursday morning rolled around with the business as usual hum of office chatter and ringing telephone background noise. Helen buzzed my intercom to announce Nick Audrey had arrived. I walked up front to escort him into the conference room. He dressed like the typical financial type right out of Wall Street. His pants and jacket were too tight, and his hair was perfectly coiffed and shiny like it was wet. Rae heard the commotion, walked down the hall to join me, and introduced herself.

Nick hooked his laptop up to the audio visual (AV) monitor and proceeded with his dog and pony presentation on his firm, highlighting the list of companies his firm took public, pointing out the rapid increase in each company's share price and the many millions of dollars each company raised through Venice Capital's fast-track IPO program. He was well-spoken and enthusiastic. We dryly went through the boring details of the arduous paperwork filing required for the IPO. He assured us that they reaped their commission of a few percentage points on the shares' selling price, so it behooved them to work hard on our behalf. That was their underwriting fee.

At the end of his polished presentation, Rae innocently asked Nick, "Isn't twelve months extremely aggressive for this type of public offering?"

Nick stated boldly, "Actually, it isn't. When our entire team proffers a company, I can positively say, like in your case, Venice could get you there in ten months."

I gave Rae a skeptical look, responding to Nick's comment, "Let's continue."

"Certainly. I'd like to see your facility before we talk about the share price offering I've worked up for you based on your government contracts and future projects." Rae and I walked Nick around our manufacturing operation so he could visually see production and assembly in process, viewing all but my off-limits testing lab. "You run a pretty tight ship," Nick remarked to me. "I see Marc Sullivan, your sales manager, is absent. I was hoping to ask him a few questions about sales projections."

"Marc had a family emergency earlier this week," remarked Rae. "I'll gladly answer your questions about sales projections."

Walking back to the conference room, I came back at Nick. "As you can see, we're out of space. We need space alone for raw materials, work-in-progress (WIP), finished goods inventory, and equipment. And as I'm sure you've read in our business plan, our delivery schedule in year two and three increases by 1.5 to 2 times production. And in this stagnant economy, I've had absolutely no luck with banks offering loans to small businesses with less than five years in business, so we're stymied without cash to expand. It's the proverbial chicken and the egg scenario."

"You hit it on the money, Logan, but Venice Capital is vastly different. One of our backers is an angel investor who looks to help the little guy rather than the bank's attitude of only lending for brick-and-mortar real estate, like shopping malls. In this economy, angel investors take more risks, but they reap bigger rewards. You will too if you want to see your company go public. Let me show you what we consider possible," Nick remarked confidently, opening his laptop once again.

He clicked on a folder titled LSComm and switched it to the AV monitor. He opened an interactive excel spreadsheet. Pointing first to the company valuation, he remarked, "Extrapolating the added value of your three government contracts and commercial distribution, according to our Mergers and Acquisition (M&A) team, your company's value today is seven million dollars. Now for example, our investment bank buys three hundred thousand shares at twenty dollars per share all for a 5 percent commission, we take all the risk. On the day of your IPO, you just made six million bucks. Our bank takes its commission of three hundred thousand dollars. Then we turn around and offer those shares for sale at twenty-five dollars per share. That's how we get our investment back. But then your shares are worth even more, and they'll continue to grow. You both would be very wealthy on that day."

"That's a lot to digest," I countered.

"I expected you may be taken off balance, Logan, but believe me, you have nothing to lose and everything to gain. If you have time, I'd like to introduce you to our angel investor. Do you have time?"

"Yes, I have time."

"I'll videoconference him so you both can meet him. It won't take long," Nick said as he initiated a live introduction from his laptop and a handsome man appeared on screen.

"Logan Scott and Rae McAllister, this is Michael DeSalva, one of our backers and our angel investor from Lake Tahoe."

"Greetings to you both. Logan, I just finished rereading the *Forbes* and *Wall Street Journal* articles on your commerce encryption technology. Nick here tells me your organization fits our business model to a T. He tells me you have three government contracts and you need capital in order to meet the contract delivery requirements," stated DeSalva.

"Yes, that is correct. We could run a night shift and meet the demands, but that won't accommodate commercial growth over the next five years," I admitted.

"Yes, I read that in your business plan. It's impressive," confessed DeSalva. "So, ah, what are you two doing this weekend, say, Saturday?" he asked.

I looked at Rae, who shrugged her shoulders and nodded yes. She could make Saturday. "Saturday is free," I replied.

"Great! Why don't you and your partner drive up for the day?" DeSalva proposed.

I countered, "Takes too long. I'll fly us into Lake Tahoe Airport. We can get a car."

"Nonsense! You're my guests. I'll send the limo to pick you up. Come for lunch. I have a spectacular chef. We'll get to know each other. See what it's like to make a fortune," he said as his cell phone rang in the background. Looking at his phone, he muttered, "I must go. I look forward to meeting you Saturday. Nick, e-mail me their paperwork and give Logan my private number." He signed off, ending the video call.

Nick ended the presentation, handing me his business card. "On the back is Mr. DeSalva's direct line." He situated his laptop in his briefcase and left. Rae and I remained in the conference room, discussing our fortuitous meeting.

"Timing sure is everything, isn't it?" wisecracked Rae.

I asked innocently, "I apologize for not asking. Are you afraid of flying in small planes?"

Grinning, Rae echoed, "Not at all. Gramps used to take me up as a kid, and we'd fly around the countryside. It was fun. He owned a Piper PA-18 Super Cub that he kept on the ranch. Occasionally, we'd fly to Anderson Lake where we'd fish for bass and crappies. Sometimes, he'd let me steer. He stopped flying when I was eighteen. I never knew why."

"I've flown Super Cubs. They're a riot. I'd love to own one. So let's meet at nine at Santa Clara County. Oh, I mean Reid-Hillview Airport. It's on Cunningham Avenue."

"Oh yeah, I know where it is."

"Park anywhere in front of Fly Aero and come inside. I'll taxi the plane over after I refuel. I'll be in a black-and-silver Mooney Rocket. It has Wile E. Coyote riding a rocket decal on its tail. You can't miss it." I laughed.

Looking quizzically, Rae mused, "Wile E. Coyote? I guess you'll tell me why."

"It's called Rocket. There are only about 140 of them. They're very fast, and not many can handle its horsepower. Originally, it was a Mooney M20K 231 that was converted in 2008 to a Rocket 305 by modifying the cowling, fortifying the nose wheel, and replacing the engine with a turbocharged Continental TSIO 520 NB, 325 horsepower engine. It's like your 911 with wings," I said, fielding her query.

CHAPTER 4

Rae and I spent most of Friday morning looking into Venice Capital. Rae called her contacts in the Chamber of Commerce, questioning her former colleagues about how our business information ended up in the hands of Venice Capital. As expected, no one seemed to have a clue, confessing that they would pass along information within the SVO district and mostly forget about it thereafter.

Following the matter-of-course inquiries into Venice Capital's portfolio, it was reported that he, Michael DeSalva, was by no means the quotidian venture capitalist. Rather, he was an openhanded gentleman who had amassed tremendous wealth and now at this stage in his life was enjoying a selective lifestyle, helping others achieve their aspirations, their slice of the American pie.

I arrived at Reid-Hillview Airport about eight twenty on Saturday morning. The weather was clear but a crisp fifty-seven degrees with a slight breeze. I needed to clean the inside, top off the tanks, and check it over before taxiing it to Fly Aero to pick up Rae. I loaded the flight coordinates into Foreflight, direct KRHV Reid-Hillview to KTVL Lake Tahoe. Zero headwind and only 127 nautical miles—it should only take about thirty-eight minutes. I was hoping that Rae enjoyed flying, and if so, I would circle around part of the lake so she could appreciate the vista.

Taxiing the Rocket up the ramp, I spotted Rae sitting at a picnic table situated just outside the back door of Fly Aero FBO (fixed-base operator). The lineman guided me to a parallel position on their ramp stop. I kept the engine idling for an extra minute to cool the turbocharger before shutting the engine down. I unbuckled and slid over to the passenger seat, opening the passenger door. Rae stood up and walked around the tail to the passenger side.

I leaned out and held the door open as Rae walked up to the right wing. "Mornin'. Step up on the retracting black step and only on the black area of the wing as you climb in, please." As Rae settled into the passenger seat and buckled her seat belt, I handed her a Lightspeed headset, pointing where to plug in. After turning on the master switch, the Garmin 530 GPS radio came alive. Speaking into my Lightspeed boom microphone, I asked, "Can you hear me?"

"Loud and clear."

"This switch controls volume. You can clip the cord to your jacket or pants to keep it out of the way."

"Got it."

"I'll be doing a run-up at the end of the runway before we take off. You'll hear me recite a checklist to myself. Don't be concerned. I flew single-seaters in the air force." I raised my finger as if to say, "Please listen," and facing the runway, I began talking to the controllers, requesting and reciting the required departure sequence into my mic as Rae listened intently.

"Tower, Mooney 776 at Fly Aero. Taxi." I kept the intercom switch open, allowing Rae to hear the controller's directions as I proceeded through takeoff sequence. I repeated the directions. "Cleared taxiway Alpha to Tango. Hold 31 Right," I recited as I taxied the Mooney down to 31 Right, holding short of 31 Right.

I started the engine run-up, boxing the controls and testing all flight surfaces. Speaking again, I said, "Tower, Mooney 776 ready to go 31 Right."

"Tower, Golf Xray 776 cleared for takeoff, 31 Right. Have a nice day," I recited as I pushed full throttle, holding right rudder. The Mooney quickly lifted off at 80 mph at a positive rate of climb of 1,500 ft per minute. I retracted the gear and brought up the flaps. Proceeding this sequence, I called NorCal departure. "NorCal, Golf Xray 776 with you 500, climbing to 4500 VFR."

After a few minutes, NorCal cleared us direct to Lake Tahoe at 9,500 feet. Looking over at Rae, I mentioned, "Let me know if you need more heat. It'll be about minus ten degrees up there."

"I'm good, thanks. This is quite a difference from Gramps's Super Cub. I used to tease Gramps that my horse, Bella, could run faster than his plane. He would have loved flying in this." Rae stared out her window at the snowcapped mountains.

"Even in the dead of winter, the mountains are beautiful, aren't they?"

"Yes, they are. Have you skied here?" asked Rae.

"I used to ski here a lot but haven't in the last couple of years. Just been too busy. Do you ski?"

"No. I'd try it, though. It looks like fun. I spend a lot of weekend time riding Bella. I've had her since she was six months old. She's almost twenty-two, so I keep her active. Do you ride horse?"

"Never tried. The closest I got to a horse was mounted police in New York," I said as I started to descend to pattern altitude of 7,200 feet for Lake Tahoe Airport. "I'm deploying the speed brakes. You'll feel a slight change in pitch. We'll be descending about 500 feet per minute. Touching down in five minutes."

The Rocket floated over the numbers, finally squeaking its tires on runway 18. I taxied over to Mountain West Aviation, turning off the taxiway following the lineman's hand signals for parking the plane. I maintained the engine idling for another minute, allowing the turbocharger to properly cool down before methodically running through my shutdown checklist. As I shut off the engine, the lineman asked if we needed fuel.

"Not at this time. Just parking for a few hours. Thanks," I replied through the vent window.

"It should be an interesting lunch," claimed Rae as she climbed out, stepping down and waiting for me by the passenger side baggage door.

As I climbed out, I spied a brawny middle-aged man in a gray suit on the ramp, walking directly toward us. Sporting a flattop haircut atop his hardened, well-tanned face, he tucked the folded newspaper under his left arm, advancing to my left. "Mr. Scott?" he asked, extending his right arm in an outward motion, pointing to the FBO entrance door. "Follow me." He was masking a slight accent. I caught a glimpse of a tattoo on the inside of his wrist but didn't pay it any mind. Once inside, I walked up to the counter, telling the young lady that we would be here for a couple of hours. She said that was no problem.

Without uttering another word, he ushered us through the lobby and out the front door where a black stretch limo was idling. The driver, a young man clad in a black suit and chauffeur's hat, had been nonchalantly leaning against the front passenger door. As we approached the limo at a brisk pace, the driver snapped upright and opened the rear passenger door. The man of little words nodded for me and Rae to climb in. Rae climbed in first, sitting with her back to the driver. I sat across from her as he closed the door with purpose. He nodded to the driver to get us underway as he walked to the front of the limo.

As we settled in the back, the fellow in the gray suit turned around and pointed to what I thought was a single malt scotch glistening over ice in a crystal highball glass monogrammed with a D resting next to a glass of bubbly champagne on the cocktail table in the middle. "Rémy Martin XO," the man remarked flatly. "Dom Pérignon for the lady." The privacy window rose between us.

Things seemed to be starting off astonishingly well. The libation I savored but couldn't afford, the best swill. I savored the first sip but decided the FAA might have something to say about it, so I declined enjoying anymore. I stretched my legs and leaned back into the rich camel-colored leather interior. Rae was sipping her champagne quietly, taking in the majestic landscape. God, she looked good in the back of this limo, like she was born for this lifestyle.

I was musing in thought over the sheer social gesture of how DeSalva keenly guessed that I developed a taste for Cognac. For all I knew, as any first-class socialite would discern, he had one of his staff purchase it to impress me, or perhaps he simply ran in the social strata that lavished themselves with only the very best at all times, except nothing but the best. I shrugged off a chary feeling as we merged into highway traffic. I had better things to focus on.

Startled by the limo's handset ring, a husky voice broke silence over the intercom. "Mr. Scott, for you." I picked up the handset.

"Hey, partner. You two are hereby ordered to sit back, relax, and enjoy the beautiful ride. Rolf is preparing an extraordinary lunch."

"Thank you. We will."

DeSalva was being the consummate gentleman, welcoming us to his sanctum while persuading us to draw in the spectacular scenery of Lake Tahoe, as he would see us in thirty minutes. *Beau Geste*! No added words.

CHAPTER 5

Lake Tahoe was a twenty-two-mile-long alpine lake at an elevation of at least 6,225 feet encircled by the snowcapped, grand Sierras, whose peaks remained crested in snow even in midsummer. Tahoe was said to mean "high water" in the dialect of the Washoe Indians. It was a pulsating playground for the rich and famous, flaunting all the opulent glamour that Vegas boasted yet unspoiled.

We drove west and north, flanking the shoreline of this pristine body of water, as I pointed out to Rae two yachts that were making their way into Emerald Bay. In contrast against the majestic Sierras as the backdrop, the yachts were insignificant in size.

We turned off just north of Emerald Bay, meandering through the giant ponderosa pines that shaded the road, descending downward toward the shoreline. The limo slowed and turned onto a long cobblestone private driveway lined on both sides with tall ornamental trees. We slowed approaching an ornate iron gate suspended between two massive stone pillars. As the gate rotated inward, the limo veered to the right, opening to an immense stone courtyard approaching a bronze statue of David by Michelangelo, poised in a tiered water fountain.

Just as the limo circled the fountain, DeSalva's villa came into full view. It was constructed of rich dark wood and fieldstone and nestled among towering pines. Before the limo rolled to a stop by the front portico, I spotted a spacious two-story boathouse with a gazebo perched on top and edged by the background of azure water. The grounds surrounding the courtyard to the boathouse were immaculate and beautifully landscaped. Its panorama was a Norman

Rockwell picture-perfect vista as I gazed across the lake at Mt. Rose and Heavenly Valley.

This place wasn't just a house, at least nothing I had ever been in. It was a mansion extraordinaire, ranking up there in stature with five-star resorts, reminiscent of *The Godfather* sequel where two went fishing and only one returned. I shrugged off that edgy feeling again as the driver opened my door. DeSalva appeared more tanned than on the video call as he approached the limo.

"Welcome to Lake Tahoe," he said, extending his hand to help Rae out of the limo. By the tone of his haughty voice, I had guessed him to be taller. Rather, he was shorter and younger than I had speculated with slicked back black hair and displaying all the gentlemanly mannerisms one would expect of an aristocrat. Even his casual attire was elegant, reminiscent of the after-dinner jackets upstanding chaps might wear at the Harvard Club as they sauntered about the library to sip good brandy, smoke cigars, and retort political banter and world economics.

As good hosts did, DeSalva escorted us through the main rooms on the first floor, pointing out his revered collection of fine art exhibits, all the while extolling the virtues of living in this vast wilderness while taking pleasure in helping others, carrying on his family's dynasty. Rae recognized famed Remington paintings and bronze statues that appointed the main hallway.

As we entered his study, he stopped and poured two snifters of Louis XIII straight up! I was speechless. At this point, all I could do was politely accept but not drink. Most likely, it didn't occur to him that I was flying the two of us home.

"May I offer you white wine, Rae?"

"Yes, that would be lovely," she said, seating herself on a tufted oversize leather sofa. I chose the same sofa a short distance away.

At first glance, his study appeared to be more along the lines of a library with bookcases to the ceiling and an oversize Baroque executive desk. He seated himself on the opposite sofa. I found it thought-provoking that the back issue of *Forbes* containing the first article about my commerce encryption technology was lying on the table between us. Rae noticed the same, nodding to me.

DeSalva continued expounding how he amassed the preponderance of his wealth in commercial real estate development in Seattle, New York, London, and Hong Kong, and his brilliant multilevel exporting program selling personal protection equipment.

"Personal protection?" I goffed. "We didn't catch that in your public relations profile."

Smirking as he lit up a Davidoff, he motioned for me to select one, and our conversation ensued by recapping the IPO investment details, noting how it would greatly benefit my brainchild, espousing his philosophy of no day-to-day involvement, boasting two examples of his ease in management style, a biotech company in Montreal and his multinational exporting commerce in Seattle. In no uncertain terms was he considered the micromanaging sort. His travels, his family, and his philanthropic lifestyle kept him far too occupied. Rather, he enjoyed being a ghost, a silent partner.

Rae interrupted. "You have a lovely family. Where are your children?"

"Why, yes. They're back east in the best schools money can buy. Gabriella and I see them quite often," he answered, pointing to pictures of his kids on his desk, then shunning Rae and turning back toward Logan.

Tapping off ashes, he leaned back, emphatically restating that I would remain the majority partner running the day-to-day operations, focusing on the next generation commerce advancement, reciting the recent articles in *Forbes* and the *Journal* and my affiliation with military and government agencies. He lauded the boon of our imminent partnership with Venice Capital, working on the IPO. In his words, Venice Capital would propel the technology's launch worldwide, which would finance advanced research for both mankind and industry. And in taking only one voting seat on the board, every quarter, we would meet as his guest to track our progress and financial growth. It was captivating. It was surreal.

Just then, the man in the gray suit appeared at the door. DeSalva nodded, and he approached. He leaned over the back of the sofa, touching DeSalva's shoulder. In an audible whisper, he stated that Senator Hicks was calling to confirm their meeting tomorrow evening. DeSalva excused himself, picked what appeared to be a satellite phone from his desk, and announced "Grady" as he walked out of the study to continue in private.

Weighing the rationalization of his comments while thinking of how connected this man was, I looked at Rae. She raised her eyebrows with a look of wonder on her face. Christ, Senator Hicks, the chairman of the House Security Subcommittee! I had briefly read about his appointment to Subcommittee after being elected a few years back.

I whispered to Rae, "This should be a grand slam! Senatorial connection! It doesn't get much better than this!" I stood up and strolled toward the window, inhaling the fumes while I etched the theme of his well-appointed study in my mind. He boasted hunting big game as I imprinted the enormity of the prized Cape buffalo trophy suspended atop the burl wood mantel of his man-size stone fireplace, like an eagle overshadowing its prey.

The Turkish rug beneath my feet was two inches thick, and the ornate jade statues, paintings, and art sculptures artfully arranged exuded impassioned wealth and power. This place was right out of *Gone with the Wind*. DeSalva returned and sauntered back to the sofa, apologizing for the untimely interruption. I reseated myself.

"Let's make this a winning partnership. You two run it, Venice Capital will bankroll it!" He held his glass up in the air, exhibiting the bold confidence of a politician. "Together, we'll make big things happen! Next year this time, you'll be publicly traded and well on your way to amassing a luxurious fortune."

As the time neared noon, DeSalva beckoned us into the dining room. His staff served caviar, stone crab claws, abalone, and roasted pheasant, a meal fit for a king! It was just the three of us in this ornate dining room that could easily accommodate a sit-down party of twenty with room to spare.

While we continued to discuss the private equity investment, DeSalva complimented me repeatedly on how thoroughly I had written the business plan, noting its five-year global projections. He was duly impressed after reading the most recent article in the *Wall Street Journal* about my commerce encryption technology, remarking he was keenly interested in seeing my encryption project burgeon globally.

I interrupted. "For the record, to ensure we are on the same page, Venice Capital will invest up to $2 million to complete the IPO filing for 5 percent commission. Venice Capital will assist us in choosing the right investment bank, which will commit to purchase an agreed upon number of shares, and as we move forward, together we will determine the optimum selling price of those shares. Is that correct?"

"Absolutely, my friend! We make it easy, as outlined by Nick. If you agree, we will begin drafting the filing. If you need cash now, I'll commit one hundred thousand dollars downstroke as a good faith gesture." At the precept of his associate in the gray suit, DeSalva excused himself and walked out of the study one last time for about ten minutes.

Reveling in the moment, I grabbed my snifter of Cognac and ambled back to the bay window overlooking the waterscape mountain view. Rae stood up and joined me. For a moment, I swirled the Cognac in its snifter, inhaling its aroma while scanning the picturesque view. I was euphoric, struggling to keep my emotions in check.

Rae whispered, breaking my train of thought, "Are we ready? I mean, is this amazing or what?" Mulling over high points of the proposition in my mind, at least we were leaving with the full commitment of Venice Capital and an angel backer to boot. I knew from experience that the courtship was almost over. There would just be a ton of legal paperwork to finish, sealing the deal.

As DeSalva walked back into his study, he audibly summoned his associate to schedule a meeting ten days from today in the private conference room at the Argonaut Hotel, near city center in San Francisco, to finalize the investment details and conclude the legalities, and he reiterated the earnest one hundred thousand dollars to cover incidentals on our side once a contract was signed for the IPO and advocating that both of us attend our first strategy meeting while directing his associate to summon the limo for our return trip to the airport. We shook hands and left.

CHAPTER 6

The ride to the airport somehow seemed shorter. We both were bubbling with an abundance of excitement, that feeling of luck like a volcano set to explode. I found it hard to conceal my excitement while trying to maintain civility. Rae's facial expression was exuberant. She would be hard-pressed to hide her natural beauty. We cheerfully chatted like two magpies all the way to the airport, hypothesizing over the interesting concoction that was about to take place and how our company's future would change forever.

Our flight home also seemed shorter. Perhaps we lost track of time as the discussion continued, neither of us paying attention to the scenery. It was tight quarters in the Rocket, and as our conversation became more animated, I accidentally brushed her breast when she was reaching for the sun visor. She didn't flinch or react negatively. Was I reading too much into this slight?

"We have a lot to think about over this weekend," I said to Rae as she stepped out of the plane.

"Yes, we do. See you Monday." She waved while walking into Fly Aero. I started the engine and taxied the Rocket over to my T-hangar, stowed the plane, and jumped in my truck, heading for my apartment in Cupertino, just west of San Jose.

I moved into this apartment complex about three years ago after my ex-wife cleaned out our bank account, borrowed against my life insurance policy, extorted money from my father, bounced numerous checks, and sued me for divorce, getting the house, the car, and a healthy settlement. I came home from a business trip to find she had even taken the clothes hangars, leaving my clothes in a heap on the closet floor. Every room was stripped bare to the bones. I should've seen it coming. She was spending money like a drunken sailor—furniture, jewelry, clothes, more shoes than the closet had room for, new social activities, modern art, and redecorating the house.

I turned on the television to catch the rest of the Kentucky Wildcats playing the USC Trojans. Wildcats was leading by eleven points. They might make the NCAA Division I championship once again. Good coaching. I made a turkey sandwich and grabbed a Sam Adams, trying to relax my mind.

CHAPTER 7

The sunrise woke me early Sunday morning. Still feeling an emotional high, I figured a long, hard run would help bring me back down to earth, so I dressed and hit the pavement. My thoughts kept returning to wondering what Rae's thoughts were about going public, about expanding the business, about how busy we would become, and about signing Venice Capital's contract. Fighting the urge to call her, I put the cell phone back in my pocket. I wanted to hear her take on the prospect but decided against it. After all, nothing would be accomplished until the workweek begins anyway. Knowing that she spent a lot of her weekend time at the ranch, I should've invited myself to watch her ride horse. I would've liked to see where she grew up.

The run was good but didn't sap enough energy, so I decided to wash and wax my truck as another way to pass the time. I finished feeling hungry, so I telephoned a buddy to see if he wanted to meet me at Grumpy's Sports Bar for a late lunch—have a burger and beer and catch up on NBA basketball. He was busy, so I showered and dressed and went by myself.

Grumpy's was a popular place. I had many weekend lunches there. Its ten televisions always played live sporting events all around the horseshoe bar. If you didn't like the Lakers, you could watch the Cavaliers or the Rockets. If you didn't like basketball, the playoffs of the NFL leading up to the Super Bowl were on.

The Rams weren't looking good at all. The Patriots were in the playoffs again. It was odd how they got such bad press despite being a great team. The Jets always got the press, but they hadn't looked good this season either. There was never a lack of entertainment, and their burgers and homemade fries were great. Rae and I had a quick lunch there before, as it was close to work.

The burger and fries really hit the spot. I didn't feel much like beer, so I settled for a Diet Coke. After watching a couple of games, it was time to leave. I hadn't done any grocery shopping in a few days, so I left Grumpy's to fill the fridge at Safeway on my way home.

It was dusk when I finished shopping. Setting two bags of groceries on the passenger's seat, I started my truck. As I backed up and stopped, I caught a guy staring at me in his driver side mirror. He was giving me the stink eye, just sitting in his car with the windows rolled down, just glaring. He was parked next to me on my left. I gave him a last look, put the truck in drive, and headed home.

The phone was ringing as I opened the front door. It was the San Jose police stating that there had been an apparent break-in at my company and requested that I come down to assess any damage and inspect and inventory the building and its contents. The police were waiting at the premises. I asked if they had contacted anyone else on the list from the alarm company. The duty officer responded that since they reached me, the on-record primary contact, no additional personnel would be called.

I called Rae at her house. No answer. I thought it might be a good idea to have a second set of eyes for this task, but if needed, I would call her from the office. It might just be nothing, so why bother her? Their phone call was so startling, so out of place, that I didn't remember the name of the officer who would be waiting at our building.

I finished putting the groceries away and headed to the office. Walking to the truck, I felt a sensation of uneasiness, like I was being watched. I looked around, saw nothing, got into the truck, and put it out of my mind. Like most people, I had become complacent, settling into a routine and believing that nothing much would happen. My life had become rather predictable.

As I turned onto El Camino Real, the reflection of high beam headlights in my rearview mirror from the car directly behind me was annoying. It was just too close for comfort. It kept pulling up right on my bumper, its bright headlights shining in my eyes. As

I turned into the parking lot, the car slowed but continued on. I thought, *What a jerk.* Just then, my cell phone rang. It was Rae.

"Hey, Rae."

"I just got home and saw that you called."

"Yeah. I'm at the office. The police called after the alarm was triggered earlier. They're here now. I just pulled in. They want me to walk through to see if anything is missing or if it was a false alarm," I said, staring at the front door while the truck idled.

"I can be there in fifteen minutes," replied Rae.

"Another set of eyes wouldn't hurt at this point."

"Okay. See you shortly," she said as she hung up.

I sat for another long moment just looking at the building, thinking about the last twenty-four hours, about the business I built, and about Rae. Her contributions helped me in so many ways. I wouldn't have been where I was today without her. She needed to hear that.

Staring at my company, a stand-alone, tilt-up, one story building that bordered a large industrial complex, I remembered how bare the building was until Rae helped decorate and fill the five thousand square feet of office space with new and used office furniture. It had an eclectic look, as Rae described it, where no two offices were alike and where little matched, but it was adequately functional.

Well-networked throughout the business community, Rae picked up good bargains to furnish this place from her repertoire of business acquaintances. The remaining thirty thousand square feet was consumed by Research & Development, a clean room testing lab, light manufacturing, and assembly of advanced electronic components.

I turned off the ignition, stepped out of the truck, and walked up to the building. The outside entryway door was ajar. Forced entry didn't seem evident as the doorframe appeared undamaged. Two law enforcement officers and a working canine were standing just inside the glass entryway.

The senior officer stepped forward. "Logan Scott? I'm Officer Blaas, and this is Officer Jenson and Rex."

"Yes. My partner Rae MacAllister, who is second in your security contact list, will be joining us in a few minutes. She's on her way now."

Officer Blass motioned for me to walk in. "It's safe to enter." Officer Jenson remained inside the lobby with K9 Rex. I proceeded in with Officer Blaas recalling the incident. "The alarm was triggered at five fifty-eight. Your security company called it in. As standard procedure, I called the canine unit in as backup. When they arrived, Officer Jenson and I found the outer entryway door ajar. Ah, it appeared to have been left open with no visible damage, at which time we dispatched Rex inside and followed, conducting a room-to-room search, all but the locked laboratory.

"No one remained in the building as Rex conducted a thorough sweep of the premises. We recognized nothing unusual, nor did we find anything that appeared damaged or missing. The back door remained bolted and locked. We would like you to canvas the building to determine if theft is involved and note anything missing or damaged for our report."

I walked directly to my office and carefully looked around. Officer Blaas stood back in the doorway. At first glance, my office seemed untouched. Nothing appeared to be missing or out of place. My computer remained undisturbed. My encrypted program and tera drives were hidden in the back of my desk drawer behind a false partition. I removed the hidden partition and counted. The entire batch remained intact. Nothing had been removed. My file drawer with its locking bar and padlock remained untouched. Everything seemed in order. Walking back out of my office, I said to Officer Blaas, "I'd like Rae to inspect her office if that's okay. I can start out back, and when she gets here, I'll have her go directly there."

"That will be fine," he replied.

We walked out back, stopping by R&D first. The cipher lock to the R&D lab was still secure. Asking the officer to step back, I punched the code in the lab's cipher lock and walked in. He stood in the doorway. The P27 algorithm testing equipment appeared untouched, so I continued through the lab and out into the assembly work area.

At first blush, everything appeared fine. Without undertaking a complete parts inventory, I couldn't guess if any semiconductor circuits or parts were missing. As I closed the heavy self-locking metal door, I heard Rae announce herself while walking in the back. I must've looked stunned when she entered the back. She was wearing equestrian clothes—beige corduroy breeches, a tailored performance top, and tall riding boots. Her hair was pinned in a ponytail. The outfit accented her shapely body. For a moment, I lost my train of thought.

Walking up to Officer Blaas, she said, "I'm Rae. Sorry for my appearance. I probably smell like my horse."

I laughed. "Would you inspect your office? You more than I would know if anything has been disturbed. I'll be back up front shortly."

"Be happy to." She turned and walked back to her office to begin a cursory inspection. She looked in the remaining offices and through everyone's workplace. With Officer Blaas in tow, I joined in helping her inspect room by room, opening and closing desk drawers and file drawers, completing all eight rooms.

We slowly worked our way back to the front office. Rae stepped aside to talk with Officer Jenson and meet Rex, who was standing guard in the front entryway. After a minute, she stopped abruptly. "Where's Helen's computer? How did we miss it? Why would anyone take the computer and leave the monitor?"

"Um, maybe whoever was in here got spooked and just grabbed something to fence," I quipped sarcastically.

Writing notes in his report, Officer Blaas asked, "Are you stating that the desktop computer from this reception desk, one piece of equipment, is missing? Can you tell me the model?"

Focusing on Officer Blaas, Rae spouted, "It's an HP, ah, HP Pavilion. I forget the model."

"I see nothing else. If we find something tomorrow, one of us will call. If this is all that's missing, then I guess we're lucky!" I replied.

Rae turned to me. "Anything missing in the lab?"

"Not that I've noticed," I said, looking to the officer.

Officer Blaas signed the report, handed me a copy, and walked outside to join the canine officer, who was now standing by his vehicle with Rex inside the back. This incident appeared to be rather routine on their part. Famous last words—"We're lucky!"—would come back to haunt me over and over again.

Rae and I walked back down the hall and glanced through the offices one last time. Rae shut off the lights and set the alarm, and I locked the door as we walked outside. It was 8:25 p.m. At that moment, I realized that all the excitement made me hungry as I hadn't eaten since lunch.

"I'm hungry. You interested in chocolate French silk pie?" I asked.

"My house is closer. I can whip up French pancakes, a kind of late-night celebratory breakfast."

"You win. I'll follow," I replied as Rae turned and walked to her car. I couldn't help but watch her graceful stride.

CHAPTER 8

Rae was spot-on. I was keyed up with yesterday's lavishness, and now the break-in. Perhaps eating and a nightcap would prove a good sedative. I had more than my share of excitement over the past few days. We arrived back at her house at 8:40 p.m. Her house was an extraordinary California hillside home, the back buttressed on stilts overlooking the valley on a one-and-a-half-acre, architecturally landscaped lot.

It was originally built as a custom home by a plastic surgeon who got divorced and sold it to Rae and her husband, only to later become a divorce settlement gift from her ex-husband, who left Rae for his very pregnant secretary. Rae had mentioned in passing that when she caught her ex with his secretary, he had the nerve to say to her face that he had always wanted someone to stay at home, not someone who wanted a man's career. Rae asserted embarrassment as she felt the house way too pretentious. It just wasn't Rae. Her ex-husband only wanted it so he could rub elbows with the right social elites and exploit her family ties in the community. She preferred the ranch where she grew up, spacious and quiet.

Sheba greeted us at the front door, tail wagging furiously. Although she was friendly, she was wary but very obedient. It was very apparent that she had serious training. Rae joked a while back that one day, she hoped her ex-husband would stop by unannounced looking for a favor where he would meet the alpha wolf in her—watchful, protective, and stealthy. *Canis lupus familiaris* described her behavior, keenly aware of Rae's whereabouts at all times. I wouldn't have chanced pissing her off. Well, at least Rae had a guardian.

Rae motioned me into the den, just off the ultramodern kitchen. From the large bay windows, you could see the city lights of San Jose in the south twinkling like a giant marquee all the way to Oakland in the north with the bay in between. In the daytime, the mountains of Fremont loomed, appearing as if they were painted on a gigantic canvas as the backdrop of a Hollywood movie set, so rich in their golden hue. How I envied this house! Who wouldn't fancy owning a house like this, alive and expensive, all the way contemporary with four large bedrooms, a billiard room, and an oversize study positioned in the back, adjacent to the left side of the deck that extended across the back, some thirty feet off the ground, opposite the master suite?

When asked, I would stop by occasionally to feed Sheba and sit on the back deck and take in the vibrant colors across the valley and watch the evening approach. It was a serene place to unwind. I never minded Rae asking me to house-sit and care for Sheba while she traveled. She had friends who lived closer, but the last few times she traveled, she asked me. She believed it good for my soul to share communal time with nature and man's best friend, claiming Sheba was far more insightful than the preponderance of people she knew and a far better listener.

While Rae was preparing the late-night nosh, I got up to let Sheba in the back door, just off the kitchen. Out of the blue, Rae challenged, "Why the hell would anyone steal the front office computer?"

"Who the hell knows? Guess we'll just have to get another one and reload from the server." Rae pointed to the oversize built-in refrigerator, asking if I would open the bottle of Veuve Clicquot Demi-Sec, semisweet champagne. I obliged and opened the bubbly, filling two glasses and setting them at the breakfast bar.

The smell of cooked bacon always seemed to arouse hunger in people. It certainly caught Sheba's senses. Rae whipped up French-style pancakes with old-fashioned home fries and bacon. I savored the late-night nosh and guzzled the champagne. We opened a second bottle, continuing our fervent discussion about our company going public. As the evening wound down, Rae insisted that I not drive the windy roads at this late hour, mainly with a high blood alcohol count. It was a sound decision. I didn't resist. She pointed down the hall toward the guest suite.

"Sheba won't mind. She'll think you're babysitting again."

"Okay. You win." Who in their right mind would want to go back to a lonely apartment when you could stay at a spa? She poured the last of the bubbly and walked over to the living room leather sofa overlooking the valley. Sheba crawled up beside her and put her head on Rae's lap. That was where I would rather be right about now. Being the consummate gentleman, I slid into the adjacent leather chair and propped my feet up on the ottoman as we continued rehashing the last four days' events. I was still on a proverbial high!

Unexpectedly, Rae changed the subject. "Why haven't you dated since your divorce?"

"Well, ah, my divorce was ugly. It's so much easier to stay busy. Anyway, ah, everyone I meet acts so damn immature. I can't relate. I've nothing in common with bar bunnies, and the older ones, hell, they're sharks just circling their prey. They're trolling for a stand-in with credentials, ah, you know, fat wallet, big house, luxury car. And I'm not into one-nighters. Besides, we're so close to success now. Who needs the distraction? We've got a genuine opportunity to make a difference. How 'bout you? You seeing anyone?"

"Nah. Ever since the fiasco with catching Jerry and then fighting his greed in the divorce over my inheritance, that made me lose complete faith in men. I've been on a couple of dinner dates set up by good-intending friends, but like you, I wouldn't even consider the bar scene. I'd rather have a true soul mate. Honesty and trust are far too important. I guess I haven't found anyone who intrigues me yet," she mused.

As I watched her roughhousing with Sheba, that arousal swelled in me again. Even after the many hours, her fragrance was still captivating. Her charm, her looks, so alluring. Was I sensing for the first time that she might be hinting something or that maybe something was brewing? Was this my secret wish for staying over?

After imbibing a lot of champagne, the rules changed—you know, the rules you made up for every situation before you had that first drink. What concerned you earlier in the day transformed in the twilight hours when one's inner beast emerged. Dismissing that torrid thought aside for the moment, I reminded Rae that she needn't bother to show me where to bunk in.

"Nonsense," she said as she popped up and summoned me to follow her to the guest room at the end of the hall. On the way she grabbed two towels from the linen closet and showed where to find the sundry items in the guest bath.

"Really, I don't need a thing."

She touched my arm. "You've earned this accomplishment. Be proud." She headed back down the hall to her room where Sheba waited by the door.

Was I in a dream? Was there something in her touch? It felt penetrating, even voltaic, though only a touch. Was I wishing another sensation was there, not just a sign of friendship between two business partners? The wonders of champagne seemed to cloud one's thoughts and made one forget the essentials of life.

Tiptoeing back down the dimly lit hallway, I waited until I entered the guest bathroom and closed the door before I turned on the light. I brushed my teeth and threw water on my face. As I looked through the cabinet, I wondered if the shaving cream had been left by her ex-husband or it was a brand she liked. Hmm. I dried my face, hung the towel up behind the door, and shut off the light.

I opened the door as Rae approached, smelling of Jasmine from a fresh shower. She was standing there with a look on her face that would melt the hardest butter and arouse the most celibate monk. Dressed in a purple satin nightgown and robe, she asked, "Did you find everything okay?"

"Yeah, thanks. Ah, time to hit the sack."

"Can I ask you a personal question?"

"Yeah, sure."

"We've known each other for, what, two years? I've seen the way you look at me, so why haven't you ever made a move?"

Jolted by her question, I stammered, "I, ah, well, ah, it's not that I hadn't thought about it. I'd be a fool not to. But I respect your friendship, what you did for me and the company. I admire your professionalism and our working relationship. Guess I'd have a hard time facing you."

"Fair enough. Sleep tight!" With that, she turned, lightly brushing my arm. What was that I sensed? I moseyed back to the room and closed the door. I plopped down on the edge of the bed as the day's events whirled through my head, letting the champagne do its job, when it occurred to me how foolish I was for not seizing the moment. Man of honor or not? Time seemed to fly as if in a time warp. Minutes seemed to pass, but in reality, it was only seconds. Oh, hell, liquid courage could be convincing.

Determined to test the water, letting the champagne guide my rationale, I opened the door and walked down the hallway. I knocked softly on her door. No answer. Was she asleep already? Had I been sitting there longer than I imagined? My courage instantly waned, and I hoped this was all a bad dream and that she was fast asleep and would never know that I had knocked. What the hell was I thinking? As I turned to walk back to my room, the door opened. Rae was standing there, radiating a coquettish look. I said to myself, "Make me strong enough to endure the humiliation!"

"Are you all right?"

"I leaned forward and lightly pulled her to me and kissed her passionately on the lips. She felt so wonderful, the softest creature in the universe yet so daunting. How was it that this five foot five femme fatale could make a six-foot guy cower from a simple glance? I didn't know what to expect, a quick slap or a sarcastic remark. Seconds passed. Her expression grew even more intense. Utter shock entwined with happiness. Dammit anyway! Had I just ruined a great relationship? Would she forgive my faux pas?

I pulled away, embarrassed. "I'm sorry. I…"

She grabbed my hand and whispered, "Don't leave." I lost the power to speak. As she put her finger to my lips, she whispered, "It's okay."

Picking her up off the floor, I kissed her more intensely and more passionately than I believed I could muster. After three years, I had finally thawed. She broke off the kiss, slipped her hand down to mine, and led me into her bedroom. She dimmed the over bed lights.

"I want to see you." She squeezed my hand. Tenderly, I slid the straps of her gown off her shoulders, letting the satin draping her body slowly fall to the floor. She squeezed my hand and pulled me to the bed. Shedding my clothes, I moved in close, caressing her. Hmm, her sweet smell was intoxicating. The look on her face was mystifying, so enchanting. I tasted her lips, her face, her neck, and her shoulders, the pace intense. My heart raced. My thoughts was consumed with desire. I had to have all of her.

Gently, I caressed her breasts, first with my hands, coveting them with desire. I kissed and ran my tongue down the flat curves of her stomach, tickling her navel with my tongue. I nibbled on her hip bones and discovered her ticklish spots. I drank in the folds of her womanhood with penetrating ecstasy. She was extremely warm, and I was eager to burst with intense desire. Kissing me passionately, she moved smoothly, pulling all of me inside her. Soft yet so strong! I was on fire, sweating profusely, breathing hard as if I ran a marathon! I lay back breathless, trying to regain my composure.

She maneuvered close to kiss me and smiled. "I'd forgotten how wonderful sex can be with the right partner," she said delightfully.

CHAPTER 9

We slept in late, but before we fell asleep, Rae called the answering service to tell them to hold messages until we arrived midmorning to the office, a trivial detail I would've forgotten. As the morning sun danced across the room, I awoke feeling jubilant. I couldn't describe the emotion, but as I glanced over at Rae cuddled next to me, she was smiling. She raised herself up on one shoulder and gave me a good morning kiss. Unlike the hurried peck I got now and then, this was genuinely different.

Without saying a word, Rae snuggled closer and softly ran her finger across my lips and down my neck. She leaned over to kiss me, and nature took over once again. I found the morning romp playful and invigorating, clearing the fogginess from the champagne out of my head. On the drive to the office, I realized that I knew the mystifying answer. I knew what she looked like in the morning, and I wanted more of her softness, more of her smell. I wanted all of her.

I arrived at the office ahead of Rae, around 9:00 a.m. As I pulled into the parking lot, that uneasy feeling surfaced, that gut reaction that something was afoul. The parking lot was empty, except for Helen's VW Beetle. As I walked through the front door, I was about to realize that all hell was breaking loose.

"Morning, Helen," I announced. "Where's everybody?"

"Logan, I need to talk to you," she said, speaking decisively.

"Okay. Just give me a minute to grab a cup of coffee." As I walked into the break room, I considered it odd that no one was around. Helen seemed pensive. *Did everyone take an early lunch? Did they park out back?* I found it strange that there was no hot coffee. Knowing it would take a few minutes to brew a fresh pot, I called Helen into my office to find out what was on her mind.

She walked into my office and stood silent in front of my desk. I sensed tension in the way she was fidgeting. Standing stiff while frowning, Helen was saying more by not saying a word. She was undeniably upset. "Helen, please have a seat," I said as I motioned to the chair. "Is everything all right at home? Are you and Jack okay?" I asked with deep concern.

"Logan, I waited until you came in because I didn't want to do this without talking with you first." She was rubbing her hands together nervously.

"Do what?" I queried.

"Well, all of us, um, all of us got together last night and discussed what's going on. Um, well, we now know that the company will not make it and—"

Abruptly I cut her off. "Who's we?" I rose in my chair. "Who are you talking to? Who's spreading this BS? Come on, is this a joke?"

"Well, ah, yesterday afternoon, Marc showed us court papers. He knows from good authority that the company's going bankrupt and none of us will get paid this week!"

"Whoa, Helen! Helen!" I snapped loudly. "Court papers? What papers? Marc is supposed to be on family leave! What the hell's going on?" I barked.

"I wouldn't do what others have done. I wanted to tell you to your face. Logan, please accept my resignation. Can I have my paycheck now?" she replied sheepishly.

"What do you mean resign? Where's your computer? Where's everyone? Dammit, Helen, what's going on? Well?" I demanded.

"Well, ah, Marc has gone to work for Mr. DeSalva, and he's offered most everyone a job at much higher salaries. He says our stock in this company isn't worth the paper it's written on and that you're being indicted by the federal government for stock fraud. He showed us legal documents. I don't know who took the computer or whatever. I don't want to get involved. Please, I just want to be left out of all of this!"

Helen was visibly shaken. She had worked for me for a couple of years and knew that my bark was worse than my bite, but this was worse than bizarre! I composed myself, settled back in my chair, and humbly spoke. "Look, Helen, I've always been straight with you. Why won't you be straight with me? Tell me what you mean by everyone going to work for DeSalva!"

"Please, Logan, no hard feelings. I just want my check and what's left of my vacation pay so I can leave."

With little left to say, I unlocked the file cabinet, took out the payroll checkbook, and wrote out her final paycheck. Politely, I asked her to reconsider, but she nervously declined. I hadn't noticed when I walked in that the pictures of her three grandkids were missing from her desk. She had already boxed up her personal items and was just waiting for me to arrive, waiting for her pay, and split.

Stunned beyond belief, I couldn't fathom what or how I would tell Rae for her to grasp the gravity of our situation as I was still struggling to make sense of it myself. In less than forty-eight hours, I screwed my partner on the same day that my business got screwed by the same guy who told me he would never screw me. Some fucking white knight purporting to slay the financial dragons once and for all!

He had to have been arranging this for some time, probably since the day he received my business plan and sent his emissary to coax us into believing he would take our company public. And the unexpected inspection, that was how he identified who was who when he asked such probing questions. That fucking bastard! Now what? No employees? How in the hell could we fulfill the military contracts on time?

At that very moment, Rae walked in dressed in a jade-green silk blouse tucked inside a fitted knee-length navy skirt. The jade green accentuated the green in her eyes. Even as agitated as I was, she was one good-looking lady with a great set of legs.

"Where's Helen going? She passed me on her way out the front door, said a quick goodbye, and told me to talk to you. What's going on? Where's everyone?" Rae asked innocently as she set her briefcase down beside the chair.

"She quit, Rae. She said she and the other employees got together with Marc yesterday, and the whole bunch are going to work for DeSalva!" I sneered, gritting my teeth. "They were told we were being indicted by the government for stock fraud, that we were going bankrupt. Marc showed them legal documents and who the hell knows what else."

"DeSalva? The man we met with Saturday? Has everyone quit?" Panic flooded her face.

"The same, and yes! You see anyone around?" I leaned back in my chair and bitingly gibed, "Well, it damn sure cuts down on payroll taxes."

"That's not at all funny," she said as she plopped down in the chair facing my desk. We bantered clamorously about our situation, exchanged ideas, discussed our options, and talked a lot about DeSalva. More and more, we realized that we had been gulled into this predicament. Trusting fools we were. From Marc Sullivan's peculiar behavior over the past couple of weeks to the theft of the company's computer database, we were experiencing a genuine *The Twilight Zone* adventure, sans Rod Serling's voice-over.

The lure of a savvy benefactor and wealth could blind one's defense mechanisms into believing that everyone was aboveboard and that everything was on the up-and-up, and what one later found out was unbelievable became truly unbelievable! We continued to parley our naive, trusting nature, asking ourselves what had triggered this malice, this injustice.

CHAPTER 10

S tartled by the telephone ring, I nodded to Rae, encouraging her to answer. She reached across my desk and grabbed the phone. I realized at that moment that it was midmorning and the telephone hadn't rung once since I had arrived and Helen delivered no messages, and this was a busy time. With a bewildered look, Rae put the call on hold. "It's DeSalva, for you," she hissed. As she stood up, I motioned for her to remain seated. I needed an ally more than ever now, a witness, and moral support.

Taking a deep breath, I picked up the handset. "DeSalva, what else do you want to fuck up in my life today?" I bellowed.

"We need to renew our conversation from Saturday to consider my new proposal," he taunted in his dry, steely tone.

"And what offer is that? The offer to take all our employees away and tell them that we're bankrupt, that I've committed fraud? Is that what you want to discuss?"

"Take it easy, my friend," he said wryly. "It's strictly business. Let's work together and straighten this out man to man. Since you're the majority equity holder, you'll make a much smarter decision than the little lady, so you speak for her. My offer is this: For your combined equity interests and intellectual property, I will pay you $250,000 and give you 10 percent ownership in the new company. I'll be president and CEO, and you can be the general manager. Your annual salary will be $100,000 plus the usual perks.

"Eh, as for the little lady, well, I suspect she's worth only forty thousand dollars a year. She can be a salesperson with no equity in the new company. If you don't take my offer, then I'll just put you out of business and get it all for free! And with no manpower, you'll lose your ability to fulfill your military contracts. So, my man, what's your answer?" he demanded coldly.

"The M&A auditors valued this company today as it sits with assets at just under $2 million and with the military contracts over $7 million, and you want me to do what? Take one-fifth of the money I already have invested in here and just roll over and let you steal the company, my intellectual property, my patents, and four years of sweat equity so you can broker the company for twenty times earnings? Fuck you, DeSalva! Just try and get my company!" I slammed the phone down.

With my chest still puffed out and my face flushed, Rae stood and leaned on the front of the desk. "Well, Mr. Murphy, what fires did Mrs. Murphy and her cow start now?" she quipped. It brought me back to reality. How brazen we humans could be when our ego was life-size. I sank back in my chair. My day of reckoning had just arrived. "With Helen and the rest of the staff gone, it certainly is dead around here. Do we even know what we're up against? Logan, I'm worried! Do you consider DeSalva dangerous?" Rae challenged tensely.

Rae's face glared with apprehension, that "What have I gotten myself into?" look. Already in hock up to her gorgeous body for the company, she was looking to get out of debt, not to increase her liability any more than she already had. Her point about DeSalva was a good one. What did we really know about him?

"You're right, Rae! What the hell do we really know about DeSalva, except the standard public relations bullshit that, ah, that Venice Capital guy, Nick, gave us. Other than what he looks like, where he lives, and a thumbnail sketch of a few of his companies, we don't know squat!"

We sat pensively staring at each other, intermittently rehashing the recent events over and over that contributed to our predicament. For a split second, I reflected on the unexpected inspection by a third-party consultant representing the military contracting office when Rae was in Washington, DC, and I was away attending my father's funeral two months back. Although I was in constant communication with this individual while touring our facility, I was assured everything was going extremely well as Marc Sullivan was providing him the sales projections and production schedule required to complete his report. What a trusting fool I was.

Recalling the multitude of trivial comments spoken when matching wits with DeSalva, I said to Rae, "He alluded to being well-connected, said he grew up in New York City collecting vig when he was young. It may be total bullshit, but why the hell would he make a reference like that?"

Rae shook her head in disbelief. "Do you remember me telling you about my old college roommate, the one whose father really is connected? Well, if DeSalva's connected somehow, Frankie will know! Let's get that worry out of the way, if that's all right with you." I was hoping to elicit a more positive reaction.

"Yes, by all means," she responded, looking less despondent.

The least I could do was to let her in on more of the decision-making so that if everything went to hell in a handbasket, she would have more time to redress some of the liability. As a good-sized equity partner, it was her money too that he was stealing. It was her dream he was crushing.

"Wait a minute!" she said, almost jumping out of her chair. "Did you ever meet my neighbor Bill Lyons?"

"You mean the retired guy who lives just down the street from you? Ah, the one who walks Sheba occasionally?"

"Yeah! Well, before Bill retired, he used to be head of the major crimes division for the Nevada state police. He is grateful for all the time I spent with his wife, Eleanor, before she passed away. If I tell him about our situation, I'll know he'll help. Hmm, maybe he could run a background check on DeSalva for us. He's like a grandfather. Since Eleanor died, he's been so lonely. He would enjoy getting to know you. How 'bout you and I get together with him tonight? I'll invite him over for dinner. Okay with you?"

Rae had that coquettish presence—you know, the one like "The cat's away, so it's time for the mice to play" look. How could I resist? "What's in it for me?" I smirked.

"You need to ask?"

I envied her. Even with all the tension and stress, she could still slip away from reality just long enough to envision something pleasurable. Why the hell couldn't I do that? "Hey, sweetie, I enjoyed it more than you know. Maybe we should take it slow, huh?" Using the reverse psychology bullshit, I convinced her I needed to be persuaded.

"You call me sweetie and you want to what?" She giggled and walked around the back of my desk, fell over the arm of the chair in my lap, and planted the sexiest kiss. Oh, that same sensation. "How slow?" she asked as she kissed me with fire.

"Uh, uh, we'll talk about it later over dinner. How 'bout checking DeSalva out? See if you can find anything published about him or his companies, anything. Here's his portfolio. I'll call Frankie."

"Ciao! Remember, I will collect!"

I found Frankie's number on the back of my business card, filed in the back of the Fs in my trusty old Rolodex. Number, no address—that was Frankie. I dialed the number, but as I expected, he was not available, and the throaty no-name voice that answered advised he would pass my message to him. Since things were dead, I attempted to come up with a fallback position for the company and recruit new employees, try to get my arms around the severity of our predicament, try to keep things moving forward.

CHAPTER 11

Rae walked in my office, interrupting my train of thought. She pulled a piece of paper from her briefcase. "Logan, you need to hear this! I copied an article I found in the *Montreal Gazette* on Biotechné, one company mentioned in DeSalva's portfolio. It describes a freak fire that destroyed their laboratory last year. The police determined that the fire was started by a firebomb and alleged domestic terrorism.

"Let me read you this quote from Rene LaVóie, the president of Biotechné, who emphatically disagreed with the suspected terrorism thing: 'Our work is not for the military. We are a leader in developing new drugs for Alzheimer's. I am devastated. I lost everything. We weren't properly insured and don't have the money to rebuild. I believe this to be a malicious act of industrial sabotage.'"

She handed me the photocopied article. "Are we next? Is this going to happen to us?" she asked with an anguished look on her face. "Read it and tell me you don't get the same sick feeling I have." She leaned on my desk. "I need to think," she said as she turned and walked back to her office.

A few hours had passed, and still no word from Frankie, and as depressed as we both were, I decided we needed to get away from the business for a few minutes, maybe grab a late lunch. To cheer me up, Rae tossed me her keys and posed, "Sushi?" Knowing how I would love to own another sports car, she let me drive her '06 Porsche 911 Carrera S Coupe. BBS wheels, midnight black, and power spoiler, what a performance car!

We ate our fill of spicy yellow fin and shrimp rolls. Outside walking back to Rae's Porsche, I felt that edgy feeling creep upon me. I sensed something but said nothing. I decided instead to change direction and drive a circuitous route back to the office, test my hunch.

As I backed up in a wide arc in the parking lot, I noticed in the rearview mirror a black Mustang with dark-tinted windows parked on the side of the restaurant close to the building. As I drove away, I watched the Mustang move around to the front of the building and follow. At two blocks down the road, I made an illegal U-turn, crossed the median, and floored it. The Mustang continued in the other direction.

"That's interesting."

"Sorry. Just thought I'd go a different way back way to the office. I forgot how fast this baby is."

When we arrived back at the office, I called the answering service to check for more messages and learning Frankie had called back. His family started their business in Brooklyn and later branched out to Vegas. Frankie and I met our freshman year while on baseball scholarships together at the University of Arizona. We roomed together three of the four years and over time created that brotherhood bond that remained unbroken today. Being bonded brothers, Frankie was someone I would call a trusted friend, someone with whom I had tested this bond and knew I could call on for help, although help could be in a manner I might deem offensive but nonetheless effective.

Frankie's father was always good to us during our spring and summer breaks. Reportedly, he was into racketeering, but that was never proven. Every year during spring break, he would give us menial jobs, like moving furniture or driving a laundry truck, and paid us a thousand bucks a week, cash! That would carry us through a whole semester.

The old man took a liking to me. Frankie said it was because I always gave his father an honest day's work, never cheated him out of a nickel, and was always respectful to his mother. I would say that was true, but Frankie's father always liked talking about improving his trucking business, particularly the over-the-road tracking software program I urged him to install. He always said to Frankie that I would invent something enormous one day and that he wanted to buy stock in it legitimately. His old man always said that if I ever needed a job, needed anything, call him.

Frankie's a short, stocky guy around five-eight, who still boasted a thick head of hair and always dressed to the nines. He was never married, but he always had a looker on his arm whenever I visited him in Vegas. His belief in relationships with women—"Never bring a hamburger to a steak restaurant"—certainly wouldn't cut it with Rae, but it seemed to work for him, so who was I to knock it? After college, Frankie joined his father in business. He and his family moved to Vegas about eight years ago. According to newspaper reports, the Justice Department's interest in their business must mean Frankie was doing very well for himself. Dialing the number, I recalled that I hadn't spoken to Frankie since his mother's funeral six months ago.

"Frankie, how the hell are ya?"

"Couldn't be better. How's it with you?"

"Well, that's why I'm calling. I need a favor."

"What, you owe money? You need money?" he countered.

"I wish it was that simple, Frankie. It's about work. Until two days ago, I was doing fine, filling military contracts and going through the normal capitalization expansion route with this financial securities house and an investor."

"Yeah?"

"There's this investor guy from Lake Tahoe who's taken a good shot at stealing my company for its technology, ah, making me an offer I can't refuse, and now he's trying to put me out of business. He's stolen all my employees, created fake court documents, telling me he will take it for free. He alluded to being connected to intimidate me. Can you check him out?"

"For my college brother, anything!" Frankie replied with his usual warmth and arrogance. "Give me his name and address, and I'll get back to you. Oh, from now on, I want you to call this number. Leave your number. I'll call you back. Nowadays, ya can't be too careful. So who's this turd?" he said, snickering in his usual guttural manner.

"His name is Michael DeSalva. He lives on the California side of Lake Tahoe, just above Emerald Bay. One of his companies is Venice Capital out of San Francisco. It's connected somehow to Pingston Financial Securities out of Los Angeles. That's all I've got at the moment, Frankie. Hey, thanks for the favor. And on the personal side, how's your father doing? His health good?"

"Yeah, still good. Thanks for asking. He's still on me. He wants grandkids, ya know? Not with my track record, I tell him. He'll be happy to hear you asked about him. He misses talking to you. And how 'bout you?"

"Well, me, well, I've finally found that special someone. She's different and a real looker. She used to be in her grandfather's construction business. Exact opposite of the gold digger! More and more, I'm believing in your philosophy, Frankie, that you meet the right one when you least expect it and only after you've been around the barn once!" I chuckled.

"You come and visit me, okay? And bring the girlfriend. I wanna meet her."

"Okay. Soon, I promise. I've got to work through this problem."

"Ciao, brother!"

"Thanks, Frankie."

As I hung up the phone, Rae walked into my office. "Frankie?" she asked coyly.

"Yeah. He'll check out what we know so far about DeSalva."

"Would it be feasible to borrow some money from Frankie?"

"Frankie would give me the money, but then I'd be no different from anyone else whom he lent money to regardless of our past. Business is business, and his vig would slay us! It would forever change our relationship and friendship from long ago. I wouldn't chance it ever! I'd never want to test that water!"

"It's getting late. I'll leave now and stop by the market on my way home. See you seven-ish? Oh, and don't forget, bring fresh clothes, remember?" She smiled and walked away. I had been suppressing my feelings for a very long time. Lust? Love? Time would tell. I closed the office, walked once around the entire facility, checked the lab, reset the security alarm, and headed out to Rae's house in the hills.

As I turned onto Sunnyvale Saratoga Road, I passed what looked like the same black Mustang with the dark-tinted windows on an adjacent road pulling onto the road behind me. Watching my rearview mirror while turning a wide corner, without warning, my truck cut to the left, yanking me into oncoming traffic. I slammed the brakes hard, regained control, and eased off the pavement and onto the shoulder. The Mustang was nowhere around.

I got out of the truck to assess the situation. The left front tire was flat. It must've blown. I didn't remember hitting anything. I looked for a nail in the tread and found nothing. The tires were less than a year old, so they were still under warranty. I changed the tire and got back in the truck. As I pulled back onto the road, continuing around a bend, I spotted that same black Mustang parked about half a mile up on the hill, facing downhill toward me. I couldn't see the driver's face behind the dark-tinted windows as I approached. As I slowed to focus on the license plate, the driver gunned it and sped away. The license plate was covered in dried mud, so I couldn't see the number.

I arrived at Rae's a little late. Rae let Sheba out to greet me. "Is everything okay?" she remarked. "I got worried. I wish you had called."

"Oh, I had a flat tire about two miles back on Sunnyvale, and I left the damn cell phone on my desk. Sorry."

"Excused," she said, smiling warmly. "Let's eat. I'm starving, and Bill won't be over until about eight thirty, so I'll save dessert until then. And save a little room. You can have dessert twice!" She smiled.

Dinner was terrific—grilled tuna steak and shrimp kebabs accompanied by a smooth Merlot. Now this girl knew how to put a quick meal together. We continued our intermingling of diverse business discussions. Sheba's ears perked. Must be Bill.

Rae introduced me, and we sat around for well over an hour, chatting about many things, among them our recent predicament. Bill said he would like to help, although he didn't seem to have a lot of assurance since many of his contacts also retired about the same time. But hey, you never know.

After Bill left, Rae disappeared for a moment. She reappeared dressed in a sexy blue teddy and summoned me to follow her outside to the hot tub. Chilling in a bucket of ice was a nice bottle of sweet German Gewürztraminer and two glasses. She stepped into the swirling warm water, and I shed my clothes, following her willingly. Another extraordinary night! I had hoped that more would come along, but the warmth of the hot tub and the alcohol quickly lulled us to sleep, neither of us waking until early morning.

CHAPTER 12

I awoke before Rae. She lay there so serene, breathing softly. I didn't have the heart to wake her to let Sheba outside. What a fascinating creature! I quietly showered and awoke Rae with a goodbye kiss, saying I would see her at the office as I needed to go home and change.

"Logan, why don't you bring extra clothes and leave them here? That way, you won't have to go home to change before you go into the office."

"I'll take it under advisement!" I said and blew her a kiss.

When I got outside, I noticed that the left front tire was flat again. As I got to the truck, I noticed the back tire was flat. As I walked around the truck, all four were flat. Someone had cut the valve stems! What the fuck was going on?

In a huff, I stormed back in the house and called out to Rae, "Are there malicious kids around here?"

"No. This is one of the nicest communities in Los Altos Hills. Not many under thirty live here, Yuppies mostly. Why?" she asked while tying her satin robe.

"Come with me and take a look for yourself."

Rae walked out of the house in her robe and over to the truck. Covering her mouth, she giggled slightly. "Well, they're really only flat on one side," she said, trying to pick up my spirits.

"Oh, you're a lot of help. Guess I'll call a wrecker or someone to repair 'em."

Rae headed back to the house. Skimming the yellow pages, Rae located Sweets Tow & Tire Repair, only a ten-minute drive down on Caribe Cay Boulevard, and called outside to tell me that the tire service was coming with a flatbed. Since I didn't belong to an auto club, she guaranteed the up-front towing charge with her AAA membership card.

At the garage, I stayed in the back and shot the shit with a freckle-faced, red-haired kid named Trevor while he replaced all four valve stems. We kidded each other about trading places when he walked over to show me that he was certain he found a bullet in my spare tire and that it was what made an unrepairable hole in the sidewall. Shit! That meant I must replace the spare. Warranty wouldn't cover this. It was more expense I didn't need.

Posing a sarcastic grin, the kid remarked that it wasn't hunting season, so what did I do, piss off somebody's husband? Conjecture? I drove with both windows rolled down, so I was sure I would've heard a gunshot. The kid handed me the bullet. Handgun or rifle? Maybe it was shot using a suppressor. There was no reason to rattle Rae's emotional state right now. No need to frighten her more.

I made it to the office just shy of noon after having the tires repaired at a cost of three hundred dollars. A quick update from Rae revealed that the telephones were still dead. On the brighter side, she affirmed that both of our military contracts were still secure—that is, our encrypted circuit boards and parts were specced into their equipment contracts as sole source procurement. Yes!

That meant the Defense Intelligence Agency and Department of Defense, including the authorized defense contractors, must continue to purchase only our specced in electronics, no substitutes! Thank God for small miracles! At least that bastard couldn't take those away! The only way to lose the contracts would be our inability to deliver according to the contracts' terms, and I refused to let that happen. I would find a way even if I had to work 24-7.

Rae suggested a quick burger, but I declined. She was heading over to Fremont to meet with a graphics design company about printing new product spec sheets and might make it back by five-ish. We hadn't made firm plans, and I could use a good night's sleep, if that was even possible.

The sheer silence was unbearable, so I called some of our distributors. The first one I called, a small company in Dallas, told me they wouldn't be doing business with us anymore. When I queried them insistently, they reluctantly related the following story: Our ex-sales manager, Marc, notified them that the company was bankrupt, that we didn't have the legal right to manufacture the parts, that the government had indicted the company, and that instead, the distributor should do business with this other manufacturer who held the technology owned by a Mr. DeSalva. The saga continued that our parts and equipment were infringing upon his patents.

His patents! Un-fucking-believable! Not only did he not understand the technology but he also didn't have one fucking patent! Now he was manufacturing them! I had been manufacturing and assembling these top secret circuits for years and was the exclusive licensee to a small connector developed and patented by another California company I used instead of making it myself, so tell me, how in the hell could I be infringing? If he was copying what I did, then he would be infringing.

The owner fessed up and told me he was simply afraid to continue doing business with my company as he would surely be included in the lawsuit that DeSalva had against me and the company. Completely taken aback, I informed him that there was no such lawsuit against the company or me. Just the same, he would rather wait to see how the dust settled before he purchased more electronics from me.

More calls to other distributors revealed that Marc had repeated the same story with varied twists to his prevarications over the past few weeks, and he did a lot of this shit right under my nose! And I thought things couldn't get worse. In the last seventy-two hours, the only bright light was my new and burgeoning relationship with Rae and Sheba.

Things were becoming more depressing. The utter stillness of the office was annoying, like the hollow echoes you hear when you speak in an empty auditorium. How I missed the buzz of office chatter mixed in with the employees talking in the lunchroom, listening to them barter among themselves, trading lunches, rehashing weekend activities, weekly Lakers office bets, playing trivia games, and hearing Rae squeal at their silly jokes. She rarely got any privacy during lunch as the employees enjoyed sharing their trivialities with her.

It was 5:35 p.m., time to call it a day, but where was Rae? I dialed her cell phone and left her a message I was heading home to watch the game. It was not like her not to check in or miss a call, but she had her own life too, and with all the stress of the last three days, she might have stopped somewhere on her way home. I would hear from her later. Time to close up shop.

I glanced around the parking lot and down the industrial park. No Mustang. Was I losing it, being paranoid? All the way to my apartment, I watched the rearview mirror. No one followed me. I parked my truck in the garage behind the apartment building and made my way to the front door. It was ajar. I didn't forget to close it. There had been too many incidents that were out of my control. I crouched down, gradually pushing the door in. I stood still, listening for at least a minute. Hearing nothing but my own heartbeat, I stepped inside, my mind racing, trying to control my breathing.

Old cop shows ran through my mind. I pictured a burglary gone bad, and I had no defense weapon! A quick scan of the living area, kitchen, and bedroom revealed nothing unusual. Everything appeared to be normal, nothing missing or out of place. Trepidation enveloped me. Could the guy driving the Mustang be the one who caused the flat tire last night? How could he have done it? Who cut the stems on my tires? Was this a warning, a threat? Had someone been here? What were they looking for? I turned on my computer and entered the three levels of security passwords and pulled up my EXL90 encryption software program. All intact.

This was really bugging me. It reeked of DeSalva through and through. That greedy bastard! I called Rae's cell and left another message, made a roast beef sandwich, grabbed a cold Sam Adams, and sat down to watch the Lakers play the Celtics in Boston. I had been a fan of the Celtics for years. There was a lot of history in that team without all the hoopla of LA. At halftime, the Lakers were outscoring the Celtics handily, so I tried Rae one more time at home. Hmm, just her voice message again. It wasn't like her to be unresponsive.

I grabbed another beer, sat down on the couch, and continued to watch the game. I found it hard to enjoy the game as my mind kept jumping back and forth between the shit that had been happening and DeSalva's antics, between Rae's smell and her taste, between Marc's shenanigans with employees and distributors, the threats of a lawsuit, lie after fucking lie!

You thought you knew what somebody looked like, all their finest details, until you tried to add them up in your whimsical dreams. Then everything got jumbled. Was her hair longer? Was that really DeSalva or someone else? Was he short or tall? Was he really connected to the mob? Was this really happening? What was really happening? I didn't remember dozing off.

I was shaken by the stark jingle of the telephone. The handset read 8:05 p.m. It must be Rae. Grabbing the handset, I almost knocked the base to the floor. "Hello."

"This is Detective Dixson from San Jose Police Department. Is this Logan Scott?"

"Yes."

"Mr. Scott, a coworker of yours was assaulted earlier this evening and is unconscious in the Santa Clara Hospital. We found yours and her business cards in her pocketbook. I assume you know a Raelyn MacAllister," he stated.

"Yes," I replied, alarmed. "Oh my God, is she all right? What happened?"

"Earlier this evening, Ms. MacAllister had stopped to pick up pet supplies and was attacked before getting in her car. She is in intensive care at Santa Clara. If you have time, we'd like you to come down to the station to help us sort out some issues."

"No, I'll meet you at the hospital!"

"Now, Mr. Scott, take it easy. We don't need you in the hospital because of reckless speeding. She's not going anywhere for a while, so I'll meet you there. Take your time and drive safely."

I grabbed my jacket and took off for the hospital. Upon arriving, I stopped at the welcome desk and was directed to the ICU. Detective Dixson was waiting outside the room. Dixson looked like an upstanding guy—clean-cut, square jaw, and in great shape.

"Mr. Scott? Detective Dixson."

"Yes."

"Ah, were you with Ms. MacAllister earlier today?"

"Yes. We work together. Your questions will have to wait." My patience was running thin. All I wanted to do was see Rae. I walked into the room. She was a revolting mess. Her forehead was heavily bandaged, and what was not covered was swollen and bruised, purplish. Some dried blood was still on her left hand. She was not cognizant of my presence. A doctor walked into the room.

"Mr. Scott, I presume?" he asked as he carefully examined her chart.

"Yes," I replied.

"The officer told me you would stop by. I'm Dr. Olivan, a neurologist on staff. May we step out in the hallway?" I followed Dr. Olivan outside the room where Dixson was standing. "I was on call when she was brought in and discussed her condition with the ER physician and ordered a battery of tests. The duty nurse found both of your business cards in her wallet and no other next of kin information. We could not locate any family and notified the police of the find. How well do you know Ms. MacAllister?" the doctor asked, curious.

"Rae and I have been friends and business partners for the last three years. I am the closest thing to family. She looks awful. What's the extent of her injuries?"

"She has contusions over her arms, which will all heal in time. She has a hairline basilar skull fracture. The CT scan shows minor petechial hemorrhaging but no brain damage other than intracranial pressure caused by cerebral edema, or slight swelling. The cut on her forehead will not require reconstructive surgery. She has three bruised ribs and a fractured wrist. In plain English, she looks worse than she is. She needs plenty of rest. She may seem a little confused upon waking as she has been given medication to sedate her. Don't be alarmed if she doesn't immediately know her surroundings."

"Excuse me. The police said she was unconscious. Is she?"

"No, that's incorrect. She is not unconscious, just heavily sedated. Mr. Scott, do you know if she has medical insurance?"

"Yes, she's covered. We're under the same group policy. I'll get whatever information you need."

"Please understand, Mr. Scott, I personally don't care about those details, but the hospital administration does. Would you stop by Admissions on your way out and answer their questions?"

"Sure. I'll take care of it. Thanks. Oh, uh, may I stay here for a while and call you later for an update?"

"I'm on call here for another sixteen hours, and yes, you can stay here for a while. You can reach me here at the hospital. Just ask one of the duty nurses. They'll page me."

"Detective, if you would give me just one moment." I walked back in the room and stood next to her bed. I spent a few minutes just staring at her, wondering how she would deal with the bruising on her face. In my experience, women could deal with almost anything and not care, but touch their face, well, putting it mildly, she looked like shit, and it was my fault. I should've been there. I walked back out in the hallway to get answers.

"I'd like more details. Fill me in please." The detective was not accustomed to being ordered about by a civilian. As a professional, he quickly regained his composure and began narrating what he knew.

"According to witnesses, evidently, Ms. MacAllister had driven her car around the rear of Valley Pet Store, parked near the delivery door, and had opened the trunk with the car running while she waited at the back door for an employee to help with two large bags of dog food. The young man at the store concurred he was to open the rear store door and help Ms. MacAllister load the heavy bags in her car.

"A customer heard the commotion and Ms. MacAllister's scream and ran around the corner of the building to see her being assaulted by a tall man of about six feet or more wearing dark running clothes and a black balaclava pulled down over his face. The customer, also a regular at the store, stated she thought the assailant was striking Ms. McAllister with what appeared to be a small baseball bat. From the description of her injuries quoted by the ER doctor, the assailant may have used a sap. Ah, that's two pieces of leather sewn together with lead shot inside to supply the energy and weight. One good blow and most folks go down.

"The customer screamed and yelled for the police, at which time the assailant ran around the opposite side of the building and

Ms. MacAllister collapsed. It appears from the location of the bruises on her forearms that Ms. MacAllister was trying to protect herself by putting her hands in front of her face, which would account for her fractured wrist. The Good Samaritan banged on the back door, and the store employees immediately called an ambulance. Most likely, she wouldn't have survived an unimpeded blow to the head.

"So far, we've determined that she was not sexually assaulted. I don't believe this was a typical mugging. Nothing appeared to be missing from her purse. Her rings and watch were not taken. I have towed her car to impound as evidence. That's why I asked you to come down and help me fill in some blanks."

I spent several minutes imparting information about the extent of my relationship with Rae to Detective Dixson, omitting the details of a more personal nature. I informed him I knew of no such nefarious characters in her background, and that was that!

"A list of her personal effects showed Ms. MacAllister was still wearing her watch, bracelet, necklace, emerald ring, and gold earrings. Several credit cards and a small amount of cash remained in her wallet. Your phone number had been punched into her cell phone, but the call had not gone through, apparently interrupted by the attack. It was found on the car seat. We matched the number against that from your business card the duty nurse located from her belongings," he reiterated, further explaining the differences between this incident and a typical mugging.

I told Detective Dixson about the recent break-in and theft at the company, meeting Officer Blaas who wrote the report, and the flat tires incidents. At least he could correlate that info. But to postulate an absolute connection to DeSalva for Rae's condition without proof might be too far-reaching at this point. I would rather not go there.

Then I asked how I might get in touch with Blaas, and he gave me the precinct's number to save time. We finished with some small talk, and the detective left. I returned to Rae's room, settled into a chair, and waited until something happened. Graciously, Dr. Olivan allowed me to remain against hospital policy.

*****

Rae stirred at about 1:00 a.m., moaning of throbbing pain in her head. I pushed the call button for the duty nurse and asked if Dr. Olivan was still around. In a few minutes, he came in to check her vital signs and commented that her headache was very normal considering the excess fluid within the brain tissue, swelling, and trauma. Her condition required close observation over the next forty-eight to seventy-two hours. I squeezed her unbandaged hand and gave her a kiss on the only place that didn't hurt. I hung around for about another hour until she lumbered back to sleep, and then as I had promised her, I left to go check on Sheba and get some sleep.

I slept in her bed with Sheba waking me around eight. There was only one message from the answering service. I would retrieve it later. I drove back to my apartment, wanting to get to the bottom of this nightmare! I couldn't get Rae's condition out of my head. I wanted to get that bastard! He was behind all this!

After showering, I went into my closet and unearthed a fireproof metal lockbox well-hidden behind clothes attached to the wall. I opened it and pulled out a Colt Mustang .380 automatic pistol and extra mag. It was perfect for close-up center mass or headshot. I checked the clip and changed out the ammo to MagSafe, a frangible bullet that killed easily within two feet.

I picked the gun up a few years back when visiting the contracting office of Fort Bragg's Army Forces Command, or FORSCOM. I answered a classified ad in the *Fayetteville Observer*, the local newspaper that served the surrounding community of Fayetteville, North Carolina, and Fort Bragg's personnel. It was a simple cash transaction from a soldier deploying overseas who didn't want to leave it stateside—no names, no paperwork, no traceability. Time to carry. To hell with the laws of California. I would rather be judged by twelve than carried by six.

I stuck the gun in my jacket pocket and headed back over to the hospital hoping Rae felt better. I wouldn't be staying long, as with Rae out, I had much to do at the office.

CHAPTER 13

I arrived at the office to get the shock of my life. The company we had the exclusive license for the mechanical firmware of had just served me for breach of contract. They demanded forty thousand dollars within ten days from the demand letter, or we would lose the exclusive license. What else could go wrong? Further scrutiny of their claims revealed that if the forty-thousand-dollar license fee was not paid within the ten days, they would continue pursuing their patent infringement lawsuit.

I now needed a lawyer. In all my years as a businessman, other than for writing and reviewing contracts, I had never needed a lawyer, and now I did. I had no idea what lawyer to pursue, and even if I did, what then? I called a bevy of friends looking for suggestions. Like me, most everyone I knew only recommended their divorce lawyer, but no one had a trial lawyer in mind, much less one whose specialty was intellectual property law. Damn! I clearly did not want to levy more bad news to Rae, not in her delicate condition. Nonetheless, I had to as her name was also listed under the heading: "Defendants, on the masthead of the lawsuit." Rae had business connections galore, so she might know of a good lawyer.

The answering service called back to relay the message I forgot to pick up earlier. This one was from state unemployment office. I called the woman back to find out more thrilling news: that it was recently reported to them that the company had more employees than was reported and that an agent from their office was coming in to conduct a complete payroll audit next week. I informed the woman that the company had never misreported or misrepresented its employment status ever! Then I asked her the sixty-four-thousand-dollar question: "Where did you receive this enlightening tip?"

As I expected, she replied that they were not obliged to tell me. However, she said it was an anonymous tip purportedly from an employee and that state law required them to follow up on all grievances. I told the woman it was strictly maliciousness by one or more ex-employees and that she could have complete access to my payroll records and that, furthermore, doing business under the contracts the company held with the federal government, their office had already conducted a thorough audit as they were required to every year! I had broken no laws and was distressed at being accused of such. And I asked her if I had any recourse if her office found nothing. She replied nothing! Some fucking justice!

Pending receipt of a very sizeable, overdue government check, I retrieved the morning's mail from the front desk inbox, and there was a certified letter from the California Workers' Compensation Appeals Board requesting a complete review of the last three years' work records to determine employment insurance fraud! Unbelievable! Another fucking problem! Already pissed off at the world, I yanked the phone and dialed the man who sent me this letter.

I went through the entire diatribe again, as I did earlier to the woman from the state unemployment office. No avail! Then I asked the proverbial question once again: "How is it you think my company has committed insurance fraud? Your office is also part of the annual audit required to maintain our government contracts, is it not?" He replied with the usual bullshit but said they must follow up on all tips, anonymous or otherwise. Yeah, yeah, yeah. That motherfucking bastard! Treachery? Criminal deceit? Damn right!

After closing, I drove back to the hospital, stopping on the way to buy Rae some sweets. I picked up her favorite chocolate-covered pecans. She would eat the whole damn box and never put on a pound! And she would be happy to hear that Sheba and I were getting along fine. Oh God, how I didn't want to levy more distressing news and the other nuisance bullshit.

Rae was partially sitting up when I entered her room, anxiously awaiting an update on her status from Dr. Olivan, who was expected any minute. She wanted to go home. Although she looked like a freight train had hit her, she was talking better, not so sluggish. I bent down and kissed her hello. Her eyes welled up. I choked a little myself. It was beyond my comprehension how someone could maliciously attack such an innocent, beautiful creature.

Dr. Olivan walked in. We exchanged greetings, and he politely ushered me away from the bed, pulled the curtain closed, and began examining Rae. I stepped outside into the hallway. Anxiety rushed over me. Thoughts zigzagged with increased intensity—the tires, the computer, Sullivan, the lawsuit, the forty-thousand-dollar demand, no employees, the Mustang, the audits, and now this! The timing, I knew it was him. He was calling the shots. I wanted that son of a bitch!

Dr. Olivan opened the curtain to levy the diagnostics update to Rae as I walked back in. She was experiencing posttraumatic shock, which incited restless, intermittent sleep. He would keep her at least one more night and rerun the same tests, and if her BSEP (neurobehavioral) test was good, then he would consider letting her go home if she had supervision. Dr. Olivan remarked that my face was rather flushed and asked if I was feeling all right. I replied that I was extremely tired and just needed sleep. I waited until the doctor left before I gave Rae her sweets. She was delighted, and since it hurt to chew, they would last her quite a while.

Rae listened intently as I explained our dire situation to her. She pondered for a moment and then replied that she thought Sean Pease might be a good lawyer for us. She knew him through the Economic Development Council of the San Jose Chamber of Commerce. She said they worked a charity event together. I vowed to get in contact with him as time was not our ally. And since she was staying at least one more day, I promised to bring her some fresh underclothes, her robe, and personal items when I returned later that night. This ought to be an interesting treasure hunt! I kissed her goodbye and headed out to her house. I couldn't say I minded the thought of staying there. It was helluva lot better than my dismal apartment.

I drove to Rae's house, watching my rearview mirror. My situational awareness training was coming back. No Mustang. No one was around! I fingered the pistol in my jacket pocket. Eighteen ounces but it felt heavy as I wasn't used to carrying it. I was thinking about acquiring something with more power, maybe a .45 caliber Kimber Ultra Carry. Why a .45? A good friend I met in Iraq once told me, "'Cause they don't make a .46!'"

I pulled into the driveway and parked the truck. No cars were in sight, and no Sheba in the window as Bill was dog-sitting at his house until I got home. The house still had her essence, wonderfully fragrant! I walked through the living room to her bedroom. I rarely took the time to appreciate her collection of Native American art before. As I opened the bedroom door, the room felt cool. I walked straight to her armoire and opened the top drawer, looking for her underclothes. Hmm, the drawer contained scented sachets that wafted a sweet, floral fragrance in the room and colorful lace bras and underwear, Victoria's Secret labels. Hmm, cup size?

That was the last thing I remembered. I awoke with sharp, stabbing pain jolting through the back of my head. I touched the back of my head and discovered a lump the size of a golf ball. My head throbbed worse than the earthquake of '94! It hurt like hell! I tried to get up but collapsed back down, still dizzy. How long was I out? I looked at my watch, six thirty!

I managed a roll onto my side. I got up on my knees and crawled up to sit on the bed. The last thing I remembered was the peach-colored lace bra I picked up that was still in my hand and woke up next to the drawer upside down on the floor, everything askew. I slowly rose to my feet and shuffled around the bed. I looked around, and nothing major appeared missing or messed up, except the toppled drawer. One of the French doors to the outside deck remained open. Whoever was in here left in a hurry. I drew the gun from my pocket and hurried through the rest of the house. No joy. Back in the bedroom, I replaced the drawer in the armoire.

Scanning the room, throbbing pain displaced sensuous thoughts. I found a small carry-on bag in Rae's closet. I stuffed it with her color-coordinated, French-cut peach lace underwear and bra, silk robe, her slim-cut Levi's, a light cotton sweater, and the usual personal hygiene articles from her bathroom. All her clothes had that gentle, sweet smell, like the fresh floral scent one smelled after an afternoon rain shower. I walked to the back door to check it as it remained locked, wishing Sheba had been in the house. What could I prove sans the knot in the back of my head? Not a goddamned thing! I phoned Bill to remind him I would fetch Sheba after visiting Rae. He was fine with that.

I arrived just before visiting hours ended and greeted Rae. She noticed something was wrong but didn't say anything as Dr. Olivan interposed for a last look for the night. I waited until Dr. Olivan walked out into the hallway, cornered him, and then related most of the events and story to him. Begrudgingly, he agreed and told me to meet him down in Emergency in twenty minutes after finishing his rounds, and he would attend to my head.

When I walked back in, Rae was slowly munching on the chocolate-covered pecans. "What's wrong?" she asked sternly. "You look troubled. What are you not telling me?"

"Oh, got one hell of a headache, that's all."

"Look me in the eye, Logan. What's wrong? Is Sheba okay?" She pushed the controls to bring her sitting upright.

"Ah, I got to the house at about 5:45 p.m. I went into the bedroom to get you some clothes and deodorant and stuff. The next thing I know, I'm flat on the floor, sporting a real pounder and an egg on the back of my head. The dresser drawer was upside down next to me with your underwear strewn all over the floor. I finally got up and walked back through the house. Everything seemed okay. Thanks to Bill, at least Sheba is okay. He's expecting me to fetch my new best friend on my way back," I answered, smiling while squeezing her hand to ease the worried look on her face. We talked for another hour, and I said, "Well, honey, visiting hours are over. I've got a date with Sheba!"

"Logan, call the police," she remarked, a quiver in her voice.

"I'll consider it. Get some rest now."

"No, I'm serious. Call them. Can it hurt to talk to Sergeant Blaas again?"

"Okay. I promise, I'll call him."

Rae smiled with that statement as I kissed her on that one spot and kept smiling as I walked out of the room to meet Dr. Olivan. I was really apprehensive. What was the intruder looking for? Pretty obvious someone wanted us out of the picture, and they were doing a damn good job of trying. I knew DeSalva was involved! As I meandered down to Emergency, that uneasy feeling welled up again.

Dr. Olivan gave me a cursory exam and checked my equilibrium and ocular motility reflexes. During the exam, I related some of the recent incidents. He cautioned me, alluding that our recent events were not everyday occurrences. He strongly advised I contact the police. I replied that I had intended to do so, but hunch didn't account for much. All the same, he wanted me to come back and see him before rounds in the morning. He agreed no report would be written up. I thanked him for the favor.

As I pulled into Rae's driveway, I saw a note stuck on the front door. I had been in such a hurry to leave. I must've missed it before. The note was from Bill that said Sheba was fine and to not worry about coming to get her no matter the hour and that he had saved a piece of apple pie for me.

I telephoned Rae telling her that I would visit Bill, but I wasn't so sure who was babysitting who. She laughed knowing Sheba was in good hands. The news lifted her spirits and ought to help her sleep better tonight. From the front door, I could see plenty of light on at Bill's and assumed he was watching the evening news, waiting for me.

Sheba must've heard me coming and poked her nose through the drapes in his living room window. I rang the doorbell, and Bill summoned me inside. Both were glad to see me, but Sheba seemed fidgety. Bill offered me a beer, and we sat chatting for another hour while I relayed the horror of the last couple of days to him. He was appalled at hearing the news and assured me he would help us any way that he could. Bill picked up a 9mm handgun, dropped the clip, and pulled the slide back, making sure the chamber was empty. He dry fired the trigger and handed me a Smith & Wesson M&P compact 9mm. I pulled the slide back and dry fired it. Bill said, "I insist."

I replied, "It's unnecessary."

"Yes, it is. I have more. It's clean." Bill smiled.

The way he adored Rae was apparent, like he was her adopted grandfather. He emphasized that he would keep a close eye on her and would nose around the house during his daily walks with Sheba. He remarked how pleased he was that I was around to protect her.

I pulled a fresh cigarette butt out of my jacket pocket, which I picked up off the back deck stairs earlier when nosing around, noting I had not touched the main part where fingerprints might be discovered. Bill remarked, "I wouldn't bother. Most likely, it's from the guy who smacked you. He's probably done this kind of thing before and wore gloves, so no prints. I'll look around for more clues, but don't get your hopes up." I proposed he not mention the cigarette butt so as not to frighten Rae. He agreed that was a wise decision.

Sheba and I left with me telling him we would have him over for dinner in a day or two when Rae felt up to it if he didn't mind my hand at cooking. He accepted, and I took off jogging, calling for Sheba to catch up with me.

CHAPTER 14

L ake Tahoe in spring was picture-perfect—there was still snow on Donner Summit and the other high peaks, trees were blossoming, and the air was cool and clean, just itching to climb to summer temps. Tourism outside of casino traffic was sparse at this time of year.

Michael DeSalva was reading the *Wall Street Journal* while catching sun out on the boat dock, enjoying the tranquility of the surrounding wilderness, when his majordomo approached with the telephone.

"Sir, I am sorry to disturb you. There is a call on your private line."

"Who is it, Thomas?" he said, breaking his train of thought.

"It is RJ, sir. Would you like me to take a message?"

"No, I'll take it." He waved Thomas off.

"Yes," DeSalva said, speaking deliberately as he stood up and walked to the railing.

A grated voice resonated, "The tasks have been completed."

"Problems?"

"Nothing I couldn't handle. Everything went according to plan."

"Good! I'll arrange the wire transfer today."

"Are you in need of further assistance?" the voice asked in anticipation.

"Not at this time." DeSalva ended the call with a perverse smirk on his face and sat back down to consume himself with more financial news.

Michael Francis DeSalva grew up in a brownstone on Trader Street in Queens Village, New York. As a juvenile, he collected vig for a local loan shark. He quickly learned how to levy the usury laws, both the real ones and the unwritten rules. Never dealing with the heavy-handed side of the business, he had the easy job. While others negotiated, he was quite satisfied being the carrier.

DeSalva had just turned thirty-eight years old, married with three children. His oldest, Emilio, was age fourteen, and his twin girls, Daniela and Gianna, were age eleven. His wife, Gabriella, was a looker but an uneducated dos and don'ts gal who lacked the social graces he worked hard to acquire. Theirs started as a shotgun marriage with a young one on the way before he could fathom the extent of his father-in-law's connections.

DeSalva had everything going his way—flourishing enterprises generating ample cash to support his flamboyant lifestyle, a shrewd accountant who masked each operation as a legitimate business, a wife who only enjoyed spending his money, the twins in a private boarding school in upstate Vermont, and Emilio in a prep school in Virginia. He had the best of all worlds with plenty of time for trysts and other venturesome activities.

DeSalva learned early on how to use the skills of the mob to intimidate people he wanted to do business with. Fear was a formidable weapon, especially in today's business. He was a coward, never venturing to get his hands dirty. He was proficient at using fear and blackmail to perform his dirty work. What was it they said? A leopard couldn't change his spots.

DeSalva wouldn't consider divorce, at least while his father-in-law was still alive. He didn't want retribution from the family. Besides, he liked her having money. It gave him ample freedom. He instead adopted the old-school ways: the outward appearance of commitment to his family and a mistress or two on the side. Clearly, DeSalva had his share—one in LA, one in Vegas, and one in Seattle. All his women were blond, buxom, and devoted to his money. He liked his women to put their mouth where his brass was, and he could well afford it! His war chest had deep pockets!

Every few months, he would attend to his exporting business in Seattle; but of late, his primary commerce was of taking over small companies with enormous potential through fear and loopholes in the legal system. Knowing that small companies seeking legitimate investment capital typically had insufficient growth capital and limited resources should they be required to defend themselves involving any sort of litigation, assimilation according to his terms was quick and painless.

Once under his control, his clever bursar would broker the company in through a shell corporation, take it public, and cash out for fifteen to thirty times earnings. It was business in the new century. Like the uncontested takeover of Biotechné, it was a cash cow when it hit NASDAQ! He reveled in conceit over that conquest! He even got laid in the process! An exhilarating way to vanquish the partners: fuck their wives!

Logan Scott's company was his latest fancy. Following the usual surreptitious investigation into the company and key individuals, he postulated a smooth transition once Scott conferred with an attorney about the cost of intellectual property litigation. Just in case, he would keep the heat on Scott, keenly engaging the assistance of Marc Sullivan for the continued onslaught on Scott's customer base, always keeping the liability at arm's length.

DeSalva had a moneyed way with weak-minded people. Persuasively confident, he would obtain private information on his prey and use it for his own gain. The feds called this extortion. He called it amusing. Besides the deceitful fabrications and bogus banking reports, DeSalva, like a pit boss, hired the engineers and the assembly line supervisor, leaving the working dolts for fodder. Besides, he knew that Marc's wife would play along. Veronica Sullivan fit the profile like the rest of his women—enticed by money and willing to play hardball to get it. But they had to play his game, what he wanted and when he wanted it. He always drummed up a trump card, even on Veronica, just in case.

His summation of Veronica Sullivan was right on. The very first time they met, Veronica solicited a sexual encounter with him. During a strategy meeting in the restaurant of the Ritz-Carlton in San Francisco, Veronica seized the opportunity of Marc's brief absence to come on to DeSalva. At DeSalva's request, Marc had excused himself for a few minutes to commiserate by telephone with key employees and incite the propaganda campaign against Scott and his company when Veronica enticed DeSalva to escort her to the ladies' room.

Out of sight from the dining room in an L-shaped corridor beyond the restrooms, Veronica suggested that they get to know each other better and pressed her breasts against his chest, slipping her hand inside the bond of his trousers. She knelt and looked up smiling while taking him into her mouth. Not expecting any of this to happen, DeSalva spent his wad rather quickly, turning red with embarrassment for losing control abruptly!

"This is just a taste of what you'll get if you call me!" she said while zipping up his pants, then dashed into the ladies' room to tidy up. DeSalva returned to the dining room and sat down at the table just as Marc Sullivan reappeared, grinning like a Cheshire cat. "The tide has turned," he wisecracked to DeSalva.

DeSalva pitied Sullivan, figuring him to be nothing more than a good soldier as he was hungry, easy to cast off when necessary. Veronica rejoined them, and the three finished a high-priced meal with all the accoutrements! DeSalva ordered another magnum of Perrier-Jouët. This was a celebration. Everyone was in his camp. It was time to execute his plan! The evening concluded with success. As Veronica departed for the ladies' room, DeSalva handed Marc a thick wad of one-hundred-dollar bills.

"It's important you have the little woman's support on this new venture as you'll be on the road a lot. Got a lot of projects for you. Now go buy her something nice and enjoy the rest of the weekend, on me! I'll show you what it's like to make real money!" He was smirking as he strolled out of the restaurant.

In the limousine on the way to Signature FBO at the San Francisco general aviation airport, DeSalva was planning his next attack. His kickback proposition to the patent holder for the technology that Scott had licensed was convincing enough, legal or not. DeSalva promised to pay all legal expenses incurred and signed a letter of intent to exclusively license the firmware technology for six times the royalty fee Scott had contractually licensed. The patent holder couldn't lose! And since Scott's company was a few days late in making their quarterly royalty payment, all the patent holder had to do was call default. DeSalva made sure that Scott's payment from the government for his first release would be delayed, lost in the hinterland.

DeSalva knew the lawyers in San Francisco were hurting, eating their young to survive, and would take this case on for reduced fare. He would get the license, the technology, Scott's company, and Scott's intellect to boot, all for a couple hundred grand, if not for free. DeSalva figured he could broker the deal easily, and $7 million was a lucky starting number. He suspected Scott's secret project was priceless! And when everything was running smoothly, Pingston Financial Securities would broker the company for as much as twenty times earnings. And with the help on Capitol Hill, he would peddle it off to a defense contractor. He smiled at his cleverness!

About twenty minutes out of Lake Tahoe airport, DeSalva called Thomas to report whether his wife was home and sober enough to fuck. She was still a good fuck now and then even though she meant little to him. Outside of fostering his kids, she couldn't raise 'em worth a shit. Thomas replied there was no answer from her bedroom. Most likely, she was passed out or at one of the casinos, looking for young meat. DeSalva liked to take his aggression out on her during sex but deftly learned to control his temper. No pissing off Daddy. Time was his ally. He couldn't lose focus. Besides, she would drink herself to death soon enough. It was a clear night. He was aroused!

CHAPTER 15

DeSalva smiled to himself while enjoying breakfast. One week ago, he met with Logan Scott to commence his coup, and today started his two-fold plan. First, he would dispatch Marc to hand-deliver lawsuit documents and other bogus papers to Scott's top five distributors around the country and acquaint them to his new company and their new supplier in Sacramento. That ought to test this soldier's mettle and keep him busy all week. Plan two was to fuck Marc's wife!

DeSalva telephoned his new conscript with marching orders at seven fifteen that morning from the boat dock. It was such an open space where all private phone calls were made. He promised Marc a brand-new BMW upon his successful mission and relocation to Sacramento. The caveat, Marc had to bat a thousand, or no BMW. He only gave Marc ninety minutes to pack and arrive at the airport, assuming Veronica would drive him. Then he would test her waters!

He didn't have to wait long. As soon as Veronica Sullivan dropped hubby off, she called DeSalva herself. Thomas walked down to the boat dock to apprise him that a Ms. Sullivan was calling on his private line. DeSalva took the call.

"Hello, Michael," she whispered softly. "The movers are coming today, so I'll have nothing to do from tomorrow on until the movers arrive in Sacramento. Wanna get together?"

"You must be reading my mind. Be ready for a limo pickup tomorrow morning at 9:00 a.m. Follow the instructions in the package the driver will give you. Never use the cell phone in the package for any other calls but to my cell phone, and never call this number again. The limo will take you to Executive Rent-A-Car where you will pick up the Jaguar I have leased for you. They will give you a map.

If you leave early, you will have no trouble finding the Sacramento Executive Airport. Wait for me inside the Sacramento Executive Jet Center. I will arrive before 11:30 a.m., and we'll take it from there." He ended the call.

*****

DeSalva was delighted that the flight to Sacramento would be a short, smooth flight as it was bright and sunny and all downhill. His pilot landed and taxied the Citation to aviation parking on the fuel ramp close to the building. Walking toward the building, he could see Veronica poised like a Greek statue in her see-through, low-cut blouse, revealing her round breasts. She appeared coked up, but he liked that in women. In fact, he encouraged it regularly. It made them less inhibited.

DeSalva signed in, Veronica chattering like a magpie as they made their way to the Jaguar. He insisted on driving. He always insisted on driving. That way, if he didn't like how things were going, he would just leave, a maneuver he played often. He never thought women could drive worth a shit anyway. They were just good for fucking and pushing out babies.

Veronica never stopped talking. She was on a moneyed high—new car, new clothes, Marc making four times his salary, and now this! DeSalva knew how to build a cavalry.

"How do you like the car?"

"It's unbelievable. Uh, it's so luxurious, and it has absolutely everything."

As he ran his hand up the inside of her thigh, he asked, "What's in the bag on the back seat?"

"Toys!" she replied awkwardly.

"What kind of toys?" he asked deviously.

"Toys for me…and you!"

*****

After two satisfying but tiring sexual bouts, DeSalva's mind drifted back to his latest fancy: how to finish Scott. Scott wasn't crumbling like the others. What was it going to take for him to fall? All these companies under his control yet only this one was taking maximum effort. While Veronica lay resting next to him, he planned the next phase of execution. He had decidedly removed that MacAllister broad from the equation, expecting Scott was intelligent enough to get the message. If Scott broke and gave in, he would know by the end of the week. *No staff, no partner, no money. How could he not?* he thought. *He'll fall soon!*

Reflecting on their conversation earlier in the car, DeSalva surmised that Veronica didn't know much at all about Logan Scott, never got close to him. She was no help, just a good screw. Apparently, Scott didn't screw around. There was no dirt to use that way, pondering aimlessly.

Veronica stirred. He closed his eyes and held his position, feigning sleep. He wasn't ready for more sex and hoped she wasn't either. Like a prowling cat, she slinked under the covers and began licking the points of his body that had no way to fight back. He remained still, but the incessant movement of her forceful tongue was more powerful than his ability to pretend. He started to grow, ending his ability to hide behind the mask of sleep. He groaned slightly, still trying to remain quiet. Veronica took him into her mouth, milking him, stripping off his strength to refuse, rapidly increasing the motion and tension, almost too callous. It was so erotic. More than the strongest could endure.

He stiffened, his jaw agape in deference to time and its surroundings. DeSalva tried to regain control, but she increased with tepid rhythm. Fighting the urge to explode, he focused on his fists, forcing his nails into his palms. She sucked harder, faster. She gripped tighter. He felt helpless. His mind raced back to the first time they met at the restaurant. He underestimated her appetite. Finally, he surrendered, a wicked temptress who rubbed him raw with her power.

DeSalva couldn't remember the last time he had sex like this, wondering if it was the cocaine or just vigorous sex. She was a hungry beast, not like his submissive concubines. How could Marc Sullivan keep this woman? No wonder she took part in extracurricular activities. Sullivan wasn't near man enough to satisfy her. Completely spent, he looked at his watch, 5:00 p.m. Shit! It was time to leave for Los Angeles. On second thought, Los Angeles would just have to wait. He was just too sore to perform again. He would leave for Tahoe instead.

"Stay the night," Veronica whined as he dressed.

"I'll be back, and you'll be praying for me to leave," he replied with a twisted grin. He called for a limo and left Veronica dreaming about the next seduction. He would absolutely fuck her again, and soon! That was a promise!

Climbing into the limo, he noticed that his groin hurt from their drawn-out encounter. Next time, he would prove to her he was more man than she could handle. He had always had to keep up that perfect, fearless posture, man over woman, never showing weakness. Thinking of Veronica, DeSalva was beside himself. His ego let no one, even a woman like that, get the best of him. His plan was intact now, ready to destroy the runt Logan Scott. It was time to charge the hill and capture Scott's flag.

CHAPTER 16

The weekend rolled around. It had been four days since Rae's attack. The hospital wasn't as busy as yesterday. She was looking better, smiling more often. Dr. Olivan might release Rae tomorrow provided he was satisfied with her progress and test results. She was anxious. So was I. There was time only for a quick visit today as I would be working all weekend to catch up and giving her time to rest.

It was tough to keep visiting her while running what was left of the business. Vendors were hounding us, all querying about getting paid, incited by calls from Marc Sullivan prophesizing the company's demise. Lawsuit, bankruptcy, federal indictments, stock fraud, you name it. I was surprised I hadn't been accused of arson along with the other bullshit.

My recruiting efforts panned out as a few of the production people agreed to return to work when they got word through the job service that new faces had replaced theirs. At least we could continue fulfilling the military orders. It would be a balancing act, but we would endure. What a fucking mess!

The lawyer Rae recommended, Sean Pease, had recently moved from Chicago. For his sanity, he left a stressful practice to join a small firm in San Jose. After a brief interlude from my tale of woe, he informed me that his hourly rate was $275, and he expected at least a $10,000 retainer. He estimated the cost of defense to be upward of $150,000, more if depositions were out of state.

DFAS (Defense Finance and Accounting) office was backtracking their missing payment, and they were slow as hell, but I needed ten grand now. I still had to come up with forty thousand dollars for the royalty. Only a few days to go! I had most everything in the business collateralized, had had for the past few years, and Rae was in hock as well. Maybe I could scrounge up a few bucks from my family.

A call to my sisters was encouraging. They were flabbergasted at hearing the situation. Both agreed to lend me their kids' college tuition fees, totaling eighteen thousand dollars, but they had to be paid back timely in less than sixty days. My loving sisters came through. I would be indebted forever. My brother had just sold his house and agreed to lend me the fourteen-thousand-dollar leftover that hadn't been committed to his new home. That left eight grand remaining. I could use some of the military money when it arrived, but that would be needed to cover payroll and running the business. This fee had to come from elsewhere, at least until the business could stand on its own two feet again.

Rae telephoned me at the office to lift my spirits. After contacting her broker, she arranged to cash in three government savings bonds her grandmother had purchased for her some twenty-five years earlier and borrowed what was left of the equity in her life insurance policy. That yielded us sixty-five thousand dollars, but it would take seven business days to receive it. It was a helpful cushion for the unexpected. What an angel!

Sean Pease suggested that we first try to negotiate with the company with whom we had a license agreement. The company, Ariel, was strictly a research and development firm with limited knowledge of mass production manufacturing, especially when quality was concerned. They were excellent at conceptualizing machinery and tooling from drawings and could prototype just about anything mechanical, but ask for a dozen and you would have a problem. Ariel's owner was Syrian. It was said that a business deal with a Syrian was like the weather in New England—if you didn't like it, stick around. It would change in ten minutes.

Sean mentioned he had trouble making an appointment for us to meet with the president in his office in Hayward, agreeing to Tuesday afternoon, intimating they were jacking us around. Since it was only a forty-minute drive, Sean suggested we ride together and strategize on the way. It would be remarkable to beat DeSalva at his own game.

Now that we had retained a lawyer, I called a long-time friend who was presently working for the Justice Department for advice. I met Pete Minot on occasion while flying the A-10 Thunderbolt in close air support for our ground troops on covert missions in Iraq. Affectionately nicknamed Warthog by those familiar with its immense firepower, boasting a 30 mm, seven-barrel Gatling gun and eight tons of ordnance, this badass was designed for attacking armored vehicles and tanks by extreme anti-aircraft maneuvers. Remarkable!

Most remember the swift demise of the Iraqi tanks and collapse of the Republican Guard in Gulf War where the A-10 crushed its opponent in record time. All throughout select ground offensive campaigns under Pete's purview, he had never confirmed or denied the rumor that he was a CIA spook with scars to confirm it. Last time we talked, he mentioned he would be working off the book for an extended period. As an equity holder in the company, Pete listened to Sean Pease's strategy and offered twenty-five thousand for the kitty, more as needed. The more I drummed up, the less money we needed from family.

A couple of business colleagues already committed their greenbacks to charity, school, and the usual bullshit. One told me to throw in the towel and take the guy's offer, rebuild the business, and cash out for a smaller portion, but I couldn't live with myself. I was responsible for everyone's hard work and support. I couldn't let them down. I wouldn't let them down. As the day wound down, I decided to surprise Rae and dine on hospital food with her. Perhaps they would let me take her to the cafeteria in a wheelchair. We would have to see.

As I walked in her room, she was busy on the telephone, conversing about refinancing her home. She was extremely happy to see me, but on the same hand, she was furiously upset after a follow-up conversation with Sean Pease. The pieces of the puzzle were coming together. We were duped, as she aptly expressed. As she put it, we were screwed without getting kissed and were prepared to fight!

I located a wheelchair and told her we would have a fanciful meal in the cafeteria. I even brought a couple of small candles from a leftover birthday cake so we would share dinner by candlelight.

She laughed heartily for the first time in days, bringing tears to her eyes from her sore ribs. Poor thing. I couldn't wait until she was well enough to...

We talked for hours as if we had been soul mates for years. She was incredibly special, and I told her I wasn't going to let her go under any circumstances. And besides, Sheba and I were quite fond of each other, and she had better watch out. She smiled and squeezed my hand. Her eyes told me how she felt without saying a word. I left feeling better despite the insurmountable problems looming ahead.

*****

After visiting with Bill and walking Sheba, I sat down to catch up on the local news and scribbled a few notes for discussion with Sean Pease for Tuesday's meeting. The news droned on, but nothing made much sense. I found it hard to concentrate, my mind a whirlpool of angry thoughts. What problem would I awake to tomorrow? Would we be firebombed if I didn't acquiesce and take DeSalva's offer? What was next, a fatal attack? When would it end? Would it end? What other nuisance bullshit would he stick up my ass? How did he do it? How could we keep going on like this?

I must have dozed off and awoke at about midnight. Sheba was resting comfortably at my feet. Time to hit the sack. At least Rae would be coming home tomorrow.

CHAPTER 17

I met Sean for lunch and discussed promising scenarios for tomorrow's meeting with Ariel. He was optimistic that Ariel and their attorneys would work with us since we had an impeccable track record with them. Sean emphasized that four years of timely royalty payments would go a long way in the eyes of the court. Ariel had made a good buck off us for doing nothing, and they were apprised a week ago that payment would be rendered immediately upon receipt of the overdue government check. In the past, being a few days late never bothered Ariel until now.

As Sean put it, tacit approval was in our favor. As I continued to bring Sean up to speed on the technology, our proprietary secrets, the military contracts, and the last four years' relationship with Ariel, I wondered myself why the sudden change of heart.

Tuesday rolled around. I picked Sean up and drove to Ariel, arriving on time. I expected a courteous greeting from Halif Aswad, Ariel's president, as every time I had met with him or his engineers, he always greeted me in person. Today was different. Instead, his receptionist escorted me and Sean into their conference room where Halif Aswad and two lawyers were seated, one on each side of him at the end of the table. He was standoffish, not acknowledging either of us. I felt like Daniel in the lion's den. So much for pleasant, long-term business relationships! Guess they had poisoned him too!

Ariel's lead attorney, Victor Weissiner, from Cabot, Weissiner & Lowell in San Francisco, opened with their demand: if we satisfy the forty-thousand-dollar royalty payment to cure the default of the license agreement within the specified time provision, that would satisfy all. Sean responded by presenting proof that money was forthcoming as the Department of Defense contracting office was backtracking its overdue payment rendered ten days earlier but not received. In lieu of this snafu, Pease respectfully requested a ten-day extension to the fifteen-day cure period stated in the license agreement given our four-year track record with them.

The trio conferred and agreed to a five-day extension with this proviso: their lawsuit would continue in force until payment had been rendered in the form of a certified check and, as a precedent, that we would also pay the reasonable attorney's fees associated with this unrequited meeting. Sean whispered in confidence that their fee should be reasonable, only a couple of hours of billing time, and recommended we agreed to their terms. I asked Weissiner, their lead lawyer, what reasonable attorney's fees entailed. He responded, "Usual contract review work. Nothing excessive."

I took Sean aside and asked him bluntly, "Do we really have a choice here?"

Sean replied, "Well, they've got you over a barrel, and from everything you've told me about this takeover attempt, I'd give them what they want. You can't legally operate under their patent as a licensee for that one component without remaining valid within the terms of the agreement. Seems like a no-brainer to me. This way, you'll keep the business alive, which affords you proper time to source the part elsewhere or make it yourself." So we agreed to their terms. Their office would inform Sean Pease of their fee the following day. As we got up to leave, as I always had, I offered a handshake to Halif as a good business gesture. He wouldn't even look me in the eye.

In the car on the return trip back to Sean's office, I gibed, "Today's meeting stank."

"It should be fine. We have their word."

CHAPTER 18

The next afternoon, Sean telephoned, informing me that he and his office had properly notified the court and opposing counsel that his office asserted power of attorney wherein all communication from hereon would be through his office. And to boot, the bill from Ariel's attorneys was $9,200.

"What'd they do, charter a fucking jet and fly to Bermuda to review the agreement? That's horseshit! They don't want to work with us. They're doing everything they can to stick it to me, to break me financially!" I slammed my fist on the desk. "That son of a bitch!"

"Look, Logan," Sean repeated with self-control, "this is standard procedure. Yes, it's excessive. They're just covering themselves. They're officers of the court. We have their word."

"Yeah, and pigs fly too! I sure as hell hope you're right." I abruptly ended the call, feeling more disgusted than ever. I had heard enough worthless news to last a lifetime. It had been eleven days since my meeting with DeSalva. I desperately needed a change of scenery. I left early to join Rae. I telephoned her asking what I could pick up at the market. Once again, I invited myself into her life.

By the time I arrived, I was mentally exhausted. Pulling into the driveway, I noticed Sheba pacing at the front window. That caused a flashback of the day I got smacked. I grabbed the 9 mm and ran to the house. Unlocking the front door, I called out, "Rae."

"Hi! I'm soaking in the tub," she called back. "Can you help me out?"

Shoving the gun inside the back of my jeans, I answered, "Be there in a minute." Sheba and I walked back to the truck for the groceries. Dropping the bags on the kitchen counter, I walked back to greet Rae. Bending down to kiss her, I gazed in horror at the enormity of the bruising on her body while helping her out of the whirl-pool tub.

"About an hour ago, Sheba started fidgeting. She's growled once and has been pacing back and forth between the back and front windows ever since." Hesitating, with a quiver in her voice, she asked, "Do you think someone's skulking around here?"

"Nah. It's springtime. The deer are eating new bud growth on the shrubs out back." I grinned hoping to ease the look on her face. Did I think so? Damn straight! But I dared not scare her anymore. She was fragile enough from the attack. She didn't need more anxiety.

"I'll take Sheba for a walk around the house and down the hill to the tree line. Should I use a leash in case we see a deer?" I responded in an upbeat mood.

"No. She'll stay beside you if you start together, but you must always look eye to eye when you give a command and she will mind you. Start by using her name and say, 'Walk.' Then say, 'Sheba, heel,' and she will walk beside you. Move your hand downward when you want her to stay put somewhere and say, 'Stay.' And when you want her to join you, bring your arm up toward you and say, 'Come,'" Rae said confidently. "You'll be fine. I need to lie down. These painkillers make me drowsy."

I kissed her goodbye and walked to the living room to fetch Sheba. She was already waiting at the back door like she had read my mind and knew I wanted her to help look for something. I rechecked the safety on the gifted 9mm and told Sheba we were going for a walk. She was excited, her tail wagging anxiously. While I could feel that something was awry, I wasn't all that eager to find anything.

We started a close perimeter walk around the house and under the back deck. I didn't know what to look for, but Sheba smelled something. Man or beast, I wondered, or one and the same? There was no way to determine footprints in the landscape rocks. Sheba led me over to the back stairway where another cigarette butt lay stomped out just below the first stair. It looked relatively fresh. As I did before, I picked up the butt, keeping my fingers from touching the filter. It looked like the last. I stuck it in my pocket and gave Sheba a pat on the head. We continued to walk around the house, increasing the width of each circle. Nothing appeared out of place. At least this afforded Rae some quiet resting time. Then I would attempt making a light meal, tend to Rae's needs, and invite Bill to join us.

CHAPTER 19

Day twelve. After arguing with the military contract officer over expediting repayment and getting frustrated, I was drained. Production was slowly getting into swing. To keep my mind off the maelstrom, I revamped the assembly area and conducted an inventory. All backup machine parts, operational and maintenance manuals, and specific tools were missing. Damn! Now we must replace the spares, rewrite the OMM, and train another line supervisor. I recalled Helen's comment on the day she quit that she intimated that things had been done, prompted, by that fucking traitor Sullivan.

Rae and I discussed the assembly situation and agreed not to hire another technician while we rebuilt our foundation with the existing orders. Rae proposed we each work extra hours at night, keeping Sheba around for company. I concurred.

We amassed enough cash to satisfy the demand payments to Ariel and their avaricious attorneys. Sean affirmed to Ariel that we would deliver our payments as directed before the close of business within the five-day extension period. Feeling better, Rae tagged along on the ride over to Ariel late that afternoon. Ariel's lead attorney, Weissiner, was not present. Instead, a junior partner was waiting in the conference room.

Sean produced the cashier's checks and accompanying documentation for satisfaction of all terms of the license agreement and the reasonable attorney's fees. Ariel's attorney acted surprised. In a scolding tone, he abrasively denied his firm offering any extension to us and that we should pack our briefcase and see them in court. We were shocked! We couldn't believe our ears. We couldn't believe what we just heard!

Sean Pease began arguing that he would take them in front of the Disciplinary Review Board and see to it they would be sanctioned! I went ballistic. Sean had to step in front to keep me from punching the arrogant little punk. With a twisted smile on his face, the young attorney turned his back to us and refused to discuss the issue further, telling us we had to leave. We left check in hand, realizing that DeSalva had us by the balls!

In the parking lot, Rae quipped to both of us in a sarcastic tongue, "Guys, isn't this the week we were scheduled for our first strategy meeting with DeSalva? I'm surprised we haven't heard from him."

I retorted, "Oh, but we have!"

The ride back to Sean's office was filled with flogging the dead horse and self-fulfilling sympathy. We didn't know how bad things were about to get—federal court, patent infringement, expensive lawyers, more harassment! Sean brought us back from the grave by telling us we needed to find a different attorney, and right away, one who specialized in intellectual property and patent law. Sean was little help as he was new to the area and had never worked on a patent infringement or IP case before. He said he would ask around and have some names the following day.

After a few attempts at calling, I was able to reach Pete Minot to relay more disparaging news about the lawsuit. Pete offered more greenbacks for our kitty, commenting that we would likely need it tenfold. Four years earlier, Pete had reviewed the license agreement and the corresponding patent at length. Pete was halfway around the world and unable to talk at length, so he recommended a new twist to our dire situation.

He strongly suggested that a good IP attorney attack the patent and its intellectual property, confident that there were similar patents out there where technology like this was utilized in the manufacture of electronic toys and games. This was a hot issue with Pete and the Justice Department, who specifically targeted foreign entities who illegally pirated American technology and manufactured copycat products, importing them back into the US for huge profits. But to fight a battle this complex, Pete explicitly remarked, "We needed to hire a good junkyard dog!" This was an old saying for the kind of lawyer who had done it all, seen it all, and was the best at skinning the cat. As we concluded our conversation, Pete remarked, "I'll catch 'em, you skin 'em."

"Maybe I should just kill the bastard!"

CHAPTER 20

The very next morning, Sean Pease telephoned me with promising news. He had asked each of his partners independently whom they recommended as a good litigator. They each advised C. Daniel Whitehead, who used to be a member of their firm and was now on his own. Flippantly, I asked Sean, "Is *litigator* another word for *alligator*?"

He laughed. "You're quick."

"Not quick enough, Sean. Not quick enough."

Sean mentioned that he would spend the time to bring C. Daniel Whitehead up to speed and would assist behind the scenes if need be as the senior partners held high regard for his ability and, most of all, his winning record. Sean said *C* stood for Carroll the Bulldog because Whitehead was known for grabbing hold of the opposition's ankles, and they couldn't shake him loose.

"Funny description. Hope he's half as good as you say," I retorted.

"Just wait till you meet him. He'll surprise you. I'll pick you up at one," he said, disconnecting the call.

I telephoned Rae to see if she was up to attending the meeting that afternoon with the new lawyer. She said yes but didn't feel much like driving yet. "Okay. I'll pick you up at noon if that works."

"That's fine."

"Gotta go. The other line is ringing. I'll call you if anything important comes up. Get some rest now. I miss you."

I recognized the number. As directed by Pete, I picked up the line and said, "Please do not continue to call this number. We're not interested in purchasing your service. Place us on the do not call list." I hung up. Walking outside, I dialed Pete's number on the encrypted cell phone Pete gave me two years ago with the proviso that I talk to him only from that phone. I waited for the buzzing and clicking relays to stop. Employing AES 128 encryption through real-time Sophos servers, all Pete's calls, in and out, are protected.

"It's safe. I've unearthed your junkyard dog. His name is Keven Ward. He's a highly regarded IP attorney from LA. Years ago, a colleague of mine went up against him and got slaughtered." He echoed some of his accomplishments: patent infringement against a Japanese auto maker, copyright issues on two blockbuster movie scripts, patent infringement on a Korean company importing stereo equipment, and the list went on.

Pete finished Ward's impressive background with his curriculum vitae: "A bachelor's degree in mechanical engineering from the Naval Academy, a master's degree in mechanical engineering from MIT, and a law degree from Yale. I'm wiring you 50K, but K.W. will eat that up quicker than shit through a duck! He's agreed to 10K up front. As I see it, he's your only way out of this trap," he replied sternly.

"You've been right about this in the past. Ah, thanks for the help. Wish you were closer. I'll keep you posted."

My call to Keven Ward in Los Angeles was expected. I was surprised that he had already reviewed the patent and the license agreement, implicitly agreeing with Pete that the only way to fight this complex problem was to simply strike at its core issue: disallow the patent.

"Logan, Pete and I have played on the same ball team together." Pete might have been on the other side of the world, but he wasted no time when it came to crucial issues.

"Let me see if I understand what you propose. If the patent is challenged and compromised, then the issue of the license goes away. Correct? And the other points become moot?"

"Absolutely."

As a favor to Pete, Ward was already working the case partial pro bono. But as he stated earlier, he, too, liked to feed his family and levied the unpleasant news. He required ten thousand dollars as a retainer plus travel and expenses, and this was billed at a discounted hourly rate of six hundred dollars. I asked him how much he thought it might cost to break Ariel's patent, and he guessed about three hundred thousand dollars.

I arranged for a telephone conference call with me, all three lawyers, and Rae for the meeting at Whitehead's office. That was fine as he felt we should act quickly and so he could outline his strategy and plan of attack to the others. Although he was the highest-priced attorney, he could not be the lead attorney on this case. According to the system, that had to be Whitehead, the litigator, requiring filing amicus curiae, "friend of the court," paperwork.

I got to say one thing for Pease: He said when you go to court, you better be sure you had filed all the compulsory paperwork accordingly, crossed all the t's and dotted all the i's. If you didn't, he said they would get you on a technicality and you would either lose your position or lose altogether. Either way, you would lose. He said of his own kind that a way of keep making money was to shuffle paper.

Despite her soreness, Rae was glad to be back at work. On the way to Whitehead's office, she vented. "I can listen to just so much music and watch just so much TV. I've had my fill of both."

We arrived early at Whitehead's office building. Sean Pease was waiting for us in the lobby with more sobering news. Ariel had been granted an emergency hearing ten days from now! Ariel was seeking a temporary injunction against us.

"Temporary injunction?" I repeated as we shuffled in the elevator.

"Yes," Sean replied and pushed the elevator button for the eleventh floor. Rae remained silent, taking it all in.

We walked into Whitehead's office and were ushered to his conference room. Whitehead looked scholarly, confident, and prematurely gray. I guessed him to be in his fifties. He warmly greeted each of us. He had prepared copies of the patent and the license agreement with a notepad in front of each chair on one side of the table. The other side of the table was his theater of war, and in the middle was a built-in videoconferencing phone.

We sat down, and Whitehead dialed up Keven Ward. At Whitehead's request, Pease brought Ward up to speed on the past few days' transactions, emphasizing the emergency hearing for temporary injunction. Ward wasn't the least bit surprised and detailed each claim in the patent for us and commiserated much of his findings to Whitehead. The conversation lasted almost ninety minutes. Ward suggested he come to San Jose first, arriving two nights before the hearing, to spend the day before working with Whitehead. We smartly agreed. Before concluding, Ward recited that all would be ready.

I learned two important principles in ninety minutes: If you wanted justice, you damn sure wouldn't find it in the system, and you would be better off putting your faith and greenbacks in a worthy attorney, not the system. Big bucks would win!

CHAPTER 21

The next ten days flew by in a fury. Part of each day was consumed by fighting more dragons. Someone sicced the IRS on us, and I received a certified letter requesting a personal audit, accusing the company of hiding assets and unreported income. More bullshit! And that afternoon, a young man from the EPA showed up unannounced, requesting a walk-through inspection of our manufacturing facility to check out the allegation that we had been using mercury in processing our electronic parts. I felt like I was at my wit's end. When was this shit going to end?

At first, I was belligerent to the young man, requiring identification and all, but I didn't know whether he was a spy or another madman! After he assured me that he was just doing his job and he had already preliminarily investigated our company and was satisfied that the accusation that had been filed was false, he said his visit was simply required for him to complete his report. He assured me that this kind of thing happened all the time, usually by pissed-off former employees.

"You can say that again!" I sneered, then I got on my soapbox again and asked the big question with a sarcastic tongue: "What do we get when you find us innocent?"

He replied with the pat answer: "Nothing!"

Other than the thirty or so hang-up calls we had been receiving daily, work had been delightful, just fucking delightful! DeSalva must have had our number rigged to an automatic dialer just to piss me off.

Whitehead was excellent at including me in his conference calls with Ward and sending me reports and court documents. Each day was like climbing stairs—there was always one more to go. The hearing differed greatly from what I envisioned. Layered with ritualistic procedures, it was formal and intimidating. The courtroom was cold and lifeless.

Ariel's attorney, Weissiner, hemmed and hawed his way through the proceedings. Whitehead passed me a note stating he gauged that Ariel's attorneys hadn't put much effort into their case, perhaps believing they thought they would win by default, as he captured the surprised look on Weissiner's face when we showed up with two attorneys. His note gave me something to focus on: their lead attorney.

Their surprise turned into utter shock when C. Daniel Whitehead pleaded our case proficiently, introducing to the court with proper paperwork Keven Ward, our intellectual property attorney. Ariel's table buzzed like an angry swarm of wasps.

Whitehead was the first in counterargument, exuding an intelligent cadence in his statements, carefully pointing out chapter and verse misappropriated use of the legal system by Ariel. He explained the four points that must be unequivocally proven for a temporary injunction to be granted.

1. There was a substantial likelihood of success on the merits of the case.
2. Ariel faced a substantial threat of irreparable damage or injury if the injunction wasn't granted.
3. The balance of harm weighed in favor of the party seeking injunction.
4. A grant of an injunction would serve the public interest.

Whitehead tasked the opposition to prove any and all these points. As for an injunction to be granted, all four must be undeniably evident, not just one or two. His poise and confidence reminded me of a work from a Shakespearean play. Whitehead recited the case history from memory like he lived it personally, thanked the judge, and sat down. At no time did he hem or haw or miss a beat. He knew his stuff cold, and it showed.

Next up was Keven Ward, attorney extraordinaire! With the aid of visual cues from his laptop computer onto a large screen, Ward exhibited how there could be no infringement as the patent examiner missed reviewing all past and current patents, articles, or other inventions going back several years preceding the granting of Ariel's patent. Ward called these missing items prior art, skillfully pointing out that any combination of two or more patents that could be combined were granted well before the Ariel patent, which should have disallowed the granting of the Ariel patent in the first place.

Ward revealed six distinct combinations with explicit case history to back up his points of argument, carefully explaining the intricacies of patent law to the federal judge as she was not well-versed in patent law and recognized that Ward was an authority with notoriety. Ward graciously thanked the judge and sat back down. What decorum this guy exuded!

The judge proceeded on and asked the complainant if they had any statements in final rebuttal. Ariel's lead attorney, Weissiner, stood up and said, "No rebuttal, Your Honor. We've been sandbagged!"

The judge stated, "There will be no injunction at this time. I will review all transcripts, testimony, and documents and issue my findings in ten business days." Then she tapped the gavel once, announcing the end of the proceedings.

CHAPTER 22

As if karma was controlling our destiny, Whitehead called my cell to relay the news from the federal judge: no injunction granted! The plaintiff failed to make their case, not even making one of the essential points required. In other words, it was utter failure on Ariel's attorneys to shut down our operation. Hurrah for the good guys!

Two days later and just to be theatrical about it, a county process server delivered another lawsuit to our front door. Now we were being sued by Ariel and DeSalva's new company together for another attempt at patent infringement shrouded under the pleadings of trade deception, Lanham Act, RICO, and several other bullshit accusations, and since they couldn't go back to federal court, they were railroading us in county court! Our small but important victory was short-lived. Our attorneys had thirty days to answer the pleadings and state our case.

The system, no matter what we were taught as children, was not "innocent until proven guilty" in the civil court structure. It was more like, "Defend yourself with as much money as you can muster as the onslaught will become drawn-out and costly." And what made even less sense was the next part of the proceedings. We, the defendants, justly or unjustly accused, must answer all the claims made by the plaintiff; however, they never had to prove or justify one word.

J'accuse, the famous French saying, was the word of the day in the US civil court system. Doubted my logic? Doubted my word? Well, then, you, average citizen, were not well-versed in discovery and depositions! Discovery was initially developed by university scholars to make the system fairer, to make all lawyers equal, but the question really was, fair to whom? The principle for us laymen was simple:

"Let's make all the lawyers equal in knowledge of the incident." Each side must have answered questions of any, repeat any, nature honestly and without reserve before going in front of a judge or a magistrate. So in essence, you were tried twice for the same incident.

This principle reduced the trial by ambush scenario where the defendant at the trial divulged pertinent information that the plaintiff or prosecution had no previous knowledge of and won. That seemed logical as it always worked for Perry Mason on television. Perry Mason played the real Melvin Belli, the King of Torts, who exonerated the defendant time after time with just seconds remaining. It would seem to me that it should be up to the plaintiff or prosecution to prove their case, and if they couldn't, then they should be penalized in some monetary form.

I rather preferred the Old West's creed: "an eye for an eye" or the "do unto others" golden rule. My father once told me that the "road to success is paved with carcasses of competitors." Well, I guess that was why I wouldn't be a bastard in business as I believed in being fair, not abusing talent or experience. Remember that statement, though, as it was a fundamental flaw in my character makeup.

Weeks after the pleadings had been answered, I attended my first deposition. They should have called it the Salem Inquisitions as they resembled the witch hunts of the seventeenth century. It was usually conducted in your lawyer's office since it was home turf or the court reporter's place of business. They tried to conduct it in Weissiner's office in San Francisco, but Whitehead adamantly refused, so it was just me, as the authorized representative of my company; C. Daniel Whitehead; Halif Aswad, president of Ariel; Weissiner; and a court stenographer. Whitehead whispered to me not to get rattled by the video equipment, that it most likely was there for intimidation purposes.

To say the least, the atmosphere was so heavy with tension I could've cut it with a chainsaw. It was by no means a pleasant environment. Weissiner began with the elemental stuff—your name, address, and social security number and if you were known by any other name. They must have assumed everyone was like Al Capone. They asked me questions that were against my better nature to answer, and then they got personal, and the way they asked each question repeatedly, rewording and rephrasing the same question to see if they could catch me in a lie, was ludicrous.

But it was the personal questions that weren't germane to this lawsuit that got to me, like the following: Did I cheat on my ex-wife? Was it true that my girlfriend slept around? Did I regularly cheat on my ex-wife? How would a normal person answer questions like these? Well, it certainly pissed off Whitehead, that was for sure.

About halfway through the deposition, the issue regarding non-payment of royalties on the license agreement with Ariel came up. They all but called me an out-and-out liar over my response about the delayed government check. That opened the door for more probing questions about the company's financial position. Given that, Weissiner had the gall to ask, "Is it true you made up the death of your father so you wouldn't be present to meet with an oversight inspector about your military contracts?"

I rose from my chair. Looking sternly at Weissiner, I replied, "Excuse me, would you repeat that question?" He repeated the question, this time with sarcasm in his voice. I wasn't about to take his bullshit any longer. With aggravation in my inflection, I repeated, "Excuse me, would you repeat that question?"

Weissiner was disgusted with me. If the tables were turned, he most likely would have told me to fuck off! For the third time, I asked the court stenographer to repeat the question. She read back the question in monotone staccato, making Weissiner even more pissed.

Turning to my attorney, I said, "My answer's simple: this deposition is over!" I got up and out of my chair. Whitehead grabbed my arm, ushering me out into the hallway. He gauged my body language and knew I was about to punch that asshole.

Whitehead walked back in, stating for the record, "This deposition is over due to badgering of my client and intimidating line of questioning. I am ordering my client not to answer your questions. Your intimidating attitude is unacceptable. We will take this matter up with the magistrate." He made sure his comments were recorded. He, too, derived pleasure in basically telling them to piss off!

Over the next several weeks, Ariel's attorneys arranged depositions all around the country, forcing us to pay for excessive travel expenses for our attorney, and we had to repeat the same with Ward when he deposed Ariel's president on patent issues. It was expensive but well worth it! Their tactics put the squeeze on us financially, trying to invoke a settlement.

Nice laws and procedures we had created. Pleadings went back and forth. New accusations replaced old accusations, ones that were incredulous! People not yet identified were added to our lawsuit, like John Doe 1–25. This allowed the plaintiff to add up to twenty-five more people at any time if they so desired. This lawsuit was really nasty!

Whitehead had become so involved in this lawsuit that he became more than just our attorney. He turned into more of a friend. He couldn't believe the bullshit they were pulling and their lack of ethics and morals, so he gave us a break and cut his billing hours by half as he knew we were struggling to survive.

We struggled through the next few months, both of us working seventy to eighty hours per week. I remembered the grief I felt for Rae when she received notification from a banking acquaintance that they found someone to purchase her house and car.

Almost five months to the day, we moved into a rental house in San Jose. The expenses of the lawsuit were bleeding us dry. Paying the attorneys had to come first as we couldn't just stop in midstream. We cashed in all our stock, bonds, and 401(k)s. We sold furniture and Rae's art collection and pawned her jewelry on occasion to make ends meet. Now we were down to one vehicle, my Tundra pickup, but we kept the business alive, always putting ourselves last on the food chain.

The last month leading up to the trial date was the absolute worst. Coordinating expert witnesses' travel arrangements, lodging, and transportation and tallying their hourly fees were enough to make our accountant, despite ourselves, sick at the rate we were spending money, and for what, to fight off DeSalva's fucking greed? Then we woke up one morning and realized that after months of being attacked, we no longer controlled our destiny. Now it was our time in court with people we had yet to meet, a box filled with strangers wondering what we had done and what was going on. They would be deciding our fate—whether we lived or died, whether we ate tomorrow, or whether we were good guys or bad guys. Nothing else mattered.

Remember this important rule: if you wanted to know who was lying in court, focus on the lawyers! Everyone in court was sworn to tell the truth, the whole truth, and nothing but the truth, except lawyers! No one made them swear to that oath! Attorneys would say the most asinine things. They would lie and tell falsehoods to make you become confused so as to agree with their position. Remember, I said their position, not the truth!

The only truth in the US civil court was that it would cost a bundle! Money decided the winner, sad but true. In this case, the trial lasted for five full days. They predicted it would last two, three tops. Six jurors and one alternate were chosen. They were chosen, most interestingly, because they fitted the flavor of your position, not because they were your peers!

We spent five agonizing days listening to hype and lies, deceit and duplicity, and petty arguments between lawyers about when to break for lunch and a whole bunch of bullshit, all at our expense. But it wasn't just the money. It was the compromising of our principles and the values and beliefs we stood for that were really being challenged and, of course, questioning whether we had the moral conviction to stand up for what we believed in.

The jury convened behind closed doors to decide our fate at 6:00 p.m.—six people, six issues, and six o'clock. I commented to Rae that I found it peculiar that there were three 6s hitched to our fate, wondering if there was something morbidly prophetic in that coincidence.

The two and a half hours we waited to hear the verdict was like waiting for our own execution. During the trial, we tried as best we could to read the jurors and the judge to no avail. We didn't know whether the six jurors had enough sense to recognize common principles of science and mechanics we all learned in seventh grade, or had those greedy bastards paid their experts to invent bizarre contraptions to promote something that didn't exist? Were we in a kangaroo court, and did it really not matter? Were we going down regardless? A very scary thought, losing—no more business, shattered dreams, no more anything. Our lives would be decimated from that moment on.

About twenty minutes after six, the anxiety became so intense while listening to DeSalva overtly boast about his custom 76' Striker sportfishing yacht with extended flybridge, large staterooms, and latest Scottstar navigation, blah, blah, blah, that he was taking delivery of this weekend so he could do some marlin fishing off the coast of Baja. It made us nauseous to hear him gloat, so much so that Rae and I got up and walked down to the other end of the building just to get away from the hungry eyes of Weissiner, DeSalva, and his pride of lions.

Trying to fill the empty minutes with small talk, Rae asked, "What did we do wrong?"

"Too trusting, I guess. I can't see that we did much differently than most people in our situation. But I tell you what, I've damn sure developed a whole new outlook on business. The new saying ought to be, 'If you can't buy 'em, sue 'em!'" Rae nodded, looking empty with disappointment.

At that moment, a bailiff interrupted to inform us that the jury had finished and that it was time to get back in the courtroom. Whitehead and Ward were already seated when we walked in. Weissiner and DeSalva positioned themselves in the aisle just so they could leer at us as when we walked past them to our table.

We stood as the jury filed in from the left side of the chambers and the judge emerged from the opposite door. With teary eyes, Rae grabbed my hand and whispered, "I hope someone upstairs has heard us." I squeezed her hand and smiled knowing we had prayed more in the past few days than we had in our entire lives.

The foreman of the jury handed the verdict to the bailiff to be handed to the judge to read. The judge read the verdict, handed it to the clerk accordingly, and instructed the foreman to read the verdict to the court. Were we guilty? The foreman audibly delivered the verdict, declaring unanimously that we, the defendants, were not guilty!

Whitehead yelled "Yes!" and leaned over and hugged Rae. Ward gave me a hearty squeeze while the four of us happily regained our composure and sat quietly while the judge issued instructions for conclusion of the case. We were elated, relieved, and alive! God, it felt good to win our life back! One big dragon slayed!

CHAPTER 23

The next month was tough. Although we kept fulfilling our military contracts, the onslaught continued from DeSalva and his hired guns. DeSalva and Sullivan continually badgered our commercial customers with legal lies and bullshit, espousing that they had filed an appeal, that there was a doctrine of equivalence law case that took precedence, and that their patent was upheld. Lie after fucking lie! We continued to be tainted, constantly defending ourselves, and we were the ones who prevailed!

By the time we had gotten wind of our customer being attacked and responded, the customer was already second-guessing why he should do business with us. Fucking business in the new century! It was like fighting the school bully. The nonmilitary customers would become intimidated and back down. Some would ask to return their first order of parts or equipment. Two of our midsized newest distributors were deluged with legal bullshit from their lawyers about a doctrine of equivalence as if we had continuing legal issues to resolve. For the life of us, we couldn't get it through to any new customer that this was all bullshit and no substance!

Despite the fact that we would immediately provide the customer with the jury verdict, the patent office documents, a legal opinion letter from our IP attorney, and even offer our attorneys to talk to, the customer would become even more confused. Further harassment mostly from Weissiner and DeSalva with legal rhetoric and threats and the customer would get totally pissed off and throw in the towel. They wouldn't do business with anyone regardless!

DeSalva's greed cost us plenty! Just as we would get a new customer, someone would attack. One step ahead, two steps back. It seemed like we kept backsliding. Our finances were becoming a mess. We did the absolute best juggling act we could to keep feeding everyone. Employees never suffered, but some organizations didn't get their fair share on time.

I had made some end roads in finding legitimate financing, but everyone was skittish about our ability to climb out of the hole quick enough for investors to get their money back. Most of the investors didn't want to wait even eighteen months for a profitable exit strategy. Our margins were good, but our receivables weren't growing fast enough for them.

Banks wouldn't touch us as neither of us had bankable collateral left. The Small Business Administration loan office was even less helpful. We were basically screwed. We had to keep plugging away at finding a white knight while pinching pennies.

Early one Sunday morning, I received a call on my cell phone from a Geoff Wuesthoffer, a retired businessman from San Diego referred by Keven Ward. He mentioned he was bored with retirement and wanted to help with investment capital and hands-on management. He asked if Rae and I would meet him that afternoon at our office. I agreed we would meet him at the office at 2:00 p.m. We drove to the office in silence, neither of us in a talkative mood, not knowing what to expect. Another trap?

Mr. Wuesthoffer was waiting for us in the parking lot. We pulled up beside his Mercedes. He got out of his car, and we greeted one another in front of the building. He was a small-framed, slim man, about sixty-ish. Opening the front door, I suggested we would be more comfortable in the conference room. He cheerfully obliged.

Wuesthoffer was a businessman first but an honorable one. He had heard of our plight through Keven Ward and offered immediate investment for a modicum of stock. The continuance of employment guidelines was simple, that he and I would attend to the finances together. He empathized with our plight, but on the other hand, he was providing us an opportunity to grow the company.

If we agreed, we could recruit additional assembly personnel and continue. Ward and his lawyers would intercede on our behalf to ensure all military contracts would be upheld, and we would work closely together so he could get his hands around the scope of the business. He was delighted that we encouraged his active participation as a welcomed respite! He, too, was looking forward to working once again.

Rae and I were dismayed but agreed that we had worked too hard not to continue, at least for the time being. Even though it wasn't just our company anymore, at least we had a vested opportunity! He invited us to dinner that evening so we could get to know him.

What an incredible sequence of events. It was hard admitting defeat as it shouldn't have ended like this! We would just have to take this one day at a time.

CHAPTER 24

Dave Flaherty was driving south from Tahoe City along Highway 89. It was a cool, crisp night, and the sky was speckled with millions of twinkling stars. He could see the glistening casino lights of the western shore reflecting off the still waters of Lake Tahoe. There was no traffic to distract his deliberate thoughts of money, plenty of money to set himself up, start a whole new life.

Flaherty's thoughts were racing faster than a speeding bullet: *How to spend it? What to spend it on? First, I'll get rid of this shitbox, then gonna buy some clothes and get laid! Shit! Been a long time since I had a piece of ass. Can't wait to get this fuckin' over. Money, money, fucking a' money. Woo-hoo! And that fuck Logan Scott called me a mooch! Wouldn't give me the promotion over his coworker. Said I didn't deserve it 'cause I didn't put in the time and effort and that he only hired me when the company really didn't have an opening. Said he felt sorry for me. Felt sorry for me? Fuck that! He should've given me that promotion! I deserved it. That motherfucker!*

Flaherty floored it, increasing his speed to 90 mph, eager to get to DeSalva's. The guardrails were flying by like strobe lights at warp speed. *Think I'll do some gamblin', maybe MGM. Drink 7 and 7, fondle some babes, and throw dem dice! Give me dem bones baby. I feel lucky tonight!'*

The car lurched to the right, closing rapidly on a tall ponderosa pine. Flaherty slammed on the brakes, swerved the car across the road, and came to a screeching, burned-rubber stop just inches from the guardrail, keeping him from the cold, deep waters of Lake Tahoe. *Shit! Gotta take it easy! Could've bent myself on that one! No more dope till I'm in the hotel. Whoa! Better check my shorts. Heh!*

He looked ahead. No cars were coming. *Good!* He looked behind. No cars. *Okay, Lady Luck's my broad tonight even if she's a slut! Heh!* He slowly pulled out, shaking his head, putting his anticipation aside until after payoff. After forty minutes had passed, Flaherty looked for the landmarks. *It's gotta be close. That's the abandoned farmhouse...maybe? Looks like only the foundation survived. There's the mailbox. There it is. Holy shit, look at that fuckin' gate! How do I get into this fuckin' place? That looks like the opener. I guess I press that button there.*

Flaherty rolled down his window, pressed the button, and spoke into the box. "Dave Flaherty here to see Mr. DeSalva." After a minute, the gate opened. *Look at this place. Nice fuckin' fountain. What a fuckin' mansion! This guy's got bucks! I knew it! I knew he had money, but not this much!* Dave parked his car and started to get out when a large man approached the car. *Man, this guy's big. Gotta weigh three hundred. Nice face! Heh! Wonder what he wants.*

"Mr. Flaherty, hand me your car keys and follow me please."

"Hey, no one drives my car but me. It's all I got."

"That'll be Mr. DeSalva's call. He doesn't like cars blocking his view of the fountain and gardens. There's plenty of garage space. Don't worry," the big man said as he mechanically steered Flaherty into the spacious foyer of the house.

Man, this entryway's bigger than my old apartment. He glanced up the sweeping staircase, admiring the richly carved accent molding, fancy tapestries, paintings, and sculptures as Thomas, the majordomo, approached.

"Mr. Flaherty, Mr. DeSalva is waiting for you in the study. Kindly follow me please." Thomas led Flaherty into DeSalva's office, the same room where Logan and Rae met with him. Before departing, Thomas politely asked, "Mr. Flaherty, what may I offer you to drink, sir?"

"Oh, a strong Seagram's Seven will do," responded Flaherty as he walked over to a sofa.

Rising from his desk, DeSalva lit up a Davidoff cigar and walked to where Dave Flaherty had seated himself. Still standing, he said, "Well, Dave, how was the ride down the lake? Uneventful, I take it?"

"Eh, no problem. Where's the missus?"

As DeSalva seated himself, he said, "She's visiting our children back east. So, Dave, let's discuss the trappings of your endeavors. So tell me, what news do you bring of Logan Scott?"

Dave Flaherty had attended the same high school as Logan Scott and had become a short-term employee of the company he worked for five years ago. Flaherty had sought out Scott after reading an ad for a telecommunications assembly worker. Flaherty claimed to be down on his luck and convinced Scott to hire him so he could skate through life with ease. Scott had taken Flaherty on but had never promised him more than short-term employment as he had no specific skill set or experience in telecommunications.

Flaherty worked for Scott for a little more than four months, but with the passage of time, Flaherty's memories weakened in truth and strengthened in fantasy. Flaherty had convinced himself that Logan would promote him if he succeeded in his employment. When Logan Scott left his position with the company and went off to start his own telecommunications company and failed to bring Flaherty along, Flaherty left under less than desirable terms. Five years had passed without the two communicating. Flaherty's hatred toward Scott intensified with each passing year.

Six weeks before the trial and with past contacts retrieved off the stolen computer, DeSalva contracted Flaherty to become a mole in Scott's organization. Flaherty had to eat a lot of crow and apologize for his deplorable behavior, claiming that overwhelming gambling debts and too much drugs and booze were the rationale behind his abrupt departure and blowup at Scott, expecting something he was undeserving of receiving. Answering the advertisement for assembly personnel, Flaherty groveled extensively to Scott, stating that he would work for a low salary, banking on Scott's good nature once again. Now to deliver the coup de grâce to Scott's company.

DeSalva counted on Scott's sense of morals to help an old friend, but what he hadn't counted on was Scott allowing Flaherty to bunk in with him and Rae for a couple of days until Flaherty could get his own place. Flaherty had sent timely communiqués to DeSalva, arming him with the foils that should have been Scott's—stealing Scott's mail, checking his telephone messages, monitoring confidential conversations between Scott and his attorneys.

Flaherty supplied customers, vendors, and new information, foiling Scott's ability to make headway, but nobody considered that Scott and his partner, Rae, would sacrifice everything to fight the battle, especially not DeSalva. He was certain that Scott would fold within a month or two of his legal attack and that he would acquire the company ridiculously cheap and that Scott and that sassy bitch MacAllister would be his charges!

Well, it didn't quite work out that way, and DeSalva's hunch was off the mark. Scott and MacAllister hung in there, losing everything personal—money, health, and peace of mind. But hung in there they did, ultimately winning with all the odds stacked against them. Flaherty moved out on his own with his ability to continue supplying information waning with each passing day as the attack on Scott's company ensued.

"Well, that bastard Scott is planning to countersue you for business interference and a bunch of other shit. He's gotten some of his old customers back, has new people, and is shipping product. Just keeps dodging fuckin' bullets. I can't fuckin' believe it. How you gonna get rid of that fuckin' prick?" he wisecracked.

"Dave, you keep getting your role mixed up. I ask, you answer, not the other way around! I'll get the bastard. Don't you worry. Tell me more!" ordered DeSalva.

"Listen, Mike, I've given you more than you asked for. You keep promising me payment, but I've yet to see a buck. No more till I see fuckin' greenbacks!"

DeSalva was taken aback by Dave's slight. An understrapper talking to him like this! "You still living at Scott's?"

"Hell no! The bastard made me move out a couple weeks ago. Didn't give me enough time to find a decent place. Had to move into a real shithole in Downtown San Jose with all the people of lesser quality. Man, pay me so I can get the fuck outta here. No more fuckin' promises! You owe me!" demanded Flaherty, raising his voice sternly.

DeSalva was viewing Flaherty in a different light. With him out of Scott's place and on the outs at work, what value did this peon have? "So how's your position at the company? Everything going as planned?" he asked.

"Eh, it's fuckin' time to move on. I've had enough of that chickenshit operation and bullshit friendship! It's time for me to start a life, like wine, women, and song and not in that order. I wanna start my own company, one to compete with Scott. I think I know how to make a product like his. Well, not as good, but it'll look just the same. What about you? You gonna stay in business since you didn't get Scott's company? Um, I could run it."

"No, Dave, you won't be running it. After tonight, you will go your way. Do what you must. Hear my words. I never—and I mean I never—want to hear from you again or hear of you again. Is that clear? But just in case you missed my drift, disappear! Capisce? And I strongly advise that you go into some other line of work."

"Fuck you, DeSalva! Just fucking pay me and I'm outta here! Don't tell me what I can or can't do. If I want to stay in this business, I will and with no interference from you! Never forget, there are people out there that would like to know what really happened." *Heh! Fuckin' A! Got 'em this time. I'm in the money.*

DeSalva's face flushed with rage. *This little twerp thinks he's strong enough to take me on. I'll teach that little fuck a lesson!* After regaining his composure, he said, "I've arranged a little libation for us, a celebration of sorts. What was that you said, wine, women, and song? Well, how about some champagne to start off the night? What do you say?"

"If you're buying, sounds good to me! How about the women and fuck the song and how about my fuckin' money?"

He strolled over to his desk. "We'll settle up when you leave in the morning," bellowed DeSalva as he opened a silver case filled with stacks of one hundreds, turning it so Flaherty could envision the wealth he was about to accumulate. "This is such a beautiful place. Why not enjoy yourself while you're here? I've arranged for some companionship. You're going to like my little present." With a twisted smile, he grabbed a stack of one hundreds and tossed it on Flaherty's lap.

DeSalva summoned Thomas to open a chilled bottle of 2006 Veuve Clicquot Ponsardin La Grand Dame. "Ah, yes, an exceptionally good year. I believe you'll enjoy this. There's plenty more, so drink up, my friend! Ah, I see your companion is here!"

Flaherty turned around to see Veronica Sullivan entering the study. His balls climbed up to his throat. He stuttered, "Veronica, I, ah, I didn't expect to see you here! Where's Marc? He here?"

Veronica closed quickly to DeSalva's side. "Nice to see you too, Dave!"

CHAPTER 25

D ave Flaherty awoke at 7:20 a.m. in a strange bed in an unfamiliar large room with a very oppressive benzos and spirits hangover, the worst. His mouth was dry, his hands shaking, and his eyes not focusing. There was the usual lament: "Never again! Oh, never again! Was I with Veronica Sullivan last night? What a piece of ass! Oh man!" Slowly, he swung his legs out of bed, placed his feet on the floor, and rested his head in his hands.

His head was swimming, his stomach rising. "Shit!" Flaherty ran to what he thought was the bathroom and swung open the door. "Shit, a fuckin' closet!" His stomach expelled into the void of an empty closet. "Oh, fuck! I feel like shit!" he mumbled. *Shit, I'd better clean this mess up before anyone sees it. He'll…he'll…oh, fuck!*

After finding the bathroom and cleaning up the mess, Flaherty dressed in clean clothes that had been neatly hung on a suit valet taken from his outdated cloth luggage. How his clothes got there was unfathomable to him in his current condition. Dizzy and dehydrated, he guided himself out the door and into the hallway. Looking over the railing, he noticed a beautiful, well-appointed room below connected to the winding staircase. Like Tara in the movies, just waiting for the actress to walk down, in his present state, Flaherty staggered over to the staircase, descending with little grace. As he stepped onto the marble floor, DeSalva beckoned to join him in the formal dining room.

"Good morning, Dave. Ready for breakfast? Thomas, bring Mr. Flaherty a mimosa. What's your pleasure? Rolf makes one fabulous omelet," DeSalva replied. He was dressed in designer clothes.

"Nah, just some toast and strong coffee. Can't get anything else down."

"Nonsense. You must. After breakfast, what do you say we take a ride over to the casino and play a little? It's on me."

"I'd like to, but, ah, it's time to go!"

"What, you deny your host's generosity?" sneered DeSalva. "Thomas, call down and get the Marauder ready."

"Eh, ah, Mike, that was Veronica last night, wasn't it?"

"Yes, it was. Did you enjoy yourself?"

"Oh yeah! Where is she?"

"Ah, Veronica left after you passed out. She's meeting us later. Please sit down," he said as Thomas served Flaherty his first mimosa.

"A little hair on the dog will help! You'll feel better after a couple of these. Now enjoy!"

Dave Flaherty had the best omelet ever with all the fixings he craved—hash browns, Virginia ham, Canadian bacon, and croissants. Washing down a benzo with another mimosa, he started flying again, the pain of the night a distant memory. He thought about Veronica, the smell of her pussy. He was becoming aroused just thinking about it. *Oh, was Marc Sullivan a lucky fuck! Or was he? Does he know she fucks around? Hmm, can use that to my advantage. Ah, who gives a fuck?'*

They departed the dining room, exiting over the exquisite stone patio as they walked down to the boathouse. The mountains of Nevada were beautiful this time of the morning. DeSalva pointed out Mt. Rose, Northstar ski area, and Heavenly Valley. The boathouse was larger than any house that Flaherty had ever lived in. They boarded the fifty-foot Marauder and cast off the lines as DeSalva's lieutenant backed the boat out of the boathouse. The water was beautiful, blue green and crystal clear. Flaherty could see the bottom. Flaherty turned to DeSalva. "How deep is it here?"

"You can almost see the bottom. Only thirty feet. The deepest part's about sixteen hundred. This is the best way to enjoy the scenery. Legend be told, more people are rumored to be buried here than in the town cemetery. Hard to believe, isn't it?"

Dmitry Fodorov, DeSalva's lieutenant, steered the boat toward the middle, passing the opening to Emerald Bay. In the distance was a picture-perfect view of Vikingsholm, a thirty-eight-roomed

Scandinavian castle built in 1929. They were heading southeast, toward Lakeside Marina, with a pickup limo to Harrah's.

"You know, all the best casinos and spas are in South Lake for the rich and famous. In the North, there's Incline Village and what was Kings Castle until it closed for mismanagement and theft. It was rumored on opening night of Kings Castle that comedian Buddy Hackett appeared nude. Now that'll get your attention! Now it's Hyatt's. And Frank Sinatra's casino, the Cal-Neva Casino, also had its share of troubles over the years when he was forced out of ownership in the sixties and lost his license to gamble. The gaming commission didn't like Sinatra's buddying up to a notorious crime boss. There are small casinos like Lakeside to the big boys like Harrah's," DeSalva said, nodding to Dmitry as he steered the boat near a natural rock outcropping inlet, slowing to idle speed in neutral.

DeSalva turned to Flaherty. "Let's get something straight."

"'Bout what?"

"Who the fuck do you think you are? Nobody calls me Mike, least of all a troll like you!"

"You motherfucker! You…!" Flaherty rose, getting in DeSalva's face.

Without warning, Dmitry struck Flaherty on the back of his head with such force that his knees buckled, and he fell, crumpling to the deck, with a deep gash bleeding severely. His eyes glassed over and rolled back, showing only the whites. His body convulsed, then seized. He lay still, giving the appearance of being dead.

"Throw that scumbag off my boat. Quickly before we turn the corner and expose ourselves. He's bleeding all over the place!" DeSalva ordered, showing no remorse for what was about to happen.

Dmitry wrapped a heavy chain hooked to a large steel anchor twice around Flaherty's chest, looping the chain through his crotch and fastening it with a shackle. Using his powerful upper body, Dmitry lifted Flaherty's anchored body onto the transom. Vaulting over the transom to the swim platform, he pulled Flaherty's limp body off the transom, letting it fall onto the platform. Leaning against the transom, he pushed the unconscious Flaherty into the water, his body disappearing from view to join the denizens of the deep for all eternity.

Dmitry sprayed the residual blood off the deck, put the boat in gear, and continued on toward the Lakeside dock at South Lake. Veronica was waiting for their arrival. As the boat docked, Veronica walked up. "Michael, where's Dave?"

"He left early this morning. I don't think we'll be seeing him again. Let's go to the casino for a day out," he answered as he stepped onto the dock.

"Michael, let's talk."

"About what?"

"About last night. I didn't enjoy fucking Flaherty. He's a disgusting pig. That's not what I came here for. I came to see you and be with you! Michael, never do that to me again! I'm not your whore!"

DeSalva closed the space between them. "Listen, you love to fuck. And besides, you love the money I spend on you. You'll do as I say, fuck who I want, when I want, or this is all gone. Capisce?" he said as he fingered her silk blouse and brandished his arm at the surrounding vista.

CHAPTER 26

Since having to accept the fate of losing a portion of their company, Rae and Logan had become demoralized. The old spunk and fire were missing. Neither believed any longer in justice or the American dream. Having lost faith in the system, they only had each other. The topic of conversation centered on righting the wrong that was dealt to them. It was evident that so-called friends and employees had sold them out, double-crossed for the modern-day equivalent of Judas Iscariot's thirty pieces of silver.

Logan was becoming more distracted each day, fixated on righting the wrong, not through the courts but as a vigilante doling out restitution. It started as a fleeting concept, one that conceded little atonement—dreams of revenge, a cathartic release, a reverie where he was the savior. He and Rae would get back what was rightfully theirs—the company and its immense potential—and finally realize their American dream with a modicum of success and peace of mind!

As time progressed, Logan planned the events, who and how. First, he wanted to get Dave Flaherty, to make him suffer as he had, after hearing Marc Sullivan's boasts to former employees who bragged to some of the old production staff that all along, Flaherty had been a spy for DeSalva. Colleagues who just had to bring up the sensitive rumors, never letting them grasp closure from the tumultuous past, friends who gained amusement from inflicting subtle psychological pain of what they considered were innocent comments, Logan's revenge dreams were embracing more of his time, both in daydream fashion when he was awake and when he was sleeping. Getting Flaherty was becoming a passion.

One morning, still depressed with little drive to accomplish anything productive, Logan left the office to search for Flaherty. He drove to Flaherty's apartment, only to find a new tenant name on the mailbox. Logan rang the bell to find out that no one was home. As he walked around the complex, he noticed the manager's office and went in, asking about Flaherty's whereabouts.

"May I help you?" asked the older gentleman.

"Hi! I'm looking for an ex-employee. He used to be in 29C, but I noticed the name on the mailbox changed. Do you know where I could find him?" asked Logan.

"Well, that depends. First, tell me who you're looking for," stated the manager.

"Oh, ah, a Dave Flaherty. Do you know what happened to him?"

"That guy's a piece of trash! He stiffed me for two months' rent. He even skipped out on the furniture rental folks. I don't know where he is. I got mail for him, though. I'm giving it back to the post office. Sorry, pal. Can't help ya. But if you find him, I'd appreciate it if you'd let me know."

"Yeah. Thanks."

As Logan closed the office manager's door, he reflected what a stupid move that was. If he was to get Flaherty, going to see his apartment manager wasn't smart. This guy was someone who could put the two of them together. Logan returned to the office and continued to search, calling old acquaintances, friends, and foes, to no avail. Logan learned that Flaherty was no longer living in the Bay Area as no one had seen him in weeks. It was as if he had fallen off the face of the earth. Rumors had him living in Las Vegas, Atlantic City, and Monte Carlo, spending the reported half a million bucks he was paid for his deception. *Someday, I'll find that bastard and get my pound of flesh. He's not getting away this easy.'*

*****

Rae walked into Logan's office. "Logan, every time I turn around, you've gone off somewhere. What's going on?"

"You don't want to know, Rae."

"Try me. We've been through an awful lot together. So?" she said, looking at Logan with purpose.

"You'll think I'm crazy."

"Well, that depends."

"Ah, I've had this burning desire to kick the living shit out of Flaherty. I'm trying to track him down, okay?" Logan responded with raised eyebrows.

"You're kidding me, right?"

"No, Rae. I've been looking for him. I keep seeing him sitting at some blackjack table, laughing at our kindness. I can't sleep. All I do is think about getting even with all of them!" He gritted his teeth and clenched his fists. He had that look!

"Hey, I'm miserable too, but don't cut me out of your life!"

"I'm sorry. I'm just really pissed. It's different now. I've failed you. I've failed everyone. I want revenge, and doing this makes me feel better."

"Why haven't you asked me to help?"

"I don't know. I guess I thought you'd think I'm foolish," he said as he walked over to Rae.

Placing her hand on Logan's shoulder, reacting with a look that Logan had never witnessed before, she replied, "Well, in some species, it's said the female can be the more dangerous beast. Let's do it together. I'd like to get the bastards too!" She looked like a cornered lioness ready to rip the limbs from her prey, giving no quarter, giving no mercy, doing unto others.

"In high school, remember, I went to a Catholic high school and studied a lot of Latin. The Romans held a creed about getting even, like from the Bible, an eye for an eye, a tooth for a tooth. You know the one. Well, anyway, the Romans called it *lex talionis*, or the law of Talion, the act of revenge! They believed that the retaliatory punishment inflicted should correspond in degree and kind to the offense committed by the wrongdoer." Rae slipped her hand down to Logan's and squeezed. "I feel as you do."

CHAPTER 27

E arly on, Rae had reaffirmed through acquaintances in the industry that four of the key positions held by past employees had been recruited by DeSalva—sales, engineering, manufacturing, and purchasing. It was a masterful quartet with the knowledge to copy Scott's product and manufacturing technique, the process, the customers, and the vendors. Essentially, these were the works to steal his business.

On Marc Sullivan's recommendation, DeSalva hired them for their knowledge, an understanding that was only half-baked. Logan Scott had never shared the complete manufacturing process, much less to the assembly workers. All they knew to do was operate the machinery. Since he designed the equipment, the intricate workings of his unique manufacturing process were only known to him. Logan might have made mistakes in character judgment but never in his design and production. Rae often wondered what would happen to the defectors if DeSalva figured out he had been duped. Hmm, maybe…

Struggling to gain more business, Rae was confronted by the likes of Marc Sullivan's antics and despised him. Dave Flaherty, however, was the shot to the heart. She found it hard to come to grips with herself about Flaherty being a plant, a pathetic stoolie for DeSalva. He always commented to Rae how incredulous this was. He could never conceive of hurting Logan. What a maggot he turned out to be! Sometimes, we heard what we wanted to hear!

Word from the industry was that DeSalva had pirated a great deal of Scott's product from distributors and passed it off as his in order to jump-start his business. His strategy was clever and underhanded. He would dispatch his number one warrior, Sullivan, to visit each distributor and intimidate them with propaganda and exhibit phony court documents. Then while Sullivan was still at the location, a telephone call from DeSalva's lawyers espousing legal bravado usually topped it off. Afraid of legal repercussion, the customer would reluctantly give up the inventory to DeSalva's mercenary or would place an order for new product from DeSalva's new company, unaware that the new product was pirated from Scott's company with cosmetic packaging changes. And as hard as Scott tried to get distributors to cooperate and join his crusade, most would just stand back with frustration and disinterest.

The next morning, in the middle of breakfast, Rae grabbed the remote control and put the morning news on mute. "Logan, how about this for a plan: disinformation! We get DeSalva to do some dirty work for us. What do you think?"

"What are you talking about?"

"Ah, suppose we put out erroneous information about his people, his business, his customers—you know, all kinds of bogus stuff—and make sure it gets directly back to Sullivan and DeSalva and even those lying scoundrel lawyers. Maybe Frankie or Pete can help us. Soon, he starts second-guessing the turncoats, especially Sullivan. The information he's hearing is completely false. He expends energy pursuing the useless. He begins to distrust Sullivan and the others. You know he's got a temper and a big ego. Let's use them to our advantage. What do you think?" Rae asked with enthusiasm.

"And, my dear, how do you start such an undertaking?"

"I think it's time we do some snooping of our own. It's time we lower ourselves to their level and get our hands dirty," Rae replied with a matter-of-fact look. "I mean it, Logan. I want to get every one of those bastards. I want them to suffer by my golden rule."

*****

Besides true friendship, Pete Minot had a vested interest in helping Rae and Logan succeed. In return, Logan awarded him adequate shares of stock in their company to ensure some modicum of certainty of him being repaid. In his early years, Pete was assigned as the cultural attaché to the US Embassy in Peru, overseeing the US government's involvement in the continuing war on drugs campaign started by Peruvian president Fujimori by training the Sinai Battalion to fight against the Sendero Luminoso, better known as the Shining Path guerillas.

It was speculated that Pete had eliminated individuals, whether they were worthy of it or not, as a field agent with the company. Hearsay had it that his tradecraft was heralded to be flawless with intelligence data and information, true or otherwise, his specialty. He had seeded the foundations for numerous incursions into unfriendly countries, helping identify and eradicate nefarious characters, leaders, or heads of state.

Sometimes his own fingerman, he proved that one could get to like his profession regardless of the duty or assignment. Pete liked his job as a field agent, missing the "days of boredom establishing the order of the job intermingled with seconds of terror while taking direct action to carry the task through."

CHAPTER 28

The electronic telephone attendant answered, "Mosby Foundation."

"Pete Minot please," voiced Rae into the payphone receiver.

"Identify yourself," replied the electronic voice.

"Tell Pete this is a friend from the land of fruit and nuts," Rae replied curtly.

"One moment."

As the buzzing stopped, the phone clicked twice. Over a speaker voiced Pete Minot. "And who does this lovely voice belong to?"

"Pete, I would say the love of your life, the one you can't have, but probably the only one, though. This is Rae," she said, laughing into the phone.

"Hello, Rae. Are you and Logan all right?" quizzed Pete.

"That's why I'm calling," Rae replied hesitantly. "Pete, we need your help. I'm hesitant to discuss anything over the phone. Can you come out here, and soon?"

"Rae, you know I'll do anything for you guys, but you've got to tell me more. This line is secure. They're monitored continually. They're absolutely secure! Now talk!" Pete ordered.

"Okay, if you're—"

"Rae, it's my business to be sure. Get on with it."

"Well, Logan and I were…can you help us by getting information on certain people, like a background check, credit card info, you know, something useful?" she asked.

"Maybe, but on who?"

"Well, we need to know more about DeSalva and his associates."

"What others? Names, Rae," Pete countered.

"Okay. Victor Weissiner, the senior partner in the law firm of Cabot, Weissiner & Lowell in San Francisco. That's all."

"Why do you want this information, Rae? What's the reason?"

"Not on the phone, Pete. I don't care if your phones are checked. Please?" she asked in her best pleasing tone. "Pete, it's really important! Logan needs your help."

"I'll call you back. You're not at the office?"

"No, I'm at a payphone in the mall! We found a listening device in Logan's office. I'll call you back. What time?"

"Call me in one hour at 990-539-5959 and use a public pay telephone in a safe area."

"What kind of number is that? Aren't you in Washington?" she asked innocently.

"No, Kuala Lumpur. That's a special number to my secure phone. It'll find me anywhere on the globe," he answered sternly. "Stop asking so many damn questions."

To the second, Rae dialed the number given to her by Pete. The phone rang, and an electronic voice stated, "Please hold." The phone clicked four times, then buzzed electronically as it searched for Pete's secure phone. Pete picked up.

"Rae, always punctual. Now fill me in," prompted Pete as he walked outside the embassy's front gate in a light drizzle of rain.

"Pete, Logan and I want to get even with these bastards. They've screwed us royally. You won't believe the lengths they've gone to destroy us, and they're still messing with us. They won't leave us alone. I'm scared for us. We want revenge."

"I'll be in tomorrow evening. I have some business to attend to in LA. Pick me up at Apex Aviation, San Jose, at seven thirty. Got it?"

"Oh, Pete, thank you, thank you, thank you! We'll see you tomorrow night."

"Oh, and bring that listening device you found. I need to see it. Don't forget, seven thirty, Apex Aviation, San Jose. Bring the bug!" With that, the phone went dead.

CHAPTER 29

Rae and Logan walked into Apex Aviation FBO, awaiting Pete's arrival. Rae was thumbing through a magazine, seated in the lounge, when Logan spotted the unmarked white Gulfstream on final approach. Walking into the lounge, he announced, "He's early." Rae laid the magazine down and joined Logan at the window, watching the Gulfstream taking the taxiway to the ramp at Apex Aviation.

The lineman and golf cart were already in position to guide the pilot to the jet's parking position and ferry the guests and their baggage off the ramp. Hardly two minutes had passed when the air stairs deployed. Pete was first off the plane followed by a crew member in a green flight suit, carrying Pete's equipment case.

"There he is," squealed Rae. "Maybe we should've worked for the government. They never seem to go without," chided Rae.

"No kidding." Pete entered Apex. "Hey, old man. Thanks for coming," Logan said, shaking Pete's hand.

"Hello, gorgeous. Been way too long," he said, picking Rae up off her feet. "Missed you two!" Pete turned back, warmly putting his arm on Logan's shoulder. "Sorry, brother. I was dark for too long and wasn't there for the two of you these past few months. Oh, hell, let's get out of here!"

Logan sidestepped to the crew member. "I'll take that now. Thank you. Now let's get out of here," declared Logan, carrying Pete's case.

Rae squeezed between Pete and Logan as they exited the building. "Have you eaten yet?"

"Not since lunch. Let's go to Original Joe's. It's an old hangout of mine, great place to talk. Not far from here, in old town. Okay with you two?" he asked warmly as the three walked abreast to the parking lot.

"Sure," replied Logan.

Nearing Logan's truck, Pete stopped them in midstride, causing Rae and Logan to turn and face him. He was somber. In a deliberate whisper, he said, "From here on, absolutely no names or any of this subject matter in the truck or house, just trivial chat or loud music. Am I clear?"

Logan spoke for both. "Got it." Logan placed the case in the back and took Pete's overnight bag, placing it in the back. "I'll put the bag and case in the cab when we get to the restaurant. Sorry, Pete, this is our transportation these days." Logan unlocked the doors.

"Don't worry, tonight's my treat. This is an official field trip." Pete winked.

"You're staying at our place. Hope that's okay."

"That's great. Let's get some grumbles. I'm famished!" suggested Pete.

They arrived at Original Joe's in the heart of downtown San Jose. The parking lot had plenty of space. Since it was three minutes to 8:00 p.m. on a Tuesday night, the restaurant wasn't that busy. Pete pointed to the oversize corner booth in the back, and the waiter seated them accordingly. "Plenty of privacy," remarked Pete. Rae slid all the way in, and Logan followed. Pete slid midway on the other side, facing them yet with an unobstructed view of the front door. "I need a dry martini, and then we'll talk," he said, shedding his light-weight jacket.

The waiter took their drink order and left. Logan and Rae each ordered Original Joe's famous frozen margaritas. Pete held his finger to his lips as he pulled a small box that looked like a hearing aid case from his jacket pocket. "Rae, hand me a napkin." He opened the case and placed a half-round device on the table, covering it with an open paper napkin. Pete kept the chitchat light until the drinks were delivered. "Okay, now show me what you've got and tell me about it. Leave nothing out."

Logan pulled out a smaller-than-a-dime disc-shaped gray-and-silver device from his jacket pocket. One side of the device had a square of adhesive attached, and the other a gray matte surface. It resembled a small watch battery with a faint geometric pattern. Pete examined the diminutive disc with precision, treating it like a dime, carefully turning it over and over between his thumb and forefinger.

"We'll talk about this later," he said and winked to Rae and Logan, placing the disc in his shirt's breast pocket. "I guess you two aren't flaking out on me after all. I was able to follow just so much while abroad. So tell me everything from the beginning."

Rae and Logan related the sordid tale from the first tire incident to Rae's near-fatal beating. Pete was aware of most of the legal details but was unable to communicate to comprehend the brutality to Rae and Logan, the break-ins at the office, Rae's house, and the continuing nuisance bullshit. Logan related the story of finding the listening device within his office.

"Where did you find it exactly?" he asked, sipping his martini.

"It was on the base of my desk phone. I went ballistic the other day over the course of events and slammed my fist on the phone. It wouldn't ring after that, so I took it apart to see if I could fix it, and that's when I found this device attached to the inside cover. I've never seen a part like this before. It's sophisticated. Circuitry appears expensive, odd conformal substrate."

"Have you looked for others in the office, at home, in the car?" asked Pete.

"Others?" Rae quizzed.

"Absolutely! Where there's one bug, there's more. I need to locate its nest. Let's see what I find when we get to your place. I'll sweep the house and truck tonight, and tomorrow, your offices. You can have it back after I look into this more."

"I wonder what menacing secrets it will reveal," Logan muttered rhetorically.

"More than you know. We'll finish this later," Pete said as their food was delivered to the table.

The three enjoyed a hearty steak dinner and the cozy warmth of friendly laughter, a social indulgence that Rae and Logan dearly missed during these past few months. The restaurant emptied by nine thirty, and Pete beckoned it was time for the three of them to depart.

Outside the restaurant, Pete turned to Rae and Logan. "Remember, before we get to your place, do not—I repeat, do not—say a word until I say it's all right to do so. No names, all right?"

"Hmm." Rae nodded concurrence.

"I'm testing the waters."

As Logan rolled the truck in the driveway, Rae interrupted, "I'll take Sheba for a short walk."

Pete waited until Logan locked the truck, heading toward the house. Opening his equipment case at the front door, he handed Logan a nondescript CD. "Turn all TVs on any news channel and put this jazz CD in the stereo and turn the volume up. This CD has embedded sound wave inversion designed to interfere with wiretapping and eavesdropping. Put it this way: there's enough white noise in this to allow us a modicum of protected conversation tonight." With that, Pete took out a portable countersurveillance case containing a nonlinear junction detector and attached an egg crate, eight-inch parabolic-shaped antennae, to the top of his spectral correlator device.

Rae opened the front door, beckoning Sheba outside. After Sheba greeted Pete, he stepped in, pointing the detector at windows, walls, pictures, lamps, in and around upholstered furniture, air vents, and accessories, watching for spiking wavelength readouts. Rae and Sheba walked around the house to the backyard while Logan watched Pete methodically work his way through every nook and cranny, beginning at the floor level and continuing to the ceiling vents. He went room to room, taking some fifteen minutes to complete his house sweeping, saying nothing, noting everything.

He walked back to the front door and opened his equipment case. In it was a telephone signal-measuring device with a data transceiver and video display. Pete unplugged the wire to the handset on the kitchen counter and replugged the same telephone wire into an input port on his device. He pressed a red button and a predialed number scrolled across the video screen. The number had a 202 area code, somewhere in Washington, DC, terminating the signal after the second ring. He repeated the same sequence to the second handset in the bedroom. Holding his finger to his mouth, Pete motioned for Logan to follow him out back.

Joining Rae in the backyard, in a soft whisper, he said, "I found two more bugs. One's on the left backside of your bathroom mirror, and one's on the underside of the microwave, right behind the fan's filter. They're well-hidden. And your phones are tapped, all right. That means there's a nest nearby. Ah, a voice-actuated recorder. Logan, with me."

Pete walked around the side of the house until he came to the electrical junction box. He pulled a multipurpose tool from his pocket and removed the screws, giving them to Logan to hold. He opened the box and shined the flashlight in and around the meter, pointing to a rectangular black case measuring about two inches by a half-inch thickness wedged behind the electric meter.

Logan watched intently as Pete gently pulled one of two wires loose just enough to break the circuit yet look as though it became unfastened by itself or unintentionally by the power company. Next, Pete pulled a small tube of clear adhesive from his pocket. Looking under the box, he motioned for Logan to observe. Under the bottom of the box, he squeezed two thin lines of clear adhesive crisscrossing each other, covering the box closure.

"You'll know if this box has been opened, and you can easily redo this ploy. Innocuous but effective. On the rare occasion the power company visits, well, either way, you'll know."

Walking around to the front yard, Pete remarked, "Now we know where it is. Let's go back in. Until I know more, we don't want to remove the devices and tip our hand. You'll just have to selectively communicate. Disinformation, my friends, disinformation."

Back inside, Logan watched as Pete swept the house once more, motioning for Logan and Rae to follow him outside once again. "They're sophisticated. Who'd you piss off other than DeSalva?" he said, smiling cleverly.

"Everyone but the pope, I guess," Logan replied.

"Well, this is getting interesting. These bugs are pretty new, used by the feds, mostly the FBI and DEA. Any reason they would be looking into you or your contracts?"

"No reason whatsoever."

"I'll let you know if this is an assignment and who's working it, dirty or not." Pete dialed a number on his encrypted satellite phone. It was a sophisticated-looking device resembling an oversize Blackberry but ruggedized with a retracting antennae and a large screen. It was shaped differently from rectangular PDA phones.

Smirking, Pete pressed a green LED button at the bottom, uttering, "Locate J.F." Pete was tapped into a restricted group of satellites within the Comintel Iridium System. Boasting some sixty-six satellites, his communiqués were well-guarded with the latest stream cipher technology accessible only to his ghost organization.

After a few seconds of hearing a resonant buzz, Pete connected. "Good, and you? Yes. I'm in San Jose. Look, ah, I know it's late, but I need a favor. I need an audio op authentication. Is the Bureau monitoring a wiretap on a Logan Scott in San Jose?" He listened to the response. "Well, I found a few XTD5s at his house. I think we should get together. Logan and I go back a few, and I want to know what the hell's going on. Hmm. Huh. Hmm. Huh. Roger." Logan listened patiently as Pete remained poker-faced. "What say we meet tomorrow? Usual place. Noon. See you then." Pete disconnected the call.

"At first blush, the FBI is not investigating you or running a tap. I'm meeting a former colleague tomorrow for lunch. I'll let you know the outcome. Remember, leave the bugs. I'll sweep everything again first thing tomorrow. You have the CD, so use it and make as much noise and chatter as you wish until I tell you otherwise."

"Sure. Hey, you're not going to hear us complain. Thanks, man." Logan slapped Pete on the shoulder.

"Eh, what are friends for? And now if you don't mind, I'm bushed. Jet lag is catching up with me. I'm calling it a night." Pete yawned and headed back in the house.

CHAPTER 30

Rae was the first up. She was listening to the six o'clock news as Pete peered into the kitchen holding the special jazz CD, motioning for Rae to remain silent. He leaned over, whispering to act as if only she and Logan were present, as he walked to the stereo and inserted the CD while sweeping the kitchen in a slow, steady tempo, covering floor to ceiling. Rae watched as Logan wandered into the kitchen.

Pete shut off his device. "Sleep all right?" asked Logan.

"Very well. I'll be bunking downtown for a few days and then on to LA. I have some things to attend to and don't want a hint of a connection to you two at this time. Never know who's watching."

Pete handed Logan a pager. "This is an encrypted pager that scrambles numbers. I'll call it and leave a 990 callback number. Do not call from your cell phone. Do not call from your office phone. Do not call from your home phone. Use this new burner phone, preferably in a populated, noisy place, like in the shopping mall. Be absolutely certain no one follows you. That also goes for your house.

"You both need to keep a sharp eye for strange vehicles driving by or a strange vehicle normally not on this street. If you do see that, be cool. Act normal and disinterested in the vehicle unless it acts out of character. The nest may be disabled, so this whoever may be just nosy enough to check. Now if for some reason you cannot call me within thirty minutes from the time I call the pager where you can safely talk, then call me from this burner. Let it ring once and disconnect. I'll call you back from a monitored scrambling line and give you instructions. Now are you two up for an adventure?" Pete asked coyly.

"Hell yeah!" Rae replied emphatically.

"What's the scoop?" asked Logan.

"A little faith, amigo," Pete said as he winked at them and smiled. "Remember, revenge is best served cold." Pete sat down to enjoy breakfast.

CHAPTER 31

The next few days were business as usual but with a twist. Both were restless, anxiously waiting like expectant parents. Rae asked her neighbor Bill to look after Sheba while she and Logan went traveling on extended business. Bill obliged without hesitation. With that task out of the way, she and Logan could concentrate on more meaningful thoughts.

Logan shared with Rae that he perfected the subsequent function of the handwriting identification analysis project he developed for the Federal Deposit Insurance Corporation (FDIC). The EXL90 was a marvel. With minimal cursive assimilation on the transmittal pad, typically one's name but as little as eight to ten characters, the handwriting of anyone could be documented and stored for worldwide safeguarding. But no one knew that Logan took it one step further.

The EXL90 had another innovation. It could duplicate bona fide signatures right down to the smallest of idiosyncrasies. One's stroke length, pressure, movement, and force were memorized within a microprocessor half the size of a ladybug. The microprocessor stored the data. Later, when the writing implement was inserted into the articulating arm attached to a special transmittal pad he created, voila! Most anyone would be capable of signing authentic congressional documents!

"That's a scary thought, Logan. I don't have words to describe how this could change the course of history, and not necessarily for good. This is life-altering. My God, it's invaluable," replied Rae.

"Pete fully understands its implications. It is light-years ahead of the pressure-sensitive LED screens presently used in department stores and some banking institutions to process credit card transactions and thwart fraud. But as Pete cautioned me, if it fell into the wrong hands, everything from stock fraud and illegal wire transfers would be child's play."

"So how do you duplicate a signature when there's no one around to sign?" Rae asked intently.

"The EXL90 employs an advanced cursive recognition software program I created that correlates to an optical character recognition scanner that plugs into the transmitting pad I developed. It will capture one hundred words in three-second increments, store, and dump the data. Pete and I suspect DeSalva may have read a little about it and wants to manipulate it for his own gain," exhaled Logan with a smirk.

"You're up to something, aren't you?"

"You bet. We'll get those bastards, but on our terms!" Logan reacted in a steely but calm tone. "Pete and I have had each other's back. Even in Iraq, he watched my six. He won't let us down. I'd bet my life on it. Sooner or later, we'll have to act. Either we give up the technology to the feds or destroy it. There is no third option."

"What do you mean destroy it?" Rae quizzed.

"Not entirely, just its OCR and duplicitous feature. The EXL90 alone is worth a pretty penny to FDIC, and I'm banking on that for us, for our future," he said and kissed Rae on the cheek.

Startled by the vibration of the pager in his pocket, Logan read the 990 number. He called out to Rae in the kitchen. "Hey, honey, I'm bored. Let's go get some ice cream!"

"I'm game." Rae giggled. "I'll race you to the truck!"

Rae whistled for Sheba and grabbed her altered new satellite cell phone, one each given to her and Logan by Pete. Rae now guarded her communiqués to Logan. At this point, all they knew about their new sat phone, albeit its sophisticated look, was that it could instantly transmit their whereabouts to a network of people when needed and that all communiqués to Pete were encrypted and secure. They would soon learn about its amazing capabilities.

Pete directed each of them to write or whisper important notes to each other on their new phone and to keep all conversations in the vehicle, the house, and office benign. Pete emphatically reminded them to use the sound inversion CD when and wherever as its abundance of static white noise coupled with excessive vibration and imbedded high frequencies impeded wiretapping and microwave surveillance. "Turn the radio volume up and sing along, joke, have fun, and be as normal as possible" were Pete's parting words, lesson one.

Logan pulled into the parking lot by the main entrance of the Westfield Mall, by the Cheesecake Factory and the entrance to the food court. "What flavor today?" asked Rae.

"Hmm, how 'bout butter pecan?" Logan smiled.

"Back in a few."

Rae walked to the end of the food court by the public restrooms, between Chick-fil-A and Swenson's Ice Cream. Scanning the area, noting just teens hanging around the phones, Rae stood by the entrance to the restrooms, pulled out the burner phone, and dialed the number displayed on the beeper. As Rae initiated the connection, she listened to several steady clicking sounds and four high-pitched beeps, and then Pete picked up.

"Pete?" Rae whispered.

"This line is secure, Rae. Can you hear me?"

"Clearly."

"Hit record."

While talking on the burner phone, Rae depressed the record data button on her new sat phone and watched it record an abbreviated version in text in one second. It read, "Apex Aviation, San Jose, 1500 tomorrow. See Manny. No names. No Qs. Warm clothes. Watch yourself." Pete's call disconnected.

Rae saved the message, cleared the screen, and walked across the food court to the ice cream store. Bouncing in her light-footed cadence, Rae smiled as she carried back the tray of goodies—double scoops of butter pecan and cookies 'n cream and a small cup of vanilla yogurt for Sheba. They drove in silence to Bill Lyon's.

Bill walked out to greet them as they pulled into the driveway. Sheba was eager to see her old pal Bill, and Rae knew she would be in good hands while they traveled. "Where must you two travel this time?" Bill asked.

"Oh, Washington again, negotiating the military contracts," replied Rae. "Then we're taking time for ourselves, an extended vacation."

"I'm so glad you still have a going concern."

Logan unloaded the dog food while Rae gave Bill her new cell number and cash for additional food and treats. "We'll be back in four weeks," she said as they backed out of Bill's driveway.

CHAPTER 32

Rae and Logan drove to the airport in relative silence, pensive about their impending journey. As they approached Apex Aviation's side access gate, a tall, dark-haired man in a green flight suit walked outside, waving them toward him. Logan rolled down the window.

"Half a mile down on your right is Hangar 10. Park nose in the back, right corner. Leave the keys in it," replied the stranger as he opened the access gate.

Rae leaned over. "Manny?"

"Yes."

"I'm Rae, and—"

"I know. Drop your bags by the rear door. Climb aboard and make yourself comfortable. We'll be off in twenty." Manny waited for their truck to pass through, then closed the access gate. Driving slowly on the access road, Logan located the open hangar and drove in slowly, steering around the left wing of the silver-and-blue-striped Pilatus PC-12 turboprop, stopping in the back corner. Rae and Logan each grabbed their bags out of the back and wheeled them straight to the plane's open baggage door as Manny pulled up in a golf cart.

"Logan, just set the bags on the compartment floor in the back and then unhook and stow the tug in the back next to this cart," Manny instructed as he rolled the golf cart into the hangar.

"Will do." Walking around the wing to the front, Logan unhooked the three-wheel tug from the nose wheel, steering it back in the hangar, impressed by the ample work areas. *This is a mechanic's dream workshop. I'd love fiddling around in here,* he thought as he pushed the tug across the epoxied spotless light-blue floor.

Rae climbed aboard the plane and chose a front-facing, second-row left seat. She was in awe at the oversize seats and luxurious interior. Each seat, covered in ivory-and-gray leather, sported its own worktable and a wall-mounted monitor that could swivel ninety degrees, allotting ample workspace. Logan rejoined to shadow Manny during his preflight check of the aircraft.

Tailing Manny's precheck of the exhaust system, then the ailerons, he asked curiously, "What's its cruise?"

"We beefed up this Pratt & Whitney to average 310 knot cruise," replied Manny, pointing to the underbelly FLIR ball.

"Nice Safire 380 FLIR ball," Logan commented as he continued shadowing Manny.

Handing Logan the fuel tester, Manny said, "It should be clean." Manny leaned inside the baggage door. "Hey, Rae, Pete thought you guys might want a snack, so help yourself."

Rae swiveled backward and stepped back to open the compact refrigerator between the last two rear seats up against the baggage compartment wall to find it stocked with hors d'oeuvres and chilled splits of champagne. "Just like Pete, eh? Always travels in style."

Logan tested the fuel for moisture accumulation, finding it clean, while Manny inspected the prop, lights, brakes, and tires. Satisfied with the preflight check, Manny motioned for Logan to climb aboard and take copilot seat. Logan obliged. After getting situated, Manny leaned around the cockpit wall. "Rae, you'll find a headset under your seat. Plug it into the wall next to the worktable."

Logan grabbed a Bose A20 headset hanging off the copilot's yoke and plugged it in. He was surprised at the clarity and noise-cancellation capability as Manny started the plane, audibly verbalizing his run-up checklist. After completing the run-up check, Manny called ground clearance for permission to taxi to the runway for takeoff. Rae and Logan listened as Manny received immediate clearance for takeoff. Astonishing electronics, the latest in flat panel avionics. It was no ordinary plane. It had more gadgets on it than they could count.

Before they knew it, they were airborne. "Short takeoff," remarked Logan.

"You'll see why soon. We'll be landing in fifty minutes. Rae, if you don't want to listen to us, the passenger seats offer a selection of music. You can locate the channels by turning on the monitor."

"I'm fine." Rae smiled. "Thanks for asking."

"Climbs fast," remarked Logan.

"She's a workhorse. Packs 1,200 shaft horsepower. Smooth running, short field takeoff, 1,800 feet per minute, climb at full gross," added Manny. "She really struts her stuff in tight spaces. Take control."

"I'd love to," exclaimed Logan as Manny released the autopilot and Logan assumed manual control.

"Pete said you two go way back, that you worked together in the sandbox," remarked Manny.

"Yep. That was a while ago. Those were some wild and crazy days." Logan chuckled. "I think Pete still is a bit crazy, though!"

"Aren't we all these days?" chimed Manny. "Enjoying the scenery, Rae?"

"Yes. Arid and desolate, isn't it?"

"That it is. It can get mighty chilly out here at night. Did you bring warm clothes?"

"Yes. Pete warned us."

*****

The time passed quickly. Manny and Logan swapped personal stories about Pete, each story better than the last. "Heads up," Manny announced. "Taking control. After we cross the Sierras, we'll bank left to our private airstrip. We'll hit dirt in a couple of minutes." Manny retarded the throttle, pulling back the prop into beta range for maximum descent.

"Logan, gear down."

"Gear down," recited Logan.

"Flaps 20."

"Flaps 20," repeated Logan.

"Flaps 40."

"Flaps 40," repeated Logan.

Manny pulled the nose up and deployed the speed brakes as the Pilatus rapidly descended. With the airstrip in sight, Manny worked the throttle down, floating just a few feet above the airstrip, squeaking a touchdown landing.

"Whoa! Bravo, Zulu," Logan hooted. "I know what you mean by strutting her stuff. Impressive."

Manny back-taxied, pulling off the runway, stopping in front of a large metal building. Keeping the engine idling for proper cooldown, Manny clicked the radio frequency button twice as the oversize door began to rise. Logan assisted Manny in completing the shutdown sequence. After the hangar door completely opened, a fit-looking man in a long-sleeved beige shirt and digital desert camouflage battle dress uniform (BDU) pants tucked into high-top tan leather Kevlar boots pushed a large aircraft tug out on the ramp and hooked it to the nose wheel. Giving Manny a thumbs-up, he guided the tug, pulling the Pilatus into the hangar.

Changing radio frequencies, Manny clicked the radio frequency button again. Neither Logan nor Rae had unbuckled their seat belt as the entire hangar floor began to descend and rotate 180 degrees. Logan turned to Manny with eyes wide as Manny teased, "Please place your tray tables in their upright and locked positions. Thank you for flying with us. Be sure to rate our service. We'd appreciate a five-star review!" Both Rae and Logan laughed as they unplugged their headsets and prepared to exit the aircraft.

As the floor stopped rotating, Logan stated, "Now that's impressive."

"Yes, it is. I rarely use this. It's only when we have other aircraft. We need to keep out of the sight of prying eyes in the sky that we use it. We never keep any aircraft outside."

As Logan and Rae stepped off the plane, the man stowing the tug walked over and introduced himself. "Hi, I'm Tom Davenport. Please call me Dav." He extended his hand first to Logan and then to Rae.

"Pleasure to meet you," Logan said, shaking hands.

"Likewise," remarked Rae, shaking his hand.

"Follow me. Pete's waiting for ya." Dav led the way through the tunnel to Sublevel 3.

Pete was dressed in the same long-sleeved beige shirt and digital desert BDUs tucked into high-top tan leather Kevlar boots. "Welcome to the Mosby Foundation," he said, giving Rae a hug. "How's the flight?"

"Quite interesting." Rae smirked. "I'd fly with these two characters anytime! What's with these stories I've been hearing about you and Logan in, what do they call it, the sandbox? And you and Manny, huh? When was the last time you flew left seat?" They walked through a tunnel to the elevator.

"Actually, last year in Angola," hissed Pete.

"Was this a power transmission substation or just made to look like one?" asked Rae.

"Hmm, quick study," he said, smiling coyly. "Come on, let's get you two settled in."

Exiting the elevator, Pete inserted a remote key FOB into the steel turnstile. After everyone had passed through the turnstile, Manny punched a seven-digit code into a keypad centered in the middle of an immense steel door and looked directly into a screen for retinal and facial recognition. Everyone was on real-time video monitors with extraordinary sound detection. The door hissed and rotated ninety degrees, opening to a circular, tiered room with sixteen eighty-inch screen monitors strategically positioned around the entire room. Manny stepped to the side as Pete led Logan and Rae into the operation's center.

Akin to the type of large flat screen monitors used by the National Oceanic and Atmospheric Administration (NOAA), Logan and Rae were speechless as they gazed at the diversity of manned computer workstations and high-tech security monitoring and surveillance equipment that was clearly visible from every angle of the room. Not like a typical square workstation with one computer and monitor, each individual seated at the operational desks resembled a cockpit crew from a spacecraft with the firepower to destroy the earth. It was apparent that Big Brother was really capable of watching you. It was mind-boggling to comprehend the variety of resources an operation of this magnitude required.

Pete began his indoctrination. "The grounds are monitored and recorded 24-7 down to motion sensor, sound detection, heat signature, and seismic measurements covering a radius of fifty miles in any direction. We're testing new surveillance equipment for the Department of Defense that can distinguish movement down to the size of a mouse. We may be alerted when a coyote walks by, but the program sidesteps all nonhuman or mechanical contact, so we're not busy sifting through unnecessary surveillance. It's far more advanced than commercial surveillance equipment, which has to be monitored by humans.

"Outside of a HALO, or high-altitude, low-opening, airdrop, it would be exceedingly difficult to penetrate the grounds. As redundancy for our operational use and security, we have five dedicated birds in the sky that keep a close eye."

In the middle of the room, four very fit-looking men clad in identical camouflage BDUs stood up from each of their respective workstations and nodded as Rae and Logan stepped down onto the first level that circled this immense cybernetic chamber. Stepping down one more level into the center, Pete began his animated introductions of his core team, each situated in their respective circular cyber station positioned at the four compass points of the globe.

"Each of these four workstations monitors one of four quadrants of the globe, rotating mission management every ninety days. The north station on my left is Skip Larsen from Joint Special Operations Command, Task Force Green. The east station directly in front is Ron Lilly from Force Recon, First Marine Battalion. The south station to my right is Alex Iglesias from Air Force PJ. And you already met Tom Davenport for our west station from Naval Special Warfare group.

"And last but not least, your chauffeur today, Manny Sapulva." He stepped out from behind them. "Hell's Kitchen Clandestine Services." Laughter filled the room. "There are a handful of others you will meet in time in the primary support room two floors down, but these guys will be your mentors for the next few weeks," he uttered warmly.

"Gentlemen, our guests for the next four weeks, Raelyn MacAllister and Logan Scott." Everyone smiled concurrently. "Now that the formality is over, let me show you to your room." Pete guided Rae and Logan to their living quarters off the second-floor balcony.

CHAPTER 33

The rooms were much like that of superb hotel suites—large-screen televisions, a well-appointed mini kitchen, comfortable living area with a double-sided computer workstation, king-size bed, and a spa bathroom with ultraviolet lighting designed to blend natural light from the outdoors carefully hidden in every room. Not bad considering it was a concrete building with no windows to the outside world.

"Freshen up if you like. Social hour is in thirty. Time to get acquainted with the group. We'll eat at 1930. Don't worry, these rooms are sacred—no eyes, no ears, no noise. Everyone and everything are sacred on this floor, I promise." He winked and backed out of their room.

*****

After unpacking and settling into their temporary living quarters, Logan caressed Rae on the shoulder. "You don't have to do this."

"I understand I don't. I've thought about this a lot. I'm here because I'm tired of being a pawn in someone else's chess game," she glared back in a matter-of-fact tone. "We've just needed a little outside help giving us an edge! Being here gives us a chance to right some wrongs! Come on, let's go meet everyone." Rae grabbed Logan's hand playfully, urging him to follow.

They joined the group downstairs in the lounge. They marveled at Pete keeping the group engaged. A few new faces from the support staff were introduced. Pete was skillful at pairing up individuals with like personality, characteristics, and interests yet clever enough to know when it was time to change dance partners. He had become masterful at managing his talent. With training and opportunity, he expected that the newcomers would prove their mettle and likewise become worthy talent.

Rae was enjoying harmless banter with Skip and Alex as Pete and Manny guided Logan into an adjacent briefing room and closed the glass door. Rae suspected it was to decide the fate of the EXL90. Maybe it was payment in kind. Nothing in life was free. There was always a price.

Pete had helped Logan recently. Perhaps now was payback time. Pete was cognizant of EXL90's handwriting duplicity features. Logan knew the day of reckoning would arrive. The government would want it. In fact, it would take it. He had to decide—forfeit or destroy? It was a momentous decision, one that affected their lives, their safety, and their future, everyone's future.

The trio talked for some time. Logan decided to kill the duplicity program, agreeing in principle with Pete that custody in the wrong hands would be devastating. Greed might sway even the pure of heart—executive orders issued without knowledge or question, Senate passing bills eroding human rights, Wall Street brokers running rampant in the market, widespread identity theft, judicial orders railroading the innocent, security in the armed forces running amok, political action groups becoming totalitarian dictators, or the private sector completely manipulating politics.

"All in all, Logan, without a reasonable system of checks and balances, utter fucking chaos will occur," Pete stated emphatically. "Why, currency manipulation alone would disrupt our commerce system dramatically. You know as well as I do that as flawed as our system is, there's still a degree of checks and balances in place to prevent this very such thing. That's our main focus here. We're a nonexistent adjunct checks and balances concern. We exist to fight for those who can't and to keep our liberty and justice for all intact!"

"So who do you report to?" queried Logan.

"A top dog at the Justice Department, that's all you need to know at this time. So, Logan, are we together on this?" he asked as Skip opened the door to announce dinner.

"Solidly so," Logan replied with a confident smile and followed Skip to join the others.

Unaware that all was going according to Pete's master plan—divide and conquer—Rae was being graded amid the seemingly harmless chitchat among the group. Tom and Ron intermittently chimed in their two cents. Everyone seemed relaxed, enjoying their cocktail of choice, but that, too, was under watchful scrutiny. Laughter was muddled by current events, trivia, politics, and agendas.

Rae's facial expressions and body language, her decorum, her knowledge, her experience, and her responses, all were on trial, being analyzed by trained eyes. Did she have conviction? Could she maintain focus under extreme duress? Was she tenacious? Could she effectively assimilate another's role? Psychological stress points were being weighed here. Did she have the moral turpitude to contribute? These were valid questions that determined the basis for rejection or induction as a plebe in the Mosby Foundation.

When Pete formed the adjunct intelligence operations center, he chose the name Mosby Foundation to honor a few men who changed history. The most noted who stood out in history, General John S. Mosby, was a feared Confederate army commander who operated outside of the traditional military structure. Mosby believed that guerilla actions were more effective in defending Virginia and the Confederacy. He was given his nickname Gray Ghost for his ability to lead his partisan rangers, strike a target quickly, and then disappear.

As a boy, Mosby was small and frail and was subjected to bullying, even in the mid-1800s. One day, at the age of nineteen, while attending the University of Virginia, he nonfatally shot a bullying student, was expelled from the university, and was sentenced to one year in jail.

During the Civil War, Mosby and his Rangers, using guerilla tactics, disrupted supply lines, captured Union couriers, provided intelligence to the general confederacy, and became a real thorn in the side of federal officers in Virginia. On occasion, he was also known for conducting his own reconnaissance and was wounded seven times. After the war, he opened a law practice and became lifelong friends with Ulysses S. Grant.

History also admired Francis Marion, who preceded Mosby by just over one hundred years. He was credited by the US Army Rangers and other special forces as engendering modern guerilla and maneuver warfare. Nicknamed the Swamp Fox, he and his men operated out of loyalty outside of the structure of the regular military, supplying their own horses, ammunition, and food. Marion's swift attacks against British garrisons and retreat back into the swamps of South Carolina defied the then strategic logic and bewildered the loyalists, which was why he and his men were so successful.

William Quantrill, another notorious and enigmatic wartime guerilla leader, led his Bushwhackers into guerilla war on the Unionist town of Lawrence, Kansas, in 1863. He was joined by the famous James brothers, Frank and Jesse, who later learned how to conduct their own guerilla tactics in bank and train robberies. The Mosby Foundation was an apt name for its mission task force, bound by honor, truthfulness, and love of God, country, and family.

Rae smiled across the table at Logan as she squeezed in between Alex and Ron. The group enjoyed a healthy meal of veal shank, potatoes au gratin, and white asparagus topped with hollandaise. To wet their palate, Pete opened a full-bodied Australian Shiraz.

"Respectable choice," Logan proclaimed, holding up his glass, acknowledging the host.

Pete nodded and continued on with his witty stories and such. Rae pondered the purpose of the stories. At one time, these guys were complete strangers to one another, yet they all shared a common bond. She pondered if it was patriotism or the thrill of the missions, or were they kindred spirits in kind, a brotherhood of philosophic ideals? And how did Pete become the Pied Piper? There were many unanswered questions.

"I hate to cut this short, but you two have a busy day tomorrow," Pete said. "We'll meet here tomorrow a.m. at 0600."

CHAPTER 34

Rae stirred as Logan lay quietly admiring her innocence in sleep. It was 5:15 a.m. Logan had been awake for some time, thinking about the challenges that faced them. He worried more about Rae, wondering how she would cope with such intense training.

"Hey," whispered Rae as she smiled upon awakening. "What time is it?"

"Almost five twenty. You up for this?" he asked innocently.

"We'll know soon enough." Rae bounced up, smiling. "C'mon, join me in the shower."

*****

They were dressed and downstairs at five forty-five. Logan noticed Pete was sitting in the briefing room and tapped on the glass door. Pete motioned for Logan to enter. "Sleep okay?" asked Pete.

"Fine, actually," replied Logan.

"Grab a cup of joe and sit down. We'll go for a run later. We've got a few things to work out." Pete opened a blue folder with "Confidential" stamped in red block letters across its front, carefully arranging the contents on the table.

Logan remained quiet, eyeing the collateral: several black-and-white eight by tens of Michael DeSalva, his lieutenant, the lawyer, Marc Sullivan, and a handful of other irreverent individuals. Pete had one hell of a dossier on DeSalva.

"How, ah, where did you get all of this?"

"He's an arms dealer for the Russians. Brokers some two, maybe three, big shipments a year—handguns, assault rifles, heavy machine guns, mortars, RPGs, anti-tank weapons, even, ah, from air defense ZSU 44s to SA-7 shoulder-fired missiles, you name it. Hell, he sells the whole goddamned gambit from Nicaragua to the Ukraine! His father-in-law is one of the organized crime bosses in New Jersey.

"DeSalva's been increasing the drug traffic for them into Nevada and the five contiguous states. Hasn't gained a foothold into British Colombia yet as the Asians have it locked up. Without backing from the Russians, he'd be dead in the water. He acquires legit businesses as fronts, launders the money, and dumps the business through Pingston Financial Securities.

"His wife spends the preponderance of her time in New York. His three children remain at boarding schools on the East Coast. He has three active mistresses, now four including your ex-employee's wife Veronica Sullivan. Other than the usual dirty linen bullshit, he's a sophisticated puppet master and a junior capo in his father-in-law's organization. We've been monitoring him and backtracking his movements. We're certain he eliminated your ex-employee Dave Flaherty."

"This might explain the firebomb that destroyed that Canadian company, ah, Biotechné that DeSalva swindled two years ago," Logan declared with amazement.

"We believe so," replied Pete. "We traced the explosives back to those typically used by the Russians."

"How do you know all this in such a short time?"

"As I mentioned before, I had just terminated an extended undercover operation in Angola and Malaysia when Rae called. I was unaware of the extent of harm that had been inflicted on you two. Believe me, had I returned a few months earlier, things would be radically different! To answer your question, I cashed in a few chips." Pete stood up to pour a second cup of coffee.

"As a personal favor, this facility will assist you and Rae in righting the wrong. We'll provide you with tools, teach you how to use them, and guide you accordingly. The rest is up to you two. You're both extremely intelligent and resourceful. Sure, you can eliminate DeSalva, but your chances of getting caught are far too risky. Think your way through this. If you and Rae accept this challenge, you must unequivocally, without question, beat him at his own game. Divert the attention to someone else and no one will be the wiser for it." Pete smiled with self-assurance.

"Who pays the bills in the meantime?" Logan asked innocently.

"Stay where you are for the next few weeks. Ward briefed me on Geoff. He checks out, so I'd safely say that base is covered. I concur that licensing the security program to the Department of Commerce is a smart move. That'll yield an income stream. As you progress, you'll realize when it's time. And when you complete this undertaking, money will never be a problem. You'll be able to replace that plane you were forced to sell with a brand-new one. So, hotshot, still do a six-minute mile?"

"Try me." Logan pushed Pete out the back door to breathe high desert air.

"A little brisk this morning," Pete quipped, leading Logan on a downhill trail behind the metal hangar. "Always easier on the way down, but it's a bugger on the way back."

"Couldn't help notice the radomes up on the peak." Logan smirked as he cut in front, taking the lead.

"This is an ECHELON Intelsat VII shadow satellite interception site. It clones the Sugar Grove, West Virginia, site that targets European and Atlantic regional communication. But here, our primary targets are Russian and Pacific regional communications. Like Sugar Grove, this site monitors cellular, landline, e-mail, and Internet traffic. Each works on the gisting principle with several Dictionary Swiss supercomputers. Each Comsat SSC collects the equivalent of 255 Mbps or well over three million words per second. The data is forwarded for analysis according to its significance.

"The dish at the crest pulls data in from intercept cables trailing behind our Wolf Class submarines. Its mind-boggling what these babies do. They even capture the temporary emanation of spurious transmissions of handheld radio signals. The intelligence analysts in Sublevel 3 assess the mundane chatter and occasionally provide us with minutes of interpretative excitement. It's the reconnaissance imagery similar to that of the National Imagery and Mapping Agency where we monitor and analyze measurements and signatures intelligence for the director of Military Intelligence and Defense Intelligence Agency that I find fascinating.

"We coordinate with all the intel sectors, the Brits, the French, the Russians, our own. Hell, at one time or another, we've talked to 'em all." Pete sprinted and caught up beside Logan on the wide part of the trail. "Ever since Khobar Towers, all intel sectors relay cache data on terrorism activity to the counterterrorism center in the Menwith Hill NSA station in the UK. We leave the crime stuff to the homeboys. And many times, we provide intel and assistance to the feds."

Logan was used to the flat asphalt in his neighborhood. As they turned the halfway point at the bottom of the second hill, he realized that Pete's trail was a lot tougher than he had anticipated. He had been so engrossed in conversation, taking it all in stride, that his calves were stinging on the uphill grade.

"Showing your age, old man?" chided Pete, who was breathing hard.

"I'll survive," snickered Logan, who was also breathing hard. "Brings back memories of us in Iraq. Any other surprises?"

"You'll see."

CHAPTER 35

Ron Lilly and Skip Larsen escorted Rae into the workout room. After several stretching exercises, Ron and Skip began by conveying their philosophy about the mental and physical conditioning required in hand-to-hand combat, stemming from extensive martial arts training. Ron followed the teachings of Ving Tsun, believing that physical combat was much like a verbal argument: always expect the unexpected. Ron believed that every encounter had a triangular space where everything offensive and defensive took place between two or more people.

"When encounters are inevitable, perpetual forward movement is necessary," said Ron, exposing step by step the vulnerable body regions. "Our job over the next few weeks is to recondition you to react effectively when encounters occur where you instinctively replace inefficient reactions with efficient movement. Our focus today will be on balance and shift of energy. As you progress, Skip will take over with open—and closed-hand attack maneuvers, use of handguns, general weaponry, and powerful, offensive personal protection techniques."

"Hmm, interesting. And how about you, Skip?" muttered Rae.

"Well, I favor Choy Li Fut." He demonstrated a few simple defense moves, completely debilitating Rae without hurting her. "It's a refined blend of deadly attack-and-destroy force maneuvers that evolved over the years from Shaolin martial arts experts that migrated from Northern China to Southern China, each area known for its unique characteristics. After you've practiced on the punching bag, you'll find human interaction more exhilarating." Ron motioned for Rae to steady the bag for Skip.

"You pack one helluva punch." She steadied her stance.

"You'll do the same with practice and concentration," alleged Ron.

Rae was unaware that the better part of each morning would be devoted to honing her survival skills with afternoons and evenings taken up with intense tutoring on subject matter she seldom gave a second thought to or perhaps only fantasized. Her days began at 0600 and ended when her instructors deemed that her mental faculties could absorb no more. Each day began with a recap of the last—more intense, more demanding, more to remember, and more to prove.

Rae rarely saw Logan during the day, except the occasional hurried meal, as their specialized training had been condensed just over thirty days rather than the standard four months. Rae was surprised her vigilance and physical performance remained sharp despite the continual barrage of information and command of her time. She found herself captivated by the myriad of electronic surveillance devices that she was learning to employ and assumed Logan was learning much of the same but unaware of the degree to which Logan was being trained and the intensity of the select subject matter.

The morning of day seven, Tom "Dav" Davenport escorted Rae into the Simunitions Training Room for inoculation of firearms and self-defense reactionary behavior. He and Rae sat at a table covered with gun-cleaning kits, oil rags, ammunition, and several popular handguns. Tom handed her a small black case. Rae opened the case. In it was a 9mm SIGARMS M11 handgun. Tom nodded, and Rae picked the M11 out of the custom foam lining.

"Keep the clip in the case for now." Tom pulled an identical M11 from a holster tucked inside his lower back and released the ten-round, double-column magazine. "We'll practice with unloaded firearms for the time being. Don't be fooled by its size. Although compact, the M11 uses the SIG top-locking block with a combination safety/decocker, maximum effective range of fifty meters. It's small and lightweight, which makes it an ideal weapon for close protection. And for you, the best way to get used to firearms is take to 'em apart, clean 'em, and reassemble 'em."

"Kinda takes the mystery out of it all, huh?" Rae replied.

"That's what it's all about."

Skip Larsen walked into the Simunitions Training Room and interrupted. "Hey, Dav, Pete needs you upstairs. I'll take it from here. Hey, Rae, time to learn about instinctive aiming." Skip motioned for Rae to move to the center of the room. He reached behind his lower back and pulled out his .45 Heckler & Koch MK 23, released the clip and the chambered round, and laid the clip on the table. "Have you dry fired a weapon yet?"

"No. I'm just getting used to gun care on the 9mm and .357."

"Okay. It's time to practice aiming and drawing your weapon. Try this side holster and see if it's comfortable." Skip handed Rae a brown leather Yaqui Slide holster. "Get used to pulling the weapon out and aiming at my chest. After you do this a couple hundred times, it will become second nature."

After the midday break, Skip turned and walked across the room and opened a large metal storage locker. "Over here." He pulled out two black gear bags and handed one to Rae. Rae unzipped the bag and pulled out padded black protective gear.

"These protective bodyguards are required for simunitions training. Start with the legs, then the vest, throat collar, sleeves, and then the head mask. It's time you get the feel of it," remarked Skip as he donned the same protective gear. "This is a modified same model 9mm simunitions SIG." He turned and handed one to Rae. "These are actual firearms that have been converted to fire small, liquid-filled projectiles that travel at three hundred feet per second. This is no game. It's as real as it gets. My intent is to get you to overcome the fear of being hit. They'll sting, no doubt about that. But with practice, your mind will assimilate that sensation. And before you know it, you'll react instinctively and become self-protective." Skip pulled on his head mask and handed Rae a loaded simunitions clip.

"Let's do it." Skip walked back across the room and turned on a simunitions training program that displayed interactive 3D holograms across the middle of the room. Skip dimmed the lights and seemed to disappear as Rae muttered, "This is so real. It's like we're in a dingy warehouse."

Smoke filled the room from the perimeter and center floor, diminishing visibility. Sensing her heart pounding, Rae stepped backward, nearing the back wall. She heard a pop and felt intense stinging in her left thigh. Then her upper right shoulder flung back and another shot in the right ankle of her day boots.

"Find me, Rae. Find me and shoot me," Skip yelled, advancing quickly across the floor. "Find me, Rae."

Looking side to side, her heart pounding, Rae dove in a quick roll toward the left side near the back wall, crouched, and came up on one knee. The surroundings seemed so real. Rae fired off a shot and missed. Skip returned fire, hitting her midchest.

"Uh!" cringed Rae.

"Come on, Rae, follow my voice, track my movement." A loud, screeching engine noise blasted, and searchlights crisscrossed the room. "Find me!" yelled Skip, who was crouched in a back corner. Skip stood up, walking quickly into the smoke. Rae caught the movement in the corner of her eye, rolled on her back, and fired.

"Gut shot, low center mass. Not bad for a first-timer. A couple hundred more times and it'll become instinctive." He extended his hand, helping her off the floor.

CHAPTER 36

After the first week of survival skills inoculation, Logan spent the preponderance of week two studying remote-controlled triggering devices and electronic tracking and surveillance with Tom "Dav" Davenport and Alex Iglesias. Logan's formal education and air force flight training made assimilating his specialty training effortless. First, Logan learned to operate handheld satellite tracking devices, listening devices, and other untraceable mechanisms he would find useful. As a former fighter pilot, his skill set was validated by situational awareness in his ability to glean line-of-sight surveillance in simulated situations and mock tailing of marked vehicles.

His day of reckoning arrived after eight days of practice when Dav and Alex hijacked Logan for a side trip for the day. A short flight of thirty minutes and they touched down on a private landing strip just south of Reno, Nevada. Two cars were waiting for the trio. Alex and Logan jumped in one car while Tom played the decoy and drove off toward the active district of Reno. Alex dallied to give Tom a two-minute head start. In the meantime, Logan initialized the mobile radio frequency detector and set up the SATRAK surveillance equipment as the three began their sophisticated game of cat and mouse.

Dav entered the Silver Legacy Casino downtown. Initially, it wasn't difficult; but once inside, tracking Dav became problematic with the interference of signal blockers designed within the ceilings and walls of designated rooms. Dav was remarkable at blending in the surroundings in a furtive manner. He donned more than one disguise, challenging Logan to locate and pin down the moving target.

From time to time, Dav jammed the homing signal just long enough to change identities. At one time, he followed the two as they entered the sublevel filled with several kiosks, restaurants, and gift shops that connected the Eldorado Casino. Dav intentionally bumped into Logan from behind and invited him and Alex to lunch. Logan shook his head as he didn't immediately recognize him. Although surprised, he expected that sort of event might occur.

Dav and Alex split again after a brief lunch to assess Logan's skills at surveillance outside, among crowds of people, between buildings, and in vehicles. Leaving Logan unaccompanied, Alex gave Logan a small handheld radio with a wireless earpiece to listen for instructions. Alex advised Logan to monitor their conversation as they would give latitude and longitude coordinates as he would be quizzed after they completed the third trial.

Alex and Dav walked outside the casino and around the side entrance to the garage. Listening to their benign chatter, he picked up the first code: "South, eighty-nine degrees, forty-seven minutes, thirteen seconds." Once they began driving, Alex advised Logan to switch equipment and follow. There was more chatter supplemented with laughter and radio music for annoyance.

Logan picked up the second code while tailing them: "North, twenty-nine degrees, twenty-three minutes, forty-six seconds." The third test was the most difficult. Finding a line-of-sight position was the toughest from the street without being detected. The dictum was, "Don't be seen, blend in, and execute a flawless escape." Dav and Alex gave Logan three minutes to get set up while they waited to begin their tête-à-tête in a street side café. Finally, the last code: "West, 136 degrees, four minutes, eleven seconds." Logan scribbled the codes on the inside of his forearm and read them back to Alex.

"That's affirmative. Now come and join us for a soft drink. I'm buying. You're flying left seat tonight, so no booze," chided Alex.

CHAPTER 37

A great deal of the equipment used at the Mosby Foundation was the forefront of technology supplied by DARPA (Defense Advanced Research Projects Agency) and select defense contractors designated by the Joint Chiefs. In addition to special operations, Pete's role at the Mosby Foundation was to oversee a first-look, multidiscipline approach when testing DARPA's latest battlefield weaponry and military intelligence networking equipment and report his findings to the Joint Chiefs. Even the FBI and other federal agencies didn't enjoy the latest innovations.

In the spring of 2002, after the launch of Operation Enduring Freedom the previous October to beef up counterintelligence initiatives against global terrorism, Pete Minot was chosen by General Latise, the then chairman of the Joint Chiefs, to create a quasi test and evaluation operation for top secret intelligence gathering and satellite tracking communications intelligence programs, like ORATORY, developed as a joint venture between a US and French defense contractor and to parlay that into a paramilitary communications intelligence (COMINT) organization.

On September 8, Pete was ordered to the emergency intelligence briefing at SOCOM (Special Operations Command) at MacDill Air Force Base in Florida. The Command had made great strides in their effort to augment technological advances through their unified combatant command, composing itself of all service branches within its command structure. Of the nine unified commands, SOCOM was the premier command at running special operations, including PSYOPs (psychological operations) and other clandestine antiterrorism operations and support.

Although Pete briefed the Joint Chiefs on his newest intelligence gathering equipment for support of the first draft retaliatory plan, Spartan Shield, the correlation of global intel gathered for select active terrorist targets in the Middle East and Asia, it was Pete's expertise with the JC-SSAT space-based reconnaissance surveillance program that would lend superb insight in the strategic planning of a combined air and ground campaign against both the Taliban and Al-Qaeda's central organs in Iraq and neighboring countries.

Beginning with telecommunications targets, power plants, oil storage facilities, and main transportation links, JC-SSAT would locate and pinpoint the arteries that fed the extremist groups' headquarters and their munitions and chemical weapons production facilities.

Conceived in 2001 by the Joint Chiefs for the purpose of unifying communication between the Armed Forces Special Operations Units, the Joint Command Satellite Surveillance and Tracking Program had and would continue to serve the primary needs of democracy, freedom, and homeland security. Scoffed at by some congressional members of the Joint Armed Services Committee as budgetary luxuries, Pete's devices would earn their keep.

On September 8, Pete's briefing to the Joint Chief's intelligence sector's agents working directly with NATO concluded with Pete's marching orders: to recruit an elite team of no more than six members from each spec ops branch and set up an intelligence enclave in Riyadh, Saudi Arabia. Shortly after implementation, Riyadh intel forced the reevaluation of a sole air strike campaign by the Joint Chiefs as being impolitic.

By the end of the year, the list boasted more than 437 prime targets. JC-SSAT was instrumental in assisting ground war planners at tracking the Taliban's movements throughout Afghanistan and Iraq and adding in Pakistan. Pete's right-hand man, Major Skip Larsen, targeted SCUD missiles and sorted weapons of mass destruction that prepped the intelligence community and Joint Chiefs for Phase III—Battlefield Preparation as a precursor to Phase IV, the ground offensive campaign.

Master Sergeant Alex Iglesias's area of expertise was to locate and destroy the production of chemical and biological weapons. Alex located a nerve and blood agent chemical weapons plant that was cloaked within a power station two kilometers southeast of Al Hillah, Iraq, on the Euphrates River. Guided by Master Chief Tom "Dav" Davenport, a small incursion team destroyed the chemical weapons factory on the eve of the pending conflict. Evidence of cyanogen chloride as a primary blood agent weapon and tabun and sarin nerve agents were later discovered when Chief Warrant Officer 3 Ron Lilly located a mass grave where human experiments were used on a mass population of men, women, and children, totaling over three thousand bodies. For health concern, the mass grave had to be reduced to ashes by a precise napalm strike.

As a precursor to present-day war on terrorism, President Bush's memorandum on January 15, 1991, to his security advisors—Security Directive 54 underwritten by the Saudis, Japan, and other wealthy allies—the US and England began their air supremacy bombardment of Baghdad at 7:00 p.m. on January 16, 1991, the first direct retaliation by the United States to global terrorism. President Bush in his television address to America cited, "Nothing of this moral importance has occurred since World War II," as Americans watched with great trepidation of what became known as Operation Desert Storm. Accordingly, Pete cited this passage from that security directive to impress upon the Joint Chiefs: "From whence the US may never envision a peaceful resolution to Islamist extremism ideology."

The Mosby Foundation received a healthy share of private funding by testing new equipment and technology and reporting the findings to the Joint Chiefs. From time to time, the Mosby Foundation provided high-level intel and security for defense contractors and counterintelligence (CI) for our own and for our closest ally, Mother England. Pete continued to work closely around the world with England's finest, the British secret intelligence service MI-6, to purge the international intelligence community of double agents.

In the embryonic stage of the Kosovo conflict, Pete Minot uncovered a directive from the chairman of the Communist Party that ordered ethnic cleansing as genocide for Muslims living in

Montenegro as the Serbs believed they should dominate the Muslims and not recognize their quest for independence. With assistance from CWO3 Ron Lilly and an Australian SASR (Special Air Service regiment) counterpart, the group captured a stockpile of soman and VX OP nerve agents in Podgorica.

With that directive came a hunt for the black market trade of deadly biological weapons through Iraq, Iran, and other rogue nations that comprised the Middle East. This time, it was mustard agents and the mass experimentation of biochemical agents and mutilation and torture of suspected dissidents. Not since the days of Josef Mengele was Pete so appalled at the horror he and his coterie uncovered and subsequently destroyed.

Pete was notorious for creating black propaganda through disinformation campaigns while sifting through the trails of his adversaries. Pete was quite at home in the spy-versus-spy business. He was naturally observant like a hawk and always conducted himself with steadfast confidence. In the spring of 2009, Pete tried to recruit Logan, telling Logan he had the very same qualities, but Logan was busy with his telecommunication manufacturing and distribution business. Logan confided to Pete that if the timing had been different… Well, so much for ifs.

Pete always knew that Logan possessed the innate intelligence and charisma to carry off the most demanding of assignments. If only.

CHAPTER 38

B y day, Logan watched training videos of explosive ordnance devices interspersed with hands-on pyrotechnic instruction by Tom "Dav" Davenport. Most afternoons, Skip Larsen acquainted Logan with bioweapons training, self-defense techniques, and attack maneuvers. By night, he studied the imposing and expanding dossier he was compiling on DeSalva, sifting for more clues. He was confident he had gained a good working knowledge of a myriad of binary and plastic explosives, focusing their blast radius and calibrating the collateral damage they would cause. Ron Lilly joined in at the end for supplemental specialty weapons training. The pieces of the puzzle were beginning to come together.

At Logan's request, Pete arranged for Logan and Rae to meet key agents from the Counter Narcotics Center, Interpol, and the Foreign Intelligence Service of the Russian Federation. They shared crucial information on DeSalva's financial and business contacts as well as his whereabouts for the past ninety plus days up to the present day. Pete's longtime associate Justin Farwell, forensics special agent, assigned on paper only to the FBI Sacramento field office, spent the final few days teaching Logan and Rae about forensic evidence.

As a recap, Justin began. "These days, it's extremely difficult not to leave some part of your identity imprint behind." This was Justin's stoic response to Rae's earlier question. "It can be done. There are plenty of horrific crimes that either lack the substantive evidence needed for conviction or ineptness of the neophytes that botch the crime scene altogether where significant clues are overlooked or destroyed in the process. And unfortunately, the latter occurs more times than we care to admit." He audibly shook his head to both Logan and Rae.

Alex interrupted the forensic lesson, motioning for Rae and Logan to join him in the conference room. Logan closed the door and sat next to Rae at the conference table. "These files contain your alternate ID collateral, bank, credit cards, and such. Study the files hard and memorize everything down to the smallest details, then destroy the files. They may save your life one day.

"Your phones are encrypted with scrambling, real-time tracking and video uplink and, more importantly, imprinted biometrically with your voice, fingerprints, retinal scan, and facial recognition data. We're still trialing a facial recognition program for DARPA. So far, it's promising. Your phones will not activate either to the center or to any of us individually if someone else tries to use them.

"They also have GSM active tracking even when you are using just the phone alone feature. This is so we can immediately switch on SATRAK and maintain accurate coordinates for downloading during an emergency uplink."

Rae smiled. "This ought to be interesting reading."

Alex walked over and opened the door. "Let's go relax."

*****

Logan and Rae spent their last evening enjoying social interaction with their four mentors, Justin, and Manny. Pete could not join in as the Committee on Foreign Intelligence had summoned him to Washington earlier in the week. There were no quizzes, no videos, no "show me agains." There simply was good food and good company, an evening of warmth and relaxation after thirty-two grueling days.

Rae and Logan had changed—still close in their bond to each other but with an intuitive outlook on life. Both viewed a macro picture of the American dream, not a "my world" dream any longer. They had evolved and were prepared for bigger challenges. Throughout the time spent with each of their mentors, Rae realized the common denominator that bonded these kindred spirits together: These mentors also believed in the American dream but a macro view, a better world for their children and those to follow. They were not fanatics, extremists, or socially unacceptable. They were all leaders with above-average intelligence and damn good at what they did. They were kindred in spirit, and each would lay down their life for the other. She wondered if she was capable of doing the same.

As the evening wound down, Logan raised his wineglass to the group. "To all of you, thank you for this opportunity and for changing our lives."

"Hear, hear," they replied in unison.

"Your lives haven't changed. They've just been enriched. And by the way, Logan, don't drink too much. You're flying home tomorrow," Manny crowed, and the group laughed heartily.

CHAPTER 39

After picking up Sheba and settling back in their rental house, Rae smiled at Logan. "We did the right thing."

As Logan inserted the inversion CD and put the countersurveillance detector back in its case, he looked at Rae and said, "Regrets?"

"None." Rae walked into the kitchen with a small bag of groceries. "I'll make brunch. Lemon chicken crepes?"

"Yes, I would love 'em." Logan sat down, poring over updates to the dossier, concentrating on the data supplied by the SVR and Counter Narcotics Center. He began contriving use of the array of equipment and weapons assigned to them by the Foundation.

Out of habit, Rae turned on the news while stirring her lemon cream sauce. "Breaking news. Three cases of Saint Louis encephalitis were reported this morning by a spokesperson of the Southern California Division of the CDC. The cases were reported after one youth and two adults were admitted to St. Joseph's Hospital in a North Los Angeles neighborhood within the last twenty-four hours. Comments from the director of the Los Angeles County West Vector Control District stated that all efforts to respray the South and West neighborhoods and all standing water ponds have begun, further warning residents to wear long sleeves and plan to remain indoors after dark."

Rae jotted a few words on a memo pad, looked over, and smiled while Logan tinkered with the cache of new surveillance and tracking equipment scattered on the table. He was aiming the SV1 antennae through the open kitchen window and at a couple walking their dog. Adjusting the volume and fine-tuning their conversation, the couple's chatter echoed audibly through the speaker before they walked past the courtyard and out of range. After a few minutes, Logan aimed at a second-story window of an adjacent duplex and chuckled hearing the Bugs Bunny cartoon character, shaking his head at proving how easy it was to "hear no evil, see no evil, speak no evil."

Rae grabbed the phone and dialed the televised number for the Southern California Division of the CDC. Posing as a writer for *Time Magazine*, Rae persuaded the receptionist she needed information for an upcoming feature article. She was transferred to the director and was granted a telephone interview. She was dumbfounded by how people were so gullible, so easily persuaded.

She began by asking what this division was doing to stop the spread of SLE and other infectious diseases prevalent in California. She asked if any affiliate organizations were seeking breakthrough cures and was urged to contact the program director at the Hysech Institute in San Diego. Hysech was a well-known political hotbed that continued to be scalded by the press for its controversial methods of infecting healthy animals in seeking breakthrough cures against new strains of SLE and equine encephalitis.

Continuing her pursuit, Rae telephoned Hysech, beginning the dialogue with Mason Purdew, program director, and was invited to tour their facility. She ended by asking if they allowed photographers into their facility, and Mason said no as it was a secure building but said that she could choose from several of their canned photographs for the magazine. She reaffirmed directions and thanked him for his time.

"Logan, let's take a quick trip to San Diego," Rae said as she served the crepes.

"I overheard your conversation. What's the objective?"

"Marc Sullivan. He's the easiest to purge."

"I'm listening."

"Infect him with SLE and let Mother Nature do the rest," she replied matter-of-factly.

"Maybe we should take a side trip to Tahoe instead and try our new equipment," Logan replied. "The Sullivan objective can wait."

"Hmm, camping and hiking. Good cover. Sheba?" she posed.

"I can get into that. Too bad I can't take Bella too. I'll even volunteer to get the gear and transportation."

"Settled." Logan smiled. "I'll call the center for an update on Dino's [code name for DeSalva] whereabouts and activate GSM tracking on our phones. Use your cover."

Rae opened the back door to call Sheba, who was lying down under the shade of a large live oak tree in the backyard. "You've got to see this. It's amazing. There are hundreds of monarch butterflies resting in the trees." She turned to Logan sitting at the table.

"I saw 'em earlier. Hmm, crepes were delicious. I'll clean up." Logan walked over to kiss Rae goodbye as she waited for Sheba.

"Sheba and I are stopping by to see Bella first." She knew Bella was in good hands back on the ranch, but she dearly missed being with her.

"Take your time. We can do the shopping thing later. Go spend the afternoon." Logan smiled.

"Thanks for understanding. When they're together, they're like two peas in a pod. See ya in a few." She grabbed the keys and motioned for Sheba to follow her to the truck.

Rae used to ride the Los Altos Hills trail with Bella and Sheba. Rae would never let Bella outrun Sheba, and after a good workout, the three would stop and enjoy a snack before the slow walk back to the trailhead. When Rae rode for show jumping, Sheba would sit quietly and watch. Afterward, Sheba and Bella would sniff each other's noses.

One Saturday morning last fall, Bella was being stubborn about getting inside the horse trailer. Rae commanded Sheba to coax Bella inside. Sheba walked up the ramp inside the trailer, turned around, and barked once for Bella to follow. Bella walked in without incident.

*****

Logan called the command center. Ron Lilly and Dav acknowledged. "Hey, guys. Anything new on our boy Dino from the next seventy-two hours?" Logan observed Dav on his phone screen key in Lat-Lon coordinates into the 1C Satellite Controller to reposition the telemetry of one of the SV4 Echelon satellites to overlay the South Lake Tahoe target. Lilly moved out of view to collect and download the latest recorded incoming and outgoing communications intel from Sub3.

"Logan, this will take a few. We'll have another Sub3 update in eighty-two minutes. Set the receive mode on X-Alpha channel. We'll scrub and transmit in twenty. You'll be able to review it shortly and uplink again after 1530 for confirm," Lilly stated, walking back into view.

"Copy that."

With his back to the monitor, Dav began reciting the prologue to the report that was scrolling rapidly on the intel VDT from Sub3. "Looks like movement planned over the next few days. His pilot called FBO. Usual personal phone traffic, and, ah, here's one between Dino and Sergei Zohdolofski. More intel coming from SVR and support." Pete walked into view.

"Do you two need anything else at this time?" Dav asked as Pete stepped in front of Dav and turned the intel VDT toward him.

"What's up, old man?" Pete interjected.

"Hey, Pete. Ah, just coordinating with Dav as we plan some selective bird-watching," beamed Logan.

"And hey, Dav, thanks for asking. Too early to tell. I'll let you know."

Pete scanned a freshly printed intel report. "Change of plans. Seems your boy's heading to Seattle in a couple of days. Look into Senator Hicks. He's the outside connection through the Pingston Financial Securities money laundering organization. He's in Sacramento the entire week for legislation meetings at the Capitol building. There will be two gallery passes at reception in your personas for Thursday morning's budget hearing. Remember to uplink every day after 0600 and before 0730 for updates. Keep your phone on GSM active A5 protocol for receiving secure data. You may have to get creative to set the uplink. Now that you're on an op, we'll keep our eyes and ears on you."

"Roger that."

*****

Six hours later, Rae returned home and backed a dark-blue Ford Expedition in the driveway. She coerced the rental clerk in allowing her to leave Logan's truck parked in their back lot for a few days. Logan walked outside to greet her and peeked in the side back window, looking over the camping equipment and supplies, as Rae put the driver's window down.

"So, Mrs. Ferguson, are we going to sing songs, roast marshmallows, and tell ghost stories too?" He grinned and snickered in comical tenor.

"Sure, if it makes you happy, Mr. Ferguson. But when in Rome, do as the Romans do." Rae winked, stepping out of the vehicle with Sheba in tow to open the back hatch to unload the food and repack and rearrange their supplies. Sheba bounced up behind her. "Here, Sheba." She gave Sheba a bag of dog treats to carry in the house, leaving the Timberline six-person tent, sleeping bags, lanterns, cooking stove, and miscellaneous camping gear neatly stacked in the back.

"We're on our first op. I'll fill you in on the details after the next uplink." Logan sidestepped Sheba trotting happily toward the front door.

As Rae continued to place items in sequential order on the living room floor, Sheba curiously sniffed in and around the supplies, sensing something was about to take place. Sheba knocked over her container of dog food and nudged it over to Rae, who was piling the supplies in sequence at the front door, as if to say, "Don't leave me."

In the bedroom and preoccupied with her mental checklist, Rae hadn't noticed Sheba's whereabouts until she nudged Rae's right hand, brushing against her leg, placing her front paw on Rae's foot. Laughing aloud, Rae bent down and nuzzled Sheba with a big hug. "No, girl, we're not going to forget you. Come on, girl, carry this." Rae grabbed the handle of a small travel bag and held it for Sheba to grab.

Logan was smiling as he watched Rae and Sheba through the arched opening to the living room. "It's nice to see that part of you again." He walked up to kiss her.

"Here." She smiled. "Make yourself useful." She tossed Sheba's dog bed.

"Yes, ma'am." Logan caught it and headed out the front door with Sheba carrying the travel bag.

CHAPTER 40

As soon as they hit the on-ramp to pick up Highway 80 East to Sacramento, Rae called the center on her new phone. Pete appeared on the screen with a lighthearted, "Hello, you two. You heed direction well."

"We try," Rae replied as she glanced over at Logan. "Thanks for the interactive map. It's terrific. We're looking to locate Senator Hicks's city residence and limo service. Oh, and any dirt on the same."

"You'll have updated intel before 0600. The Capitol was recently renovated, adding sophisticated security monitoring in and around the grounds. Justin Farwell is expecting you at the San Joaquin Guild located on Ninth Street, two blocks from the L Street entrance. I'll transmit the address. It's a safe place to hang your hat. Only a short walk to the Capitol building.

"Going in on foot limits the number of times you will be photographed, skipping the parking garage. They're testing a facial recognition program, but your new IDs go deep and are valid. You can uplink from your room as well as the data center. Tomorrow, consider entering off the L Street entrance and exit through the basement rotunda and out to Tenth Street. Dav here will download the diagram before the next uplink. I'm off tomorrow to the Pentagon. Alex and Skip are on duty. Be safe," replied Pete.

"Travel safe, and again, thanks for everything."

*****

Several hours later, Logan turned into the driveway on the south side of the building, leading to the parking lot in the rear. There were only two vehicles, both black SUVs. "Hmm, no wonder

Pete recommended this place," remarked Logan as he parked next to a government vehicle. "This ought to be interesting."

"This entire trip should be interesting," Rae retorted as she opened the right rear door to grab her equipment bag and beckon Sheba. Logan followed her lead, not wanting to disturb the carefully placed camping gear that covered their surveillance equipment behind the rear seat.

Rae walked ahead of Logan as they approached the front entrance. Sheba stayed right by her side, keeping pace with Rae. "There's surveillance on the vehicles and building perimeter. Everything should be all right." Logan opened the front door for Rae.

They were startled by a quick hello. "Justin!" Rae gave him a quick hug. Sheba stared at Justin in silence. "Justin, Sheba is highly trained. Don't worry." She signaled Sheba to follow.

"Nice companion," Justin replied.

"Hey, guy," Justin extended his hand to shake Logan's. "Yes, there's surveillance on the vehicles and building perimeter. This is a safe house."

"You heard us?" asked Rae.

"Yes, I did. Outside only." Justin grinned.

"Nice seeing a friendly face," replied Logan.

"How 'bout a bite to eat? On me."

"Great," replied Logan.

"Let's get you two situated, and we can meet back here by seven thirty. Okay with you two?" he said as he walked in the back and appeared behind the counter. "Will there be three of you joining me this evening for dinner?"

"Nah, just two. Sheba has her own plans. Cozy looking place you have here," remarked Rae as Justin handed her an electronic key FOB that resembled her old Porsche key with a square stem.

"You three are in 2B upstairs, off the elevator to your left." Justin handed Logan a manila envelope. "If you need anything, I'm in 4B, opposite corner." He motioned for Rae and Logan to follow him into an adjacent room. "Breakfast is as early as 6:00 a.m. You can order light fare all day long until about 10:00 p.m. After that, you're scrounging on your own."

"This looks nothing like a hotel dining room." Rae chuckled as she tugged on Logan's jacket while Logan gazed at three big screens playing C-SPAN covering government hearings and twenty-four-hour news mounted on the wall above three flat screen workstations.

"Most of the time, I keep busy on the homeboy stuff," retorted Justin. "Occasionally, though, I get to help Pete with more interesting assignments. Now go get ready for some good cooking. My treat. Ha!" Justin pointed to the elevator.

Rae stepped back into the lobby and waved a hand signal to Sheba, who promptly ambled to her side. They joined Logan, and the three walked to the elevator as if they had been there a thousand times. Rae stepped ahead of Logan into the elevator. "Our days just get more interesting, don't they?"

"Uh-huh. They most certainly do." He punched in a text message: "Keep your guard up." Rae nodded in agreement, ruffling Sheba's ears. If she hadn't remained so quiet, one would hardly notice her presence, except for her silver-tipped white coat. On occasion, people had mistaken Sheba for a wolf because of her coloring and eerie silent behavior. Besides extensive obedience training, Rae spent time with Sheba at a guide dog school so she would be at ease with people in close quarters, honing her obedience skills in verbal and nonverbal commands.

Logan opened the door to 2B and stood in amazement at the plush surroundings and the vast size of the living quarters. Rae shuffled in, glancing upward at the balcony bedroom in awe. "These rooms make the Grand Plaza suites look ordinary," remarked Rae as she turned in the center of the living area, admiring its architecture and design.

"Guess we've been on the wrong side of the fence all these years." Logan chuckled as he flicked on the wide-screen television in the entertainment center. "I expect plenty of surprises are ahead."

Rae walked into the kitchen area and set up Sheba's food and water. "I'll take her for a quick stroll around the building. Back in ten." She kissed Logan on the cheek.

CHAPTER 41

The faint beep from his phone downstairs awakened Logan. The green numbers on the clock radio read 5:56 a.m. The sun wouldn't rise for another twenty minutes. He leaned over and smiled at Rae, admiring her in motionless slumber. He slid out of bed and tiptoed down the spiral staircase. Sheba stirred but remained on her pad at the foot of the bed. He picked the phone out of its recharging case sitting on the credenza next to the breakfast bar. The text message scrolled across the screen was, "Uplink GSM A5 Protocol."

Logan unzipped the leather case and assembled the SV-4 data transceiver. He switched on its signal locator and carried the unit through the French-style patio door. He placed the unit on top of the patio table, attaching its antennae. Its antennae automatically rotated seventy degrees and stopped. The blinking red LED light on its base changed to a steady green light as Logan watched the SV-4 data transceiver rapidly scroll data on its screen.

The scrolling stopped with the text message blinking, "Acknowledge receipt of transmission." Logan depressed the End key twice and watched the screen fade to black. He picked up the SV-4 data transceiver and walked back in and placed it on the credenza next to the open manila envelope. He picked up the envelope and walked to the breakfast bar.

The automatic coffee maker had just finished brewing hazelnut, and the smell permeated the kitchen area. Logan poured a cup of coffee and sat at the counter, fingering through the pile of pictures and data on DeSalva. One picture from the middle of the pile stuck out among the rest. It was of an unknown face shaking hands with DeSalva, who was standing next to Sergei Zohdolofski. On the picture was a Post-it note scribbled with, "Intro, 2340 hrs, 02/06/11, Terminal 25, Seattle, Michael DeSalva, Sergei Zohdolofski, unsub."

He sifted through more of the pictures, and he noticed an unusual marking on the inside arm of the unsub. A fraction of the tattooed marking remained covered by the unsub's jacket sleeve but appeared to resemble a biblical symbol. He stared at the symbol. It reminded him of a cross between a Chinese character and the modern abstract of an angel with wings spread. Logan circled the symbol with a red marker and continued sifting for more clues.

He examined each picture and noticed one view was in front of a container ship but could only read the last few letters as Sergei was standing in such a way that it blocked the ship's full name. Logan circled the two lines of letters—OLSK and HSTAN—below. He knew that Kazakhstan was a small commercial seaport and surmised that the ship most likely was registered in Kazakhstan but would confirm.

Logan knew these pictures would be useful collateral. He unpacked his camera and shot close-ups of each circled areas. He plugged his camera into the SV-4 data transceiver and uploaded the pictures for analysis by the center and CIS (Counterintelligence Service).

Logan knew he needed to confirm his conjecture before proceeding. Senator Hicks was profiting. He surmised others who had recently crossed his path were also connected to DeSalva's drug trafficking, gun running, and money laundering operation. He was so affixed on the picture of the unknown that he hadn't heard Rae walk down the stairs.

The morning sun had lifted and was shimmering throughout the upstairs balcony area as Rae sipped Logan's coffee. "Hmm, been busy?" she muttered with a light peck on Logan's cheek.

"Look at these. Does that mark mean anything to you? It seems familiar."

"At this moment, I'd say late twenties, early thirties, so I'd rule out gangs. Something with more order," replied Rae as she turned on the kitchen light to study the picture. "What else have you uncovered?"

"I have close-ups of the symbol and ship already uploaded and ready for the next uplink. Do you have anything?"

"Not until I digest breakfast. I'm famished." She tended to Sheba's food and water. "Let's join Justin for breakfast downstairs. I'd like to quiz him for more info."

"You tend to Sheba and get ready. I'll send the uplink." Logan reassembled the SV-4 for the uplink. He picked up his phone and called the center. Alex appeared on screen.

"Mornin'," declared Alex.

"I uplinked two pictures from intel collected by Justin recently. I need confirmation on the symbol and identity of the bearer from Alexei Iakova from CIS, and anything on the container ship would be helpful," replied Logan.

"Roger that. Is there immediate urgency?" asked Alex.

"No."

"I'll forward downstairs and contact Alexei. You'll have something within the hour."

"Thanks. Transmitting A5 in thirty," Logan added as he walked out onto the balcony with the data transceiver.

*****

Rae appeared a few minutes later donning her new persona—bronze-colored wire-rimmed eyeglasses, a chin-length chestnut pageboy wig, a shapely blue sweater, faded slim blue jeans, and boots. "Does make a difference. What are you wearing today?" she asked while adjusting the wig in front of the hallway mirror. Sheba was puzzled by Rae's appearance, tilting her head in bewilderment as she watched Rae intently.

"Mustache and wire-rimmed glasses is all I can do for this visit. I'll wear the Blue Jays baseball cap and act like a Canadian tourist in the gallery audience."

"I'll buzz Justin while you shower." Rae pressed the 4B intercom button on the wall.

"Good morning" resonated through the speaker.

"Do you have time for breakfast at, say, seven fifteen?" asked Rae.

"Seven fifteen it is," replied Justin.

"See you then." Rae clicked off.

*****

Justin was robustly talking on his cell phone as Rae and Logan walked into the dining area. Doing a double-take, he motioned them to sit at the dining table covered with an assortment of breads, pastries, and fruit. Putting his call on mute, he whispered, "Help yourself. There's hot tea, coffee, and juice."

"Nice personas," Justin said as he walked to the table. "Your choice of apple crepes, eggs Benedict, or the cold stuff. Follow me." Rae and Logan followed Justin into the kitchen to meet Maria. "Maria is our house mother," Justin said, and Maria turned away, blushing.

"Nice to meet you, Maria. I'm Rae, and this is Logan. It's your kitchen. What do you recommend?"

Maria turned back around, exposing a ghastly scar on the side of her face. "My favorite would be the crepes, Ms. Rae."

"Crepes it is. I trust your judgment." Rae smiled at Maria.

"Mr. Logan, would you like crepes too?"

"Thank you, Maria, but I'll have the eggs Benedict instead," replied Logan.

"Oh, Mr. J, would you like eggs this morning?" asked Maria.

"Thanks, Mom, but I'm just having muffins. I'll be leaving for the day, so I'll take a lunch to go, though."

"Yes, Mr. J. One sandwich or two?"

"Two will be fine," replied Justin as they walked into the dining area.

"Turkey and ham?"

"That's fine."

*****

As the trio settled into breakfast chatter, Rae asked Justin about Maria and the San Joaquin Guild. "Initially, this was a safe house for witness protection giving the outward appearance of a historical foundation. Remodeled two years ago with influence from Pete, it's now an off-site office and provides housing for very select transients. The entire basement level is the safe house. Not many feds know about this place, and that's a good thing." Justin chuckled.

"Maria was a housekeeping servant for Juan Bustamante, a drug lord from Colombia now residing in San Diego. DEA wants him for drug trafficking. We want him for organized crime, kidnapping, murder, and trafficking illegals. During the raid, Juan escaped through a hidden tunnel under his house. Juan's son Ernesto stayed behind and used her as a human shield at knifepoint while interrogating her husband. He cut the side of her face before we could take him out.

"She and her family were illegals held against their will, working for Juan to pay off their freedom. It took us several months to gain her trust with one of ours. They would meet in the grocery store where she was allowed to shop two to three times a week. We had planned the family relocation in witness protection, but the raid went horribly awry when Ernesto shot Maria's husband and two children in a fit of rage," he commented, remorseful. "Maria started in witness protection but later asked to remain here legally. She's become our adopted mother and looks after me."

"I wish I hadn't asked," remarked Rae. "Oh my God, poor thing. I can't imagine anything worse. That must have been horrible."

"I can't imagine…killing kids," Logan interrupted, shaking his head.

"Don't try," remarked Justin. "I'll get that bastard one day! You two set for the day?"

"I believe so," Logan stated.

"Proper IDs?" asked Justin.

"Yes," they both responded and grinned.

"Staying the night?" asked Justin.

"Probably will want to organize our thoughts and data."

"Good idea. We'll recap at dinner, then." Justin got up from the table and walked toward the data room.

"Hey, Justin, why are you still with the Bureau?" Rae asked as she stood up from the table.

"I was wondering when that question would come up," he said as he turned to face her and Logan. "Pete and I go back a few. I served under him for five years. I was placed here for a reason. Only a handful of need-to-knows and the director himself know what I do here. For now, let's just say I'm another helping hand." He smiled and walked into the office.

Rae slipped her arm through Logan's and leaned on his shoulder. "That makes me feel better. And you?"

Nodding in affirmation, he answered, "We were sent here to learn, so…" Logan tilted his head and winked at Rae, sliding his arm up around her shoulder as they walked to the elevator.

CHAPTER 42

Logan completed the second uplink at 0837. He repacked the data transceiver and handed Rae his phone, and she put it in the backpack. Rae grabbed the backpack as they strolled out the door to the elevator. "Do we look enough like tourists?" Slipping the backpack over her shoulders, they exited through the side door and onto Ninth Street.

"The glasses make a difference. Don't forget your Blue Jays hat. Their surveillance cameras are mounted high, looking down. Remember the facial recognition thing," remarked Logan. As they turned the corner, they could see the Capitol from over a block away.

As they crossed the street at the intersection, Rae pointed out, "This is a Renaissance Revival-style design, reminiscent of our US Capitol. I suspect it was built around the late 1800s."

Entering the Capitol building through the L Street entrance, Rae dallied by the entrance, picking up several pamphlets on local tourist attractions, noting tours of the Capitol. She caught up with Logan standing at Reception, picking up the gallery tickets for Cynthia and Roger Ferguson from Toronto, Canada. The staff assistant was providing guidance on the floor plan map to the Gallery. They walked down the corridor to the elevator.

As they exited the elevator, a Capitol police officer and his German shepherd canine partner checked the ticket stubs at the lobby entrance. The officer advised them to put their loose change, keys, cell phones, and all personal belongings in the plastic bins and place them on the belt of the X-ray scanner and to walk through the metal detector as instructed. Rae stepped first and made it through. Logan followed with no delays.

They gathered their personal belongings and walked into the lobby. They were advised that no flash photography was allowed and to maintain silence decorum throughout and try not to leave the Gallery until scheduled breaks every ninety minutes. The officer opened the Gallery door for Cynthia and Roger Ferguson as they smiled and walked in as instructed.

They sat quietly at the end of the bench, waiting with the small tour group, trying not to intermingle with the others. Most of the senators were seated with their aides and staff still milling in the front of the Gallery pulpit. The president pro tempore, the individual voted in by the other senators whose additional responsibility was to chair the Senate committee on rules compliance, announced the opening proceedings, commenced roll call for the hearing, and introduced the first speaker, State Senator Grady Hicks, District 11. Rae and Logan would get plenty of time to observe the senator in his element.

Senator Hicks opened the budget hearing, acknowledging the newly elected junior senator from District 3, and began a diatribe that would last nearly twenty minutes before meaningful budgetary questions were posed by opposing party members. Senator Hicks's proposal alleged to first double the annual vehicle registration and the inspection tax fee as well as to increase the tobacco and alcohol sales tax each by 1 percent, stating that the increase in revenue was required to beef up security and personal protection in state buildings. The opposing senators booed and heckled him throughout his speech.

At 10:30 a.m., the president pro tempore used his gavel to cease the meaningless banter, calling a twenty-minute recess. Rae stood up and walked to the Gallery pulpit where Senator Hicks's aide was seated behind a desk and introduced herself as Cynthia Ferguson from Toronto.

"Would it be possible for Senator Hicks to sign an autograph for my niece? My niece is in eighth grade and is studying American politics and would very much like to have an autograph, perhaps with a sentence or two on state government so she could turn this in with her class project," Rae said, smiling.

The young man excused himself and walked up to the pulpit and whispered in Senator Hicks's ear. Senator Hicks grimaced begrudgingly but acknowledged her request. The aide motioned for Rae to walk behind the desk on the lower level below Senator Hicks's microphone.

"Mrs. Ferguson, do you have something of significance that I can write a note on to your niece?" asked Senator Hicks in a phony sort of way.

"Yes, sir. She'd love to have you write a short sentence on this blank card. She'll frame this to hang in her room." Rae smiled. "Oh, please use her favorite pen. We gave it to her for Christmas last year. She will enjoy telling her classmates that a famous United States senator signed this with her pen." Rae smiled and handed Senator Hicks the silver ink pen.

"Nice pen, eh? Maybe this will get me reelected." He laughed aloud to his aide. "What's your niece's name?"

"Jessica Ferguson."

Senator Hicks wrote the following:

Ms. Jessica Ferguson,

The business of state politics is dynamic and ever-changing. If you choose to follow a path of politics, be wise to always keep your options open, make many friends, and remain neutral on all controversial issues.

State Senator Grady Hicks, Second Term
District 11
San Francisco, California

Rae reached up as the senator handed her the autographed card and pen over the pulpit counter. "Thank you, Senator. All the best." Rae smiled and turned and walked back to Logan, who remained seated in the back row.

"You sly devil," he sneered with a grin. "Let's take a walk."

Rae followed Logan out to the elevator. Most everyone had already departed or disappeared to the snack bar. Logan and Rae made their way to the basement rotunda and stopped just outside the snack bar.

"Want something to drink?" asked Logan.

"Yeah."

"Coke, water?"

"Water." Logan walked to the counter and bought two bottled waters as they hustled toward the rotunda exit.

CHAPTER 43

L ogan pointed to an empty park bench across from the Capitol courtyard. "Let's sit close to the water fountain." Rae picked a good spot on the opposite side of the noisy fountain that blocked their view and provided good background noise.

Logan opened their backpacks, grabbing both phones. He placed each, facing each other on the bench, and turned on their infrared links to transfer data from his to Rae's. The transfer took three seconds to complete. "Let's review the latest intel," he spoke softly.

"It can't hurt to err on the side of caution," she responded as she began scrolling the intel report Logan received earlier that morning. "Hmm, I wonder how busy our boy's been," Rae muttered. They both began reading the following intel report:

Data report A5 0622 04.22

- Grady Walter Hicks, the Barrington Club, 2425 Labrea Avenue, Sacramento (map target 1)
- Metro Limo, 1124, S. Market Street (ground-level parking garage behind Capitol)
- Leases dark-gray limo, license no. 357M122
- Residence. 348 Marino Circle, Mill Valley (map target 2)
- POV black Range Rover, license No. D11C38
- Wife, Sandra, POV silver Mercedes 300, license no. 344Sl33
- Hicks's admin assistant Lee Anne Wheeler (DL pic in recall), 1108 Largo Street, Apartment 42 (map target 3)

- Wheeler POV red Ford Mustang convertible, license no. 316SJ33
- EOT

CIS report A5 0847 04.22

- Unsub Ilia Zohdolofski, age twenty-eight (pic in recall)
- Youngest son of Russian diplomat Sergei Zohdolofski (pic in recall)
- Sergei Zohdolofski, Russian organized crime
- Ilia emigrated from Umirzak Village, Aktau, Kazakhstan, 10.09.99
- Runs the Vory in Grozny, Chechnya
- Symbolic tattoo, the Mark of Cain
- Member of Angel of Death Blood Brotherhood
- Ilia linked to prostitution, gun running, Afghan heroin, human trafficking
- Container ship Zavadolsk, registry, Kazakhstan 1987
- Owned by Caspian Shipping & Transport Ltd., Seattle, Building C, Terminal 25
- Ship is transport of aforementioned

"Hmm, some real undesirables," muttered Rae as she scrolled through more information.

- AODBB began after 1990s Russia breakup
- AODBB proclaims secret mbr of Russian death squad
- Social outcast/soldier of God
- AODBB discovered in 1988 by Russian government
- AODBB penetrated all levels of government/politics
- Markings, tattoo—heart-shaped face between angels' wings
- EOT

"That's it, the angel wings. I remember where I saw the tattoo. It's on the guy's wrist who picked us up at the airport, DeSalva's goon," Logan said with contempt. "Let's check out the limo service. We can park in the same garage and go from there."

"Okay. Let's get our equipment." They started back to the safe house.

"How good are your eyes and ears?" Rae grinned and raised her eyebrows.

"In need of practice." Logan grinned back.

CHAPTER 44

Logan pulled into the parking garage and grabbed the ticket from the auto attendant machine. He drove to Level 4 before locating an empty parking space. Rae grabbed her backpack and closed the rear side door. Walking toward the elevator, Rae stopped to glance at the parking complex directory.

"Logan, Metro's on the east side, ground level. Let's meander our way to Biacchi's, the Italian restaurant just down the block, for lunch. Good cover."

They walked in front of the six stretch limos parked next to Metro's office cubicle. Rae stood at the counter window, waiting for the young man talking on the telephone to notice her. Rae tapped the silver bell to get his attention. He turned and nodded acknowledgement and concluded his conversation.

"How can I help you?" asked the eager young man.

"We're checking out limo services for our wedding in October. You do weddings and special occasions, don't you?" Rae asked innocently.

"Ah, yes. We're mostly business leases, but we have two off our fleet dedicated to airport runs and general rental. They're specially done up if you know what I mean," he said, grinning sheepishly.

"Perfect. We'll need two limos. May we look inside?" Rae turned toward the cars.

"Sure. Everyone's different. They're all open."

"What's your charge?" Logan asked as he lagged behind.

"Minimum is three hours at sixty-five dollars per hour. Half days, or twelve hours, is $595, and full days are a flat rate of $1,100 a day. Business leases are flat rates by the month."

Rae began by sitting in the back seat of the limo parked closest to the office. Logan would stand by the door, partially blocking the view to Rae. Rae peeked in the window of limo two and three and walked around the rear and stopped in between limo five and limo six. Logan stepped a short distance away from the cars to glance at their license plates. He stopped at the rear door on the driver's side of the gray limo, opened the door, rested his arms on the hood, and bent his head down to peek inside.

"This is it," he whispered.

Rae reached in her pocket for her plastic gloves and the tiny wireless microphone enclosed in the fold of a soft case. She slipped on the gloves and opened the case. It resembled a thin chip from a PC board stuck on a straight pin like a miniature lollipop. It was tiny, no larger than a quarter of an inch in diameter.

"Rear deck middle. Tuck it behind the fold of the leather seat and rear deck," Logan said, speaking softly as he turned to look back at the office, his body blocking the view from the office window.

Rae forced the microphone pin deep in the rear deck fabric, wedging the microphone just behind the rounded fold of the leather seat where no one would notice. Logan stood up from his bent-over position, stretched his back, and turned back toward the office to see if the young man was watching. The young man hadn't paid them any mind.

Logan stepped back and shifted one step to the right and looked in the back window. Rae was already getting out of the car. Logan bent down on one knee, pretending to be tying his sneakers, as he slipped the GSM magnetic tracking device just above the inside of the left rear wheel well. He stood up and waited by the trunk and winked as Rae approached. They ambled back up to the counter window together. The young man finally looked up as they stood at the window, Rae locking arms with Logan.

"So what do you guys think?" asked the young man.

"We both like the second and fifth limos," replied Logan.

"You can have one or two, but not five. Three through six are strictly for business, especially three and five. They're both leased."

"What do you mean leased?" Rae asked openly.

"They're on call twenty-four hours a day for Senator Hicks and his staff," the young man replied.

"So where's the driver?"

"His office has two drivers depending upon time of day. They stay upstairs in the lounge till they're needed or their shift ends. We only need ten minutes."

"That sounds rather boring."

"Yeah. They watch a lot of TV."

"Hey, ah, what do you know about Biacchi's?"

"Good food. Very expensive. Lots of rich folks go there."

Logan guided Rae away from the window. "C'mon, honey, I'm hungry. We'll check it out and get back to you on the rental thing. Thanks for your help." Their arms were locked as they ambled out of the garage and on toward Biacchi's for lunch.

*****

A quick glance around the restaurant revealed that Biacchi's was a local watering hole for business acquaintances and the affluent. Logan asked they be seated by the window and were accommodated as the restaurant had not yet filled with the lunch crowd, the hostess leaving two menus and a wine list.

A few minutes later, a clean-cut young man greeted them politely, asking if he could help with the menu and take their order. "What looks good to you?" Rae peeked from behind the menu.

"Um, maybe the veal piccata. You?"

"I'm thinking the manicotti with a small Caesar will do," she replied and handed her menu to Logan.

Logan handed both menus to the waiter. "For the lady, she'll have manicotti with a side of Caesar salad. I'll have the veal piccata and side Caesar as well. The lady will have a glass of chilled pinot, and I'll have your Yellow Tail Merlot."

"Right away, sir. Your lunch will be ready in about twenty minutes," declared the young man.

Adjusting her wire-rimmed glasses, leisurely gazing around the room, Rae asked, "What's next?"

"Let's get Sheba and try our eyes and ears out tonight." Logan grinned, fingering his newly acquired mustache, as the waiter delivered their wine.

Waiting for the waiter to walk away, Rae sipped her pinot. "The mustache looks astonishingly real. I'm game."

"We'll park down the street just south of the exit and wait."

CHAPTER 45

L ogan turned up the volume on the remote microphone speaker clipped to the air vent as the driver mumbled over the sound of the engine.

"Dispatch, how long at Glenview?" asked the driver.

"Schedule blocked for four hours," replied the dispatch voice.

"Got it. On to the Capitol. Out."

"That's pretty clear considering we're hearing the dispatch voice over two-way radio from the back seat." Logan slowed the Expedition and pulled to the curb a half block behind the parked limo.

"We'll know soon enough." Rae smiled, leaning back to pat Sheba.

As a car door opened, faint chatter and footsteps grew louder. "Should be a nice evening for your fundraiser, Senator," boasted a young male voice as he climbed in the limo behind Senator Hicks.

"As nice as one thousand dollars a plate will give us. I've got a meeting after the fundraiser. Arrange for transportation home," Senator Hicks expressed wryly.

"Senator, will you need any of your staff at this meeting?" asked the young voice.

"No!"

"Will Mrs. Hicks be joining us this evening?"

"No! She's away."

Rae piped in, "Sounds like something's up."

"Bet on it." Logan maneuvered back into traffic, following three cars behind the limo.

Rae placed the GSM tracking monitor back in its base plugged into the auxiliary twelve-volt power source. She turned to Logan. "I set the memory log to transmit in five-second intervals with first-in and first-out memory log and to data log and save all repeat stops and repeat locations to the network. We're good for one thousand hours on the battery, so when we leave, I'll forward to the network."

"What RF identifier?"

"I'll tell you momentarily," replied Rae.

"GSM Alpha 7 is the uplink frequency. The data log doesn't tell us when the random radio frequency changes occur, but they change according to cluster frequencies in the area used by the feds and local law enforcement agencies. When you see two back-to-back blinks of the red light, the frequency changed."

Logan slowed to allow another car to get between them and the limo. Rae watched the blinking red dot move over the monitor screen. Sheba's ears perked. The short-lived silence was broken by the high-pitched ring of the limo's mobile telephone. The young voice answered on the second ring. "Robert Allison, aide for Senator Hicks. Just a moment. I'll ask the senator."

"Who is it Bobby?"

"Lee Anne. She wants to know if you need your breakfast meeting notes."

"Yes. Tell her to take them home, and I'll swing by and pick 'em up around nine thirty."

"The senator requests you take the notes home with you, and he will pick them up on or about nine thirty this evening. Yes. I'll relay the message," replied Bobby.

"What message?"

"Your eight o'clock breakfast meeting with the junior senator has been cancelled."

"Good! Don't be in a hurry to reschedule."

Rae spoke over the chatter as she pressed the memory key to trace their movement on the moving map screen. "Turn right at the next intersection."

"On second thought, Bobby, call the bastard back and reschedule the breakfast meeting by week's end! Set it up for seven thirty!"

"The executive restaurant, sir?"

"Yes! I want a report on his campaign issues on my desk tomorrow morning! Anything important I need to know?"

"Sir?"

"Hand me the goddamn guest list! I need to know who to schmooze tonight!"

After a few minutes of silence, Logan slowed the vehicle and stopped about forty yards before the turnoff to the guest entrance security checkpoint as the limousine bypassed the checkpoint, rolling into the Glenview Country Club entrance circle and stopped. The valet opened the right rear car door as Senator Hicks and his aide exited the limo, walking briskly into the country club. The driver rolled the limo slowly to the opposite side of the water fountain entrance and stopped at the outer perimeter of the circle. He picked up the handheld radio and reclined the front seat.

"Dispatch."

"Go ahead."

"Arrived Glenview five forty-five. On standby. Will call when leaving."

"Copy and out."

"Looks like he'll be there awhile," remarked Rae, looking through binoculars.

"Let's go back and connect with Justin, then." Logan turned the vehicle around and headed back into the city.

*****

Back in their room, Logan buzzed Justin on the intercom. "We just returned. How about we meet you downstairs, say, six thirty?"

"Six thirty it is," replied Justin.

Maria was busy setting the table as Rae and Logan, still donning their personas, walked into the dining area. She smiled shyly while arranging the place settings and hors d'oeuvres.

"Hello, Maria. What wonderful surprise do you have tonight?"

"Ms. Rae, we have lobster bisque, grilled sea bass topped with a spicy mango chutney, and rice and grilled vegetables. For dessert, coconut crème brûlée."

"Boy, that sounds absolutely wonderful." Maria blushed. "You can spoil me anytime."

Logan stuck his head around the corner and motioned for Rae to join him in the data room. Justin and Logan were discussing Senator Hicks as Rae walked up to join them, standing over a handful of black-and-white eight by tens of Hicks and another seated at an outside restaurant along the pier strewn on a desk.

"He's one of ours gone bad. Been rogue for some time. Bureau is clueless. Pete and I have enough on him to move but waiting for the right moment to bring the whole house of cards down. Hicks, DeSalva, the Russians—he's the one who planted the listening devices. Probably your attacker, Rae." Justin looked first at Logan and then fixed on Rae.

"How?" posed Logan.

Justin raised his hand in silence. "His name is Royce Joulbert. Goes by RJ. Been with the Bureau ten years. We traced a one-hundred-thousand-dollar wire transfer to a bogus account in the name of Agnes Joulbert, his mother, who died four years ago, the day after your attack. The funds came from DeSalva's trading company account, Caspian Shipping & Transport. You have the address. Confirmed residence is 133 S. Freeman, a townhouse in south Milpitas. Drives an '08 black Mustang.

Logan stood upright, tensing his jaw muscles, slowly moving his head. "That's the son of a bitch!" The words rolled out in deep rhythm through gritted teeth.

Rae reached over, touching Logan's arm, interjecting, "If you know he's bad, why haven't you taken this higher in the Bureau?"

"At this time, I'm the only one who knows within the Bureau. No hurry on this. We'll get our kudos on this one. Bureau doesn't like bad publicity, and a rogue agent to boot would generate plenty. Pete and I are in agreement. Time will lead us to the big fish. One swift takedown and the whole house of cards falls. That way, everybody has skin in the game. And that way, everyone gets an attaboy! It'll happen soon enough."

"How did you find out?" Rae asked, sidestepping Logan toward Justin.

"When I delved into the two of you at Pete's request," he said, assenting acceptance by nodding his head between Rae and Logan.

A stone-cold grin appeared on Logan's face. He grimaced again, tensing his jaw and relaxing, gradually nodding concurrence. Logan piped up, "Pff, this guy's a small-timer, mere foot soldier in the over-all picture. If you're right, attacking the link between them will cause them all to implode and fall like dominos." He pushed the eight-by-ten photo to the side and spread the remaining few openly on the desk, exposing all eight photos.

"You're right on the mark with one exception," beamed Justin, touching DeSalva's photo and then tapping his finger on the rest. "We bring down each parcel in orchestrated succession."

"Who first?" Logan queried with curiosity.

"While I'm sure Pete will propose tally, but knowing Pete, he'll leave most of this up to you. But use me as much or as little as nec-essary. It's your op. You effect the assessments." Justin turned to walk into the dining area. "Bring your package. We'll discuss more over dinner."

"I'm curious, Justin," Rae interrupted. "Why RJ and not one of DeSalva's goons?"

Justin turned back. "Because you're alive, Rae. Your attack wasn't lethal. It was spontaneous, a little sloppy. Meant to take you out of the picture, that's all. If it had been DeSalva's lieutenant or one of the Russian mob, you'd have been abducted, raped, and tortured to death and then dumped, um, probably in the North Bay area or the desert. Either way, you wouldn't have been attacked in broad daylight in such a public place. This guy knew how to strike and kill. He chose to strike, not kill."

"I can't argue with your point," chimed Logan, shaking his head in agreement.

"Hell, Rae, if DeSalva had sicced the Russians on you, the least they'd have done is cut off one of your fingers or some other body part and deliver it to Logan, assuming, of course, DeSalva still wanted Logan to acquiesce or give up to someone or something. Mark my word, they don't play nice! Their rules garner the unthinkable. As for RJ, eh, don't worry about him. I'll gladly bust him for you."

"Thanks anyway, but I want my pound of flesh from that fuck-ing bastard!" Logan sneered coldly.

"Of course you do, but don't compromise the big picture! Logan, let him hang himself! Let his own greed take him down! It always does! I'm telling you, my friend, lose the emotion now, or it'll kill you! I've struggled with this myself. Don't ever think I'm not damn emotional over the killing of Maria's family! Don't ever think I didn't take it personally, because I did! Don't ever think I don't feel guilt because I do!

"Christ, I wanted to pursue that bastard more than anything! I wanted to rip his fucking heart out! I wanted to take down his entire empire that very moment! I wanted to burn the flesh off his body! But I didn't. No, not yet! If there's one valuable lesson that I've learned—and I learned it solely from Pete—it's that. Lose the emotion! He who lets emotions rule is ruled by weak judgment! End of speech. Let's eat."

The three seated themselves comfortably. Justin further amplified the percussion of their discussion by asking poignant questions designed to invoke emotional outbursts. He pushed hard, expecting flippant answers from both. "Pete's right. You two have come a long way. You're not letting your emotions get the best of your ability to make sound decisions. And I did my damndest to provoke each of you again."

"Thanks for the vote of confidence," Logan responded. "Back to the situation. So far, we have two knights and a handful of bishops in this chess game."

"That's the way I see it," replied Justin. "You get Hicks on the money laundering and DeSalva on the gun running, money laundering, and drugs. Everyone else is cannon fodder, prep work, good target practice, with one exception."

"Who?" asserted Rae.

"Sergei," replied Justin. "Do not underestimate the Russians! You're not ready. Leave Sergei to us homeboys." He raised his eyebrows and grinned. "Ya know, we homeboys need to justify our existence from time to time." Refilling his wineglass, Justin paused for a moment, glancing sternly at Logan and then at Rae across the table. "How far do the two of you want to take this?"

"Is there really an end or only a series of ongoing conquests?" Rae asked.

"Aptly asked. I'd like to think there's an end to every crusade. Some are smeared with platitudes and disappointment but mostly self-gratification and accomplishment."

"Aptly answered," she replied, glancing at her watch. "We'd better get back to our eyes and ears for the night."

"If you need anything, call me on my private cell. It's secure. I'll be nearby." Justin handed Logan a folded piece of paper. Without looking, Logan stood up and slipped it into the right front pocket of his blue jeans.

"I know, don't interfere, stay clear, and call if we need backup." Rae and Logan nodded as they walked to the elevator in silence.

CHAPTER 46

"Do we have time for an uplink?" asked Logan.

"Hmm, eight twenty. Yes," replied Rae as she refreshed her disguise and changed into a pair of black Levi's and a black turtleneck sweater.

"I'll give Sheba a quick snack." She walked over to the credenza and grabbed a pouch of beef-flavored treats. Sheba happily chowed down. Rae picked up the camera bag, pulling the strap up over her right shoulder. She checked her sidearm and slipped it into a hidden pocket in her backpack. She walked over to recheck her new look in the mirror while Logan called the Ops Center, looking for Pete.

"Greetings. Hmm, nice 'stache! Pete's in Sub3 if you need him. Update, your boy Dino's on the move. Uplink ready?" Alex asked as he replotted the uplink coordinates.

"Ready."

"Coming to you on A5 in four, three, two, now!"

"Copy that. Anything significant?"

"Yes. Dino's coming to your present location. Scheduled to land 2100, Valley Jet Executive. Hicks is meeting him 2130 at Valley Jet."

"Interesting," murmured Logan.

"Don't try anything. His lieutenant's with him."

"Copy that."

"They're both marked. Eyes on 'em!"

"Thanks, Alex. I'll uplink again later." Logan ended the call. "Ready?" Logan turned to Rae, who was scratching Sheba's ears.

"Let's go." Rae stepped ahead of Logan, opening their room door to the corridor. She gave a hand signal to Sheba, and Sheba followed like a guide dog at Rae's side. All three walked in silence toward the elevator. The only noise in the corridor was the muffled chaffing of Rae's backpack rubbing against her jacket and the spongy whoosh of their footsteps on the thickly woven carpet fibers that was slowing in its tempo as they approached the elevator. Sheba walked quietly.

Logan was lost in thought, staring at the quilted green-and-navy pattern in the carpet. As he looked up, reaching for the down arrow button, he turned and whispered, "Dino's meeting with Hicks at Valley Jet tonight at 2130."

"Hmm," Rae muttered softly with equal caution as the elevator door opened.

Rae and Sheba stepped in the elevator. Logan caught her arm. "You have protection?" She turned and nodded in silence. Logan stepped in beside Rae and turned to face the door. Sheba quietly remained on Rae's far side. "The long-range camera?"

"Yes."

Logan stepped out of the elevator and looked around. The first floor was quiet. He presumed Justin had already left. Apparently, no one else was bunking in at this time. Logan led the way with Rae and Sheba ambling close behind. He opened the side door while Rae and Sheba picked up their pace until they reached the SUV, quickly stowing their gear.

Sheba jumped in Rae's side and lay down in the back seat as commanded. Rae closed the door and climbed in the front passenger seat, plugging the GSM tracking monitor back into an auxiliary twelve-volt power source, hunting the Alpha 7 frequency. Rae waited for the two back-to-back red blinks as the monitor searched for an isolated frequency.

"Tracking's on." Rae closed the door as Logan maneuvered the Expedition out of the parking lot and onto Ninth Street, heading back to the country club. She checked her watch and clipped the remote speaker to the air-conditioning vent and turned the receiver volume up. Rechecking the time log memory, she said, "No radio or dispatch transmissions in the past three hours." She leaned back to pat Sheba.

Tracking the previous GPS trail, Logan slowed the Expedition as they approached the entrance to the Glenview Country Club. The limo remained in its parked location. They rolled past the side road entrance about fifty yards and steered into the middle turning lane. Logan made a quick U-turn and pulled into the parking lot of a small strip shopping center comprising eight stores opposite the country club's entrance.

He rolled the Expedition by the first few stores, looking for an unobstructed view. Nearing the end of the parking lot, he diagonally cut across to the perimeter row in front of a RadioShack store and eased into a spot farthest from the store's entrance, facing the road. Their position afforded them an unobstructed view of their target.

Logan surveyed the parking lot, observing most of the stores had closed for the evening, leaving theirs and only three cars left in the entire parking lot. Other than light traffic on the road, their position was ideal for egress without being noticed as anything other than a late-night shopper or employee.

Logan reached behind Rae's seat, opening the equipment case. Setting aside the handheld parabolic microphone, he grabbed the shotgun microphone from the bag's side pocket. Shotgun mics were less noticeable and more practical for aiming straight line base to target. He screwed a long-curled cord into its base and the other end into SATRAK. The long cord permitted a wider range of placement from either window, even with its power transceiver behind Rae's seat plugged into a power converter in the back of the center console. Logan was pointing the shotgun mic out the window when Sheba's ears perked at the electronic crackle of the two-way radio call, which broke the silence.

"Driver, dispatch."

"Go ahead, dispatch."

"Keenan, the senator will be ready in five. Drive him to Valley Jet Center on Alameda."

"Affirmative. Valley Jet Center, five minutes. Over and out." The young driver started the limo and got out and walked around the back and stood by the rear door, waiting for the senator.

"Guess we'll postpone this till later," Logan said as he pulled in the shotgun mic and dropped it on top of the bag.

"When we stop, I'll set it up on the roof."

Rae pulled the long-range surveillance camera out of its leather case and began focusing the zoom lens on the limo. She switched its light amplifier to autofocus as there wasn't enough light from the overhang to clearly see the driver's face. She refocused on the driver and captured the frame and stored it as a time stamped high-res picture. "I'm surprised the light amplification enhancer captures his face so clearly." Rae turned the small screen to Logan.

"It impressed me when I first tried it on Skip and Ron back in the sim room under low light and smoky conditions. Somewhat similar to night vision image intensification but much better. Not like any other camera I've used before."

Rae closed the viewfinder and rechecked the Alpha 7 frequency. "We're good to go," she said, shoving her backpack down by her feet.

Logan started the ignition as they watched the limo pull out of the side road, crossing right in front of the shopping center. Waiting until the limo had passed, Logan backed up and rolled out of the parking lot four straggling cars and a good distance behind them. Rae punched the history button to track and store the route. SATRAK was capable of storing two hundred routes before required purging, comprising no more than five hundred hours of cumulative tracking time. As little as one route or an entire batch could be categorized and uploaded to the Ops Center's supercomputers and could be recalled from history on demand either individually or in clusters through satellite uplinks. Rae maintained vigilance on the tracking screen.

"Right turn coming up. They're on Alameda. We're 1.3 miles from Valley Jet Center." as Rae punched in the code for Valley Jet, and an inset map of the airport and access roads appeared in the lower right-hand corner. "I wonder where Justin is." She turned to Logan, who was keenly looking for access roads.

"Hopefully covering our six." He turned right onto Cargo Road. "Are we veering too far away?"

They stopped. Rae pointed. "There's the FBO. We're here by the utility hangers. If you continue on Cargo Road, it winds around to the other side of the FBO where the jets are parked."

"We need to stay on this side. Is there line of sight to the front of the building?"

"Yes, beyond the next hangar. There's a parking area in front of the last hangar, southeast corner, about three hundred feet," whispered Rae, focusing on the display.

Logan shut off the headlights and rolled the SUV gradually into the end parking space, jockeying for the best visual posture, and killed the engine. It was a suitable position. Their exposure was limited. A mere sliver of the front quarter panel would barely be visible to onlookers. They were surreptitiously cloaked by the eclipsed shadow, like an invisible wall of darkness behind the perimeter floodlights poised on the rooftop corners of each hangar pointing down on the walkways that stretched between each building connecting the taxiways and parking areas.

On their way in, Logan counted only two vehicles that were still parked in front of the hangars. Even at this late hour, it was completely normal for vehicles to be parked for several hours outside hangars. You could often drive by hangar doors and see folks working on their airplanes after work. Most of the time, hangar doors were closed while pilots racked up flight time, better known as putting hours in soloing.

Logan handed Rae SATRAK's shotgun microphone as she rolled down her side window just enough to slip her hand out and set the magnetic base on the roof, aiming it toward the limo, awaiting optimum signal strength.

"Aim it thirty degrees." Logan leaned over and hit record. They watched in silence as the limo backed up, turned, and stopped. A few seconds passed as the limo rolled forward to its final stop, perpendicular to the double glass door entrance. Rae watched as the young driver stepped out of the limo and walked around the rear to open the right rear door as Senator Hicks stepped out and walked briskly into the building. Refocusing the camera, Rae clicked on the autofocus light enhancer, adjusting the lens to thirty times magnification, capturing clear, time-stamped close-ups of the senator exiting the limo and walking into the FBO. Logan fine-tuned SATRAK's amplifier and plugged in a headset.

"They're coming!" Logan signaled for Rae to restart the paused audiovisual while she was capturing several stills of Senator Hicks strolling out the right front door with DeSalva to his left and his lieu-tenant two steps behind. Scanning the monitor for signal strength, Logan leaned over. "Point the mic ten degrees north," he instructed as the dialogue he was listening to was faint and scratchy. Reaching her hand up through the open window, Rae pointed the mic slowly to the left.

"More. More. Good!"

The young driver was holding the rear door open as Senator Hicks and his guests approached. "Hey, son, take a walk for ten," ordered Hicks. The young driver nodded, turned, and walked toward the building.

Without saying a word, Logan leaned over the center console to view Rae capturing time-stamped high-resolution pictures of Hicks getting into the limousine. As DeSalva seated himself across from Hicks, the lieutenant handed him a slim black briefcase, stepped back, and closed the rear door. He turned around and faced the building with his back against the rear limo door.

"Rae." Logan tapped the headset, giving a thumbs-up that the conversation coming through the remote microphone from the back seat was clear, and gestured cutoff of SATRAK as it was causing fre-quency interference with conversations overriding one another. Rae nodded and paused SATRAK while scrolling through several stills captured on all three players. For an instant, the background com-motion grew loud and waned quickly as DeSalva settled in the seat. A distinct clacking sound resonated.

"Your frosty as requested, Grady." DeSalva handed Hicks a fat bag of cocaine as another clack sound was heard.

"Very much obliged, my man."

"Anything changed, Grady? Dock security, protection?"

"Nothing's changed. Everyone's in place."

"Distraction?"

"The north end warehouse in Terminal 18 a week from this Sunday night as planned."

"Good. That'll back up unloading. Cause delays. Create havoc." DeSalva grinned.

"Where's the pickup?"

"Terminal 51, offloading with all the reefers."

"Refrigerated container? That's brilliant! Truly cold steel!" Hicks hooted at his play on words.

"Funds in place?"

"Indeed. Do you want the split the same as last time?"

"No. This time, seventy-thirty. Seventy to Shanghai Commercial, Hong Kong, thirty to GBC San Fran, and nothing to Seattle. Transfer when you get the page."

"So what's in this shipment?"

"Small arms this round. Mostly Kalishnikovs, AK-47 and AK-74 carbines, 105s, Tokarev pistols, and eight thousand cases of 7.62s. Is it important?"

"What's the word on the heavy stuff?"

"In the works."

"What do I tell my diplomatic associate when he asks for the date?"

"Grady, I always keep you informed!" This was spoken with a twinge of raspiness.

"Same fee?"

"Yeah."

"Nice doing business with you, Michael. Up for some late-night entertainment?"

"Rain check." DeSalva tapped the window. Dmitry opened the door as DeSalva stepped out and turned back to address Hicks. "Clear your calendar next week Thursday for a long weekend of brotherhood and fishing off Cabo. It'll be our last trip for this season. Captain Popov here tells me this time, black marlin will be running. Plenty of billfish. We'll fetch ya here at ten and fly straight to Cabo. Dmitry will provision the boat, including your favorite single malt. Gotta move 2200ks of pure Hindu Kush and atom bomb arriving Sunday week. Time to do your part. Arrange it." Dmitry closed the limo door as he and DeSalva marched toward the front door.

In the background, Logan heard the muted ringing of a telephone. A faint voice answered. Hicks heaved a belabored sigh. "I'll be there in a few, and, ah, clear my calendar from next Thursday week until Tuesday." A muffled response ensued but was indiscernible. "Just tell Bobby to take care of it!" More muffled words as the senator exhaled with sheer exasperation. "Dammit, just do it!"

Logan pulled the headset down around his neck. "Get ready to move."

Rae pulled SATRAK's mic base off the roof. "We're ready." Logan leaned over in time to watch the young driver walk straight back to the limo. After getting in the limo, the young driver put the opaque privacy divider down and turned around to speak to the senator directly. "Where to, sir?"

"Go to Meadows Condominiums on Largo Street." Hicks leaned back and loosened his tie.

"Yes, sir. Is that all, Senator?"

"For now. Go! Just go!" he ordered as the privacy divider rolled upward and the limo pulled away.

Logan eased into traffic well behind the limo. Rae was tagging all the chatter from the limo and matching it with time and date for each of the photos and the recordings. "This alone is enough to end his career," quipped Rae.

"It should be enough to put him in jail, but not yet. There are more rooms in the house of cards that need to topple." Logan drove past the limo as it veered right into the front valet drop-off area. "We know where he's going." Logan slowed, following well behind the limo. "Looks like a better view from over there." Logan turned left and stopped adjacent to a park playground and the condominium building. "Better view from here."

Rae repositioned SATRAK's mic base back on the roof, aiming the antenna at the limo, keeping their eye on Senator Hicks as he walked swiftly toward the condominium building. The doorman held open the lobby door as Senator Hicks brushed past him in a flurry, ignoring the gesture and heading straight for the elevator. Rae listened to the dispatcher acknowledge the interim stop and time.

Six minutes later, the senator exited the elevator, envelope in hand, walking straight through the lobby with little care for those around him. As he settled in the back seat, he opened the envelope as the limo pulled away. He was reading by the ceiling lights in the back seat as Rae and Logan prepared to follow.

"Goddammit!" He grabbed the phone and dialed his aide. "Answer the damn phone," he uttered to himself. "Move my breakfast meeting back with what's-his-name one more week. I still want his report on my desk." He hung up.

Rae pulled the headphone off her left ear and leaned toward Logan. "It'll be my pleasure to see him crumble." They continued to follow him all the way back to his office residence. It was an opulent building that resembled the Dakota Building that overlooked Central Park West in New York with the social accoutrements afforded the rich and famous, like John Lennon and Lauren Bacall. Logan drove past the stopped limo and turned left into a covered parking lot, stopping in a reserved spot. They watched the doorman graciously open the limo door for the senator and follow him through the revolving door as the senator scurried to disappear into the elevator.

"So much for that saga. He could use manners among other things."

"His wake-up call is coming," replied Logan as he maneuvered the SUV out of the parking lot. "We've got a lot to do tomorrow."

They rode in silence as Rae packed up the equipment. "Should we follow him tomorrow?"

"Nah. We know where he's heading. We have plenty to coordinate."

*****

As they pulled into the parking lot, Justin was just getting out of his SUV. He walked over as Rae opened her rear side door to unload. "Pete's set up a briefing. Ten minutes." Justin patted Sheba lying on the back seat, waiting to jump down.

"Roger." Logan nodded as Justin leaned in and grabbed the SATRAK shoulder bag from the back seat floor.

"Thanks, Justin. I'll be there in a few." Rae ordered Sheba to follow.

Logan grabbed the remaining bags from the back. Following Logan up the steps to the side door, Justin murmured, "Pete briefed me on your idea of getting DeSalva and Hicks during next week's fishing excursion. Hmmm, short window. A lot can happen. Not much time to plan an exit strategy." Justin and Logan set the bags down inside the hallway and walked into the conference room.

"Appreciate your concern," replied Logan.

CHAPTER 47

Eight minutes later, all three were sitting on one side of the conference table, watching the three audio-visual (AV) screens come alive. Pouring Logan a cup of coffee, Justin advised, "Perhaps you shouldn't try this by yourself." Just as Logan was about to respond, Justin whispered, "Hold that thought." A real-time Milstar image of the Baja California Peninsula displaying the Gulf of California and the western coastline of Mexico south to the Pacific Ocean appeared on the center monitor.

Ron Lilly appeared on the left AV screen. "Logan, Rae, Justin, on center is real-time satellite imagery from the Air Force Satellite Communications Wing." Lilly typed another command on the keyboard from his workstation. "And now I'm overlaying three of our geostationary birds' orbital patterns." Imposing red, then yellow and green dotted lines appeared sequentially, left to right, across the entire topographical image. Splitting the center AV screen, he instructed, "Eyes right."

Pointing to a red *X*, he said, "This is an abandoned cartel airstrip located seven miles northeast of San Jose del Cabo. This will be our egress point." He circled the *X* with a yellow marker. "Logan, building off your fishing excursion concept you discussed with Dav, we've located a fifty-five foot Nordhavn yacht we can retrofit to clone the *Antares del Sol* oceanic research vessel." He split the right AV screen, imposing a picture of the Nordhavn yacht on the left and the genuine *Antares* research vessel on the right.

The left AV screen split as Tom "Dav" Davenport joined in from his workstation. "The *Antares del Sol* of Patagonia registry was sponsored last year by Right Alliance for Oceanographic Research and is one of the recent vessels known for documenting migratory patterns of humpback whales in the Gulf of California along the Mexican Coast. US Coast Guard cataloged it as running these waters for days last spring and fall."

Hearing keystrokes in the background, a mock-up print of what the modified Nordhavn *Antares* clone would look like when completed appeared on the left, replacing the earlier picture. Dav continued. "By week's end, she'll look like this. When you compare the two, there's nothing to question. This disguise as a research vessel permits unrestricted movement and foregoes any suspicion."

Pointing back to the satellite image screen, Dav drew an elongated area with his index finger. "The deepest part of this strait spans some 160 miles north to south. We want to aim for this area here," he said, finger-drawing the elongated circle on the screen again.

"Logan, you and I will be marine scientists en route to our research vessel. Manny will drop us in La Paz on Tuesday. There, we'll pick up a vehicle, provision with local food and supplies, and drive to the marina." He circled the San Jose del Cabo Marina on the satellite image.

Lilly interjected, "After dropping you and Dav, Manny and I will continue on to the airstrip. Manny has arranged armed escort to transport us and the payload the seven miles from the airstrip to the marina."

Glowering, Logan was about to interrupt when Lilly said, "Hold one, Logan. You're thinking, why not two armed vehicles from La Paz? Discussed the same challenge. Consensus, it's far easier to follow and ambush a vehicle or two than it is to ambush an unexpected aircraft flying over uninhabited landscape. Can't afford equipment falling into the wrong hands. We'll dedicate a bird to monitor the airstrip. In the event of uninvited guests, the armed escorts will have advance notice and will fly the plane elsewhere and return when summoned to pick us up later. They'll return your La Paz vehicle as well.

"Manny will be the registered vessel's captain. He'll retain all documentation, permits, registration work papers, and such. Logan, you'll play the role of Roger Ferguson. We three will continue using our real first names but different last name identities. You and Dav will be trialing a new DPV—scooter, as we call it—under review by

DARPA. This one is a modified high-tech torpedo type but with a conical body shield, plug-in diver suit warmth that travels fifteen to twenty knots. Our plan is to make our way east and south, passing Cabo by midday Wednesday." He drew a yellow line through the middle of the Gulf of California out into the Pacific.

"We will endeavor to delay Dino's departure time until at least 1500 on Thursday. The later they launch, the less catching up we do. Depending upon their heading and speed, we'll continue to criss-cross a grid pattern in this area here, south and east of Cabo, until we can intersect within a mile or two of the *Opulenza* just before sunset. According to his chatter, Dino doesn't make headway after sunset, which works in our favor. We'll be monitoring the *Opulenza* from both our boat and Ops." He put a grid of pictures of DeSalva's new Striker sportfish yacht up on the right screen as Pete stepped out from behind Lilly to interrupt his **OPBRE** (operation briefing).

"Rae, you're sitting this one out with me here. You'll be assisting Alex, Skip, and Alexei in monitoring all tracking, geolocational movement, and comms." Pete turned away to read another **SITREP.** Turning back, Pete carried on. "You need practice time, and we have a lot of collateral to craft. Need you both here ASAP. Assume you're driving, be here NLT tomorrow night."

"Fair enough," replied Rae. "Would bringing Sheba be an imposition?"

"I'll allow it on a trial basis. Justin, you and I have a house of cards to tumble," commanded Pete.

Justin acknowledged, "You're on."

Stepping back in view, Ron Lilly picked up where he left off. "If all goes as planned, we'll position ourselves so the *Opulenza* passes us running south-southeast parallel to Mazatlán. We'll adjust our Lat-Lon position to converge with our boy here at dusk when they go into auto-drift, idling mode for the night." He continued the yellow line and drew a 360-degree circle as he marked another *X* directly below Cabo some one hundred miles from either coast.

"There's a deep trench that runs along the Rivera and Cocos, bisecting fault lines." He drew an elongated oval in red around the circled *X*. "Anywhere within this trench is your best shot. It's on the fringe of commercial navigation satellite reach, so closer to Mazatlán, the better," he added.

"How hard to disable their comms?" Rae interjected.

"Good question. Besides marine VHF radio frequencies, that part of the peninsula area south also uses single side band. It broadcasts widely, so we must disrupt that frequency band as well to be safe. That's where you and Ops come in. You guys will toggle coordinates from bird to bird, transversing our airspace as we'll be on a fringe area for tracking. Your timing will maintain optimum thermal tracking, especially critical as we're not the only country with birds in the sky. Timing is absolutely crucial. No mistakes."

Logan interjected, "Assuming Dräger rebreathers, how much time to prep, and how long can we stay under?"

Lilly stated, "Dav, on point."

Dav asserted, "We'll be shallow, max twenty feet. Once our vessel establishes a parallel intersect when the *Opulenza* begins drift-idling for the night, I estimate our time at seven to ten minutes each way, depending upon distance. Based on oxygen consumption, thirty-seven to forty-five minutes. These scooters cruise comfortably at fifteen knots but will easily go twenty, so I estimate about one-third of our time transiting, two-thirds doing the deeds."

"What do we do with the scooters when we make contact?" asked Logan.

"Refer to the top row, middle picture, of Dino's yacht. Using your bungee idea, attach 'em to the bracket on each corner of the swim platform, or we carry a self-inflating fender and tie that to the platform. I'll get a close-up to reaffirm. On board our vessel, Manny will have thermal-augmented day scope to watch from afar and the eyes from our SATRAK devices onboard. They won't know we're watching."

"Can we get a schematic of Dino's boat?"

"You'll have it before arrival tomorrow."

"Logan, see you at Ops."

"Copy that."

"If nothing else, signing off." The video monitors went black.

After postponing a discussion with Justin, Rae and Logan sequestered themselves in their room. "I say we leave early tomorrow morning and drive this rental to Ops." Logan handed Rae a glass of Chartreuse while pouring a glass for himself.

"I'm a little jumpy." Rae took a long swallow. "This may settle my jitters."

"I'd be fooling myself if I didn't admit I'm nervous too. After all we've been through, the least we can do is put our training to work for us," replied Logan as he took a big gulp.

"It'll be nice to have Sheba with me in your absence. I won't be calm until this mission is over and you're back safe."

"I'll be safe, and I promise you, it will be over," he said, downing the last mouthful. He set the glass down, picked Rae up from her chair, and carried her over to the bed. "This is our last night here. Let's make the best of it." He kissed her with the passion of their first encounter.

CHAPTER 48

L ogan loaded the bags in the Expedition as Rae uploaded all pictures and batched data to Ops before saying goodbye to Justin and thanking Maria for the homemade dog treats. Justin joined Logan, handing him an envelope. "We'll discuss after you guys get settled. If you need anything, call me. I've got some hole-and-corner work to do. Now get outta here."

After breaking free of city traffic, Logan hit I-80 E ramp by nine thirty, anticipating arrival at Ops Center around three that afternoon after a fuel stop east of Reno, Nevada. After settling the Expedition in a steady rhythm while Rae was scrutinizing their recent photos, Logan interrupted her train of thought. "Justin gave me an envelope this morning. It's in the pocket behind my seat. Want to have a look at it?"

"Sure." She retrieved the manila envelope. Opening the clasp, Rae smiled. "I just knew it. I knew he'd come through."

"What?"

"It's pictures of several months of Grady Hicks's personal calendar, um, his appointments, who he's been meeting with, names, locations. This is awesome!"

"Anyone you recognize?"

Thumbing through several pages, she said, "Hmm, this is interesting. He's met with a Leonid Bocharov, looks like more than once. I bet that's the Russian diplomat Hicks was referring to."

"Yeah, he's the foreign minister. Got that from Alexei in CIS," remarked Logan.

"How does implicating him in this house of cards work with diplomatic immunity?" asked Rae.

"That's a question better answered by Pete," replied Logan.

"He's met with a lot of influential folks. Um, I'm willing to bet many of these folks may not want their name associated with him after next week, especially if they get a call from the feds. I'm guessing a few of them were at his fundraiser. Oh, how I'd love to be a fly on the wall and watch it all go down."

"Ditto." As they approached the higher elevation of Truckee, the temperature dipped to forty-six degrees, and light rain began sprinkling. "At least there's no snow or sleet to deal with today," shrugged Logan as they continued driving through the mountain pass and toward Reno, Nevada.

"You know, Pete was pleased with your overall training report. On our second to the last night, he confessed that he was leery about you at first. He didn't expect you to grasp it all so quickly or excel as fast as you did," Logan cautiously replied.

"I'll take that as a compliment," said Rae. "He's no slouch when it comes to his instincts. I won't let anyone down."

"I expect nothing less."

*****

They stopped at a rest area east of Reno after refueling for a late lunch break. Rae and Sheba took a quick walk before the three sat down to eat a packed lunch made special for them by Maria, Justin's house mother. Each bit into their club sandwiches while Sheba snacked on some chicken, rice, and peas. The wind and rain had subsided, and the sun warmed the air. Anxious to get to their destination, both hastened their lunch break.

"We're about fifty minutes from the turn off to Highway 50, and from there, it's another hour or so of two-lane driving. Alex or Skip will text us the gate passcode," said Logan as they climbed back into the Expedition.

"I'm eager to get settled. You think Pete's in today?" asked Rae.

"As far as I know, he is. I expect he'll have us fully engaged shortly after arrival."

At 2:40 p.m., Logan's phone beeped with a text message: "Approaching a two-lane gravel road to the north in 3.2 miles. Travel

5.5 miles to the first gate. Passcode is 572018. Press Enter. Eyes and ears on. See you in twenty. Skip."

"It's really desolate out here, isn't it?"

"Yeah. Seeing it from the air versus driving makes a helluva difference." Logan slowed and turned onto the unmarked gravel road. Each side of the road stretched for miles with cactus and sagebrush and scattered spruce trees.

As they approached the first gate, Rae remarked, "Look at the size of that video screen. I count four cameras." Logan punched the six-digit code, and the gate opened.

"I'll bet there's more hidden all along the way." Logan rolled the Expedition through the gate, stopping on the other side, watching it close in the rearview mirror.

They drove another twelve minutes, rounding the base of a hill. Hidden in the basin, not visible from the road, was the second gate with a security fence that had to be at least ten feet high and capped with razor wire atop that protected the Ops Center. To an innocent bystander, it looked like protected native reservation land from the highway with No Trespassing signs posted every quarter mile. To Logan and Rae, it was the endpoint to an exciting outlook on life.

"I see why these guys fly in here. Driving takes forever," replied Logan.

At 2:56 p.m., Logan's phone beeped with a text message: "Same passcode. Enter west side sublevel, back of the hangar building. Park anywhere. Skip."

Logan drove through the gate, up a hill, and around the back of the neighboring hangar building, entering the underground parking and pulling into a corner parking spot facing south. He was amazed the lot was filled with so many cars and SUVs, some with government plates and others depicting mixed states, most likely POVs (privately owned vehicles) by workers in the sublevel intelligence areas.

As Rae and Logan climbed out of the Expedition, Skip walked out of the elevator pulling a rolling cart to greet them. Sheba remained quiet in the back seat, waiting to jump down and greet the new face. Skip helped Logan load the bags onto a rolling cart as Rae beckoned Sheba to come and meet Skip.

"Hey, Logan. Hey, Rae." Skip gave Rae a quick nod. "Justin mentioned you have a highly trained dog. Purebred?" asked Skip.

"Yes. She's papered out of the Czech Republic," replied Rae. "You won't even know she's around." Rae ruffled Sheba's ears. Sheba jumped down and came to heel at Rae's right side, facing Skip. Rae spoke to Sheba. "Sheba, friend." Sheba sat, offering her right paw to shake with Skip.

"A few years back, I worked with a SAS counterpart that part-nered with a Dutch shepherd out of Germany. It's amazing the things they can do and how many lives they've saved because of their instincts and skill set. I'll enjoy getting acquainted."

"She's easy to enjoy," remarked Logan as they walked toward the elevator, Rae and Sheba shadowing quietly.

"We have you back in your same room." Skip pushed the ele-vator button.

"Nice-sized elevator," said Logan.

"Yes, it is. Has to be large enough to move equipment in and out," replied Skip. "Very few outsiders are allowed in."

"Guess that makes sense."

As the elevator arrived at the top floor, Skip said, "Get cleaned up if you wish. Dinner is at 1800. I'm sure you'll enjoy the company."

CHAPTER 49

Rae and Logan unpacked as much as they could, settling in their room. Feeling more at ease this time, Logan gave Sheba a few of Maria's homemade treats. "You'll like this cooler temperature tomorrow," he said as he scratched her ears while she nudged his leg and stood on his foot.

"Rae, you want to run with us tomorrow morning?"

"If it's early, I will."

Thirty minutes later, Logan and Rae caught up with Skip in the hallway leading to the dining area just as the rest of the team meandered in from the opposite side for a get-together working dinner. They both noticed the atmosphere in the dining room felt different. They were no longer guests where team members went out of their way to be nice just to be professional. It was evident they both had earned their due respect from each member of the team even though they were newbies.

Rae and Logan looked at each other and smiled. Graduation had come and gone. It was now time to pitch in without being asked. Time to earn their stripes. Dav was sitting down at one end of the long table. He motioned for Logan to join him and Ron. Likewise, Rae sought Pete out for the same reason, a given that ideas, suggestions, and up-to-the-minute details for the mission would be discussed.

"Received the hydroskins, fins, and wrist gauges yesterday. The full-face mask we're also trialing has built-in low light vision, customized for zero visibility and night diving. We'll test 'em before we depart," Dav said to Logan as he sat down.

"So where do you dive around here?" asked Logan.

"Lake Mead is one, but I know this commercial dive instructor at Polytech in San Diego. We dove the Tigris in Baghdad together. We can use his pool anytime. He runs advanced dive programs, and I've tested a lot of equipment there. They do it all, from underwater welding to hyperbaric medicine. And if time permits, we can wreck dive the HMCS Yukon," replied Dav. "That'd give us good open water practice timing the DPVs from a half mile or less."

"No arguments there. Can't have enough drill time," expressed Logan. "I've used scooters before, but they tend to be heavy and place a lot of pressure on the arms. How well do these maneuver at fifteen knots?"

"You see through a clear conical shield that extends beyond your elbows, protecting your upper body. Lilly and I tried them about a month ago in San Diego. It makes turning so much easier, and your arms don't get so tired. The shield is removable, but I wouldn't. It's an asset. You're not feeling the force on your face mask, especially if you have to bolt."

Lilly butted in. "You're an advanced rescue diver with PADI. You'll have no problem. These tools will shortcut your objective. Tomorrow, we'll look at the schematics and determine optimum placement of the charge. Then we'll run a mock-up drill and set the timer. You can choose remote detonation or time set detonation. Your Op, your choice."

"Remote from the boat?" asked Logan.

"Possibly, or remote from a modified dragonfly drone," replied Lilly. "We'll play with it tomorrow. We can adapt it to deliver the message or just use it for observation. It's another close-up eyes on our boy. I've practiced with the dragonfly following a car from a car at night. Practically invisible. And you can switch from night vision to thermal easily."

"How long can it stay up?"

"Last trial, over two hours and still had 35 percent residual batteries remaining."

"What altitude?"

"I flew it most of the time at 120 plus feet above the target, tracking Skip running at night. He couldn't find it most of the time, even knowing it was above him. It gives off a whisper of sound because it uses the same quiet fan jet propeller blade design as our Pilatus."

Dav interjected, "I'd say that's more than we need for this op."

"Agreed. If we need more than that, we're in trouble," replied Logan.

*****

Pete and Rae strategized how to entangle the triad of evil—DeSalva's villainous operations, Hicks as the go-between, RJ and the culpable—a murder of crows to pay one's dues for their dirty deeds.

"Justin gave me Hicks's appointment book contents. From that, I'll interweave the connections and collateral to RJ, the diplomat, DeSalva's father-in-law, and implicate mob connection. Am I missing anything important?" Rae asked Pete.

"Implication is all that's needed. Justin and the homeboys will take care of Zohdolofski, the Jersey syndicate, and the Russian mob."

"Your thoughts on replacing his appointment book with a replica or hide a black book of secrets?"

"Rae, I think a conversation between you and Justin will sort that out," replied Pete. "He needs his kudos as well."

"I assumed you'd say that."

"You're on point all day with Alex and Skip tomorrow." The dinner waned for the evening, and Pete stood up to leave.

Skip, sitting across from Rae, said, "First thing tomorrow, report to SubLevel 3 for your BDUs and microchip and then my station by 0830."

"Will do."

"We'll break midday. I'm interested in seeing Sheba's level of training firsthand."

"Sure. Be happy to."

Alex chimed in as he was picking up his dinnerware, "I'd like to watch as well." He walked out of the dining area.

Skip reiterated, "Everyone pitches in."

"Point taken. Should be that way," she said, picking up her dinnerware and nodding to Logan as he was still engaged in heavy conversation.

Rae walked swiftly to their room to retrieve Sheba for a stroll around the building. Sheba was more relaxed than Rae expected, perhaps sensing that Rae herself was more self-confident. Tomorrow will be intriguing.

L ogan was first up, drinking a quick cup of coffee before a short run. Sheba was waiting for him at the door as Rae came down to the kitchen area dressed for the run.

"Coffee?"

"Not yet. Where are you placing your microchip?"

"The inside of my left bicep." He took a long sip of coffee.

"That's a good place," she replied. "I'm ready when you are." The trio headed for the elevator.

Outside in the crisp, cool desert air, they jogged three abreast to the road leading up the hill to the radomes when Logan pointed ahead. "Skip runs this trail all the time. It's 1.5 miles to the radomes."

"Skip's too fast," remarked Rae. "I can't keep pace, especially uphill. He wants to see how well Sheba is trained," remarked Rae.

"I'm impressed."

Rae continued, "He's worked with a military working dog on a previous mission. Did you know they have a rank?"

"Yes. Assaulting a working dog is no different than assaulting a soldier or a cop. They're referred to as guardians of the night. They were on guard duty 24-7 at every flight line I was assigned overseas."

*****

Two hours later, Rae and Logan had completed their indoctrination in SubLevel 3, heading back to their room to change clothes and begin their first workday, Logan catching up with Dav in the training room and Rae heading to the heart of Operations.

Rae peeled off the bandage where the subcutaneous microchip was injected on the inside of her left bicep. The skin around the chip still felt a little tender but would be fine in a day or two. Walking up to the door, she placed her right hand on the biometric screen and looked up, awaiting access into Operations. The door hissed open, and Rae walked over and down to Skip's workstation where a chair awaited her presence.

"Remember from Lilly's brief a couple days ago, we employ three navigational geostationary birds. They're sequenced to overlap each other so we gain the greatest footprint for monitoring and tracking images live. The top row of function keys controls the sequencing province that flashes the digital countdown of each bird's viewing prefecture as the earth rotates in a sidereal day, or twenty-fours.

"The first is Geo1, depicted by the higher latitude red dotted line and its coordinate numbers show visible at the bottom of the screen. The second is Geo2, showing up by the middle latitude yellow dotted line and coordinate numbers at the bottom. The third bird is Geo3, represented by the lower latitude green dotted line and coordinate numbers at the bottom.

"When you press this function key, you see a blinking white dot. That's where the bird is in its orbit. When time comes for you to alter or reposition an orbital pattern, this manual shows any operator the sequential steps required to reposition the orbit for each bird," he said, handing Rae the manual.

"Why three birds?"

"Redundancy is imperative for national security."

As Rae perused the manual, she posed, "It says here SATRAK functions in a higher earth orbit that provides longer dwell time for communications."

"Yes," replied Skip.

"How does it stay operational for so long?"

"Different type of orbit. This bird is in what is known as a tundra orbit. The pattern looks like a bowling pin, or an elliptical eight, with the larger ellipse remaining over a chosen geographic area much longer. SATRAK's position over the northern hemisphere covers the large ellipse, the small ellipse is below the equator.

"If you ask too many technical questions, I'll have no choice but to send you downstairs to one of the aeronautical coordinators."

Skip laughed. "Operationally speaking, it's imperative to be vigilant, especially watching those numbers when its mission critical as tracking could be life or death. Tomorrow, we'll be downstairs, learning how to program jamming, cloaking, and killing cell phone and radio signals. That's kinda tricky, but for now, you need to learn how to request a **SITREP** as well as an updated **SITREP**." Skip depressed a function key on the keyboard and asked Rae to type in the keyword "Dino" in the dialogue box.

Rae did so, and a new **SITREP** report popped up on the screen from SubLevel 3. She hit the print command and walked over to the printer to retrieve it. She shared it with Skip. The **SITREP** read as follows:

- Dmitry Popov wanted for crimes in Russia
- Identified by Mark of Cain tattoo
- Cousin to Ilia Zohdolofski, also wanted for crimes in Russia
- Diplomat S. Zohdolofski runs Minister Leonid Bocharov
- Bocharov received two wires (two sets of fifty thousand dollars from CS&T)
- $14 million deposited SCB Trans 15099289; $6 million deposited GBC Trans 15099296
- Dino at CS&T Seattle; leaving for Tahoe end of day today
- Confirmed firebomb Sunday Terminal 18 located, feds notified
- Hicks in Sacramento
- Weissner law firm under scrutiny by DOJ
- EOT 0950

Rae laid the report on the desk. "Is most of this coming from Alexei in CIS? How do you know so much?" Rae asked openly.

"Yes. Alexei manages the brainworks of Ops. We're capable of cross-device tracking all devices, so we're capable of monitoring every type of communiqué possible, sans visual sign language. We could interpret that too, if we captured it, but that's another part of tomorrow's training. At any time, you can tap into the ongoing eavesdropping and wiretapping of Dino's phone calls, texts, etc. Your job is to cleverly incorporate the incriminating evidence so they suffer the consequences of their misdeeds, all while doing so at arm's length, letting someone else do the dirty work."

"I like that."

"In my humble opinion, you're in a position to effect positive change in everything you do," espoused Skip.

"I see what you mean. Everything that goes on here has one concentric formula: seeking the overall good for mankind," said Rae as Skip nodded his head concurrently.

"You're in a position to positively affect this team in ways we have yet to learn," noted Skip.

"What do you mean?" she asked kiddingly.

"For the past few years, we've only had our viewpoints and experience that shaped our approach to problem solving. You and Logan bring fresh, untainted perspective and insight. That's a plus," replied Skip.

"Thank you. I didn't consider our past would play into this that much."

After over three hours of intense surveillance charting, Pete walked out of the elevator from Sublevel 3 (Sub3) and interrupted. "It's 1215. I've got overwatch. You guys break for lunch."

Skip replied, "Works for me."

As Skip and Rae walked to the dining area, he stated, "Someone's always on duty. Even when missions required the entire team, Sub3 assumes coverage to man overwatch."

CHAPTER 51

Rae finished an early lunch and went back to her room to retrieve Sheba. Grabbing her lead harness, Sheba looked at Rae as if to say, "You know I don't need that." They walked around the hangar building for exercise and fresh air, ending up at the outdoor range where Skip and Alex were seated at the picnic table.

Rae, with Sheba keeping pace on her right side, walked up to the guys and commanded Sheba to lie down as she sat on the end of the bench next to Alex. Rae asked, "Are either of you familiar with CSVs in the German shepherd world?"

Alex shook his head while Skip replied, "See a lot of shepherds on bases and with local police but never owned one myself."

"Sheba is a silver-tipped Czechoslovakian Vlcak, which is actually a new cross-breed between a German shepherd and a Carpathian wolf. This new breed began in 1955 to capitalize on the top characteristics of each breed to create a better-working dog. In Sheba's case, she seems to have slightly more shepherd characteristics as she is very obedient."

Rae commanded Sheba by raising her arm to come to Rae. Sheba stood up and walked over to Rae, who scratched her head affectionately, saying, "Good girl." Rae lifted Sheba's head slightly, "Notice her facial bone structure is slightly different than a typical GSD. Her back is straight, not slanted. Her chest is large and flat with a strong, drawn-in belly. Her legs are longer, so her canter stride is longer. Notice her front paws are slightly turned outward." Rae ran her hands down Sheba's back. "Her coat is slightly different than most dogs as it sheds dirt easily. She rarely needs bathing."

Skip asked, "Honestly, I didn't really notice the difference. I just thought she was a big breed."

Alex asked, "Does she bark or howl?"

"Actually, she doesn't do either. I had to teach her to vocalize. Rather, she makes guttural vocalizations. Ah, we'd describe it as a short outburst, like a woof. When she is in protection or suspicion mode, she makes a low-toned, guttural growl, like when the deer used to come in the backyard. When she's running alongside Bella, my horse, it's a higher-pitched, drawn-out utterance. That's more like a pack thing. She is very stealthy, even for her size. Many large dogs are noisy walkers. She's not."

Skip asked, "What kind of training has she had?"

"I started with her when she was seven weeks old. The first thing was imprinting. She had to know I was the alpha female in the hierarchy. There wasn't a part of her body that hadn't been touched by me. When she was twelve weeks, we began basic disciplinary training. She was easy, but if she didn't get exercise, she got bored. I was lucky that I had a neighbor who was a canine officer who trained shepherds and malinois for service and protection. So after several weeks of disciplinary training, we attended another eight weekends of dog guide school to get her used to being around people in close quarters."

"How old is she?" asked Alex.

"Just over three," responded Rae as she hand-signaled Sheba to sit.

"Do you use German or Czech commands?" asked Skip.

"Neither. I prefer action language, with and without verbal."

"Does she fetch balls and such?" asked Alex.

"Not really. She enjoys chasing Frisbees," replied Rae. "Mostly, she really loves to run alongside Bella. It's a pack thing. She and Bella have been close since she was seven weeks old."

"She's highly trained," replied Skip. "I watch her run with Logan, and she keeps pace and heels without having to use a leash."

"Yes. That part of the training was easier than I expected. I've been told it has to do with the pack mentality and yielding to the alpha leader," replied Rae.

CHAPTER 52

Logan, Dav, and Lilly experimented most of the morning with varying weight differential, utilizing putty that resembled the consistency of composition B explosive and detonator attached to the dragonfly drone. After several takeoffs and landings outside the building, Logan emphatically stated, "This isn't efficient. Too much drag. Too hard to control. Need to rethink this." They walked back into the training room.

Logan picked up the *Opulenza's* lower deck schematics and laid the illustration on the worktop as Dav and Lilly looked on.

Logan asserted, "I'll construct a magnetized shaped charge similar to a Limpet mine as the hull is steel." Pointing his index finger to the outline of the engine and exhaust, he said, "I'd place one charge between the engines forward of the fuel tank here." He slid his finger upward. "I'd place the second charge forward of the main cabin here, so any last-minute movement between the main cabin, the fly bridge, or the back deck should catch all three in the undex. Comments?"

Dav interjected, "If she's drift-idling, I suggest we come upon it from behind, split off, and match its forward speed mid hull. Ascend to just below the hull and approach from the side and plant the charges. We'll only need about five to ten seconds. Have to be damned careful of the propellers, though. They'll only be about ten to twelve feet behind where we place the engine charge, and the shaft and props will be rotating. Once in place, we dive, do a 180, and bolt."

"I'll assemble a quick release strap for carrying each charge," said Logan.

"I'll flip you for the engine placement." Dav reached in his pocket for a quarter.

"No, I'll do it," countered Logan. "I know it's dicey."

"How long will it take to assemble them?" asked Lilly.

"A couple of hours, maybe," replied Logan. "The two-part mastic to weld the magnets to the waterproof cases was the hardest to find. It arrived yesterday."

"Sounds like a plan," countered Lilly. "We might be better off using dragonfly for surveillance."

"We need to trial this without detonators and time ourselves," declared Logan.

"Roger that," replied Dav. "We'll do so on Wednesday."

"The big question is, how much time should I set?"

Lilly responded, "My guess is sixty to seventy-five minutes. Ample time to swim over and back."

"I've rerun my calculations three times. I estimate each shaped charge will carry 1.5 lb. of compound B with magnetized case five pounds," Logan affirmed.

Dav responded, "Oh yeah! That'll make a helluva splash!"

"I'm making them disc-shaped so they won't be hard to wield underwater."

"Copy that," replied Dav, looking at Lilly.

"It's a plan," Lilly replied openly.

"Where's our boat now?"

"Puerto Vallarta. It'll be at the marina Monday afternoon."

"Tomorrow, you can fly us three to Montgomery Field in San Diego. We'll get a courtesy car and go test the gear," replied Dav.

"What time tomorrow?" asked Logan.

Lilly replied, "Seven in the hangar. Okay with you two?"

"Seven it is," replied Logan.

Dav nodded. "Roger. Seven."

*****

Logan spent a couple hours shooting the SIGARMs M11 at the outdoor range behind Operations, all the while contemplating the worst-case scenario: eliminating one or more of the vile trio. As he double-tapped the silhouette, he pictured DeSalva in his mind and smirked knowing that the end was nearing for him and his past criminality. He was calm yet eager—calm in the sense that he was confident the mission would be a success and eager in the sense that he felt it couldn't happen soon enough.

Logan was reloading for another practice round when Lilly walked up and tapped him on the shoulder. Logan turned, lifting one side of his Peltor electronic earmuffs off to hear Lilly say, "Pete's got an update for us in his office in ten." Lilly stood behind Logan, watching.

"Got it. Ten." He turned and resumed emptying the last clip into the silhouette. After the last shot, Logan walked out and unclipped the silhouette from the target, noting the preponderance of holes were center mass.

"You like the M11?" asked Lilly.

"Liking it the more I shoot it." Logan and Lilly walked back to Ops.

"What's your choice?"

"Same."

Lilly and Logan walked in the back door and headed into Pete's office. He and Manny were reviewing a **SITREP** from late yesterday. "Grab a cup." Manny raised his cup of coffee. He was sitting next to Pete. Neither Logan nor Lilly took the coffee offer. Instead, Logan grabbed two bottles of water as he and Lilly joined in.

Pete elaborated from last night's **SITREP** from the wall monitor in front of his conference table. "These tasks are scheduled to commence after mission completion. The house of cards will begin crumbling Friday and successive days thereafter. Hold your comments until the end."

- BATF skd raid/bomb sqd Terminal 18 Friday—"They'll find the firebomb, no damage. This will recoil on Dino, the Russians and Hicks."
- SEC skd raid Pingston Financial Securities Friday—"This is just the beginning of fraud, RICO, and other financial crimes linking our boy and Hicks."
- CS&T to be raided Friday by FBI/BATF—"This will start the cascading of all involved with our boy."

- USCG escort the Zavadolsk into Terminal 51—"The Coast Guard will board the Zavadolsk and accompany it into the harbor, ensuring nothing is dumped so when the feds confiscate the contraband, all those involved will go to jail."
- BATF & DEA confiscate contraband—"Answered. The turf war begins here. Each will want their fifteen minutes of newsworthy fame."
- Evidence and cocaine in Hicks's office NLT Thursday links Dino, father, NJ syndicate, payoffs, and Russian collusion—"Rae is compiling the evidence, and Justin is executing delivery."
- CIS notifies SVR of RJ and Hicks's blackmail to NJ syndicate and Russian mob—"Alexei assures our Russian counterparts will leak this info to key individuals. All hell should break loose. This becomes Justice Department and State Department territory."
- FBI to have proof of RJ and Hicks blackmail collusion—"The DOJ will give FBI dirty deeds from RJ."
- FBI raids Bocharov's office Friday, payoff evidence revealed—"Bocharov will panic and probably spill his guts."
- FBI visits Russian Embassy looking for Zohdolofski—"After Bocharov spills his guts, this should put the Russians in a tailspin. Wouldn't be surprised if Zohdolofski returns to Russia under the guise of personal emergency. His immunity won't keep him from us forever."
- DOJ raiding Dino's three banks Friday, linking to Russia and national security risk—"The DOJ will claim any link to Russia is a national security risk, thereby confiscating funds and intel from Dino and Hicks. This should make for startling news. I guarantee you some of this will be leaked."
- DOJ raiding Venice Capital and assoc for collusion as national security risk—"Answered. The DOJ will coordinate with the SEC. That will cascade into a news frenzy involving our boys."

- DOJ and FBI investigating Weissner law firm—"Ward's law firm has wind of this and will assist."
- For now, Dino's in Tahoe, and Hicks is in Sacramento until Thursday—"Downstairs is keeping tabs on our boy scout and the Joker."
- EOT 12.20

"Comments, gentlemen?" asked Pete.

Manny piped in, "As you know, a lot has transpired in the last forty-eight hours. I expect we'll be seeing a lot more activity by week's end. Logan, Lilly, your thoughts?"

Logan glanced over at Lilly as Lilly spoke first. "We're on target. Logan?"

"Obviously, a lot of backend work has been accomplished to get this far. We're trialing the new gear tomorrow. Is there something more I can do?" he asked the group.

Manny answered for Pete, "Nothing at this time. While I'm sure this mission lacks some personal gratification, the way we do things here is to ensure nothing comes back at any of us, so let's keep it that way. It's a mission, and missions are accomplished together as a team."

Speaking deliberately, Pete stated, "I'm confident it will go as planned. Manny, how long to restore the boat back to its original state and get it picked up?"

"Once we get back to the marina, unload, and leave, my contacts will remove the bogus equipment, decals, flags, etc., clean it inside and out, and then they'll sail it back to Puerto Vallarta. One full day tops, including sailing time."

Lilly interjected, "Good move not returning one vehicle back to La Paz."

Manny followed, "We'll leave all excess food and drink with the boat."

"That's why we provisioned in La Paz. No connection to the US," affirmed Logan.

"Hmm, quick study," Manny joked.

CHAPTER 53

L ogan rose early, dressed in civilian clothes as Roger Ferguson, carrying his new identity, pilot's license, and all he should need if he were to be unexpectedly ramp-checked by an FAA inspector in San Diego. He kissed Rae goodbye at 0615 and ruffled Sheba's ears while she gazed at him with curious eyes. She knew he was leaving without her, so she trotted over to the door for a last pat on the head.

Logan met up with Lilly and Dav in the dining area for a quick breakfast. "The flight is only 420 nautical miles. It shouldn't take more than eighty minutes to KMYF Montgomery Field. I loaded it into Foreflight on my iPad this morning after checking the weather. Weather's always sunny in California, and today looks to be perfect. We'll fly VFR at 14.5, fourteen thousand five hundred feet. Smooth all the way. That way, no one knows who we are or where we're going. No flight plan, just the way you like it."

The three finished breakfast and walked to the elevator to the sublevel tunnel and adjacent hangar. Once inside the hangar, there was no mistaking the purpose of the Mosby Foundation. Logan felt pride once again as he opened the inside door bearing the large navy-blue emblem encircled by gold stars. Inside the circle that crowned the bald eagle were the words, "United States of America Overwatch."

Logan grabbed the chocks and stacked them against the wall. Lilly loaded the three dive gear bags in the baggage area. Once the hangar door was open, Dav started the remote-controlled tug that guided the nose wheel, pushing the Pilatus PC12 backward and out of the hangar. The PC12 displayed a blue caduceus on both sides, signifying it as a medical flight. Logan surmised this disguise would

232

allow them to fly to San Diego as an Angel Flight, another great way of masking the plane from curious onlookers.

Once outside of the hangar, Logan continued the preflight check of the Pilatus. He checked the ailerons, rudder, and lights. All looked ready to go. Lilly echoed, "No water in the fuel. Oil is full. Prop is clean. Tires look good. All surfaces are fine. Ready to go!"

"Copy that," noted Logan, who finished the outside preflight check and climbed into the aircraft, taking left seat. Dav released the tug from the nose wheel, returning it to its station, and closed the hangar door while Lilly buttoned up the last of their gear, securing the baggage door. Dav and Lilly climbed aboard, Lilly taking the copilot seat.

Although there was no tower or ground clearance to contact, Logan noted that they would depart from a restricted area, passing through two inactive military restricted areas, R4803 and R4810. Restricted areas were airspaces that were designated outside of general aviation airspace to segregate commercial and general aviation traffic from areas of high security. Today's flight was cleared to pass through these areas. Manny had loaded in the base radio frequency to check for clearance before takeoff, which Logan called to check. Their flight today, call sign Angel One, was cleared direct to destination through both restricted zones.

Loading in the flight director, which would bring the GPS heading 159 degrees true direct to KMYF Montgomery Field, Logan completed a double-check of switches, mains, lights, and speed brakes. He mumbled to himself, "All set." The others looked perplexed that he was talking to himself. "Sorry, habit. Just used to flying solo with no one around to answer me!"

He taxied the Pilatus out to the runway when Dav teased over the headsets, "Well, at least you're good for something, Logan. Now we'll see if you swim like a girl."

"Yeah, yeah, yeah." Logan laughed.

Logan set the breaks and ran the PC-12 up to test for TIT (turbine inlet temperature) and fuel flow. He boxed the controls and stated, "Everyone set! Ready to go!" He pushed full throttle, and the

Pilatus turbine roared down the runway, taking off at 0715, climbing swiftly to altitude.

*****

One hour and twenty-two minutes later, Logan landed the Pilatus with one quick squeak of the wheels as they touched down at Montgomery Field outside of San Diego. Lilly talked to Ground as Logan taxied off the runway heading to Gibbs Flying Service FBO.

Lilly reminded Logan before the aircraft came to a stop. "Your nickname is Ferg for this trip."

"Got it. Ferg," replied Logan. "And no, Ferg doesn't swim like a girl. Ha ha!"

After a ground service lineman guided the Pilatus to its parking position, Logan set the breaks, allowing the TIT to come down, and shut down the engine. After stowing his Bose A20 headset, he exited and walked into the FBO to check the aircraft in using his new ID. Lilly was already unloading the gear into a trailer attached to a golf cart that Dav borrowed immediately after deplaning.

Approaching the counter, Ferg said to the clerk, "We'll be here most of the day. We need a courtesy car for the day." He gave her a credit card for the landing and parking fee.

She replied, "We can't lend a courtesy car all day, but there are rental cars available. Just see that guy over there and you'll be on your way in minutes. We're open 24-7, so if you need fuel when you return, it won't take long for the fuel truck. Just let one of us know." She swiped Ferg's credit card.

Ferg replied, "Top both sides, Jet A, and please service the lav and the interior. See ya later!" He turned to walk over to the rental car desk.

"Oh, ah, help yourself to coffee, water, or soft drinks, and there are fresh cookies in the lounge," she said, smiling coquettishly, hoping to catch Logan's attention.

Logan approached the rental car desk as the young man looked up and smiled. "We need a large SUV, if possible, for the day, two days max." He handed the young man Ferg's driver's license and credit card.

"Sure. I've got three large vehicles, a Tahoe and two Suburbans. All gassed up and ready to go."

"We'll take a Suburban. Don't care which one. You pick."

"Yes, sir. White Suburban okay?"

"That'll work." The rental agreement was printed out, and Logan initialed and signed.

"It's brand-new, and there's no damage. If you want me to walk around with you, I'll gladly do so," he said, smiling at Logan.

"Not necessary. It's noted on the agreement." Logan was handed the keys and walked out the side door to the parking lot.

Tossing the keys to Dav, he said, "You drive. You know where we're going."

"Roger." Logan tossed him the keys and walked to the rear of the Suburban to help Lilly load the gear.

"You'll like this training facility," Lilly expressed to Logan.

"How much practice have you had with these scooters?" Logan asked Lilly.

"Once, here in their big pool. Dav's been out with it in open water, so this'll be a first for me as well."

"What's your take on this equipment?" he said, speaking to Dav.

"Best I've tried so far. Hardest thing to get used to is relaxing while the cone protects you from excessive force. Normally, you gotta have your face mask really secure, and your arms get stressed after a while. You'll see."

CHAPTER 54

After commiserating with Justin via live AV screen late yesterday and first thing, Rae spent the rest of the morning in Sub3 reprinting pictures and transposing notes in Hicks's handwriting from Logan's EXL90 programmed pen, compiling the evidence Justin would hide in Hicks's office. She was careful not to transmit fingerprints or other telltale forensics on the collateral itself.

Rae's cache was comprised of pictures of Hicks receiving half a kilo of cocaine from DeSalva at the airport, of the Zohdolofskis by the Zavadolsk ship, of DeSalva and Veronica, implicating her and Marc in DeSalva's drug business; three years of bank transfer photocopies from CS&T and money laundering in three banks, photocopies of money transfers to RJ, and notes on the firebomb of Biotechné in Montreal, linking DeSalva, Venice Capital, and Pingston Financial Securities; notes crafted in a new black book on DeSalva's father-in-law, expanding the drug business in the southwest, and his rank within the New Jersey drug syndicate; notes incriminating RJ as a hit man, and corresponding payments hinting connection to the drug syndicate; and finally notes, incriminating the Zohdolofskis and Bocharev by Hicks. This daytime drama would soon unfold.

As Rae completed her parcel, she carefully placed the contents in a large envelope and carried it upstairs to Pete for a last review. Wearing latex gloves, Rae tapped on Pete's glass office door. He motioned for her to come in. "Do you have a minute to look through this collateral to see if I've omitted something of importance?" asked Rae.

"Spread it on the table. We'll look at it together," replied Pete.

"I have plastic gloves if you need them."

"No. You can show me each page and picture, assuming there are notes on the back showing dates and times, etc."

Rae nodded and began sequentially with four pictures: (1) Dmitry and DeSalva exiting the airport to the limo, briefcase in Dmitry's hand, (2) Dmitry handing DeSalva the briefcase in the limo, (3) DeSalva and Hicks in the limo, Hicks holding the cocaine, and (4) DeSalva exiting the limo with the briefcase. Pete continued to scrutinize the next group of pictures of the Russian diplomat Sergei Zodohlofski and his son Ilia Zodohlofski standing in front of the Zavadolsk cargo ship. Pete studied the pictures without conversation.

"I discussed this at length with Justin this morning. I have plenty of time to change or transpose more notes or reprint as he won't arrive here until tomorrow afternoon."

Pete grinned at the newest picture of DeSalva and Veronica, dated recently, as Rae watched intently. This was a photo Rae had not seen until she received it yesterday. Pete moved on through the photocopies of electronic bank transfers in and out of Caspian Shipping & Transport Ltd. and the three banks associated with DeSalva's arms and drug shipments money laundering.

"The feds will have their heyday with this evidence. Do you know why we went back three years?"

"To keep Logan and me from potential involvement?"

"Absolutely. There's a slim chance that involvement may happen all on its own as a tertiary matter of investigative procedure way down the line, but only if law enforcement or the feds get wind of you two through sheer digging into past corporate business issues. But you and Logan are only the innocent victims of a fouled corporate takeover attempt. You have a well-documented history—winning a temporary injunction, lawsuits, lawyers, court appearances, and your own business story—to relay should it ever come to that.

"Your lawyers will be your best witnesses of fact, and don't forget how quickly your former employees will squeal like pigs when the shit hits the fan and they hear about their old workmate Sullivan and DeSalva being involved with drugs. What do you think will happen when they get visited by the feds or local cops? Odds are, they'll sing like canaries within the first five minutes, and you two will be exonerated before you're involved. You're clean as a whistle," remarked Pete as he continued, ending his review as he perused the names, addresses, and meeting dates and times along with ancillary notes written by Hicks in his little black book of secrets.

"This is very thorough. All of this will be corroborated by third-party witnesses. That's very good. As I said before, once the feds sift through this, the shit will hit the fan! Between the feds and local PD, each will be chomping at the bit to dig into everyone's personal life—friends, family, coworkers, and staff. This is high-profile stuff. Careers are made and wrecked over stuff like this. There will be turf conflict between the homeboys and the feds. Especially, BATF and DEA will have control issues. That is, until the Justice Department steps in. Besides search warrants and raids, all those that are or were connected to Dino and Hicks will find their life turned upside down. Hell, they'll probably subpoena the damn mail carrier, for Christ's sake." Pete chuckled heartily.

"That's funny. Good enough for me."

"I'd say this is bulletproof. It's not too much, just enough to stir up a hornet's nest. That's all that's required. And after this mission is over, you and Logan should feel that justice has been served." Pete smiled.

"We're both happy to see justice served all across the board. By chance, did you give Justin the idea to link Marc and his wife to drugs?"

"Yes, and that rogue agent with that biotech company from Montreal. Again, misdirect. Get him for his crimes without involving you and Logan."

"It's quite brilliant. And thank you. It saves us from more heartache," Rae said sincerely.

"Since our boys are off at summer camp taking swim lessons, why don't you and I and one of those two break for lunch?" Pete looked out on the floor of Ops, noting Alex and Skip were on duty. "We can flip a coin and see who wins." He walked out, announcing that one of the two would be lucky to have lunch with the boss. Ha!

Skip, donning a headset with boom microphone, was busy talking intently to someone on screen and waved off. "I guess you're the lucky one, Alex." Rae laughed as the three ambled down the hall to the dining area, saying to Pete, "One could get very spoiled working here. The food is quite good."

"There are days that boredom seems unrelenting, but there are also days where you'll beg for just one minute of peace," said Pete.

"Hear, hear," said Alex, nodding. "You just haven't been here long enough."

Walking beyond the appetizer selections, Alex cited, "You're right, the food is good here. Hell, I don't eat this good at home."

"Nothing to complain about here." She requested the lasagna and a side salad to one of the cooks serving today's specials.

As they each made their way to a table, Rae asked Pete, "These two weren't here yesterday. Do you experience high turnover? I mean, do a lot of the support staff travel here daily?"

"No. Just like Sub3 analysts, they work 4-3—four full days, three days off. You've never seen the living quarters beyond Sub3. It supports up to thirty people. While they're here, though, they're on call. They earn 40 percent higher salary with good benefits. For many, it's an opportunity not found elsewhere. Those that commute in from Reno have moved their family from other states for this employment opportunity."

Just then, the kitchen manager walked over to their table to meet the newcomer. First acknowledging Pete, his boss, then sidestepping beyond Alex to greet Rae holding out his hand, he said, "Hello. I'm Adolfo, the kitchen manager."

Turning sideways in her chair to shake his hand, she responded, "Very nice to meet you, Adolfo. I'm Rae. You certainly know how to spoil us here."

"Thank you. I am pleased to hear that. I just wanted you to know that we enjoy it when there are special occasions to celebrate, like birthdays and anniversaries. We only need two days' notice, and we'll be happy to make something special for you."

"That's very kind of you. I'll keep that in mind," remarked Rae, smiling as Adolfo acknowledged Pete for the interruption, and retreated to the kitchen.

Looking at Alex, Pete asked, "When are you starting net interference?"

"Right after lunch," replied Alex. "The rest of today and all of tomorrow, then it's baptism by fire. She's about ready for a full day of desk duty."

"Good," replied Pete as he got up from the table with his dinnerware.

"Alex, are you giving me too much credit?" Rae asked hesitantly.

"Why do you think I am?"

"Not sure. You guys all have so much field experience. It seems so easy for you."

"Yes, field experience, not overwatch experience. We all learned it the same as you will."

"That makes me feel better."

"Believe me, we all had issues with one thing or another. Electronic surveillance, multiple computer programs, aerospace technology—it's all mind-boggling at first, but we have great people downstairs that are immensely helpful. Hell, I still can't type worth a damn, but I get the job done," he said, chuckling in his reply.

"Thanks. I don't feel so inept now. I actually like it."

"I know you do. That was one of the high points of your psych eval."

"Psych eval? Really?"

"Yes, really. We all had the same psych eval. We have eval every six months. They indicate strengths and weaknesses," replied Alex as he picked up his dinnerware. "I'll meet you in Ops in thirty."

"I'll check on Sheba. See you there." Rae finished her meal.

Alex turned back. "If she's as quiet as everyone says, go ahead and bring her."

"Wow. Okay, I will. Thanks."

CHAPTER 55

Rae liked the feel of her BDUs and tactical work boots. They were comfortable yet practical with side leg pockets. The boots provided all-day support but weren't clumsy. She hadn't thought about their other business for days. As she opened the door to their room, she realized Logan was right all along. Geoff Wuesthoffer was a great manager, good for the company, and the business was humming along just fine without her, so guilt did not enter her thoughts as Sheba greeted her with enthusiasm.

"Come, girl, let's go for a walk." She grabbed some treats as they walked to the elevator. With a few of the guys absent, Ops seemed rather noiseless as they bypassed the entrance to Ops and continued down the hallway to the back door patio. The sun was high in the sky, warming the landscape. They ambled beyond the patio and the shooting range and walked up the hill toward the radomes. Sheba walked off trail and swiftly did her business, and the two hustled a fast-pace half-mile walk back to Ops, Sheba sniffing the fresh scents of the arid surroundings.

Sheba kept an even pace with Rae by her right side as Rae opened the back door to Ops and walked over to Alex's workstation. Alex looked up as Rae commanded, "Sheba, friend." Sheba sat, lifting her right paw for Alex to shake hands. Alex obliged and shook her paw and patted her on the head. "Sit in my chair and request an updated SITREP." Rae sat, and Sheba lay quietly by Rae's chair.

"You've done a great job with her," claimed Alex.

Rae pressed a function key and typed "Dino" in the dialogue box. Up on the screen popped the SITREP from yesterday afternoon. Across the top of the SITREP were the characters N/C. Rae asked Alex, "Does N/C mean 'no change'?"

"Yes. What does it say at the bottom?"

"OPBRE 1510."

"What else?"

"Pete's initials and three others," replied Rae.

"Yes. That means Pete held an Ops briefing at 1510 yesterday and brought Lilly, Dav, and Logan up to speed. Their initials are below Pete's as he was the briefer and they were attendees. Skip and I have read this as a matter of course. Our initials appear in the Read Only box. When you're on overwatch, you're required to be up to speed, interpret, and act on information in the SITREP during a mission or, when required, a minimum of twice daily. If you're not part of a briefing, you'll place your initials here where Skip and I placed ours yesterday, showing Pete and the team we are also on the same page as they are. Information in SITREPs is our lifeline," expressed Alex.

"Understood." Rae read the entire brief and added her initials in the Read Only box. "This is so well-orchestrated," she commented to Alex.

"You know, Pete's just not another pretty face." Alex acknowledged Skip walking back in from a lunch break.

Rae acknowledged Skip as he stopped and knelt by Sheba. "She knows you're a friend. You won't have to worry about her." Skip scratched behind her ears, and she moved her head, enjoying the attention.

Skip sat down, picking up where he left off, as Alex began instruction on DEIS Directed Energy Interference Source. "We're testing a new energy beam control device from DARPA. As a new type of cyber warfare, this device is highly effective at jamming, capable of completely disrupting communication and operations of opposition forces. These devices typically require a lot of electrical power, but we'll scab some energy from the boat for this short window. Right before Lilly aims the beam at the *Opulenza*, you'll give 'em a new SATRAK frequency, keeping our comms up. You may be toggling between two birds, but this op shouldn't take that long. The device will be covered by a hollowed-out ice cooler on the back deck.

The only thing you'll have to watch closely is monitoring the margin around the *Opulenza* so it doesn't interfere with our comms."

"How does it work?" asked Rae.

"This device will be dialed down to under 100 MHz to disrupt radio frequencies through a series of pulses. It blocks incoming and outgoing radio signals."

"Will Dino know it?"

"Not unless they're trying to call another boat."

"What about Dino's sat phone?"

"We'll be watching and can dial the beam up to 500 MHz to jam any outgoing call. Even if Dino is lucky enough to get a call out, they'll be shark bait."

CHAPTER 56

Dav pulled the Suburban into the parking lot of the school's commercial dive building. "This will just take a few. Come on and meet a buddy of mine." Lilly and Logan followed Dav. They walked down the hall beyond the classroom to the instructor's office.

They stepped inside. "Lyle, I want you to meet a buddy of mine." As the three walked in, Dav pointed out Logan to his friend.

Logan stepped up. "Roger Ferguson," he said, shaking Lyle's hand.

Staring at Lilly, Lyle kidded, "You still having to babysit this knucklehead?" He put his arm around Dav, goofing passively.

"Yeah. You know how it is." Lilly was grinning sheepishly.

Dav interjected, "Lyle here is lending us a boat so we can get some open water time."

"That's super," replied Lilly, laughing. "Maybe we'll finally teach him something."

Lyle stated, "Just put some fuel in before you leave."

Logan replied, "Absolutely. Nice to meet you." The three left to go trial the new equipment.

Back outside, Dav asked, "Catch the deep round pool?"

"Yeah. I guessed underwater welding and commercial diving pool."

"Right on, brother," replied Dav.

Thirty-five minutes later, they were parked in front of a charter service where Dav's friend Lyle kept a Breaux commercial dive boat the guys were borrowing. "Sizeable winch," noted Logan as he carried his scooter and dive bag to the boat.

"Yeah. Lyle's known for finding all kinds of crap."

244

Lilly asked, "We're using Dr*ä*gers, aren't we?"

Dav replied, "Yep. Need to take 'em to their drop-dead time." He started the engine.

Lilly untied the boat from the dock, and they launched. Dav piloted them through choppy water, bypassing the NOSC Tower Wreck. After fifteen minutes, he throttled back to neutral, placing them five miles off Mission Beach. Lilly threw out the dive buoy and pole flag and pulled another flag up off the back winch. "Time to suit up," Dav chimed as he unzipped his dive bag and began suiting up. The other two followed suit.

"You ever use a rebreather before?" Logan asked Lilly.

"Nope. Only tanks."

"If the rebreather fails, switch to your standby bottle by turning this nozzle counterclockwise," he said, demonstrating how to turn on the standby compressed air valve attached to the side of the BC (buoyancy compensator). "This gives you about ten minutes of compressed air breathing."

After all three were suited up, Dav demonstrated where to insert the closed-circuit rebreather in the bottom slot of the full-face dive mask and set the timer on his dive watch. The others followed suit. Dav hooked a bungee to his DPV, dropped it in the water, and rolled off the back of the boat. He popped up, treading water, awaiting arrival of the other two. Logan hooked a bungee to his DPV scooter, dropped it in the water, and rolled off the back of the boat, popping up, awaiting further instructions. Lilly was last and hooked up to his DPV, dropped it, and joined them in the water.

"Comm check, everyone. Logan?"

Logan responded, "Crystal."

Lilly responded, "Clear."

Dav stated, "Face mask tight?" He received a thumbs-up from both. "Okay. Let the air out of your BCs, and we'll get neutral at twenty." As they descended slowly, Dav began again, "Watch how I slip inside the cone and start the scooter. I'll keep it at idle and let you know when to increase your speed. It'll show on this display." He pointed to a digital display gauge in the center. "We're going for fifteen knots today. If you have trouble, yell." Dav grabbed the edge of the shield, pulling himself inside, grabbing the left side of the yoke and starting its propeller. Looking left, he noticed Logan had successfully maneuvered inside the shield and started its propeller. Lilly followed suit, and all three were idling at twenty feet, awaiting further instruction.

"Turning ninety degrees. Speed to five knots. Logan, my left. Lilly, my right." Dav led the trio toward shore. After three minutes, he said, "Now ten knots. Turning ninety degrees." Lilly and Logan picked up their speed, remaining within Dav's peripheral vision. "Follow me." Dav descended fifteen feet. "Now pick your speed up to fifteen and back up to twenty feet." Neither Lilly nor Logan bumped Dav for the next thirty minutes as the threesome zigzagged underwater almost as if they were in formation as Dav kept them diving and turning frequently.

Lilly announced that his heads-up display showed 14 percent air exchange remaining. Logan's display showed 22 percent remaining. Dav announced to Lilly, "When you get to 7 percent, tell me and we'll head back to the boat. I'm keeping us within a half mile so we can get back without having to surface swim."

Climbing back aboard the boat, Dav stated to Logan, who was the first to board, "Lilly went thirty-eight minutes and still had 3 percent left. He's a heavy breather. We shouldn't need more than twenty tops, out and back."

"Agreed. I show 15 percent left." He reached down, pulling Lilly up on deck. Lilly chuckled to Logan as he pulled off the dive mask. "I guess you're just long-winded, eh?"

"Yeah, yeah, yeah." All three cackled while removing and storing their gear. Dav started the engines while Logan retrieved the dive buoy and flag.

Dav asked Logan, "What's your opinion of the equipment?"

"I thought the hydroskin was going to be cumbersome, but it wasn't. No complaints. Overall, I was quite comfortable. I thought I'd have to take in more air than I expelled, but that wasn't the case either, and I'm really surprised there was no fogging."

"I thought the same thing initially. The scooters are easy to maneuver with the cone. Neither of you seemed to have difficulty." Dav turned the idling boat back toward the Mission Beach inlet.

"It should go like clockwork on Thursday. We'll come back and dive the Yukon another time. No deep diving and flying right after." Dav pushed full throttle, heading back to the marina.

"I'll top off the fuel tank." Logan slapped Dav on the shoulder before he stepped to the back of the boat.

"Good. I always do the same."

Approaching the fuel dock, Lilly lassoed the front dock cleat to tie the bow of the boat to the dock while Logan secured the back as Dav throttled the bow thrusters and shut down the engines. Logan jumped out and walked down to the fuel shack. The attendant was orderly, stepping out of the fuel shack. His appearance reminded Logan of Parrotheads, the nickname for Jimmy Buffet fans, because of his wispy blond hair, Hawaiian shirt, yellow golf shorts, and untied green canvas shoes concealing a well-tanned body. As Logan approached, he expected to hear "Margaritaville" or another popular Buffett song playing on the radio inside the shack.

After topping the tank, the attendant handed Ferg his copy of the credit card receipt. Ferg thanked him and walked back, unhooking the line from the back cleat and jumping aboard. Lilly unhooked the front line, pushing the boat away from the dock, as the threesome made headway to Lyle's slip in the marina.

*****

Lilly and Logan finished loading their gear in the back and climbed in the idling Suburban, ready to head back to Montgomery Field. As they were driving, Logan rechecked winds aloft after loading the inverse flight plan GPS heading 339 into Foreflight on his iPad. He remarked to the guys, "We'll fly back at 15.5, fifteen thousand five hundred, picking up a twenty-eight-knot tail wind. That should get us in just over one hour."

"All right, then," remarked Lilly. "That earns you the right to buy the beer. Don't you think, Dav?"

"Hell yeah!"

"Beer it is," bade Logan as he laughed along willingly. "I can easily get in trouble with you two."

"Nah. Close, but no cigar," snorted Dav.

"I wouldn't bet on that," teased Lilly.

Logan interrupted the laughter. "It looks like both MOA's (military operational areas) just went active. We'll vector around 'em and come in from the northwest, so add another eight minutes."

"Well, then, given this unsettling news, now you'll absolutely have to buy the beer," mocked Lilly as they continued to razz each other.

CHAPTER 57

During a midafternoon break, Rae checked with Alexei in CIS for an updated status of DeSalva's whereabouts. Alexei advised her that all chatter regarding Dino had remained unchanged. There were a few minor updates, noting there was no overwatch action required until the morning **SITREP** and **OPBRE**. She would request a **SITREP** first thing tomorrow before net interference training.

Justin called Rae via AV live on her phone, updating her on his pending arrival the next day. After a few minutes, Rae commented, "You've been bird-watching, I see."

"Yep. That's why they pay me the big bucks. Should've been a private investigator. Could've enjoyed catching cheating spouses." He chuckled.

"So what time should we expect you?"

"Between two and three."

"All right, then. See you tomorrow afternoon." Rae signed off. Apologizing for the interruption, Rae asked Skip, "How often do you live track the guys during a mission?"

"Depends. It's 24-7 during covert missions but intermittently during mission set up at prescheduled checkpoints and time checks, unless one's been missed, then it's all eyes and ears."

"For this upcoming mission, what would be your suggestion?"

"I'd suggest you monitor the team intermittently on Tuesday after establishing checkpoints, their arrival in La Paz, the airstrip, the marina. If all check-ins are without incident, then as needed until mission launch. We can jump on Milstar and watch them drive, but that's wasted time. If an unexpected situation occurs, that's when we turn on all the channels."

"You mean if someone or something impedes them, then it's all eyes and ears to feed their lifeline?"

"Yes. For instance, if the boys need eyes all around to ensure no interdiction occurs in hostile territory, then we'd be on point, watching them live, traveling at night, absolutely. Even Sub3 watches. They're passing through cartel country. They don't need anyone going all narc on them."

"Understood."

"So let's go ahead and check in on our swim team." He walked over to Alex's station where Rae was working. "What bird is on point now?"

Rae checked the time readout on the bottom of her monitor and punched a top-row function key. "Geo2." A live satellite image of a topographical circumference surrounding San Diego appeared on one of Alex's station monitors.

"Now how would you hone in on their location?" asked Skip.

"Since I'm not aware of any active SATRAK device, I'm guessing input one of the team's microchip is the most accurate over phone locator."

"Yes. Phones and devices can get lost or destroyed. The drop-down window allows you to choose who to track." He pointed where to click on the screen with this trackball mouse.

"Okay. I'll choose Lilly." Rae clicked on Lilly's name in the window. She stared as the live satellite picture coming in from space rapidly shrank and panned across several square miles encompassing city buildings, homes, roads, land, beach, and ocean, shrank and panned over an outgoing container ship and a handful of fishing boats in the ocean, then finally zeroing in on the boat Dav was piloting toward the inlet. She could see them clearly as if a drone was directly above them using a high-resolution video camera.

"It looks like they've finished diving and are headed inland." Rae observed the wake spreading behind the boat.

"Good deduction, Watson." He smiled. "Don't forget to keep an eye on the time when the visual pattern wanes and Geo3 takes point.

"There's twenty-seven minutes and forty-three seconds counting down before transition."

"Now switch to I-Vision thermal and tell me if you can quickly distinguish who is who," stated Skip.

Rae depressed the Function T10 key, and the live broadcast turned black and white of the boat and crew. Rae mentioned, "It's not hard to distinguish one from another. This is super high def. Lilly's sitting in the back, Logan's port side, holding the bridge ladder, and Dav's piloting the boat."

"Good."

"Why is this video feed so much clearer than the thermal imaging we viewed at Justin's?"

"I-Vision was presented to the Marine Corps a few years back. Tested at Nellis Air Force Base in Nevada, it beat all participants' tests hands down, 100 meters to 1,500 meters, moving vehicle to vehicle, wireless. The corps specced in the handheld versions, but the Pentagon overseers awarded the contract to a big corporation, who still can't produce this type of resolution. Even the commandant couldn't get it through. They had the nerve to request this chap provide his proprietary-targeting software to the corporation that received the award. The chap smartly refused and told 'em to blow it. Personally, I would've done the same. If those at the Pentagon hadn't been compromised, there'd be far less soldier lethality today as this is the best I've ever used. Pete got wind of it through DARPA, and here we are."

"Is there ever a need to switch birds early?"

"Possibly. There may be a time when solar flares interfere, which can scramble the signal, but it's highly unlikely. We boost our signal strength over all commercial satellite systems," remarked Skip. "It's nothing like the pixilation problems that occur during thunderstorms when watching TV."

Just then, Rae's phone buzzed with an onscreen AV call from Lilly as the boat moved at wake speed through the inlet. "We'll be landing in about two hours. Logan lost the sales contest again, so he's buying the beer. You three wanna join us?"

Rae held her phone up so Skip and Alex could chime in. "I'm going for a run first. Count me in," replied Skip. Alex gave a thumbs-up, standing behind Rae at his workstation.

"At 1800 for bevvy it is." Lilly signed off.

Rae looked bewildered. Alex sat down next to her smiling, "You'll get used to the wordplay. This isn't a party, it's a team thing. Camaraderie and information exchange in a casual setting. That's all," replied Alex.

"It's never boring, that's for sure."

"Let's take a short break and get some fresh air at the range out back," replied Alex. "Grab a couple boxes of ammo from the storeroom and meet me in ten."

"Shall do," replied Rae as she looked over at Skip who had sat back down at his workstation.

"How will Sheba react to gun shots?" asked Skip.

"She isn't frightened by thunder and lightning. What do you think Alex, should I bring her?"

"Yes."

Rae summoned Sheba to walk down to the storeroom with her and out to the shooting range. Sheba seemed to enjoy the fresh air and ever-changing scents.

Rae and Sheba walked out to the stanchions as Alex was double tapping the targets with his M11. Rae intently watching Sheba's body language as the closer they approached the recoiling noise of each gunshot intensified. Rae stopped twenty feet behind Alex, commanding Sheba to sit and stay. Sheba complied. Rae pulled her M11 from her holster and let Sheba smell it and walked up next to Alex.

Alex gave Rae a paper silhouette and she walked downrange to set it up next to Alex's. Starting off at twenty-five feet, she walked back to the stanchion and began double tapping the target. After she emptied her M11, she looked back at Sheba, who hadn't flinched. Rae and Alex reloaded another clip, and both began double tapping their silhouette targets together. Rae looked back at Sheba, elated to see her watching them with no appearance of distress.

Alex commented, "She seems to be taking this all in stride."

"I'm shocked. I expected her to fret or run," replied Rae.

Rae walked back to check on Sheba. Sheba sniffed the M11 that was back in Rae's side holster while Rae knelt nuzzling her head in reassurance. Rae gave her a couple of treats and walked back to practice drawing and shooting.

After running through their ammo, Alex called it a day. Rae summoned Sheba up to the stanchion to walk with her to retrieve their silhouettes and both jogged back to catch up with Alex walking back to Ops.

"I suggest you bring her closer next practice round, a little at a time, finally having her sit next to you," stated Alex. "I think you'll find she'll assimilate quickly."

"I'm hopeful," replied Rae. "She's surpassed my expectations," as they entered Ops and Rae and Sheba walked back to Alex's workstation.

Rae had just finished reading and initialing an updated SITREP on screen when Lilly called into Ops via live AV from the cockpit. Alex reached around Rae and turned up the volume as both Logan and Lilly were on screen with Dav crouching down behind them in the doorway. Lilly spoke through his headset mic, "Landing in thirty. Luke Skywalker here is buying the beer tonight. See you in the sky lounge for dinner. Rae started laughing and chimed right in, "So, is the force with Jedi Skywalker?"

Dav piped in, "Yeah... The force is with him," as Logan laughed and shook his head.

Skip joined in, "I feel like a Michelob Ultra. Catch you later."

"Any SITREP changes?" asked Logan. Sheba's ears perked up hearing his voice.

"No changes. Do you need a hand unloading?"

Dav said, "We're good. Thanks."

Still grinning Logan said, "See you shortly," and ended the call.

"That's cool," replied Rae.

CHAPTER 58

The time was 6:06 p.m. Skip and Alex had departed earlier for an evening run. Rae could see Pete commiserating on the AV screen in his office. He looked resolute. Rae and Sheba were the only ones left in Ops. Rae had been tracking their inbound flight. She checked with Alexei before she switched overwatch to Sublevel 3 for the evening. She stood up from Alex's workstation and spoke to Sheba. "Let's go see Logan." The guys were less than two minutes out.

As Rae and Sheba walked down the hill to the backside of the hangar, Logan had just taxied the plane off the runway, stopping in front of the hangar. He set the brakes and began his shutdown checklist, allowing the engine two minutes of cooldown time while Lilly operated the remote switch, opening the hangar door.

Dav was the first out, retrieving the tug used to maneuver and park the plane. Lilly began unloading their gear as Logan stored the headsets, conducted a double-check of all switches, and shut down the engine before exiting.

Sheba perked up as Logan walked up to greet them. He knelt and nuzzled her. Rae mentioned, "She handled herself remarkably at the range today. She didn't get spooked when Alex and I shot a couple of rounds."

"She's something. How was your day?" asked Logan as he picked up a gear bag, walking into the hangar.

"Jam-packed and interesting. Justin will be here tomorrow afternoon."

"I'm looking forward to seeing him," replied Logan.

"Me too." Rae grabbed the cart and rolled it over to where Lilly had dropped the gear bags and DPVs. "Any more gear bags or equipment?" she asked.

"This is it," replied Dav as they loaded them on the cart.

"Storeroom?" asked Logan as Dav was closing the hangar door. "That'll work."

Logan and Lilly finished storing the gear and walked back to the elevator. On the ride up, Logan said to Lilly, "I'm gonna take a quick shower. Meet you in ten."

As the door opened and Lilly turned back, he responded, "Ditto."

Sheba was busy eating and Rae was changing into casual clothes when Logan walked in. He picked her up and put her over his shoulder as he walked toward the shower, laughing. "You've had a fun day." She giggled while struggling to break free of his grasp.

"I missed you," he said as he set her down in the bathroom and turned the shower on. "Join me." He pulled her into the shower with him.

"You stinker!" she teased as she succumbed to kisses under the warm water.

*****

The casual evening kicked off at about 6:30 p.m. in the dining room. As each arrived, they grabbed a cold beer and sat down at a large table and began nibbling on appetizers the kitchen had prepared while they reiterated the day's events coupled with spurious mission updates. Manny stopped by to query the guys about the equipment trial as it related to the upcoming mission.

After Skip and Alex straggled in, Rae reiterated the latest intel from Alexei. Talk of the mission unintentionally became more focused when Manny asked Dav to engage Lilly and Logan to convey their take on the equipment audition and how the equipment would influence the mission. Lilly expressed his confidence in the new DPVs performance and how well Logan functioned as a first-timer. Logan echoed the same about the DPVs and dive gear but insisted that he and Dav conduct a run-through and that all four conduct a mock exercise before launch as timing was crucial. Manny was keen hearing the sweet words of Logan's resolve.

As an aside to Skip and Alex, Rae mentioned that Mazatlán was both a cargo and cruise line port and that ship traffic could potentially be more active than previously considered. She asked both of them, "Hypothetically, what if ship traffic is either too frequent or too close to successfully pull off the mission as planned?"

Skip acknowledged, stating, "I'll task a couple of analysts to govern for contingencies."

"So the guys most probably would delay the launch based on unexpected interlopers?"

"Yes," replied Skip.

Alex pulled Manny into the conversation, posing, "Any thought to contingency if one or more ships that pass by are too close?"

"Yes," replied Manny. "There should always be contingencies. Logan and I discussed a couple. First, cut communication, lob poisonous gas onto the boat, and sink it without using explosives. That takes far more time than I'd be willing to sacrifice. A hit on all three, but that leaves too much evidence. The Houdini plan, the disappearing act, is by far the least traceable."

Logan interjected, addressing the others, "The only problem I foresee could be too much traffic nearby. How would you sink the boat quickly without explosives?"

Alex jumped in, saying, "Ever wield an underwater saw? It'd work, but it's heavy, clumsy, and dangerous, especially at night without practice. The plan as it stands now is perfect, but we all know how quickly things go south. That said, we only have seven hours to complete our mission. That really lends only a five-hour window with two hours to exfil."

Manny interjected, "The Coast Guard will be busy preparing to intersect with the Zavadolsk and have rerouted additional vessels, so they'll be patrolling just outside the harbor. No worries there. All eyes will be watching north—and south-running cargo liners. The moon will be a waning crescent, so not much light. We can run dark."

"Any concern about unexpected bad weather?" asked Rae.

Dav piped in, "That'd work in our favor."

"Yeah, it would," affirmed Lilly. "Missions can be more successful as targets usually retreat in bad weather."

"Should bad weather develop, our exposure is minimal at best. We'd take full advantage of it," replied Logan confidently.

Manny added a last comment. "Let's finalize a plan B by Monday morning's **OPBRE**. Until then, enjoy the weekend." He got up to grab another beer.

The social interaction continued all through the evening meal. Rae and Logan called Justin via AV on her phone. He answered. "Hey, Rae. What's up?"

Logan spoke. "You got plans tomorrow night?"

"Not really. Pete and I have some catching up, but that won't take long. What's on your mind?"

Rae responded, "We thought it might be fun to go into Reno under disguise and thought you might want to tag along."

"I'll know more tomorrow after meeting with Pete. Let's say a tentative yes for now."

"Good," said Logan.

"Okay, then," said Rae. "See you tomorrow."

Before departing for the night, Rae asked a couple of the guys who had just witnessed their conversation with Justin, "Are there rules or policies about going into Reno for a short time prior to a mission?"

Alex responded, "We never leave Ops the day before launch, but for a short time this weekend, it's not a problem. Use your new IDs."

Skip piped in, "If you need someone to take Sheba outside while you're gone, I'll take care of her."

"Thanks. She has both a collar and a lead harness. Either would be the safe route. We'll know more tomorrow," replied Rae.

CHAPTER 59

Logan and Rae rose early to get a good run in before breakfast. Sheba was excited to explore up by the radomes, especially early morning. The sun was warming the landscape as they walked out the back door and began stretching. Sheba was sniffing the morning scents, eager to get some exercise.

"Why don't we practice at the range after breakfast and see how she reacts?" Logan asked as he set a nice rhythm for them.

"That's a great idea," replied Rae. "I expect she'll be fine with you there."

After ten minutes, Logan whispered, "Let's pick up the pace and let her run."

"I won't be able to keep pace with you uphill for long, so go for it."

"Sheba, let's go," commanded Logan as he started sprinting. Rae kept pace for about twenty seconds as Logan and Sheba were outpacing her. Sheba could easily outrun Logan, but she remained close by his side as they sprinted together the half mile. Logan slowed the pace until they reached the top of the hill where he stopped to let Sheba walk about while Rae caught up. They kept a nice, easy stride on the downhill return.

After breakfast, Rae and Logan took Sheba to the outdoor range. Logan set up the silhouettes at thirty feet. Rae remained about twenty feet behind with Sheba as before. Rae knelt next to Sheba while Logan started shooting his M11, reloading and double-tapping through a second clip.

Rae pulled her M11 from her side holster, letting Sheba sniff it. Then Rae stood up and commanded Sheba to accompany her as they walked up behind Logan, who finished double-tapping through a second clip. Logan turned around, letting Sheba sniff his M11. Praising her, he knelt and nuzzled her. She seemed calm.

"I'll stay right here with her off to your side," replied Logan. "You step up and shoot a few, and let's see what happens." Logan commanded, "Sheba stay." She sat immediately.

Rae stepped one stride forward and shot one round, turning around to look at Sheba. Sheba was watching intently but had not flinched. Rae turned back and double-tapped the silhouette twice in a row and turned around again to check once again. No flinching.

Logan stood up and stepped up next to Rae. "Let's both shoot a couple of rounds." He emptied his clip just before Rae and turned back to see Sheba sitting calmly and stepped back, letting her sniff his M11. No apparent fear. Rae followed, letting Sheba sniff her M11. They both praised her with fond nuzzling.

"I think she just passed the test," replied Rae.

Logan said, "I'd bring her out to get used to higher caliber noise to be sure."

Just then, Skip walked up, hearing Logan's comment. "I've been watching from the patio. She's not skittish." He scratched Sheba on the head.

"I'm surprised," replied Logan. "Never having been around guns, I expected her to be gun-shy."

"She's a good girl!" Rae praised Sheba affectionately.

"It usually takes time to get them used to the piercing noise without repetition and positive reinforcement," said Skip. "It took me a solid week with my pointer before I could rely on her fetching the pheasants, not running for home."

"Besides Central California, is there good bird hunting around here?" asked Logan.

"Yeah, north and south of Reno. Carson City is also good and near the border."

"After this is over, we should plan a couple of days," said Logan. "Do the other guys hunt?"

"No bird. Deer and elk mostly."

"Do you hunt, Rae?"

"Nah. You guys should go." Rae stood up, looking at Logan. "I'm going in for an update. You want to keep her here?"

"Go ahead and take her in. I'm going to shoot some more," replied Logan. "Join me?" he asked Skip.

"Sure. I'll go back and get more ammo and pick up the .45s." Skip caught up with Rae and Sheba heading into Ops. "Feel free to sit at either mine or Alex's."

"Okay. Thanks," she answered as they entered the building.

Rae and Sheba walked over to Alex's workstation. Alex had left Rae a Post-it note to notify all if anything new came in from Alexei or Sub3 analysts. Rae sat down and requested an updated **SITREP**. As she read through the **SITREP**, she was relieved that there hadn't been any changes in the past twelve hours. She annotated her acknowledgement of the N/C **SITREP** and noticed all but Skip and Logan had previously acknowledged the no-change **SITREP**. She sent both a quick text.

*****

Rae spent an hour reading the data log of Dino's communiqués for the past twenty-four hours. Dino had received two drawn-out voice messages from Veronica Sullivan last night, whining to him to come and have sex with her. She missed him, she wanted more cocaine—same old story. Dino hadn't replied to either message. He was laying low in Tahoe. Rae surmised Dino might be getting tired of little Ms. Sullivan and her pathetic antics.

Only a few days to launch. Rae felt a wave of anxiety flush over her thinking about the gravity of the mission. She put the thought aside as she received a text from Justin, who was fifteen minutes out. She texted Logan, who had been working with Dav since lunch at recalibrating the rebreathers and rechecking and repacking the dive gear and protective equipment. Lilly was testing the inflatable dinghy, starting its motor, and packing emergency survival gear.

Looking at Lilly, Logan stated, "We don't need this emergency position-indicating radio beacon." He placed it back on the shelf.

"Nope," Lilly responded. "EPIRBs are registered. That'd draw emergency response, and we sure as hell don't want that."

"How much ammo?" asked Logan.

Dav replied, "Three to four clips for your sidearm. Lilly and Manny will assemble the hardware."

"What's your thought about plan B?" Logan asked Dav while examining the detonator intended for the shaped charge.

"Me, I'd go for three headshots and blow it fast, but explosions draw attention. Even weather satellites may pick it up or the International Space Station. That's why I prefer us to be one hour, preferably two, in the opposite direction."

"Copy that. How hard is it to breach the hull, avoiding the fuel tanks, sinking it quickly?"

"This isn't a ten-footer. It's a sportfish. They're built pretty solid."

"We're still on track for placing undex between the fuel tanks one-third of the way from the back and mid hull?"

"Yeah. That's where I'd place them. It should sink quickly."

"Fire?"

"Oh yeah," sneered Dav. "The fuel may burn on the surface for a while, so it blew up. Shit happens. Even Forrest Gump says so."

"I keep arriving at the same conclusion. Anything that takes more than a few seconds to affix is a waste of time," replied Logan. "All we need to do is get there, place it, get back aboard ASAP, send the dragonfly over, watch it light up the sky, go dark just before, and run dark initially on our way back."

"Roger that. I'm on the same page," declared Lilly. "For plan B, though, I like RPGs, quick and dirty."

Dav insisted, "No RPGs. We need to keep our distance."

"I'll handle the hardware," replied Lilly. "It'll be a blast." They laughed in unison.

*****

Still reading Dino's communiqués, Rae was startled when Justin's face appeared in a window on the screen for entry into Ops.

She initiated opening the electronic door as Justin walked in. "Hey, stranger," uttered Justin as Rae stood up to greet him. Sheba's ears perked up, and she stood from lying down by Rae at Alex's workstation as Justin walked over.

"She's been hired too?" Justin asked spoofingly.

"She's been well-accepted."

Just then, Pete and Manny walked off the elevator from Sub3 straight to Pete's office, Manny motioning for Justin to follow. "Later," Justin said as he walked to Pete's office. Rae sat back down, signaling Sheba to lie down.

A few minutes later, the threesome was conversing with someone on Pete's AV monitor. Rae finished rereading the SITREP and decided she and Sheba needed to take a break and get some fresh air. Rae commanded Sheba, "Let's go for a walk." Sheba accompanied her out the back door.

CHAPTER 60

Monday rolled around like clockwork. Rae awoke early, sensing Logan was not next to her. Logan had arisen a full hour earlier and was on his second cup of coffee and going over his notes, preparing for the **OPBRE** at 0900 today. Rae tiptoed by Sheba at the foot of the bed, but she stirred regardless. Rae slipped on jeans and a T-shirt and walked over to Logan, who was intently reading, saying, "I'll take Sheba outside."

"Thanks, babe. I'll brew a fresh cup for ya."

Both experiencing nervous energy, it did Rae good to get some fresh air. She let Sheba wander about for a good fifteen minutes before returning to their room. Closing the door behind her as they walked in, Rae asked, "You feel like running this morning?"

"Not really, but I think it'd do us both good." Logan got up to pour Rae a fresh cup of coffee.

"Let's enjoy breakfast. We can always run later." She placed her hand on his shoulder.

*****

Rae and Logan left for breakfast a full hour early. Expecting to be the first in the dining hall, they were surprised to see all but Pete and Justin sitting together. Skip motioned to join the team, and they obliged. With their breakfast trays in hand, Logan turned to Rae. "Is it my imagination, or do you feel energy in the room?"

"I'm sensing it, almost like electrified ions before a thunderstorm." As they settled in, the pending mission trumped talk of the weekend activities. Excitement among the team was clear.

Skip asked Logan, "What's your plan B?"

"I'm with Dav on this one. Plant the charges, take 'em out, set *Opulenza* on a course for Mazatlán, swim back, and watch the fireworks. Thirty minutes tops."

"I hear ya. That's what I'd do. I like simple," said Skip.

Overhearing Skip's comment, Manny piped in, "Got my vote. No complications."

The chatter continued. Logan was back in his element. Glancing at her watch, Rae signaled Logan that she was going to Ops. He nodded as she departed for Ops, leaving Logan and the team discussing secondary issues. Walking to their room, Rae wished confidence would replace her apprehension. Struggling to mask her concern, she was thankful for Sheba.

*****

Pete summoned Logan to his office before the operations briefing. They discussed the business back home and Pete's concern about Logan's ELX90 and its disposition. Logan reassured Pete he eliminated any chance of his technology falling into the wrong hands.

"Wise move. You've made the smart choice," replied Pete. "This mastermind of yours is far too valuable. Even using it for this mission is risky. Only the three of us know of its existence."

"How about Justin? He's read the crafted notes in Hicks's handwriting," asked Logan.

"He believes Rae is very artistic. He knows no more. Let's keep it that way. Now go summon everyone for our mission briefing," directed Pete.

*****

Punctual as usual, Pete started the mission briefing, pointing to the center AV monitor. "The following updates are as follows. Hold your questions until the end."

- OPBRE 0900.

- No location change of Dino and Hicks. On target for launch at 0700 tomorrow.
- "Beginning Friday are the following."
- DOJ and SEC raids Venice Capital and Pingston Securities & Weissner.
- FBI raids Hicks's office; FBI raids Hicks's home.
- DOJ hands off raid of CS&T to FBI/BATF.
- DOJ/FBI visit Russian Embassy for Sergei Zohdolofski.
- BATF/DEA coordinate contraband arrival on Zavadolsk with USCG.
- FBI raids Bocharov's office.
- Russian CIS and SVR notified of RJ and Hicks's blackmail of NJ syndicate.
- USCG Gulf of California vessel diverted to San Diego for maintenance.
- USCG Station Seattle on plan to intercept Zavadolsk.

Just then, Justin walked up to Pete's office. Pete nodded, and Justin walked in and sat next to Rae. "Before we discuss the mission, let me recap the pending sequence of events. The trigger is pulled first thing Friday with simultaneous raids on Dino's securities companies. Those raids implicate Hicks. Hicks's office is raided, exposing drugs, racketeering, gun running, syndicate involvement, and capital crimes. Dino's shipping company is raided, pulling in the BATF, DEA, and Justice Department. Now enters the Russians and the diplomat. A BATF/DEA joint task force will discover the firebomb. They'll confiscate the contraband arriving on the Zavadolsk.

"The Russians will be looking for Dino, Hicks, Bocharov, and Zohdolofski. Dino's father-in-law will be looking for him too, most likely before his home is raided. Hell, they'll be looking for RJ too, if the Russians haven't already found him. They don't like loose ends. The Coast Guard, well, they're not a factor in the Gulf of California, and the cannon fodder will get their due when the homeboys question them about drugs, racketeering, and so on. Comments?"

Skip spoke first. "Analysts in Sub3 report two freighters inbound for Mazatlán on Thursday. No transit time as yet. North-bound transit pattern averages ten to fifteen miles off the coast. Most likely not a factor. We'll monitor ship traffic until exfil."

Alex interjected, "Weather will not be a factor. For eyes in the sky, the Brits have their birds over a suspected terrorist cell after last week's suicide bombing was foiled in Trafalgar Square. The International Space Station passes over Northern California midafternoon. No factor there. Water temp is 67 °F. I'd plug in the suits and use the waterproof bags for your sidearms."

Rae challenged, "There will be a handful of cruise ships passing between Mazatlán and Cabo Thursday night in both directions. We'll be watching traffic, but just one of those ships could affect your window of opportunity. Any concern?"

Manny answered, "If they transit nearby, we wait until the vessel is at least twenty miles away, say, forty-five minutes, then launch."

Lilly, nodding in agreement, replied, "We have a five-hour window, adequate time to gauge best angle of attack. What's your take, Dav, Logan?"

Dav spoke first. "About the same. We'll be tracking their movement. That'll tell us how to approach."

Logan assented agreement and added, "Once we know their route and speed, we should be able to gauge where to generate our grid. Worst case, we feign disabled vessel and call Dino's boat for help or call and ask if they've seen any whale pods, see how they react. We just might get up close and personal."

Manny replied, "That's more like a plan B but a good misdirect."

"Speaking of plan B, Logan?"

"We're all in agreement. One or both of us will board, take out the trio, plant the charges, set the boat on a course to Mazatlán, swim back, and watch it go down. Go dark on exfil if needed."

Pete asked, "Manny, where are we?"

"The *Antares* clone is at the marina. It will be ready by midday tomorrow. If the guys arrive by 3:00 p.m., we'll load and launch early."

Skip spoke up. "As of this morning, the abandoned airstrip shows no activity."

Manny replied, "Let's hope it stays that way."

"Here are your IDs, documents, and Mexican pesos." Pete handed Manny a large envelope. He asked, "How are you transporting your sidearms?"

"In the false bottom of two sonar-tracking devices," replied Lilly.

"The charges?"

"Same, hidden inside electronic equipment," replied Logan.

"Good."

Manny interjected, "There are M4s and grenades on board. We shouldn't need anything heavier. If we don't use them, they'll stay with the boat."

"You're cloaked as an Angel Flight?" asked Pete.

"Affirmative, and we have an EMS kit on board for effect," replied Logan.

Amused with his comment, Dav exclaimed, "Hey, I'll be the sick one."

Pete replied, "That's all we'd need." The group chuckled.

"Logan, you square with everything?" Pete asked.

"Affirmative."

"Everyone else?"

Manny replied, "All squared away."

"Good. Rae, go ahead and post today's Ops briefing." Pete shut down the monitor and turned to everyone. "Good luck and Godspeed."

As the team left Pete's office, Alex caught up with Rae, saying, "It's easy. Just pull up today's briefing and recheck it for accuracy, then add anything discussed but not documented, sign, and issue. It's that easy."

"Thanks. I would've asked you or Skip to double-check it anyway," replied Rae.

"No problem. Everyone does it. Part of the drill," sighed Alex. "No one's exempt."

"Anything special you need me to do after that?" asked Rae.

"Practice with our birds. Check in on Dino, see what he's up to. Catch up with Alexei. I'm sure he'll have a **SITREP** update. You and Skip have watch. There's plenty to do," replied Alex.

*****

Logan, Dav, and Lilly spent the morning rechecking their gear and equipment while discussing what ifs. Dav taught Logan how to pack the dive gear bag for easy access. When they were finished, Dav and Logan loaded all but their personal bags in the plane for the morning's flight. Manny wandered down to the hangar while Logan and Dav were loading the plane.

Handing a leather case to Logan, Manny stated, "Place this under the copilot's seat. We'll divvy up the cash when we land."

"Got it," replied Logan.

Justin walked down from Pete's office to where Rae was sitting at Alex's desk. Sitting behind Rae, Alex was observing her practice redirecting the satellites to hone in on specific targets. "I just stopped by on my way out to remind you that if I can help, don't hesitate." Justin turned and walked to the main entrance.

"Thanks for all the help," Rae replied. "You know I will."

"Say goodbye to Logan for me," replied Justin.

"Will do. Keep me informed please," replied Rae.

"The minute something happens, you'll know," Justin said as he walked out of Ops.

CHAPTER 61

Logan was at the hangar with Dav and Lilly, checking the plane over before launch. Manny, Pete, and Rae ambled down at ten minutes to 7:00 a.m. Manny conducted a last-minute walk-around, advising Logan he would be copilot. Lilly and Dav had buttoned up the baggage compartment, stowed their personal bags, and climbed aboard. Manny gave Pete a thumbs-up as he climbed aboard as pilot in command, taking left seat. Rae stood quietly next to Pete, watching their readiness pace speed up as they prepared to launch.

Logan winked at Rae and climbed aboard, taking right seat. He had previously loaded the flight plan to La Paz and began echoing the preflight checklist with Manny. Pete turned to Rae and said, "Don't be nervous. Anxiety clouds the mind. It's just another walk in the park."

"You're right." They watched Manny taxi the plane for takeoff.

"They'll be back here before you know it. Have you eaten yet?" Pete turned to walk back to Ops. "Join me for breakfast. Skip's got watch."

"That sounds good." Rae caught up with Pete. Rae smiled at Adolfo, who was overseeing two cooks prepare omelets, as she made her way through the buffet line. Shuffling her tray along, she stopped to grab a fresh cup of coffee and joined Pete at a corner table in the back.

"You've displayed high-level skills in data and surveillance analytics. You have a knack for it," stated Pete.

"I'd like to do more."

"Good. Spend the day with Roman and Alexei downstairs," Pete said as he sipped his coffee.

"What about watch?" asked Rae.

"Skip's got it covered. You'll grasp how we garner intel faster in Sub3. It's the brainstem of our operation. Even the Pentagon is envious. You'll like it." Pete smiled.

"I will."

"If anything, relating to Justin is relevant. Apprise him immediately."

"Absolutely. And you as well?"

"Critical issues only. I'm apprised automatically."

"I've never met Roman. What does he do?" Rae asked.

"Roman Egorshin emigrated to the US when his father was appointed as the Russian ambassador to the UN. He was recruited right out of college at Oxford and trained in counterintelligence by the former FSK when Yeltsin transitioned the FSK to **Federal Security Service** and expanded their responsibilities, especially on foreign counterintelligence. The FSB has a lot of hangover control from the old KGB. After emigrating here, Roman worked for the CIA for almost a year before Alexei recruited him. The CIA was not happy."

"So Alexei is more of a foreign intel analyst, like MI6, and Roman an internal intel analyst like MI5?" asked Rae.

"Yes, somewhat, but their paths cross-pollinate frequently. But different from most other agencies, we don't pigeonhole talent. They work together without stepping on each other's toes. No egos and no fiefdoms here. I ought to know. I broke away from fiefdoms years ago." Pete glanced at his watch. "I've got things to do. Enjoy your day downstairs." He picked up his food tray and walked away.

"I will," Rae proclaimed.

Walking back to their room, Rae decided to take Sheba up the hill for morning exercise. She met Alex in the hallway and was about to tell him that Pete redirected her to Sub3, but he already knew.

"Pete sees something in you. Skip and I got this covered, so go do your thing," replied Alex.

"It'll be interesting," she responded as she walked on.

Rae and Sheba spent at least twenty minutes walking up toward the radomes. She felt better about going to Sub3 to confront her day rather than be distracted thinking about the mission and things beyond her control.

CHAPTER 62

Manny landed without incident at the airport in La Paz. As they were descending, Lilly echoed over the headsets, "It's a lot like Cabo—great fishing, pretty coastline, and decent restaurants." Directing his comment to Logan and Dav, he added, "Looks like about a ninety-seven-mile drive to the marina. California 1 all the way. You'll turn east at San Padre and shoot straight down to San José del Cabo marina. Estimate about ninety minutes after you provision."

Dav goffed, "That's if pretty boy here doesn't get hung up with senoritas. Ha!"

Manny spoke up. "Okay, time to divvy up. Lilly, hand out protection. Dav, you and Logan split the funds and docs. Beware of being watched when provisioning. Mugging tourists and kidnapping are still quite common."

"Copy that," replied Logan.

Lilly was first off the plane, walking toward a short guy sporting a bright-colored tropical shirt standing by a nondescript brown Ford Econoline. As Lilly got close, the short man stepped toward him with his hand extended. "*Hola*! I'm Arturo."

Lilly responded, "Hi. I'm Ron from Toronto, Canada. Eh, nice to meet you. You already have my driver license?"

"Yes. The copy is right here. Your picture matches. *Gracias*. This is your rental van. It is full. You can go 350 miles on this tank," replied Arturo.

"Good." Lilly walked around the van, stopping back at the driver's door. "We'll be returning it back here on Friday, possibly after closing."

"No hay problema." Arturo pointed first to the gate and then to the building. "After 6:00 p.m., just drive in this gate and leave the keys on the floor."

"Thank you," replied Lilly.

"*De nada*," replied Arturo as he handed Lilly the rental paperwork and walked toward the building.

Lilly drove the van over to the plane. Dav and Logan were unloading the equipment cases and bags, setting them on the ground next to the plane. Lilly opened the back of the van, placing the pseudo sonar tracking equipment toward the front, leaving the critical cargo in the plane. Lilly helped Dav pack only the equipment they needed for cover in the event they would be stopped while driving to the marina.

As they loaded the equipment, Logan positioned each case in the back so any local, state, or federal police who might stop them en route and check the van could easily read the equipment cases were from the Marine Institute of Vancouver, BC, Canada, matching their documentation.

Before Logan and Dav set out to provision in La Paz, they climbed aboard the plane and listened to the first check-in. Manny called into Ops. Skip answered on screen. Manny spoke. "Logan and Dav set to provision. Will call when landing at checkpoint two."

"Copy that," replied Skip.

"All transmitters in place?" asked Skip.

Manny looked at each team member and received a nod from all. "Comms in place and working."

"Guys, the speed limit averages around 60 mph on these highways. Don't be surprised if you're stopped and have to graft your way out of a speeding ticket," stated Skip. "You're in bribery country."

"Copy that," replied Logan.

Dav interjected, "Tracking device active."

"Got you," said Skip. "You look like every service van."

"Good," said Dav. "We don't want to be conspicuous."

Alex chuckled, "Don't forget your clipboard."

Logan replied, "Sorry, must've left it at home."

"We'll update you on Dino as it becomes necessary. For now, travel safe," replied Skip.

"Roger. Out," replied Manny, ending the call.

"Good shopping," stated Manny as Logan and Dav exited the plane.

Dav asked Logan, "Ever driven in Mexico?"

"Nope. You want to drive?"

"Yeah. I've been to Mexico a few times diving with Lyle. Lyle taught me a few tricks with the locals. Maintain 360 always. Never know who wants trouble."

"Copy that." Dav drove the van through the gate. Logan pulled up the Oxxo grocery store location closest to their highway route south.

"It shouldn't take us long to provision. They have great pineapple and fresh fruit. It'll be tough to take a lot of perishables," replied Logan.

"Agreed," replied Dav. "I don't mind eating from a can."

CHAPTER 63

"Stopping here should be less conspicuous than a store in the countryside," stated Logan. "We might even see a few gringos." Donning his Blue Jays baseball hat, Logan opened the van door in the parking lot of Oxxo.

"I'll stay with the van," stated Dav. "Use small bills when you can."

"Beer?" asked Logan.

"Sure. We gotta have some fun."

Thirty minutes later, Logan pushed a shopping cart out to the van and loaded five bags of groceries, a case of Modelo, two cases of bottled water, a large Styrofoam cooler, and two bags of ice. Logan added six beers, bottled water, and ice into the Styrofoam cooler. As he climbed in the van, he handed Dav a cold bottle of water for the ride.

"Anything suspicious?" asked Dav.

"Hard to tell. The checkout girl was very curious, asking where I was from," replied Logan.

"Okay. Any loiterers?"

"Didn't appear so."

"I didn't notice anyone loitering outside." Dav put the monocular scope in the side leg pocket of his cargo pants and drove out of the parking lot.

Glancing at his phone, Logan said, "Turn left in three blocks for the highway. Posted speed limit is 90 km. We should be at the marina in just over ninety-five minutes." Logan texted Lilly on his sat phone for an update. Lilly replied they were at the marina. Logan stated they were ninety-five minutes out with provisions and no incidents. Logan checked in as Alex appeared on screen. "We're heading down Highway One." Logan held up the phone so Dav could see.

"Traffic isn't heavy ahead. Boys are starting to unload," stated Alex.

"We should be there in just over ninety minutes," replied Logan. Dav spoke up. "Any tails?"

"Negative," replied Alex.

Looking at a map, Logan asked, "Anything to watch for through the mountains before we get to La Ribera area?"

"I'll keep watch. Actually, San Bartolo area would be a good spot for a trap."

"Copy that. Out." Logan ended the call. He fought the urge to ask about Rae, thinking it wise for not mentioning. She was part of the team now and couldn't be treated special. She would pull her own weight.

*****

When Rae arrived downstairs, Alexei walked Rae around the room, offering a cursory introduction to seven additional analysts besides himself and Roman. He was careful not to say much about each analyst's duties, nonetheless covering the complexities of intelligence gathering. Before she was to sit with himself and Roman, Alexei showed her the brains behind their operation.

"I assume you are the person in charge," Rae queried Alexei as they walked into the computer room.

"Yes. I've been in charge since Pete recruited me." Alexei stepped aside while Rae gazed at two rows of huge supercomputers. Short of jaw dropping, Rae was speechless. Alexei began his short dissertation on the academics of his prized encephalon. "While most of the feds and military use super Crays, Pete and I chose a Swiss supercomputer. Outside of it being one of the most powerful supercomputers in the world, it is also one of the greenest as it employs energy-efficient P100 silicon. It outperforms the Titan, which may still be at the Oak Ridge National Laboratory.

"We use the latest twelve-core Xeon processors, and these babies process information a million times faster than the blink of an eye. A bit hyperbolic on my part, but you get the idea. Each supercomputer is set up for specific intelligence data management." Alexei began walking down the aisle.

"For instance, these first two are dedicated to human intelligence. They're linked to other systems from the military to the NSA, DIA, CIA, and so on. They gather information from communiques between foreign intelligence assets—ah, like diplomats, attachés, etc.—to counterintelligence organizations across the globe. As we move down the aisle, the others are dedicated to imagery intelligence, measurement, and signature intelligence. That's the most complex of all as it has so many subdisciplines. It's hard to keep track of them.

"You know, we work closely with the air force. They are the ones who have dissected MASINT into the subdisciplines. There's signals intelligence, geospatial intelligence, nuclear, electro-optical, radio frequency, materials, and the list can go on. I'm sure you get the picture," declared Alexei.

"I'm overwhelmed. I can see why this room runs 24-7. This is the brainstem of overwatch," replied Rae.

"Yes, but we're not intrusive. Our success is plying the data that's already out there. Unless we're compelled by national security or direct threats to people do we listen to communiques to eliminate the threat." He nodded his head to Rae.

"I had no idea how complex your job is."

"It's not just a job. It's a dream job. I was so stifled in my previous job. I didn't dare offer my opinion or make suggestions. It was basically boring," replied Alexei. "And when you really get to know Roman, you'll chuckle at the crazy way his mind works. I tease him that he's a savant, but he can put pieces of a puzzle together faster than anyone I've seen so far. I'm not certain he's from this planet." Alexei shook his head, laughing. Alexei steered Rae back to where Roman and the other analysts were working. Roman had pulled up a chair beside his workstation and was waiting to give Rae an elemental tour through his maze.

After almost two hours of sitting beside Roman with Alexei shadowing, Rae's head was spinning while listening to Roman speak another language—parlaying his drawn-out explanations of intel methodologies as they watched data flow from one screen to another. Roman pointed out his area of expertise and the omnipotent resources available with a few simple keystrokes. Similar to the workstations upstairs in Ops, however, Roman's and the other analysts' station each employed six monitors.

"I expected this room to be dark to compensate for eye fatigue, but it looks as though each of you control your work environment," commented Rae.

"It's a newer form of ambient lighting with glare-free, dimmable LEDs. Each of us can control the light for each monitor when needed," replied Roman. "If I need to expand an aerial photograph from a satellite, I can adjust the light to amplify the picture. It's useful when we're tracking with thermal imaging at night. It helps not having to guess when the picture is grainy or weather interferes."

"But since I'm a complete novice in this realm, what can I learn without having your educational background and experience?" asked Rae.

Roman looked to Alexei, and Alexei leaned closer to Rae. "Pete believes you have a knack for the surveillance and data gathering. Yes, you do not have the training, but Pete wants you to gain an understanding of the depth of data that can be captured as he believes you will be an asset as a go-between Sub3 and Ops. Once you know all the crayon colors, it's easier to paint the picture, so to speak," replied Alexei.

"Is this some kind of test?" asked Rae.

"No. It's to get you to think outside the box, to be daring, to open your mind to the potential sources at your fingertips to solve a puzzle."

"I don't know whether to say thank you or, 'Are you kidding?'" Rae laughed.

Roman stated, "It all seems overwhelming at first. Spend a week or two with us and you'll think you just tapped into more gray matter in your brain. Trust me. Every day, it seems that I come up with another way to view a problem. It may affect your sleep, though. Once I get hooked on a problem, it takes hold."

"With so much data to sift through, how do you find the time to manage the other analysts?" Rae asked Alexei.

"They're a special breed. Most of them are what you'd refer to as nerdish but techie. They would rather sit behind a computer than interact socially over a cup of coffee. They're absolutely in their element communicating with their computer—not literally, but then again, some utter words now and then." Alexei laughed. "Just ask Roman. He talks to his computer and himself now and then." Alexei rolled his chair back to his workstation, mentioning it was time they take a break for lunch.

"Can I access a **SITREP** from here?" asked Rae.

"Certainly. Be my guest," replied Alexei.

"I'll check quickly, and then we can grab lunch." Rae pulled up the updated **SITREP** to check on the boys' status.

"I'll make Roman tag along. You can pick his brain." Alexei waited for Rae to read the report. Alexei nodded to Roman, who placed his monitors in sleep mode and stood up, waiting for Rae to initial that she had read the latest report.

CHAPTER 64

"Notice that beat-up blue Camaro that's been behind us for about ten miles?" Logan quizzed. "They came barreling up on us, then slowed and has been matching our speed for the last ten minutes."

"Yeah. Young, teens, early twenties, tatts all over. Could be a setup."

Logan leaned back and retrieved his sidearm from his bag. "You want yours?"

"Yeah."

Logan called Ops. Skip answered on screen. "You see that blue car behind us?" asked Logan.

"Hold one. Ah, yes, I see it," replied Skip.

"What can you see?" asked Logan.

"Hold one. Zeroing in. I see…two young males, teens maybe."

"There are three. Sending pics. License plate is 64 21 Bravo Delta Romeo," Logan read off.

"I'll see what I can find out. Back in five," replied Skip. Not even five minutes passed when Skip reappeared on Logan's phone. "Could be a couple of small-timers. Nothing popped up. I'll text the info."

"Copy that. Thanks." Logan ended the call. Logan read his text to Dav. "Driver, Dario Garcia, age nineteen. Passenger, Luis Garcia, age seventeen. Address, Calle Ortiz de Domínquez 644, 23060, La Paz, Baja, Mexico. Mother, Maria Rose Rodriguez Garcia, age forty-one, teaches eighth grade at La Paz Middle School. Father, deceased, fishing accident, June 2007. Sisters, Maria Isabella, age fourteen, Yolanda Rose, age ten. Same address. No known employment. What's your take?" asked Logan.

"They appear interested in us. Been arguing and pointing," replied Dav, placing his sidearm under his right leg. Traffic was sparse as they approached the mountains. "How's your Spanish?" asked Dav.

"Fair." Just as Dav was about to speak, the blue Camaro passed them, accelerating at a high rate of speed, increasing its distance. Within one minute, the Camaro disappeared out of sight. "I wouldn't be surprised if they aren't stopped up ahead," Logan uttered.

"As long as they're not sporting automatic weapons, we can handle it," said Dav.

"Probably looking for a quick buck."

Five minutes later, Dav slowed the van as they approached what appeared to be a small pickup truck parked on the shoulder with a spare tire leaning against the left rear tire. A teenage girl was waving a white scarf rapidly while standing by the tire.

"She looks barely old enough to drive," whispered Logan. "Your call."

Dav slowed, crawling their van forward, stopping ten feet behind the pickup. Dressed in a tube top and shorts, the young teen walked to Dav's door as he rolled down the window halfway. Speaking in suitable English, the girl griped, "My tire's flat. Can you help me?"

"Hmm, English, huh? Where's your jack?" asked Dav.

"My what?" she replied.

Logan leaned left and forward of Dav, conveying a menacing look to the teenager. "Maria Isabella Garcia, where are your brothers Dario and Luis? They just drove by. Why aren't they helping you?"

Turning beet red and wide-eyed, the teen stuttered, "How… how you know me?"

Sneering ominously, he answered, "We know all about your family. Your mother, Maria Rose, teaches eighth grade at La Paz Middle School where Yolanda Rose goes to school. Your father died in a boating accident. You live with your mother at Calle Ortiz de Domínquez 644 in La Paz. You're fourteen. You should be in school, or are you waiting to call Dario and Luis to come back and rob us?" Not breaking eye contact, Logan placed his sidearm on the dash for her to see.

Dav slowly rolled the van backward. "Maria, I strongly suggest you put the tire back in the truck and go home. We'll be watching you!" He put his sidearm on the dash. "And don't try this again. We can get to all of you anywhere, anytime." Dav floored the van, peeling away from the truck.

Skip appeared on Logan's phone. "That was interesting."

"Yeah. A teenage trap that crashed and burned." Dav chuckled. "Did you know we have Houdini among us?"

"I gotta hear this." Skip laughed.

"Logan hoodwinked the youngster, who just happened to be the younger sister of the kids in the Camaro. They were probably hiding somewhere ahead, waiting for their sister to call, expecting us to be an easy mark. It was just a hunch, but our cowboy here foiled their plot."

"Do you two ever have a quiet day?" asked Skip.

"Wouldn't be any fun if we did." He and Dav continued up the road without incident.

"Five-minute delay. Looks like we're about forty-five minutes out," buzzed Logan.

"Update from the boys?" asked Dav.

"On the boat. They'll be ready to launch when you arrive."

"News on Dino or Hicks?" asked Logan.

"Rae just updated today's SITREP. Looks like no activity. Still on for Thursday departure," said Skip.

"Copy that. We'll check in at launch," replied Logan and ended the call.

CHAPTER 65

As Dav parked the van at the marina, Logan completed their second check-in. Manny and Lilly had already stowed everyone's gear. Lilly was busy setting up the munitions and electronics. Logan and Dav unloaded the provisions and their masked detection equipment. Logan set down the DEIS equipment case on the back deck while Dav undid the spring lines and jumped on board. Logan released the bowline as Manny put the transformed *Antares del Sol* Nordhavn engine in forward, slowly moving away from the dock.

Stepping up onto the bridge, Logan declared, "Good move getting us out early."

Manny turned to Logan. "It's all a masquerade."

With the marina well behind them, Logan heard Lilly whistle and turned to see him motioning to join him on the foredeck. Logan joined Lilly, who was stabilizing the DEIS communication weapon case on the makeshift strongbox in the front. "Hold this side while I lock it in place."

"Would it work better on the flybridge?" Logan asked, holding the heavy side of the case.

"Too hard to get to quickly. DEIS will be more effective up here," replied Lilly.

"Makes sense," replied Logan while Lilly locked the case to the strongbox.

Snapping open the cover, Lilly uttered, "Looks like harmless sonar tracking, doesn't it?"

After plugging the device into the electric outlet, Logan watched the green screen light up. "Sure does."

Lilly lifted off the false screen cover, revealing the communications interference weapon, depressing a button on its base. Logan watched the device rise fifteen inches and lock in place as Lilly rotated the pulsing rod left to right. "Now that's line of sight." He lowered the weapon, replaced the screen cover, and closed the case.

Dav joined them up front. "SATRAK is up. Undex and gear are in the engine room. All okay." He looked at Logan.

"Let's check in for an update." Logan led them to the bridge. Alex appeared on screen while the team stood next to Manny.

Before Logan could speak, Alex uttered, "Status quo."

"Copy that," replied Logan. "Okay. We're on standby for the night." He signed off, then looked to Manny. "Since dusk is upon us, how about we split helm watch in four-hour shifts?"

Manny replied, "Works for me. I'll take first shift."

Lilly jumped in. "I'll do midnight. Dav, you or Logan can take the 4:00 a.m. Let's get some chow."

"You guys go ahead. I'll set the CARD alarm and join you shortly."

Dav interjected, "Make sure the backup AIS monitor is set for both VHF channels. I'll tell Rae to have Sub3 monitor those channels as well. Don't need any vessel straying too close."

"Works for me," replied Logan as they headed to the galley. Logan turned back to say, "You guys up for a hearty sandwich? Turkey, beef, or ham?"

Both Lilly and Dav uttered, "Beef." Logan radioed Manny on the intercom, affirming a turkey sandwich and beer.

Dav opened the refrigerator. "Beer?" Both Logan and Lilly nodded as Dav pulled cold Modelos for all and as Logan began making sandwiches. Manny joined the group just as Logan carried the plate of sandwiches to the lounge.

As the evening wound down, Manny started his first shift, and everyone relaxed for some shut-eye. Logan called Rae on screen. She and Sheba were settling in for the night. Asking of any news or changes, he was happy to hear the calm before the storm was nada. Less than twenty-four hours from now, he would be actively pursuing Dino. As their conversation drew to a close, Rae sensed Logan's fearless assurance that the mission would be a success. They said their goodbyes for the night.

CHAPTER 66

D av slept only a fraction of the previous evening. Instead, he joined Logan on deck at 0615 with fresh coffee and Danish awaiting the first sliver of sunlight. Manny radioed the bridge; he would take the helm within half an hour. Dav sat next to Logan, directly behind the second navigation system monitor.

"I'm setting up this scanning system that tracks and maintains our course within this preset twenty-mile-wide grid. Assuming, of course, that our boy heads east-southeast as predicted, we'll be able to calculate a rendezvous point once we know his launch time, projected path, and speed."

Logan watched intently as Dav inputted commands overlaying their present coordinates on the chart plotter, inserting the parameters of the Lat-Lon positions of Cabo to Mazatlán up to sixty miles east-southeast. Drawing an oval with his finger over the chart plotter, he said, "This screen tracks our position within this grid. We'll be able to calculate an intersect point within a few miles once Dino launches and we plot his course heading and speed."

Zooming out fifty miles on the first navigation screen, Logan said, "No traffic within thirty miles. What do ya say we get our feet wet and do a fast trial run at ten o'clock?"

Lilly overheard Logan as he joined them on the bridge. "I'll jump in the dinghy and time ya."

"No more than a mile each way," choked Dav. "No need to expend excess energy."

"Agreed," said Logan.

Manny announced that breakfast goodies were on the table and that he would take helm watch from hereon. All three left Manny on the bridge and headed to the main cabin for breakfast. As they seated themselves in the circular booth, each phone pinged simultaneously with an updated SITREP.

"No changes!" Logan noted aloud as he gulped the last of his first cup of coffee, lifting his cup to Dav for a refill. Just then, Manny squawked over the intercom, "Logan, looking pretty calm out here. Running two to threes and rolling for the next hour or so. Traffic, nil. Suggest you move up your trial run."

"Roger." Logan looked at Lilly, then at Dav. "You up for nine-ish?"

"Be ready in thirty." Lilly grabbed a Danish and left the lounge. Dav sat back down for his second cup.

Logan walked over and punched the bridge intercom. "Manny, trial run's moved up. Launching in thirty."

"Roger."

CHAPTER 67

Logan and Dav suited up and were in the water before Lilly was ready with the dinghy. Before submerging, Dav motioned the direction while treading water. "We'll go against the current out for maximum friction."

Logan nodded. "Copy."

Lilly started the dinghy's motor, raising his arm, tapping his wristwatch, yelling, "On the clock! Turn your scooter lights on so I can pace you."

Dav and Logan turned on the scooter lights. Dav motioned to submerge, and the duo began their one-mile underwater challenge.

"Scuttle to fifteen feet, 110 degrees, and fifteen knots for one mile."

"Copy that." Logan maneuvered next to Dav, maintaining wingman proximity.

Lilly spoke into their comm system. "At three minutes, surface in twenty-eight seconds?"

Looking to Dav, Logan spoke. "Already?"

"Coming up on one mile, Houdini."

"What do you say we sprint back at twenty?" Logan grinned.

"Catch that, Lilly?" uttered Dav.

As Dav and Logan surfaced, Lilly dropped two bungees to stabilize their scooters to the dinghy as each grabbed the side rope.

"What about the lights tomorrow night?"

"We'll be watching. If anyone's outside to notice, we'll advise," instructed Lilly.

Dav pointed out, "We'll be fine without 'em."

"Ready to sprint?" He looked to Dav.

"Ready." Dav and Logan submerged and began sprinting back toward the idling *Antares*.

*****

Rae had been in Sub3, monitoring DeSalva's whereabouts and launch time. She buzzed Ops. Skip answered. "Hey, Rae."

"Hey, Skip. Can you patch me into Logan and Manny?"

"Absolutely. Hold one." He patched Rae, himself, Logan, and Manny to her computer screen. As each appeared on her screen, she began, "Morning, everyone."

Manny spoke first. "Mornin'. Where's our Boy Scout?"

"Dino just took off. ETA in Cabo is 1425, your time," stated Rae.

Logan interjected, "Little behind schedule. Ah, close enough. Anything else?"

"There's a lot of chatter from the Russians. They're looking for Bocharov. The turmoil should commence anytime now. Nothing else at this time."

"Copy that. Anything from Justin?" asked Logan.

"Not yet. I suspect he's instigating something," replied Rae.

Manny interrupted, "Let us know when the *Opulenza* launches."

"Will do. Expect an update with course coordinates in a few hours," assured Rae.

"We'll be looking for it. Thanks. Out." Logan winked and ended the video call.

CHAPTER 68

After cloaking the *Antares del Sol* from all oceangoing vessels opposing radar within a twenty-mile radius, Manny full-throttled the *Antares*, unobtrusively catching up to the *Opulenza*, paralleling its idling speed from a distance of two miles. It was time for Lilly to perform his magic and the boys to fashion fireworks. The *Antares* was stealthily running dark, even from most satellite detection.

Lilly set the image-stabilizing Carl Zeiss binoculars on top of its case as he needed both hands to lock in the 132 degrees point of compass aimed at the *Opulenza*, setting the DEIS energy pulsation and frequency at maximum. Lilly opened all channels, announcing, "Dino's comms disabled."

From the helm, Manny replied, "Roger."

Glancing at the live thermal image of the *Opulenza* on his laptop, Lilly opened all channels, speaking into his boom microphone, "I repeat, Dino's comms disabled. Position check."

Dav voiced, "Three minutes to target."

Logan followed. "Any souls outside?"

"No souls outside."

"Lights visible?" asked Logan.

Grabbing the binoculars, Lilly responded, "Hmm, barely visible. All inside."

"Copy that."

*****

Back in Sub3, Rae and Alexei were monitoring the operation when her phone buzzed. Noting it was Justin, Rae stood up to walk away. "Hey, Justin."

"Delivered the family reunion photos for songbird and completed my civic duty."

"I knew you'd pull it off. Complications?"

"None. Your disguise idea worked like a charm." Justin chuckled. "How's the op?"

"Monitoring as we speak." Alexei grabbed Rae's sleeve. "Justin, I gotta run. I'll call you later. Thanks," she said, ending the call.

"We've got movement," echoed Alexei as Rae turned back to his monitors. They watched Hicks stagger out and stumble on the back deck, holding a satellite phone. Rae punched in Lilly's phone. Lilly answered. "Got it, Rae. Comms are down."

"Lights are visible. He'll see them," barked Rae.

"Hold one, Rae," he said, setting his phone down.

Pushing the private channel transmit button to Dav and Logan, Lilly called out, "Go dark! I repeat, go dark! Hicks is on the aft deck."

"Copy that," replied Logan. "Going dark. Sixty seconds out."

Glassing the *Opulenza* again while intermittently watching his laptop, Lilly picked up his phone, still connected to Rae. "Gauging by his body language, I'd say he's pissed that the phone isn't working."

"Agreed," affirmed Rae.

All were watching Hicks sway and struggle to relieve himself off the back deck. Lilly began laughing as he called back on the private channel to Dav and Logan, "Heads up, golden flow, port side, aft deck. Such class."

Dav snickered. "Hmm, warm shower, sounds inviting."

Rae whispered to Alexei, "Too bad he doesn't fall overboard."

Closing the gap between him and Dav, Logan read his navigation gauge. "Breaking right in ten." He vocalized incremental countdown.

"Slow to idle. We'll drift to target," stated Dav.

"Copy," replied Logan, pointing up to the platform. "We can hook the scooters to the bracket underneath it."

Fighting the strong current, Dav slowly pushed forward until he was directly below the swim platform on the starboard side. Logan followed, pushing forward until he was directly below the swim platform on the port side. Dimming their face mask lights, Logan gave Dav a thumbs-up. Dav complied as they both ascended, each popping up underneath the bobbing swim platform. Stabilizing themselves with the platform, they collapsed their scooter cones, clipped the bungee to the yoke, and hooked the bungee to the bracket, letting the scooters dangle for quick egress.

As Dav and Logan broke the surface at the swim platform, Lilly pushed the private channel transmission. "Dino's sitting first in on the left. Dmitry is four feet in on the left, and Hicks is at the wet bar, far right wall. Dmitry is packing IWB, his right side. No other visible weapons."

Logan acknowledged, "Roger. Dav, you cover Hicks."

Dav replied, "Copy."

Logan pulled off his face mask, wedging it behind the corner platform bracket. Watching Dav do the same, Logan gently pulled himself up onto the swim platform. Slouching, each removed their fins, leaning them against the transom. Making eye contact, both simultaneously unzipped their wet suits, freeing their sidearms from the waterproof bag.

Logan peeked over the transom for a quick look, signaling all clear for them to methodically crawl over the transom at each corner. Logan motioned to move forward, both crouching low. Stepping quietly along the inside of the gunwale, they each made their way forward to the salon wall.

Leaning against the wall on the right side of the sliding glass door, Dav silently counted down. "Three, two, one." Grabbing the sliding glass door handle, Dav slammed it open as Logan leapt into the salon, aiming his M11 directly at Dmitry. Instinctively, Dmitry reached for his gun, pushing himself forward with his left arm, as Logan double-tapped him center mass. He fell backward onto the sofa.

Stepping forward in front of Dmitry's bleeding body, Logan fired the third shot in his forehead, spraying blood and brain matter on the back wall. His body slumped sideway on the sofa. In the traumatic few seconds it took DeSalva to register what was happening, he watched Hicks, who was pouring another scotch at the wet bar, turn around.

Dav stepped right and double-tapped the illustrious senator, and his glass of scotch shattered as it hit the marble floor. Stunned for a second, Hicks gazed down at the blood oozing on his Hawaiian shirt. He swayed, dropped to his knees, and fell forward. Stepping forward, Dav fired a third shot in the back of Hicks's head.

Logan stepped left in front of DeSalva, who was screaming and waving his hands, palms out, "Don't shoot! Please!" Stepping forward, Logan shoved the M11 barrel against DeSalva's forehead, pushing DeSalva's head back.

"Remember me, DeSalva?" Logan snarled.

"Yes, yes, I… I… I know who you are!"

"Do you now?" Logan swung his M11 down, shooting DeSalva in his right thigh. Screaming in agony, frantically waving his arms, DeSalva shrieked, "Please! Please! Don't shoot! Please, I beg you!"

Pressing the barrel harder against DeSalva's forehead, he said, "You think you know me? So, asshole, how much did you pay RJ to assault Rae?"

"I didn't. I don't know who you're talking about!" exclaimed DeSalva.

Shoving DeSalva's head farther back, in a guttural tone, he asked, "How much? 50K? 100K?"

Dav walked behind the sofa and picked up a cell phone lying on the counter. "Hmm, let's see whose name is in here." He scrolled through the contacts. "Gee whiz, lookie here, it's RJ." Dav smirked.

His chest heaving, DeSalva gasped, "I… I, ah, I have millions. I'll give you whatever you want! Don't shoot! Please! Please! I have children! Please!"

Logan turned to Dav. "Maybe RJ should put the hit on Hicks or maybe his father-in-law. Let's send him a text. Let's put the price up to half a mil. What do ya think?"

Dav replied, "I like squirm but forgot the duct tape!"

On the private channel, Logan whispered through his earpiece to Lilly, "Shadow. Shut off jammer for two minutes starting now. Advise."

Lilly replied, "Off. Two minutes."

Looking over at Dav still scrolling through DeSalva's cell phone, Logan uttered, "Let's have some fun! Maybe we should accidentally text Gabriella telling Veronica how much you love her and, oh, how wonderful sex is with her and to meet at 7:00 p.m. tomorrow night at the Argonaut and that you promise you're getting a divorce."

Dav replied, "I like it!"

"Send it!" sneered Logan.

Dav finished typing the text. "Done!"

DeSalva was shrieking, "Who are you? Who set me up?"

Aiming his M11 at DeSalva's left leg, Logan demanded, "Answer me, or I'll shoot you again. How much did you pay RJ to assault Rae?"

Dav interrupted. "Let's text his father-in-law that our Boy Scout here is taking over his territory."

"Go for it!" Dav texted DeSalva's father-in-law, stating that the old man was too old to be effective and that DeSalva was taking over his territory.

Smacking DeSalva across the face with the butt of his M11, Logan growled, "Last chance, asshole! How much did you pay RJ?"

Bleeding from his mouth, DeSalva cried, "I didn't hurt anyone. I… I can make it up to you. I can give you millions. Please don't. Please."

"Yeah, sure you can." Logan double-tapped DeSalva's center mass, putting the last one in his forehead.

Logan turned to Dav. "I want Dino's cell phone." Dav tossed it to him. "Ready?"

Dav responded, "Let's go." They walked through the salon and up to the bridge. Dav reset the *Opulenza's* idling course eastward, toward Mazatlán. The sportfish yacht began slowly turning east-northeast at about sixty-five degrees.

"Fireworks?" asked Logan.

"Roger," replied Dav, accompanying Logan down from the bridge, through the salon, and out on the back deck, climbing over the transom.

CHAPTER 69

S itting on the swim platform, Logan removed the SIM card from Dino's cell phone, stowing it with his M11 in the waterproof bag, then unzipped and slipped the bag inside his wet suit. Dav stowed his sidearm as well. They put their facemasks on, turned on their lights, and pulled on their fins. Logan was first to slide off, submerging a few feet, kicking hard, then circling around the outside of the rotating propellers against the current. Dav was doing the same, both kicking hard back to mid hull.

Ascending to touch the hull while fighting the strong current and neutral buoyancy, Logan unhooked the shape charge from the Y-sling strapped to his left leg. Manhandling the device, he rolled faceup, clutching the magnetic charge against his chest. Inching his way down the hull with his free hand, Logan pushed his knees against the hull, slowing his pace, working his way toward the rotating propellers.

Tilting his head back, Logan strenuously guided himself to the point forward of the rotating propellers. Releasing his clutch on the charge, he pushed it against the hull, flipping the electromagnetic switch. Testing its adherence, Logan grabbed the charge and pulled. It didn't budge. Logan did a 180, descending between the rotating props, kicking hard to get back to Dav, who was hanging on mid hull, waiting for Logan.

Dav twisted, raising his left leg up toward Logan. "Got it," Logan huffed, releasing the second charge from the Y-sling attached to Dav's leg. Stabilizing himself, Logan repeated the same maneuver—turning faceup and clutching the charge against his chest. This time, he inched his way down the hull, placing the charge and flipping its electromagnetic switch.

After pulling on the charge, Logan said, "Let's get the scooters." Logan flipped, diving down and swimming around the rotating propellers to come up to the swim platform. Dav swam around the rotating propeller, popping up to join Logan a few seconds later.

Logan was almost inside his scooter cone. "Exfil ten at twenty?"

"Roger," replied Dav, turning on his scooter light as they submerged to ten feet, gliding swiftly back to the *Antares*.

"Shadow. Beginning exfil," echoed Logan, reading his navigation dial. "Back in sixty."

"Copy that," Lilly said, still scanning with his binoculars. "I see your lights."

Looking at Logan, he said, "Let's fly." Dav pushed the scooter speed beyond twenty-two knots, easing ahead of Logan.

"What, you think you're at the speedway?" Logan chuckled, catching up to Dav.

*****

Back at Ops, Skip advised Rae to watch for their underwater lights reappearing during exfil. She and Alexei waited patiently until the lights appeared. "Boys are two minutes out."

"Thanks, Skip. We see 'em now," replied Rae, who stepped away to call Justin back.

Justin answered on the second ring. "Hey, Rae."

"Apologize for cutting it short. Boys are two minutes out."

"I know. Been watching. Okay, so here's where the fun begins." Justin chuckled.

"I'm listening," she whispered with excitement.

"So you know those recordings of the whining harlot, ah, a couple of days ago begging for sex and snowflake?"

"Yeah!" Rae giggled.

"Well, there's this mysterious envelope containing intimate pics of our singer and our Boy Scout at the Argonaut Hotel and a thumb drive with her debut song. But wait, the crackerjack surprise is years of protection insurance collateral from our illustrious civil servant about our Boy Scout and his father-in-law expanding their biz in Nevada, implicating his new mules."

"That's unbelievable. Where? How?"

"Well, the peddler will find this gift taped to his windshield tomorrow morning." He snickered.

"How about the civics teacher?" asked Rae.

"Oh, that was more fun. Everything I've derived about our distinguished civil servant tells me his arrogance is his Achilles' heel. He believes he's untouchable! Anyway, found the false bottom in the desk and the wall safe. Hell, a first grader could get into it," remarked Justin.

"And the white stuff?"

"Funny you should mention that. Ah, when the SRA folks get there, they'll have a heyday, especially finding his connection to the Russians. The insurance collateral he collected from the last few years, let alone his direct involvement to the contraband on the Zavadolsk, is enough to put him and our Boy Scout away for good. And the snowflake, well, hell, that's just frosting on the cake. They'll swear he lives on it!"

"Oh, I'd love to be a fly on that wall!" replied Rae.

"Yeah, it'd be quite enlightening to hear their comments, the offshoot, the potential cover-up, and of course, the official story for the press."

"Justin, from both of us, thank you! Seriously."

"Eh, what are friends for anyway? Besides, I needed the practice. Later!" he said, ending the call.

*****

Back on board, Dav and Logan stowed their gear before joining Lilly in observing the digital countdown for each charge to detonate so he could shut down the DEIS. Manny had previously cloaked the *Antares* from sonar detection and since closed the distance to the *Opulenza* to one quarter mile—not too close for the undex over pressure. The closest marine traffic, a cargo ship heading 240 degrees, was thirteen miles and was no factor. During the remaining four minutes to detonation, they were completely cloaked and running dark. Unless one was specifically using thermal imaging, Manny and crew were invisible. Manny readied the *Antares* for full throttle exfil back to the marina.

Lilly remained fixed on the *Opulenza*, awaiting the fireworks as the countdown continued. From the flybridge, Logan kept his binoculars zeroed in, waiting patiently for the charges to ignite the engine's fuel tanks and breach mid hull, quickly sinking the sportfish.

Alexei showed Rae how to tweak SATRAK to follow the *Antares* while running dark. Everyone at Ops watched the digital countdown live on their monitors, awaiting successful conclusion of this op. Pete walked into Sub3, stopping behind Rae and Alexei to watch the culmination of their game plan. As the seconds ticked down from ten, Rae held her breath. As the sky lit up with a bright-orange glow, cheers erupted from the boys on the *Antares*, Skip and Alex in Ops, and everyone working in Sub3. More cheering continued as pieces of *Opulenza* scattered under the orange cloud as the bow was sucked into the deep, dark ocean.

"Hurrah! Score one for the good guys!" Pete congratulated all through his wireless earpiece. Speaking off all channels, Pete remarked, "Rae, your handiwork will make for stunning headlines very soon."

"And well-deserved," remarked Rae as Skip relayed an updated message on channel to Pete that the boys were full speed ahead, scheduled to dock at the marina in under nine hours.

While Pete remained standing behind Rae, Roman, Alexei's top analyst, announced aloud that several passengers aboard the cruise ship *Splendor*, sailing to Mazatlán, reported seeing a big orange ball on the eastern horizon. The *Splendor*'s captain notified the US Coast Guard at 2207 with the report.

"That'll start the fervor," uttered Pete. "It's late. Get some rest," he said, nodding to Rae and Alexei as he left the room.

As Rae was walking Sheba before turning in for the night, Logan visually called. "I'm smiling. I hope you're feeling relieved. I know I am."

"My butterflies are gone. Yes, I'm relieved. Tomorrow should be interesting. Can't wait for you to return. I miss you!

"Miss you too!" Dav quietly made faces to Rae over Logan's shoulder.

Rae started laughing. Dav smiled. "Hey, ya know, Houdini here really doesn't swim like a girl."

Logan shook his head, laughing. "Night, honey. See you tomorrow." He ended the call.

CHAPTER 70

After almost two hours of headway, Manny uncloaked the *Antares*. It was just after midnight when Logan called Justin. "Hey, Logan."

"I have Dino's SIM card. I'm thinking a text from Dino to RJ demanding him to meet him and Hicks right away at a secluded location in Sacramento. You choose the location. You can get your hands on chloral hydrate or another surface injectable to incapacitate him. Keep him hooded and tied up until we arrive. We'll divert so I can get my pound of flesh while questioning him. Hmm, maybe we don't let the feds have him after all. It should look like the Russians got to him, but only after the feds find what's in Hicks's diary. Your thoughts?" asked Logan.

"Your idea is intriguing, and I applaud your gallantry, but I'm with Pete—quit while you're ahead," retorted Justin. "We're only hours away from him being arrested. He's clueless. I guarantee he won't be going anywhere. Trust me, flat tires don't run well. The DOJ will get him early tomorrow morning," stated Justin.

"I figured you'd say that."

"So why not have some fun with Dino's cadre, as in texts?" hinted Justin.

"Actually, Dav and I already did so before the fireworks."

"Now that's what it's all about," beamed Justin.

"Gotcha. Dino will text RJ to conduct a hit on Hicks as Hicks is going to blackmail DeSalva to the Russians, reminding RJ that he owes the favor since he was paid for a dirty deed but he didn't deliver. When they arrest him and look at his text, well, sealed with a kiss!" Logan laughed.

"You want to make him squirm? That's the way," hinted Justin. "The feds will revel in that."

"I'm glad I could help you complete the last episode in your stage show," replied Justin.

"Thanks. Appreciate it," Logan said, ending the call.

*****

The time was 0030 Friday morning. Logan, Dav, and Lilly were enjoying a cold beer in the lounge while Manny pushed the *Antares* at full throttle back to the marina. Logan inserted Dino's SIM card into his Roger Ferguson burner phone. Logan reread the texts that Dav had typed on behalf of Dino while on the *Opulenza* aloud before scrolling to find RJ's cell phone. Logan recited the text he was typing to RJ: "Take Hicks on a one-way trip. Double fee. You owe me. Acknowledge."

At 0049, RJ texted back, "When do you need this done?"

Reading the response aloud, Logan began typing while reading aloud, "ASAP. Call when complete."

Lilly held up his Modelo, urging a toast. "Good work!" They clinked beer bottles.

Logan took a long draw from his beer. "Guys, couldn't have done it without you. Thank you from both of us!"

"Hear, hear!" uttered Dav and Lilly.

CHAPTER 71

Friday morning's fracas began just after sunrise. Alexei's analysts were collectively monitoring the early morning raids sequentially. By 0640, the BATF's bomb squad K9 unit had located the firebomb that had been planted in Seattle's Northwest Seaport, Terminal 18. From Ops, Alex and Skip had been viewing the activity live, watching one of the explosive ordnance disposal techs place the bomb into a ceramic and metal box and secure that box inside the containment vessel for safe transportation and detonation.

Two news channel vans arrived with reporters and camera crew, each reporter a bit disheveled yet both scrambling to question the agent in charge as they watched the bomb squad depart, towing the containment vessel to its disposal grounds. The local police closed the terminal to all operational traffic, maintaining lockdown perimeter control, holding dock workers and bystanders at bay.

Alex texted Rae before 0700 that Sub3 was buzzing with activity and that the boys were twenty minutes from the marina. The armed escort reported no incidents, and barring any unforeseen delays, the boys would arrive by midafternoon. Rae acknowledged telling Alex she was taking Sheba for a run up the hill as they both needed to expend pent-up anxiety. Over the past two days, Sheba had sensed Rae's uneasiness, and the run would do them both some good.

Skip and Alex were tracking a Seattle-based USCG interdiction vessel that had detained the Zavadolsk cargo ship heading into the Northwest Port, Terminal 51, as Rae and Sheba walked in the back door of Ops.

"Hey, Rae," muttered Alex. "We're watching the ATF/DEA Joint Task Force board the Zavadolsk."

Rae and Sheba walked over to Alex's workstation, silently watching the raid take place. Rae watched for several minutes until the Coast Guard vessel got underway, leading the Zavadolsk into Terminal 51, where the remainder of the task force waited.

"I'd hate to be that captain," muttered Skip. "Poor guy probably doesn't have a clue what's about to disrupt his life today. The ATF and DEA will each want to interrogate him and each crew member as they conduct a full sweep of the ship and locate and unload the contraband. That'll surely attract more news media."

Just as Rae was about to leave, Justin called Ops. Skip answered. "Hey, Justin. You're on speaker with Rae and Alex."

"Hey, everyone. The JTF is raiding Caspian Shipping & Transport looking for DeSalva. His office advised that he is with Senator Hicks fishing in Mexico until Tuesday. The FBI has requested Coast Guard and aerial surveillance from Marine Corps Base Camp Pendleton. They've been attempting to contact DeSalva and Hicks via ship-to-shore radio, getting no response from cell phones, etc., so they're pulling out the big guns, all because Hicks is a senator.

"Agents are on their way to Hicks's office, home, and condo. Agents were able to reach DeSalva's pilot, who is in a beach resort hotel in Cabo, awaiting their return. The agents who interviewed the pilot disclosed in their report the pilot's statement revealing that DeSalva traveled with his lieutenant as they picked up Hicks yesterday morning and flew directly to Cabo. The pilot drove the rental car to the marina and watched as the three boarded DeSalva's new sportfish yacht later that afternoon. Now the mayhem starts. Will keep you posted," stated Justin.

"Appreciate it," said Rae as Skip ended the call.

"I'll let you know when RJ is arrested, which should be any moment now," declared Justin.

"We'll be waiting. Thanks, Justin," said Rae. "I'm going to shower. Be back shortly. Have the guys been apprised?"

"Absolutely!" replied Alex. "They're making good time."

*****

Pete was commiserating with the director of the FBI on his AV screen. When he concluded, he walked out on the Ops floor, directing Skip and Alex to include Sub3 and visually call the boys via Logan's phone. When Logan answered, Pete announced to all, "Presently, Pingston Securities, Venice Capital, and Dino's three banks are being raided by the SEC and DOJ.

"Concurrently, FBI agents searching Hicks's office have discovered incriminating pictures of Hicks, pictures of DeSalva with a suspected Russian arms dealer and diplomat, a bag of cocaine, and a book detailing months of payoffs, bank transfers, notes involving the NJ drug syndicate, money laundering, and more. It seems Hicks kept blackmail insurance to keep himself useful to DeSalva.

"Hicks implicated RJ in the firebomb incident in Montreal a couple of years back. The director is including the JTF, and the DOJ continues to expand their investigation into all associated with our Boy Scout, and the homeboys are chomping at the bit to get their fifteen minutes of fame. Rae, excellent craftsmanship! Please commend Justin as well," commanded Pete.

"Thank you. I will," she said, smiling back.

Manny slapped Logan on the back as everyone hooted their exuberance. Pete stepped in close to the monitor. "Good job, everyone!" Then he walked back to his office, leaving everyone the chance to converse.

CHAPTER 72

Rae texted Justin "Good job" as directed by Pete. Justin immediately called her back. "Internally, the FBI is keeping quiet as they're about to arrest RJ without fanfare, handing him over to the DOJ. They're trying like hell to keep this under wraps," remarked Justin. "It'll be interesting to see if he goes willingly."

"I hope they hang him from the rafters," snarled Rae. "He deserves that and more."

"Speaking to the choir. He'll get his for sure, especially in a supermax. The worst of the worst are there, and they don't like feds," replied Justin. "You and Logan want him to pay. Well, think about having to look over your shoulder each and every day and sleep with one eye open every night for life or an awfully long time. Now that's payback."

"You have a point. You still keep tabs on him?" asked Rae.

"They're at his townhouse as we speak. They'll be arresting him in a few minutes," Justin stated.

Just shy of 0940, Alexei buzzed Ops, apprising all that FBI agents were interrogating the diplomat Bocharov over the facts scribed in Hicks's journal and that the Russian Embassy was deflecting the whereabouts of Zohdolofski, and word on the street was, the Russian mob was all up in arms, looking to clean house. Even Dino's father-in-law was visited by the Russians.

Logan called Ops, declaring they were loading the plane and would call thirty minutes out, arriving early afternoon. Skip updated Logan on the raids, the pending arrest of RJ, and the actions of the Russians.

"All in a day's work," stated Logan.

"Ditto. I'm buying tonight! Fly safe," replied Skip.

"You're on." Logan ended the call.

*****

Rae and Sheba were waiting outside as Logan made the final approach to the runway. Sheba sat quietly, watching intently as the plane glided down to the runway, squeaking the tires and taxiing the Angel Flight up to the hangar. Dav was the first one out, followed by Lilly. They began to unload the gear while Manny assisted Logan for a few minutes, letting the TIT cool while they completed their shutdown checklist.

"Hi, guys! Can I help with anything?" Rae asked Dav and Lilly as they walked off the plane.

"Got it covered," Lilly replied.

Dav snorted as he unloaded the gear bags. "We could use a cold beer or two!"

"Can do." She was smiling while she and Sheba waited for Logan and Manny to deplane.

CHAPTER 73

Rae had been scrolling through the morning news stations as one reporter interrupted her normal local news and weather to report, "Just in. The Coast Guard is searching off the south coast of Baja—between the Islas Marías, Manzanillo, Mexico, and Cabo San Lucas—for a missing yacht reportedly carrying Senator Grady Hicks. The seventy-six-foot Striker sportfishing yacht *Opulenza* is owned by wealthy businessman Michael DeSalva of Lake Tahoe.

"Michael DeSalva and Senator Hicks are reported to having connections with a Russian organized crime here on the West Coast. A spokesperson for the ATF/DEA Joint Task Force report they have confiscated a container full of illegal weapons disguised as perishable food and, in a second container, two tons of cocaine with a combined estimated street value of $25 million.

"The FBI has not ruled out foul play, stating that their inability to locate Senator Hicks or Michael DeSalva for over twenty-four hours via ship-to-shore radio led them to telephone the Coast Guard. More news at noon."

"Once one channel has it, everyone will want that dirty linen." She was smiling while pouring Logan and herself a second cup of coffee.

Rae's phone buzzed, indicating an incoming text from Alexei: "Gossip mongers out in force. Reporters clamoring to get to Hicks's wife, his staff, colleagues, anyone at the state house. Like cockroaches. Stalking anyone connected. Leaking all pics to Crime Tips, Sacramento PD. Later."

Rae flipped through more channels. Each channel portrayed a section of the same story. One reporter ambushed Mrs. Hicks live but got the front door slammed in her face, saying, "No comment!"

Another channel reporter portrayed a gaggle of reporters staggered on the steps of the Capitol building, microphones in hand, awaiting unsuspecting colleagues to stray in their path for their ambush tactics.

A sports channel reporter standing outside the gate of DeSalva's house in Lake Tahoe was parading the opulence twist of what illegal drug and guns trafficking could buy, reporting no one in the house answered his request for an interview.

Justin texted Logan. Logan read Justin's text aloud to Rae as they were eating breakfast in the cafeteria: "RJ wants immunity. Willing to give up the Russians for a deal."

"I hope he rots wherever he ends up," snorted Rae.

*****

Rae and Logan were walking up the hill with Sheba when their phones buzzed simultaneously, indicating an incoming text from Pete: "Urgent intel. Briefing room 1045. Pending incursion: Boston Harbor. Suspected terrorist target: LNG Tanker. EOT 0930."

"Who's working today?" asked Logan.

"Skip and Alex. Let's stop by and see what they know," hinted Rae.

"Sure. Tomorrow brings new challenges. It's all a masquerade." Logan grinned.

Where were you on 9-11? Were you in the E-Ring of the Pentagon with members of the Secret Service presidential detail and the FBI when the infamous plane hit? I was. I was there meeting with high-ranking US and NATO army officers in charge of NATO's bomb disposal detection technology. Hence, my experiences, intimate knowledge, and technology are interwoven throughout this present work.

A former member of the USAF spec ops community, thereafter in my business career, I continue to work with spec ops personnel advancing technology designed to reduce soldier lethality and enhance their mission. If you enjoy real-life adventure, you will relate to the characters in this escapade.

CPSIA information can be obtained
at www.ICGtesting.com
Printed in the USA
LVHW030840170821
695475LV00001B/47

9 781636 927299